THE TARGET

A LANCE SPECTOR THRILLER

SAUL HERZOG

AUTHORCONTACT

rturs Alda taxied onto the runway at Rumbula Air Base and checked his gauges.

Fuel. Okay.

Pressure. Okay.

Engine. Okay.

He was in the cockpit of a forty-year-old Antonov An-2, and it rattled around him like the cage of a rickety fairground ride.

This was the aircraft his father had flown.

It was the aircraft his father died in.

For Alda, it was as much a part of who he was as his own name. Its controls were an extension of his limbs.

When he was a boy, there'd been a picture of its designer, the Soviet aeronautics engineer, Oleg Antonov, on his father's desk. For the first eight years of his life, Alda had believed the man was his grandfather.

The plane was a simple, sturdy thing, a utility plane used for agricultural and forestry duty. It was far and away the most successful aircraft ever put into production by the Soviets. Over eighteen thousand were built, and they were as common in the former Eastern Bloc today as they'd ever been.

They were hardy. Durable. Easy to maintain.

As was Alda himself, or so he liked to think.

The plane had a long history of use in the Latvian Forestry Department. It began service in 1947, and to this day, was the only plane the department ever operated. The mechanics affectionately called them *Kukuruzniks*, or crop dusters, and the nine-cylinder Shvestov engine, they bragged, was cheaper to maintain than the department's own Latvian-built tractors.

Alda opened up the throttle and revved it.

It was early, just after dawn, and the cloud was dense and low, gloomy even by the standards of a Latvian January.

It had started to drizzle, and he wondered if he'd be able to take off. The runway was a travesty, notoriously bad, and decent visibility was required just to take off without hitting a pothole.

"What do you think, boss?" he said into his radio.

His supervisor, a corpulent, grizzled old man named Agranov, who'd known his father, didn't respond. Alda knew he'd heard him, but union rules, and civil aviation regulations, didn't allow him to order Alda to take off in these conditions.

"I can hardly see the barriers," Alda said.

The light in front of him turned green, indicating he was cleared for takeoff, and he sighed.

He had a glass bottle in his coat, and he pulled it out and unscrewed the cap.

Vodka.

The very cheapest kind.

He bought it at the gas station outside the airbase every morning and took swigs throughout the day. He remembered when a bottle had been enough to get him through an entire week's worth of shifts. These days it barely lasted the day, and he had to buy a second bottle on his way home in the evening.

The runway was vast, one of the largest in Europe, and he couldn't see to the end of it, two miles off in the distance. It was built to handle the very largest Soviet strategic bombers, and if the Cold War had ever come to blows, the enormous, hardened hangars still buried on either side of the runway would have opened up to release an entire fleet of Tupolev TU-95's.

Those aircraft were over a hundred-fifty feet in length, and their four Kuznetsov propellor engines made them the loudest ever produced. When powered up, just sitting on the runway, they could be heard from the chamber of the Latvian Supreme Council in central Riga, eight miles away. The tips of the propellor blades moved faster than the speed of sound, which was what made them so ungodly loud, and they could carry payloads of up to twenty-four-thousand pounds.

If the Cold War had gone nuclear, they were the planes that would have delivered *death from above* to the entire US Eastern Seaboard. This expanse of rotting concrete was where they'd have taken off.

And before they ever returned, all of Latvia, all of the Soviet Union, would have been obliterated.

Alda sometimes thought of that, of those pilots, and the state of mind they'd have to be in to carry out that mission.

He wondered, were it him, would he even bother to return after he dropped the bombs.

There would be nothing to return to.

No runway.

No country.

No people.

Better to fly on to Cuba, or South America maybe. Ditch in the jungle. The depths of the Amazon. Live out the whole thing with the Indians and pretend he had nothing to do with the strange clouds forming in the distance, getting closer by the day, as the world got colder and a nuclear winter unlike anything seen before, or to be seen again, set in.

There was nothing about the runway now to suggest such an ignoble history.

Potholes the size of bathtubs pocked the concrete, and entire sections had been cordoned off with concrete barriers. Those areas were now used by local high schoolers learning to drive, or car dealerships testing new vehicles.

Alda rubbed his eyes and revved the engine.

He was tired.

He was hungover.

The morning before, he'd had yet another fight with his wife, and she hadn't been home when he got back after his shift. She'd left the heat off, and the apartment was as cold as a refrigerator.

No note, no message, no dinner in the oven.

He'd have been worried if it hadn't happened before.

He called her cell, and she didn't pick up, so he called her mother's house and her mother picked up.

"She's not coming home this time, Arturs. She's had enough."

"We have a two-year-old child. Has she lost her mind?"

"That's between you and her."

"Then put her on."

"She knows how to get hold of you," the old woman said and hung up.

Alda slammed the receiver so hard he broke it.

He couldn't lose her. He couldn't let that happen. He wouldn't be able to live with himself.

But then, he didn't think he could be the husband she wanted him to be, either.

It was the drinking that did it.

That and the sleeping around.

He took another sip of the vodka and screwed the cap shut.

Then Agranov's voice came over the radio. "Alda? You going to shit or get off the pot?"

Alda knew the runway like the back of his hand. Every stray chunk of concrete, every pothole. He didn't need to see to take off.

He opened up the throttle, and one-hundred-seventy yards later, he was airborne. The monochrome, Stalinist expanse of Riga's southern suburbs stretched out in front of him.

He followed the line of the Daugava River over the city, and a few minutes later, he was out over the gulf, its gray waters blurring into an icy mist that gave the Baltic a distinctive chill known to sailors from every corner of the globe. They cursed it. They never forgot it.

They called it the Baltic kiss.

He hugged the coast northward until he saw the mouth of the Gauja River, and from there, flew two miles inland to the Adazi and Dzelves-Krona forests.

If they could even be called forests at this point.

Loggers had taken so many trees that they looked more like the scarred wastes of a battlefield.

He flew in low and flicked the switch to turn on the cameras. His plane was fitted with a set of three high-definition, multi-spectral cameras. Each picked up a different segment of the electromagnetic spectrum, infrared, ultraviolet, and normal. When the three feeds were stitched back together in the lab, they revealed an image of the forest more detailed than anything ever made by satellite.

Alda didn't know how they worked. He didn't really know what use the scientists at the University of Riga made of them. All he knew was how to fly the plane.

He might not have flown it sober, but he flew it well.

And cheap.

And low.

He flew very low.

Lower than regulations permitted.

The department never came out and said it, but the lower he got, the more they liked it.

On this morning, with the mist and the rain and the low cloud, and the thought of Anya nagging at him, he flew low even by his own standards.

The tops of the trees were so close that they whipped away violently from his exhausts.

He was so low he hit a bird. A stork, he thought. He never saw it.

The clang against the hull shocked him to attention, and the plane swayed and yawed on its axis before leveling.

He took a long swig of vodka and gave himself a little more altitude for the rest of the run. When he got back to base, the cloud had cleared a little. He approached from the north and landed on the final two hundred yards of the runway, cocky as ever, jamming to a halt, the plane's pneumatic brakes screeching loudly.

Before he was even back in the hangar, he was checking his cell for messages.

Nothing.

He tried calling Anya.

She didn't answer.

"Easy on that stuff," Agranov said from the metal staircase overlooking the hangar.

Alda hadn't seen him there. They could trust each other, but he wouldn't have taken the sip if he'd known Agranov was watching.

"Anya slept at her mother's again," he said.

Agranov lit a cigarette. "She'll come home when her wallet empties."

Alda shook his head. "I don't know," he said.

Agranov made his way back up the steps to his office. "Well go easy on the drink," he said over his shoulder. "I need you to go out again."

"Oh, come on."

"You'll get overtime."

"I shouldn't have gone out on that last one. I almost killed myself hitting a stork or some blasted thing."

"You look fine to me," Agranov said.

Alda sighed. He took another swig and looked at his watch. It was still before noon.

The plane had its own fuel pump, and he went outside to get the hose. Then he checked the fuselage for any sign of the stork. Everything looked fine and, after refueling, he went up the stairs to Agranov's office to warm up before heading back out.

There was a small mauve-colored propane heater in the corner of the office and he stood next to it.

"Coffee?" Agranov said.

Alda nodded and sat down. There was a pack of smokes on the wooden table and Alda said, "Are those yours?"

"I don't know whose they are," Agranov said.

Alda helped himself to one.

"Try not to look so glum," Agranov said when he handed

him the coffee. "If you knew how many times my wife walked out on me…".

"So you're the standard?" Alda said.

"I'm just saying…".

"Your wife divorced you."

Agranov sighed. He lit himself one of the cigarettes and sat on the other side of the heater. Alda topped up both their cups with a little vodka, and they sat staring at each other.

"No lunch today?" Agranov said.

"Anya makes my lunch."

Agranov laughed. "Of course she does."

Alda took a long sip of coffee and sucked in through his teeth to cool it.

"Are you refueled?" Agranov said.

He nodded. "Where's this second run?"

"You won't like it."

"I already don't like it."

"Gruzdovas mezi," Agranov said.

Alda sighed.

Agranov nodded.

Latvia was not a large country, but the flight to the Russian border was still over a hundred miles, right at the limit of their area of operation.

Alda tried Anya's cell again and then her mother's house.

The mother answered.

"It's me," he said.

The old woman coughed before she spoke. "I already told you, she doesn't want to hear from you."

"Will you at least tell her…".

"Tell her what?"

Alda shook his head. It was no use.

It was nothing more than he deserved. He'd always hated his father. Now he flew the same model of plane, from the same runway, and fucked around with the same women, at the same two-bit bars.

He even had the same drinking buddy.

"Tell her, I understand," he said.

Agranov had prepared a flight chart, and he spread it on the table.

"Good thing I wore my wool socks," Alda said, looking at it.

"You'll be back before you know it."

"I'm taking these," Alda said, taking the cigarettes from the table and putting them in his coat pocket.

He also filled his mug with fresh coffee. It would be cold before he got to the plane, and he couldn't stand cold coffee, but he brought it with him anyway.

The weather hadn't improved but he got back up into the air and set a course due east. He passed the ribbons of Riga's outer highway system, the thinning out of its suburbs, and in just a few minutes, he was out over virgin forests of spruce and pine, interspersed with boggy marshes and lakes.

Latvia's forests were among the oldest in Europe, and it was not uncommon to see eagles, otters, beavers, lynx, even packs of wild wolves. As forests in other countries continued to dwindle, Latvia's were growing.

And gaining in economic importance.

Hence the need to scan them.

Alda altered course northward when he saw the Lubans Lake, one of the largest in the country. Soon, he was over the forested hills that marked the frontier between Latvia and the enormity of Russian territory.

It was all land that had been fought over, that blood had

been spilled over, that had changed hands so many times that even the locals could no longer say for certain whose side they were on. Empires had come and gone, ebbed and flowed. When Alda was a boy, the entire country had been part of the Soviet Union. Today, it marked one of the few places on the planet where a fully-fledged NATO member came up directly against the border of the Russian Federation.

It didn't look it, but this forest was one of the most carefully monitored places on the planet.

Not for science.

Not in planes like the Antonov An-2.

Not by pilots like Arturs Alda, working for the Latvian forestry department.

Far away, in the Pentagon, in Moscow's Ministry of Defense, were entire teams, active-duty personnel who would never set foot in the region, who would never breathe the air, or taste the food, or smell the peaty fires that burned in the houses of the villagers. And those people knew the name of every lake, every hill, every river and stream and bog and road. They knew every inch of the terrain, the widths of the bridges, the shapes of the church steeples in each village as if they'd lived their entire lives there.

Under the terms of the Baltic Air Policing mission, top-of-the-range NATO fighter jets, fully loaded and ready for combat, took off daily from Siauliai Airport in Lithuania, patrolling a sky that everyone knew the Russians coveted. It was not unusual to sight US F15's, Belgian and Danish F16's, French Mirage 2000's, German Luftwaffe F-4F Phantom II's, British Eurofighter Typhoons, and Czech Saab Gripens, rushing by in spectacular flybys, the sound of sonic booms echoing through the valleys behind them.

Far, far above, over a hundred-fifty miles up, the US's

most advanced surveillance satellites, the Evolved Enhanced Keyhole/CRYSTAL class, operated by the National Reconnaissance Office and piloted remotely by a round-the-clock team out of Chantilly, Virginia, had the area on their absolute highest level of priority.

They liked to brag that if a wolf pissed, they saw it before it hit the snow.

From those heights, their cameras, which relied on the most perfect mirrors ever made, resolved wavelengths of 500 nanometers and provided a diffraction resolution of 0.05 arcsecs. That was almost enough to recognize a human face.

The Russians countered with constant Il-20 surveillance incursions of their own.

They also sent supersonic Sukhoi Su-24's, which played a dangerous game of cat and mouse with the NATO jets, crossing the border and running back before the incursion could be confirmed visually. Those runs were regarded by all pilots involved as the ultimate test of nerve.

And skill.

But mostly nerve.

Those scenes from Top Gun, with the jets being pushed to their limits by pilots so shot up on adrenaline and chutzpah that they were willing to risk their lives, and more importantly, some of the most expensive machinery ever assembled.

Those scenes played out here.

As well as the jets, the Russians were also fond of sending over the occasional Tupolev Tu-134, which rumbled through the sky like a freight train and made the front page of every local newspaper in the region.

It was constant.

A challenge to Russia's tiny, recalcitrant, former Republics in the area.

A refusal to recognize NATO's claims.

And it was of absolutely zero concern to Arturs Alda.

He was in a clearly marked Latvian forestry craft whose top speed was less than one-hundred-forty knots. The plane's capabilities were so modest that it was actually capable of airspeeds as low as thirty-miles-per-hour without stalling. Flying into a strong wind, its ground speed could even go negative.

Meaning it would be flying backwards, like those hopeless seagulls in a strong gale.

No Russian pilot worth his salt would give the craft a second glance.

Alda checked his chart and got down close to the treetops, flying as low as he dared, right along the Latvian side of the international boundary.

When he reached his altitude, he lit a cigarette, flicked on the cameras, and began the scan.

He'd gone a few miles when he saw a strange read on his monitor. The signature was like nothing he should have been seeing out there, nothing that had any business being that close to the border.

Immediately, he pulled up and turned westward.

He was in trouble, and he knew it.

And then he saw it.

The distinctive, almost comically flimsy takeoff of what was, in fact, the deadliest man-portable surface-to-air missile ever created.

A 9K333 Verba.

The Russians called them willows.

And it popped out of a tube on the shoulder of an un-uniformed man standing in a clearing about five hundred yards away. For the first few seconds of its flight, it looked like it wouldn't even clear the tops of the surrounding trees.

But once it caught its stride, there was no questioning the outcome. Its infrared homing system didn't miss.

And Alda knew immediately that his forty-year-old Antonov An-2, and his forty-year-old self, had flown their last flight.

2

Agata Zarina didn't mind working weekends. She was an early riser by nature. Went to bed early. Kept on top of her laundry. The inside of her refrigerator was straight out of a commercial, with green bottles of mineral water in neat rows in the door, an unopened bottle of white wine on one shelf, and a packet of low-fat Babybel cheese on the other.

Her apartment was modern, neat, a little expensive, but not egregious. It offered sweeping views of the river, the ferry terminal, and the eye-catching Vanšu bridge.

A brief glance at her kitchen would show she liked espresso coffee, fresh flowers, and maybe apples, although they might have been for show.

The white silk blouses she wore to work were her trademark. She had to send them out to be professionally laundered, but she loved the smell when they returned. She wasn't required to wear a uniform, but she had that laundered too. It had pride of place in her closet, its neat creases perfectly crisp, every button polished.

She was a career woman.

Focused.

Dedicated.

She knew how to have fun, but that was firmly on the second tier of her priorities.

As was dating.

The nightlife in Riga was better than her hometown, but she was still back at her apartment with a glass of wine or a cup of camomile tea by midnight most nights.

Occasionally, she let things go later.

Very occasionally, she would hook up with a guy at a bar and bring him back with her. Always her place.

She'd read far too many crime novels ever to go home with a stranger.

The night before, she'd gone out after work with some of the cadets, and one thing led to another. She should have known better. She was their superior officer and was supposed to set an example. The strapping young man in the bed next to her was proof she was incapable of that.

Apparently, he was on the university swim team. He looked it. He looked like a Calvin Klein model, with chiseled abs and a jawline that could have landed him a role alongside Burt Lancaster.

Every woman in the bar had noticed him, and if word got out that she'd taken him home, well, it wouldn't do her reputation any favors.

She looked at him now, sleeping heavily.

She let herself out of the bed carefully, rising on her arms so as not to wake him.

She had a headache.

She'd slept in her makeup.

It looked like it had been applied with a pack of crayons by a two-year-old.

She wanted to get out of the apartment without talking to him. He was a big boy. He'd figure out a way home.

She looked at her phone and saw it was already past ten.

She locked the door of the bathroom and got ready as quickly and quietly as she could. She ran the shower hot. She dispensed with the blow-drier. When she came back out, he was still asleep.

She went to the kitchen, made herself a quick coffee, and took it with her.

The weekend traffic was light, and the day was as gray and drab as they came. She drove into the historic center of the city, an area of cobblestoned streets and throngs of tourists in plastic rain ponchos, and found a parking spot. She didn't have her own assigned spot yet, but that was something she was working on.

The headquarters of the Latvian State Police was a vast, concrete monolith, built in the Stalinist style, and it looked out of place among the medieval buildings on the square. She flashed her lanyard for the guards at the front entrance, and they waved her through.

In the elevator, she took out her compact and quickly checked her makeup, a pointless endeavor since no one at all was in the office.

She walked through the empty reception, past the seating area with the snack machine and coffee maker, and straight to her desk.

There were usually a few files waiting in her tray, items flagged by the regular police and sent up to her floor for closer inspection. This morning was no different. She grabbed the files and brought them back to the seating area, and put on a pot of coffee.

Then she opened the first file.

Some fishermen had spotted something off the coast at

Liepaja. They'd taken photos, and Agata recognized the distinctive profile of a conning tower immediately. It was from a Russian Kilo-Class submarine. The fishermen said they were inside Latvian waters when the pictures were taken, and Agata didn't doubt it, but there was little she could do. Given the proximity of those waters to the Russian Baltic Fleet in Kaliningrad, incursions like this were far more common than they were supposed to be.

She pulled out her cell and called her liaison at Naval Headquarters in Liepaja.

"What have you got for me?" he said when he picked up.

Agata had never met him, but from his voice, she pegged him at about her age, maybe a little older. He had a slight accent, which she liked, and there always seemed to be something muffling his voice slightly that she thought suggested a beard.

Her voice grew chirpy, flirty even, when she was on the line with him, but she'd never have admitted that.

"A Kilo-Class, about two miles off Liepaja."

"We tracked it," the liaison said.

She nodded. It was in the Navy's hands then. They could decide if it warranted reporting up the chain to NATO. She doubted it would.

She got up and poured herself some coffee. The snack machine contained a row of individually packaged cookies, and she looked at them longingly before going back to her seat.

The next report was an armed robbery on the outskirts of Riga. She couldn't see why it had been sent to her, no fatalities had been reported, but apparently, the responding officer thought the weapon used might have been military in origin. Nine-millimeter casings were recovered from the scene, but given how widespread they were, Agata really didn't see what she was supposed to do with it.

She put in a request to the armory at the Ministry of Defense to account for its stock of Heckler and Koch MP5's and any other weapons chambered for a 9x19mm Parabellum, and moved on.

The third report was for a forestry aircraft that had failed to return from a standard survey flight along the Russian border. She read the report, which had been filed by the flight supervisor at Rumbula, and then gave him a call.

"Mr. Agranov," she said when he picked up. "This is the State Police...".

"It's about time someone called back," he barked, cutting her off. "My guy's been missing twenty-four hours. What kind of outfit are you running over there? Connect me ASAP."

He spelled out ASAP. Articulated each letter.

"Connect you, sir?"

"To your boss or whoever? Put me through to the officer."

"Put you through?"

"I don't have time to spell this out to a secretary. I put in a call to the National Security Division. This is urgent."

"Eh, sir, this is not a secretary. This is the call."

"You're with...".

"I'm Corporal Agata Zarina of the State Police, National Security Division, and I've been assigned this report. Now tell me about your missing plane."

Mr. Agranov was put out.

"Oh, well," he stumbled, "I was waiting all night for you to decide to pick up a phone."

"Mr. Agranov. Let's not waste any more time."

He proceeded to give her a rundown on what had happened. A small, rickety, forty-year-old biplane took off in poor weather, its second flight of the day in conditions the pilot's union would have deemed unsafe, and somewhere close to the Russian border, it disappeared.

"Did it cross your mind, sir, that this may simply have been a crash?"

"A crash?"

"Pilot error. Mechanical failure."

"Pilot error? Not this pilot."

"That would make him the first," Agata said.

"Are you saying this was *his* fault?"

"Of course not."

"Because it sure sounds...".

"Mr. Agranov," she said, moving things along, "it says here the plane was over forty years old."

"*Miss* Zarina," he said, emphasis heavily on the first word. "Are you trying to imply that I sent up a plane that was not airworthy? Because I assure you, I have maintained every nut and bolt of that craft since before the likes of you were even allowed to..."

"Allowed to what?"

"Allowed to impugn the integrity of things you clearly know nothing about," he said. "I've been working on these planes for four decades. How long have you been doing what you do?"

"Mr. Agranov," she said, saying his name in the most sickly saccharine tone she could muster, purposefully trying to irritate him, which, it appeared, was working very well. "I'm simply trying to determine why this report has arrived on my desk. My job is to identify potential threats to this state's national security. From the report you've filed, all I see is one missing pilot. Have you tried checking with other airports in the vicinity? Maybe he just wanted to get away from things for a few days."

Things like his flight supervisor, she was thinking.

"Are you suggesting he's taken a holiday?"

"I'm just looking for more facts, Mr. Agranov."

"You pencil pushers are all the same. You're looking for a reason to pass this on to someone else. That's it, isn't it? Check a box on your form. Use your rubber stamp. Log your overtime."

"What made you report this to us and not to Aviation Safety?" Agata said.

"Have you read the report? You *can* read, can't you?"

"I can read, Mr. Agranov."

"Look at the location."

"I see the location."

"You *do* know what's across that border, right? They *do* still teach history in the schools? Tell me you've heard of the USSR, and Stalin, and the Gulag."

"Mr. Agranov. That's quite enough."

"Do you even know how many good men died so people like you could live without fear of the KGB every minute of the day?"

"People like me?"

"Yes, people like you. Young people."

"You think we're all soft."

"I think you don't have the faintest clue how dark things can really get. How slippery the slope is. How quickly you can find yourself in the basement of an unmarked building, strung up on a meathook, with electrodes taped to your chest and a wet sack over your head."

Agata knew this man was speaking from experience.

She knew the things that had happened when Latvia was just another republic of the USSR.

And she knew he was right. Young people in Latvia today, they didn't think about the past. They took their freedom for granted.

But she was not one of those young people.

She worked for the National Security Police.

"All right, Mr. Agranov," she said. "Let's look at this clearly for a minute. I assure you, I'm not brushing you off. I just need to make sure I'm not squandering resources. Do you understand?"

"Fine," Agranov said, calming down.

"We get a lot of reports. Someone has to filter them."

"I said fine."

"So this pilot. Arturs Alda. That last time you saw him was yesterday afternoon?"

Agranov sighed. Then he said, "He took off at around noon. He should have been back three hours later. Tops."

"Okay. And let me just back up a little before that. The report says this was his second flight of the day."

"That's correct."

"Is that normal? To perform two flights on the same day?"

"It's not unheard of."

"And the weather? Your report said there was a lot of fog. Visibility was compromised."

"Do I need to explain to you that it's January?" Agranov said. "We're not exactly on the riviera here."

"I see," Agata said. "And this pilot, Alda."

"Arturs Alda. Yes."

"How would you characterize him as a pilot?"

"How would I characterize him?"

"His second flight of the day. Bad weather. Poor visibility."

"If you're suggesting this was anything he wasn't able for, you're sorely mistaken."

"I see."

"That boy's been flying planes since he was twelve years old. He could have made this run in his sleep."

"And the craft. I see the maintenance record is up to date, I'm not saying the plane was neglected, but it also says it's a very old plane."

"The plane was airworthy. You have my word as a mechanic and an engineer on that. Look up the record of this department. I've been lead mechanic, like I said, for a long time. Eight planes. No money. No budget. But no mechanical failures. Ever."

"This particular plane was in for repairs seven times in the last eight months."

"So have all our planes. That's why I can say with absolute confidence they're airworthy."

Agata scanned Alda's civil record. His wife had made a few calls on him. The phrase 'drunk and disorderly' peppered the police reports.

"Had he been drinking, Mr. Agranov?"

"I beg your pardon."

"Lying to me is a criminal offense, Mr. Agranov."

"Arturs Alda wouldn't be caught dead drinking on the job. He's the best of the best. So was his father."

"He was a drinker, though."

"Not around here, he wasn't."

"Marital problems?"

"Listen," Mr. Agranov said. "Arturs has been flying runs like this his entire life. He knows the terrain. He knows the sky. He knows the plane."

"And yesterday? What do you think happened?"

"You know what I think happened."

Agata said nothing. There was nothing she could say.

This was her problem now, not his.

"All right, Mr. Agranov, thank you for taking the time to speak to me."

"Are you going to do anything about it?" he said.

"I can't discuss that with you. You know that."

"Just tell me," he said, "because if you're not, I'm going to go out there myself and find out what happened to him."

"I would strongly advise against that, Mr. Agranov."

"I don't care what you advise. I only care what's being done. I owe him that much."

"I'll see what I can do."

"You'll need to be quick."

"I understand," she said.

"I sure hope you do," he said, then hung up.

3

Lance Spector threw his cigar butt off the end of the pier and watched it arch toward the water like a comet.

"I can't believe you're going back," he said.

Laurel shrugged. She had a beer in her hand and took a sip.

"It's different for you now, I guess," he said.

She'd been made director of the Special Operations Group, Levi Roth's elite covert unit, and that made her, apart from the director himself, the most important person in the CIA's entire paramilitary apparatus.

"What's that supposed to mean?" she said.

He shrugged extravagantly. Exaggeratedly.

She shook her head, then turned and began walking away from him, back toward the house. Lance realized he'd gone too far.

"Laurel," he said. "I'm sorry. I didn't mean that as an insult."

"I know how you meant it."

"I was just saying...."

"You were saying that I'm putting my career, and the prospect of being in power, ahead of my principles."

"It's none of my business what you choose to do with your life."

He was trying to appease her, but everything he said seemed only to make her angrier.

"Oh, fuck you, and your sanctimonious bullshit, Lance. We can't all afford the luxury of going back to our cabin in the mountains every time something happens that we don't like."

"Is that what you think I do?"

"Every time we need you, Roth has to come groveling on his knees, like serving your country is somehow beneath you."

"Serving my country and doing what Levi Roth asks are two very different things."

"He's director of the CIA, Lance. It's not like he asks you to go pick up his laundry."

"Roth and I have a lot more history than what you've been let in on, Laurel."

She said something under her breath that he didn't quite catch. He knew he should have let it go, but he couldn't.

"What was that?" he said.

"I said, cry me a river."

Lance let out a mirthless laugh. "In case you didn't notice," he said, "the President of the United States just tried to pin a vicious terrorist attack on me. He had every agency in the country hunting me down. He called me a traitor to the nation on national television."

"You know he was doing what he had to do."

"And what was best for his reelection campaign."

"So you want him to go to war with Russia? To go to war

with China? Our two most powerful rivals. Just tear the whole world to pieces, burn it all to the ground, to save your reputation? Is that what you're saying?"

Lance shook his head. He wasn't sure what he was saying. All he knew was what he'd known for a long time. What he'd been telling Roth, and Laurel, and anyone else who cared to listen, for a long time.

That he was no hero.

That he was no soldier.

That he didn't even deserve the dignity of the name.

"Look, Laurel. I'm not going back. That's it. I wish you the best of luck. I wish Roth the best of luck."

"The best of luck?"

"Whatever the appropriate phrase is."

"Appropriate phrase?" Laurel shook her head. "I just don't understand you, Lance. You signed up for this life. This world. You've risked your life for it. You've even killed for it. But now, it's as if the things we do, the risks we take, the operations we lead, it's like all of it disgusts you. Like you're ashamed of it. Like you're ashamed of us."

"I'm not ashamed of you."

"You know better than anyone that the job we do is necessary. It's ugly work. It's bloody. It feels like butchery. Believe me when I say I understand, Lance. But, the terrible truth is, someone's got to do it."

"It's not that, Laurel."

"A clean kill. That's the best we can deliver. And if we don't do it, I guarantee you that someone else will. And they'll botch it. And then there'll be even more blood, more needless suffering, and more innocent death."

"That's not it, Laurel. That's not it. None of it."

"Then what is it? What else is there for you, Lance? This is your life. This is who you are. This is what you are."

"Maybe it was once."

"It doesn't change, Lance. I'm sorry, but there are certain things in this world you don't just get to walk away from."

Lance looked at her for a long moment and wished he could believe the words she was saying. She misunderstood him, his motives, but he understood hers. And he wished more than anything that he could still believe the things he'd once taken as immutable facts. He wished he could still be the man he'd started out as.

But he couldn't.

One man started the journey.

But it wasn't the same man who ended it.

Like she said, the events of a man's life, the things he did, the blood he spilled, it changed him. It stained him. Permanently. And he couldn't just walk away from that.

His deeds would follow him.

To the grave.

"Well," he said, "you can see things your way. I'll see them my way."

She let out a long sigh, then said, "You want to know why I'm going back? You want to know my way of seeing things?"

Lance pulled a small metal box from his shirt pocket and took out another of the cigarillos. He'd purchased them in the village, some local, Mexican brand he'd never heard of, and he held it to the flame of his lighter.

Laurel said, "Did I ever tell you how my father died?"

Lance knew the story. Laurel's father had been an army colonel. He was shot in the back by an Afghan soldier at Camp Qargha. Laurel was fourteen when it happened. Her mother was already dead. She spent the rest of her childhood in the Alabama foster care system.

But the experience didn't defeat her.

She ended up with a scholarship to Harvard.

Or maybe it was Yale.

Either way.

"I don't think so," he said.

"You know what happened."

"I've read your file."

She nodded. He couldn't make out the expression on her face. He'd have thought she'd be proud of the story, but he knew the truth was more complicated.

"My daddy had a drinking problem," she said.

Lance nodded.

"Not just like it was bad for his health," she said. "He had a real problem."

Lance nodded again.

"He was... let's just say, he was not a happy man."

"I'm sorry," Lance said.

"I'm not trying to get your sympathy."

"All right."

"I'm just telling you, they made a big deal about my father when he was shot in Kabul. They draped a flag on his coffin. Brought him to Arlington. Had a seventeen-gun-salute over the casket or whatever it was. A riderless horse. A brass band. It was dignified."

"I thought..." he said.

"What?"

"Nothing."

"What were you going to say?"

"I heard you didn't attend the funeral," he said.

"That's not the point."

Lance didn't know what to say.

There was a pack of cigarettes in the back pocket of Laurel's jeans, and she took one out and lit it.

She was a little drunk. She didn't often smoke, and she

didn't often talk like this. He knew she'd regret it in the morning. She'd be shy around him. Apologetic.

She preferred to keep people at arm's length.

"The point is," she said, "there was a dignity in his death that had never existed during his life. At least, as far as I could tell."

Lance nodded.

"That's all I'm trying to say."

"I see," he said, not sure what it was she was trying to say at all.

"And I feel," she continued, "that the least I can do is find that same dignity."

"So," he said, "you're saying, you're going back to Langley so that you can have an honorable death?"

"No, Lance."

"That's what it sounds like, Laurel."

"I'm saying, everyone dies. All of us. Eventually."

"That's the truth."

"And when I die, I want...".

"A salute? A brass band?"

"I want my life to have stood for something. Even if I mess up every other part of it. Even if I fail in every other way. Even if there's no one left who loves me."

"You're not your father, Laurel."

"Maybe not," she said, "but I am his daughter."

He couldn't argue with that.

He finished his cigar and flicked it off the pier. It singed in the water.

They both sat there in silence for a while, the moon directly in front of them. It was January, and there was a slight chill in the air.

"Playa Bagdad," Lance said to fill the silence.

"It's a strange name," she said.

"This place was a big deal during the Civil War," he said.

She nodded disinterestedly. She was thinking about what she'd said.

He was speaking so that he didn't have to.

"Cotton from every state in the confederacy made its way on wooden carts down to this beach. There used to be a big town here. Three-story stone buildings. And a port."

"Where is it all now?" Laurel said, looking out over a desolate stretch of beach that extended as far as she could see in each direction.

There was no sign at all that any town had ever been there, not a hundred years ago, not a thousand years ago.

"Under the sand," Lance said. "Gone. When the war ended, so did the blockade, and the blockade runners, and all the other adventurers and desperados their gold attracted."

"And the whores, I'll bet."

Lance nodded.

A whole world had been there. And now there was nothing at all.

He'd been to towns like that in other places. Other parts of the world. Some of them had emptied just hours before his arrival. The people had run off, hiding in the wilderness from whatever desolation had come prowling their way, and Lance, like the wolf in a child's tale, knew they'd been there from the still-warm bowls of food on their tables.

"There may have been for your father," Lance said, "but for me, there's no atonement in war."

Laurel sucked on her cigarette, flicked away the butt, and lit another.

"How can you say that?" she said. "Surely, for someone like you, war is the only path left."

Lance shook his head. "Even war requires a certain

degree of faith in humanity," he said. "War is for people who still have something left to fight for."

"You're too wrapped up in yourself," she said. "It's not about you and what you've got to fight for."

"Laurel."

"For the record," she said, "No one gives a flying shit about your faith in humanity."

Lance didn't know how to tell her what he wanted to say, so he said, "All the fight's gone out of me, Laurel."

"That's a cop-out, Lance. You're just pissed at Roth for what he did."

Lance shook his head. "I'm not pissed at Roth. I'm pissed at myself."

"What are you talking about?"

"You know he ordered your predecessor's death."

"Of course I know," Laurel said. "Clarice Snow. Your handler. The woman Roth thought you were in love with."

"And a woman who you coincidentally look uncannily similar to."

"Let's not get into this."

"Well, if we're talking like this, we might as well be clear, Laurel. You looked like her, and then you had the idea of undergoing cosmetic surgery so that you would look even more like her."

"I was doing my job."

"You were fucking with my head."

"I didn't even know who you were back then."

"But you knew what you were doing was manipulating a man who, how should we put this, had *issues*."

"Fine. You got me. That's what I did."

"You came after me, knowing full well that I didn't want to come back. That I'd been AWOL for two years. Roth didn't hear a peep. I wasn't ever going to cause him trouble. I wasn't a security risk. I'd just swallowed enough of the government's bullshit to last me a thousand lifetimes, and I was done with it."

"Roth said he needed you. He said it had to be you."

"And what I had to say about it didn't matter?"

"I thought you'd had enough time to get over your issues."

"Get over my issues? You don't even know what happened."

"Yes, I do, Lance. Yes, I do."

"You couldn't know."

"I know more than you think."

"What do you know?"

"I know Clarice Snow was pregnant with your child when Roth ordered her killed."

Lance had been in the process of lighting a cigar, and he stopped.

"That's right, Lance," she said. "Maybe you weren't in love with her, but she was pregnant with your child when Roth ordered her killed. That's why you're not coming back. Because you're traumatized. You're traumatized about what Roth did. He killed your woman. He killed your baby. And difficult as that is to swallow, you're allowing it to defeat you. You're allowing it to destroy everything you are and everything you still have to offer."

Lance shook his head. "That's not it, Laurel. That's not it."

"What?" Laurel said.

"You're wrong."

"Don't tell me I'm wrong."

"That's not it," Lance said again. "That's not it at all."

"It's all right, Lance," Laurel said. "Any man, under those circumstances, would find it difficult to come back. But eventually, you've got to move on with your life. You've got to get over what happened. I know he made a mistake, but you've got to find out a way to forgive him for what happened."

"Forgive him?" Lance said, letting out a laugh.

Laurel looked at him. The way she was looking at him, he could tell she was beginning to lose patience. She could only try for so long to pull him back. She could only hold out so much hope. Before his eyes, he was watching a woman lose her faith in him.

And he didn't care.

"Look, Lance," she said. "This ship is ready to sail. I've got clearance from Roth and the president. I'm going to return to DC and set up the team that I think is capable of defending our country. The team that is capable of standing up to the threat posed by Russia and China. If you want to be part of that team, there's a spot for you."

"They gave clearance for me too?"

"Yes, they did," Laurel said. "Of course they did. They know you didn't do the things they accused you of."

Lance shook his head.

"Fine," Laurel said. "I'll do it without you, Lance. There are other operatives. Other assassins. Other men in the military who will risk their lives for the safety of the rest of us."

She turned and started walking away. Lance stayed where he was and smoked his way through the entire box of cigarillos. Two hours passed before Laurel came back down to the pier.

"I'm leaving at dawn," she said. "My offer still stands. You can come with me, or go back to Montana, or you can disappear completely and never talk to any of us ever again. The choice is yours. I won't come looking for you. You have my word on that."

Lance looked at her. She was so young. So full of hope, of confidence, that something could be done to make a difference in the world. It was something he was incapable of ever feeling again.

She was about to leave again when he said, "Hey, do you know who found out Clarice was selling secrets to the Russians?"

She shook her head.

He swallowed. What he was about to say was difficult. It was something he'd never told anyone. Something he'd never said aloud. Something he wasn't even sure he'd processed in his own mind.

"It was me," he said.

"You?"

"There was a GRU agent in New York. I'd been ordered to follow him, to find out who his contact was."

"And you found out?"

"I followed him to a diner near Times Square, and I saw Clarice drink coffee at the table next to him. They never spoke, but she left an envelope on her table when she left."

"Which he picked up?"

"Which he picked up," Lance said.

"And you intercepted?"

He nodded.

"What was inside it?"

"It was..." Lance said, then he stopped.

"Lance," Laurel said.

"It was a photograph," he said. "At least, that's what I thought at first. It was blurry. Black and white. Then I realized it was an ultrasound. The original. From the hospital. It had an identifier on it showing the name of the obstetrician. Someone in the maternal ward at Johns Hopkins. It had a date from a few days earlier."

"Wait," Laurel said.

"And it had Clarice's name in the top right corner," he blurted.

"You mean?"

"I knew, Laurel."

"You knew?"

"It all came to me at once, Laurel. Clarice was pregnant. She was the one selling secrets to the Russians."

"And the baby...".

"And she'd gotten pregnant by me on purpose, Laurel. So that they'd have something over me. Something they could use against me."

"Lance."

"Kompromat," he said. "The baby was their kompromat. They were going to turn me. And Clarissa was in on all of it."

"I never heard of anything like it," Laurel said.

"Well, now you have."

"And you knew all of it."

Lance laughed again.

"Lance," Laurel said. "You didn't do anything wrong. You were duped. That's all. And everyone else was too. She was your handler. She duped Roth long before she ever got to you."

"You still don't understand," Lance said, shaking his head.

"I do," she said. "The assassin. The man Roth sent to kill Clarice. He was found dead two weeks later. You went after him."

"Went after him?"

"Sandra Shrader had proof. She used it to try to convince the president you'd gone rogue."

"Shrader?"

"The NSA Director."

Lance let out a long sigh. "You'd think she'd have better information than that," Lance said.

"What better information?"

"I didn't go after the man who killed Clarice."

"Lance, you don't need to lie to me. I've got your back on this."

"I didn't go after the assassin, Laurel. I am the assassin."

All the blood drained from Laurel's face, and she turned white as a ghost.

"What?" she stammered.

"I'm the man who killed Clarice Snow."

Her face was blank as a sheet of paper, like she couldn't comprehend his words. Then, slowly, her head began to shake from side to side.

"Laurel," he said, but she was already stepping back from him.

"What did you say?" she said at last.

"You heard what I said."

"But ... but how?"

"Those were my orders," he said. "Roth didn't know she was carrying my child, but I did."

"You should have told him."

"Maybe I should have," Lance said, "but I was trying to be a good soldier."

"What kind of man?" she said, still shaking her head.

"What kind of man kills his own child?" Lance said, finishing the question for her.

She was speechless. In shock. It was all she could do just to look at him.

"I obeyed the order, Laurel. And it took me a while, but now I know that I shouldn't have. And I swear, as long as I live, I never will again."

4

Agata stopped at a gas station outside Riga and filled her tank. She drove a new Mercedes hatchback but went into the station anyway and asked for the mechanic. She didn't want to get out to the border region and run into car trouble. The mechanic checked her oil and tire pressure and sold her a gallon of washer fluid.

Inside the store, she used the ATM to withdraw cash, she didn't want to be reliant only on cards, and stocked up on snacks. She grabbed chips, a candy bar, and a selection of sandwiches from the refrigerator, one with a cream cheese filling, one with ham. She also picked up some sparkling water and a large cup of coffee.

When she got back to the car, she poured the coffee into her thermos and put it in the cupholder. Everything else, she put on the passenger seat next to her. She programmed her GPS with the coordinates of the police station in the village of Ziguri, then pulled back onto the highway.

Ziguri was in the extreme northeast of the country, an area of dense forest where wolves still roamed in packs, and the villagers were more likely to carry rifles than cell phones. She wasn't sure her cell would work when she got there, so she called her captain, Alfreds Kuzis, and left another message.

She wouldn't usually follow up on a lead like this without speaking to him first, but she'd been trying his cell all morning, and he just wasn't picking up. She knew the reason. He was up at the cottage with his wife, and reception out there was sketchy at the best of times.

Agata knew because she'd been out there herself.

Just once.

The cottage was beautiful, one of those family retreats everyone in Riga seemed to covet, with its own dock and a two-bedroom boathouse for guests, but the visit had been a disaster.

Back when she first arrived at the department, Agata had a problem with Kuzis. He would whistle at her when she walked by his desk, or leer, or make inappropriate comments. Once, in the records room, he'd pressed up against her from behind while she was searching for a file.

He was quite a bit older than her. She was twenty-nine. He was forty-eight. He had also just recently married, and the entire situation made Agata extremely uncomfortable.

A successful career in Riga's national security community was difficult enough for a woman, and Agata had worked too hard to let some dalliance with a superior ruin it all. Especially one as singularly unattractive as Alfreds Kuzis.

He had money. He made sure to make that much obvious. He wore expensive suits and enough aftershave to rival the cosmetics section of a department store, but everything else about him screamed mediocrity.

He'd apparently come to the conclusion that Agata was having trouble settling into city life, and kept insisting she come up to his cottage in the lake district to get away from the hustle and bustle.

The invitation made her uncomfortable, but he extended it so many times that turning it down grew to be more uncomfortable.

She had doubts about his motives, but he was still her commanding officer, and if she couldn't find some way to get along, there would be implications for her career.

She told herself his wife would be there, and she didn't think anything untoward could happen given that fact. She even thought that perhaps, by meeting the wife, she would be able to move her relationship with Kuzis onto a more professional footing.

So, one Friday after work, she bought a few bottles of expensive wine, packed a weekend bag, and made the drive up to the cottage.

From the moment she arrived, Kuzis's wife, a woman exactly the same age as Agata, who'd apparently done a little modeling in high school, treated her like they were sworn enemies. She was so threatened, as if Agata were some sort of temptress, intent on seducing Kuzis and stealing him away from her, that she flew completely off the handle.

Agata listened awkwardly from the enormous living room, beside a roaring fire, with a stunning vista over one of the region's most beautiful lakes. At the same time, Kuzis and his wife argued loudly in the kitchen.

Kuzis claimed there'd been some sort of mixup. He said he'd intended for Agata to show up with a date of her own. Agata distinctly remembered him making sure she wasn't bringing anyone.

Anyway, the wife stormed off in Kuzis's enormous BMW,

and Kuzis swore and broke some dishes before leaving the house and chasing after her.

Agata took the opportunity to escape, and back at work the following Monday, she and Kuzis never mentioned a word about the entire incident. Things were a little awkward for a time, but Agata figured it wouldn't take long for him to get in bigger trouble with another girl in the office. About a month later, she was proved right when he started an affair with one of the administrative assistants.

Ever since, Agata had been allowed to focus on her job.

She had it in her mind now that she could make it out to Ziguri, write up a full report, and get back to the city before anyone even noticed she was gone.

Maybe she was overreacting, but something about her conversation with Agranov had left her very uneasy. She needed to find out what happened to that plane, and the longer she waited, the colder the trail would get.

The threat from Russia was ever-present, and this incident was too close to the border to ignore.

There was a local cop who'd reported seeing something. She would get his statement, locate the crash site, and confirm that it was an accident.

If everything went according to plan, she'd be back at her desk by Monday.

As she left the message, it put her mind at ease to know someone knew where she was headed, even if that someone was Kuzis.

She turned up the volume of the electronic music she was listening to and switched into the fast lane, overtaking as many trucks as she could before clearing the city.

The A2 highway went in a straight line northeast from Riga all the way to Pskov in Russia. It began as a wide, newly-paved, four-lane road, but by Sigulda it had reduced to just two lanes. From there, the going was slower as she was forced to share the road with larger agricultural and forestry vehicles.

By the time she reached Aluksnes, the last town of any size before her destination, it was already getting dark. She'd hoped to make it to Ziguri by nightfall but now wondered if it might be better to stop for the night.

Ziguri didn't strike her as the kind of place with a lot to offer in terms of lodging, and the road ahead would get increasingly treacherous as it wound deeper and deeper into the forested hills of the region.

Carrying on in the morning would make sense, but as she got into the center of Aluksnes, and saw the vacant, boarded-up buildings, she felt distinctly unwelcome. The streets were devoid of people, as if the entire town had been deserted, and there was an uneasy quiet about the place.

The entire eastern portion of the country was sparsely populated, and she'd heard that this area in particular was in decline, but she'd never imagined it was so bad. She couldn't spot a single building that didn't have a 'for rent' sign in the window.

She'd never been fond of that part of the country. It was as if the nearer she got to the border, the darker and more dismal everything became. It was as if the immense gravity of Russia, the largest nation on the planet, which stretched from this border on the fringe of Europe, all the way to Korea, sucked up everything that came within its orbit.

All that territory, the sheer vastness of it, became like a black hole, with a gravitational field too strong even for light to escape. The fact that her country, and the entire eastern half of the continent, had suffered decades of oppression at the hands of a cruel and distant regime in the Kremlin only added to that impression.

She drove on until she got sleepy, and pulled over at a little roadside restaurant about an hour from the border.

"You're from the capital," the waitress said to her when she sat down.

"Not originally," Agata said, "but I am now, yes."

"What brings you out here?"

The question was perhaps a little direct.

"I'm a state police officer," Agata said.

The waitress raised an eyebrow and looked her up and down, as if determining whether or not to believe her.

She left, and when she returned, she had a mug of hot tea. Agata usually drank it black, but tonight she added sugar and milk. She also had pork cutlets with a thick mushroom gravy. The food was good, and Agata cleaned her plate.

She noticed that the restaurant also offered lodging, there were a few small cabins with steeply-peaked roofs out back, but she knew she wouldn't sleep a wink in a place like that.

It was too desolate. The kind of place they might film a horror movie about a woman who came in off the road for food and shelter and never left.

She finished her tea and left some money on the table.

She was determined to make it to Ziguri, but almost as soon as she left the restaurant, it began to snow. The road grew darker, and quieter, and progressively less traveled.

She went fifteen minutes without passing a single other vehicle. Then she lost cell signal, and the music she'd been streaming through her cell data stopped abruptly.

She drove on in silence, and the silence seemed to grow and grow the further she got. The trunks of the trees, illuminated in her headlights, leered at her menacingly from the side of the road.

She tried to focus her mind on what she would say to the police officer in the morning. What would it mean if the plane really had been shot down?

Latvia, like every country that bordered Russia, faced a constant, existential threat. It had been part of Russia in the days of the Czar. It had been part of the USSR.

The Kremlin had let it slip from its grasp at a moment of weakness thirty years earlier, but everyone knew it wanted it back.

It wanted it back, and it grew stronger by the day.

People felt it. The constant pressure. The weight of all that history. It was tectonic. Glacial. You could look away from it, but you couldn't stop it.

You could join NATO. You could join the European Union. You could ally with the United States.

But eventually, Russia would return, seeking what it had lost, what it considered its own.

At the dawn of the twentieth century, Latvia was part of the Russian Empire. Nicholas II was Czar. Ethnic Russians made up most of the population in the cities, and Baltic Germans controlled the state bureaucracy and administration.

Ethnic Latvians were an afterthought. They were the serfs. They lived in the countryside and worked as laborers.

If you stopped at a newspaper stand in the capital, daily titles were available in Russian and German.

Not Latvian.

It was not until 1918, and the immense upheavals of the Russian Revolution, the Czar's execution, and three million Russian casualties in World War One, that Latvia was allowed to emerge as a nation of its own.

And it was a nation that was not to last.

Like the phantom limb of an amputee, Stalin felt what he had lost, and he wanted back every inch of it.

In 1940, he came to get it.

It started with the killing of some border guards and the delivery of a six-hour ultimatum.

Two days later, a full military invasion was complete.

Three days after that, political prisoners in Riga were being forced to march in so-called 'processions of thanksgiving' dedicated to Stalin.

Over the next four years, the ebbs and flows of Nazi and Stalinist forces ravaged the land. Countless unspeakable atrocities were committed. Hitler's holocaust of the Jews took root. The rivers ran red with blood, the soil was sodden with it, and when the dust settled, Stalin's armies were back.

And this time, they weren't going anywhere.

Stalin didn't even bother to create a puppet state. He swallowed the tiny nation wholesale, subsuming it into the USSR. He made it akin to a province, in what was to become the largest territorial empire in history.

When the Kremlin faltered, and the USSR collapsed, Latvia escaped again.

But the question on everyone's lips was, for how long?

Between a quarter and third of the population of Latvia was ethnically Russian. Those people had grievances, the incoming Latvian government refused to offer them automatic citizenship, and it was to Moscow that they turned.

That made them a ticking time bomb, and Russia could use them to foment unrest, instability, and ultimately, a pretext for invasion, whenever the time was ripe.

Russia was a prowling predator, a wolf stalking a pen, and Latvia was the sheep.

It was not a question of if the wolf would pounce, but when.

And that was why Agata, and the other officers in her division, even Kuzis, took their jobs seriously.

They were like seismologists on a fault line. They knew the big one was coming. They knew they weren't ready for it. They knew it could level everything and leave nothing but a desolation in its wake.

They just didn't know when.

Agata was rounding a bend in the road when a blinding, white light flashed across her windshield. She jammed on the brakes, and the car skidded and swerved. She spun the wheel, trying to regain control, but crashed up onto the bank at the side of the road. The car tore through the mud, ripping deep ruts in the ground, and just before it slammed into a sheer rock face, came to a halt.

Her chest pounded so hard she thought she was having a heart attack.

The car had spun one-eighty, and she was facing back in the direction she'd come from. Before her, through the misty beams of her headlights like apparitions in some mystical fairytale, an entire herd of deer was prancing and leaping across the road.

5

Agata woke with a start.

She had not slept well. The bed was narrow, the mattress was hard, and she couldn't for the life of her understand why anyone in a climate like that would ever make a blanket so thin.

She was in room 101 of the Ziguri Grand Hotel, and she supposed she should count herself lucky she'd made it at all.

It had been after midnight by the time she finally managed to crawl into the village. The car ran okay, but her hands were shaking so much that it was difficult to hold onto the wheel.

The place had greeted her like a ghost town. Nothing was open. Not the sole grocery store, not the two bars at the square, not the restaurant next to the church. The police station had also shut for the night, as had the Ziguri Grand Hotel.

She was so tired that were it not for the cold, she might have just leaned her seat back and spent the night in the car. All she wanted was to shut her eyes and get the day over with.

She'd woken the proprietor of the hotel by banging on the door with her fists for fifteen minutes. He was an old man, and he answered the door in a thick robe and slippers. Eventually, after she'd agreed to pay double the usual rate, he'd allowed her to check-in.

As she followed him up the stairs and along the narrow corridor, she got the impression she was the only guest.

She stared up at the ceiling. A light brown stain was forming in the plaster around the light fixture. She tried not to think about what might be causing it and got out of the bed. She went to the window, bringing the blanket with her, draping it over her shoulders like a cape.

She couldn't have imagined a gloomier scene.

The street was paved, but barely, and thick, brown water filled the potholes. Mud ran down the sides of the street, and two tractors with massive tires slowly chugged past the hotel with drivers who looked like they'd been dressed by the costume department of a period movie of the Russian revolution.

A man stepped out of the house across the street, looked directly up at her window, and a sudden shiver ran down her spine.

The expression on his face wasn't friendly. This area was almost entirely Russian, ethnically speaking. Most of the people hated the government in Riga, and she didn't think her fancy city manners and government badge were going to win her many friends.

She would go to the police station, speak to the officer who'd witnessed the crash, and get the hell out of there as quickly as possible.

That was the plan.

She did a quick scan of the room for the coffeemaker

before accepting that there was none. Then she got into the shower, which was ice cold, and scrubbed her skin as vigorously as if she was in a delousing shed.

She dressed in the same clothes she'd worn the day before, and as she pulled on her expensive, leather ankle boots, she realized that she was about to ruin them beyond recognition.

She went down to the dining room, where the proprietor's wife served her a plate of rye bread with butter and boiled eggs.

There was a coffee urn on the sideboard, and she poured herself a cup.

She saw no other guest.

She finished her breakfast, left the hotel, and went straight to the police station. It was close enough that she didn't need her car, but far enough to do the predicted damage to her boots.

She told herself she'd be out of the village in an hour.

The police station was a drab, concrete, Soviet-era structure with square windows overlooking a narrow porch. It reminded her of the sheriff's office in a western movie. She pushed open the front door, and a bell chimed above her head.

In front of her was a receptionist's desk, and behind it on the wall was a utilitarian-looking clock. It reminded her of her school days, and she checked her watch to see if it was set correctly. It was. A large leather-bound logbook with dates and notes scrawled on its pages was open on the desk, and next to it was a computer with an old, cathode-ray monitor.

No one was at the desk, and Agata leaned over to peek the papers and computer screen.

"Can I help you?" a stern voice said from behind her.

She turned to see a middle-aged woman in a buttoned-up, high-necked blouse, and gray skirt bearing down on her.

"I called yesterday," Agata said.

"A lot of people called yesterday."

Agata smiled thinly. They both knew this wasn't the kind of place where the phone exactly rang off the hook.

"I called from State Police in Riga."

"So you're the national security officer?" the woman asked skeptically.

"Yes, I am," Agata said. "And you are?"

"I'm Jana," the woman said. "I run the office here."

Agata reached into her pocket for her notebook and flicked it open.

"I'm going to need to speak to Baskin," she said, scanning the notes. "Officer Guntis Baskin."

"Of course," the woman said, glancing at the clock. "He eats breakfast at the diner down the street. He'll be there until eight-thirty."

"Down the street?"

"You're welcome to wait here," Jana said, and she managed to say it in a way that convinced Agata that another traipse through the mud was worth the effort.

The restaurant wasn't difficult to find. It had a single gas pump out front, and in the window was a neon sign advertising state lottery tickets. Below the sign, about two dozen dead flies lay scattered on the plastic ledge inside the glass.

Agata entered, and another overhead bell chimed.

A dog was roused by the commotion and tried to come at her. An old man, sitting in a booth by the window, yanked the dog back by the leash.

The man was smoking, and the ashtray in front of him was full to the point of overflowing.

There were a few other men spread around the room.

All seated separately. They were devouring big plates of breakfast or smoking and sipping coffee. Four wore heavy, forestry overalls and large, tan-colored boots with black rubber soles.

The fifth wore the uniform of a police officer.

He was sitting at the counter, and his ass was so wide it sagged over the sides of the stool like a pair of saddlebags.

Agata walked over and sat next to him.

He was about fifty-years-old and had a fork in one hand, a piece of sausage dangling from it precariously, and a lit cigarette in the other.

"Don't tell me you're eating and smoking at the same time," Agata said.

He turned slowly and looked her over, head to toe. "You're the girl from Riga," he said.

"And *you* passed detective school."

He pushed the piece of sausage into his mouth and looked at her again. "You're funny."

Agata took out her notebook again and glanced at it. "You're Baskin," she said.

He nodded and signaled to the waitress to bring over an extra cup of coffee.

"Thank you," Agata said.

He nodded again.

She took a sip off the coffee, which was passable, and said, "So, I'm just going to jump right in, if that's okay."

"Shoot away," Baskin said.

"You filed a report yesterday about a plane crash. Did you see it personally, or someone reported it back to you?"

"I never said it was a crash," Baskin said.

He was spreading jam on his toast, taking great care to get it into all the corners.

"What was it then?"

He looked at her knowingly, then raised his hand and flicked out all his fingers at the same time in the manner of an explosion.

"Poof," he said.

"An explosion?"

He nodded again.

"Why didn't you put that in the report?"

"I thought I did."

"You said, a plane went down."

"It did go down."

"Baskin," Agata said, dropping her voice, "was that plane shot down?"

Baskin sucked through his teeth and leaned back, stretching. He looked around the room, and Agata looked up for the first time.

Every set of eyes in the place was fixed on her.

"Well?" she said. "I hope you didn't get me to come all the way out here just to..." she mimicked the little explosion he'd made with his fingers, and said, "...poof."

He looked around the room for support.

She fixed him in her gaze. "Well?" she said, her tone insistent.

"I didn't get you to come out here at all," he said.

"But I'm here, Baskin. Because of the report you filed. Why bother writing it if you didn't want me to come?"

He sighed. "Look," he said. "Around here, we've kind of just learned to take things as they come. You know what I mean?"

"No, I don't know what you mean."

"I mean," he said, "maybe it was shot down. Maybe it crashed. I can't say for certain."

"You can't say?"

He did that thing again with the fingers. "Poof."

Agata was getting frustrated. "What is that? Poof, like a magic trick? Like it disappeared?"

"Look," Baskin said, "I just know what I saw, and to be honest with you, I thought someone in Riga would have had the sense to send more guys."

"More guys than just me?" Agata said. "Well, I'm sorry to have disappointed you."

"What if it *was* shot down?" he said, "What then? What are you going to do about it? Write it in your notebook?"

Agata was beginning to worry. She'd been holding out hope that some sort of mechanical issue, or pilot error, had brought down the plane. From what Baskin was saying, however obliquely, it seemed like that wasn't the case. She was no aeronautics engineer, but an explosion in the sky didn't sound like a common mechanical issue for a forty-year-old crop-duster.

"Is there something you're not saying to me?" Agata said, clearing her throat.

The men at the other tables weren't menacing, exactly, but they weren't smiling either. And they were making absolutely zero effort to hide the fact that they were listening to every word of the conversation.

"Look," she said, raising her voice to them. "I'm not here to cause trouble. I just need to know what happened."

It was the old man with the dog who spoke. He spoke in a thin, raspy voice, like his vocal cords had been left out to dry in the sun.

"Perhaps if you'd come a little sooner," he wheezed.

"Sooner?" Agata said. "This only happened yesterday."

"And this morning," the old man said, "the monitoring units on our side of the border started pulling out of their positions."

"What?" Agata said, rising to her feet.

The old man nodded. So did the others.

"That makes no sense," Agata said. "Those units are permanently positioned. They'd never pull back, unless..."

"Unless what?" one of the lumberjacks said.

Agata shook her head. "I don't know," she said. "It just makes no sense. They wouldn't do that. Not for any reason."

"That's what I said," the old man said, and then he turned to the lumberjacks. "But these men saw it with their own eyes."

"When?" Agata said.

"This morning," a lumberjack said. "Before dawn."

"Did they tell you anything?" Agata said.

"They said they got orders."

"But their orders are to monitor the border."

"Well, their orders now are to monitor the border in another sector."

Agata slumped back onto her seat. She looked at the cup of coffee. There was a chip in the enamel, and the rough ceramic had turned brown from wear.

She pulled her phone from her pocket and was about to call Kuzis when she remembered she had no signal.

"I'm sure they know what they're doing," she said, trying to sound more confident than she felt.

"Well," Baskin said, slapping some bills on the counter. "I've done my part."

"Your part?"

"I told you what I saw."

"You've been pretty vague, Baskin," Agata said.

"Maybe if the army wasn't pulling out," the old man said, "people's memories would be a little clearer."

6

Agata drove out to the area where Baskin said the plane came down.

She'd asked him to accompany her, but he was, in his words, *otherwise engaged*. He'd warned her not to go out there either, but at this point, she was constitutionally incapable of backing down.

She had to know what was going on.

She tried one last time to call Kuzis before leaving the village, but her phone was still without signal.

It was raining again and, ahead of her, a smokestack from a small factory rose up above the trees like a waypoint. Its red brick walls and metal-rimmed windows reminded her of factories from a century ago.

After the factory, there was a small cluster of houses with hay bales piled next to them. She saw no people, but there were cows, and they stared at her vacantly as she passed.

Baskin had given her detailed directions, and after passing the factory and houses, she broke off from the road onto a forestry track that brought her eastward, closer to the border. She had to be careful. Those tracks crisscrossed back and forth, and if you didn't know exactly where you were, you were likely to inadvertently cross the frontier.

Doing so was dangerous.

She drove along the track slowly, careful not to damage her car or get it stuck in the deep ruts of mud. A metal sign with two bullet holes in it told her she was entering the border region and that it was a criminal offense to cross the border other than at an authorized crossing.

A little further on, there was another sign. This one had a picture of a soldier holding a rifle and the word 'Danger' written on it in Latvian.

She checked her coat for her State Police credentials and put the badge on the dashboard.

She had the GPS programmed with some coordinates Baskin had come up with. They were his best guess at the exact position he'd seen the plane go down, and she was less than half a mile from the red dot on the screen.

The road forked, and she didn't know which branch to take. She was long past the point where her standard-issue Mercedes GPS package still showed details.

She took the right fork, and when it forked again, she took the right again. It looked from the GPS as if she was veering closer and closer to the spot she was aiming for.

When she was about as close as she thought possible, she stopped the car.

She could see now what he'd meant about not being able to find the crash site. The forest was very dense, and the track was a sodden, muddy mess. She was lucky she'd made it this far without getting stuck. She'd be luckier still if she managed to get back out.

She opened the window and listened to the sounds of the forest.

It was eerily still, and a chilly mist rose from the ground like steam from a winter lake.

The ground sloped upward on both sides of the track, and ahead, the terrain only seemed to get softer and muddier.

The drizzle of rain that had been falling all morning had stopped.

She stepped out of the car and checked her service pistol, a Glock 17, to make sure it was loaded.

Wolf attacks were rare but not unheard of in those parts, but it wasn't wolves she was afraid of.

She went to the back of the vehicle and opened the trunk. There was a plastic case, and she opened it, removing a pair of binoculars and one of those old GPS units hikers used to use before phones became ubiquitous.

She put both in her jacket and began making her way further up the track. She wasn't sure what she could hope to find. The plane could be twenty meters away in the trees and she wouldn't have seen it. But she wasn't ready to go back to Riga. She had to find something concrete to show Kuzis.

Whoever had reassigned the monitoring units needed to be told what was going on, and those people didn't listen to the likes of Agata unless she had something concrete she could show them.

She walked on carefully, stopping every ten yards or so to listen. She'd never been a lover of the wilderness, and her proximity to the Russian border made every snap of a twig, every creak of a tree, even more sinister.

From a small crest in the road, she could make out an opening in the trees off the path to her right. She left the road and pushed through branches that seemed to claw at her cashmere coat as if intentionally trying to wreck it.

When she reached the clearing, she saw that it was actually another, narrower track. In the mud were fresh tire marks.

They looked like they'd been made by a fat-tired motocross bike.

She followed the path in the direction that, to the best of her bearings, went eastward. It brought her uphill, and just beyond the next ridge, she saw a small, wood-framed structure.

It was like a carport, with open walls and a flat roof. Camouflage netting had been spread across the top to hide it from above, and inside were wooden skids with large crates on them.

Agata immediately dropped to one knee and drew her pistol. She listened. Apart from the sounds of the forest, she heard nothing.

She watched the structure for about ten minutes and saw no sign of movement.

She looked back in the direction she'd come.

This was crazy.

She had no business being out there alone. She hadn't even ensured Kuzis knew where she was.

Anything could happen to her out there, and it would be days before he came looking.

The structure could belong to anyone.

Drug traffickers.

Human traffickers.

Poachers.

But something told her it belonged to the Russian military.

She looked back down the path in the direction she'd come from. She knew that the smart thing would be to go back to the car and get the hell out of there.

But she couldn't do that.

She had to know what was going on.

Cautiously, she made her way down the slope toward the structure. She tried to open the first crate. It was nailed shut. She looked around for something to pry it with. There were some six-inch nails that had been used to erect the structure, and she managed to get one of them in under the pine lid of the crate. Using a rock as a hammer, she hit the nail and slowly managed to pry open the lid.

Inside the crate, there were smaller wooden boxes, and stenciled faintly on top of each in Cyrillic script were the words:

Advance Provisions Department
Military Technical Academy
Saint Petersburg
Russia

She lifted one of the boxes out of the crate and pried off the lid. It contained 5.45 x 39mm rifle cartridges, the most common cartridge used in the Russian military. It was used for the AK-74, as well as the newer AK-12.

She checked the next crate, again prying open the lid with a nail and rock, and sure enough, it contained dozens of the new AK-12 assault rifles.

Agata's department tracked every detail of Russian armaments, and she knew all too well that the AK-12 had been brought into service just two years earlier. It would eventually replace the older AK-74M, but production delays meant that only the highest priority units had so far been issued the new weapon.

Priority for delivery was based on one factor.

Likelihood of imminent combat.

She knew what it meant that the guns were being stock-piled here.

Her heart pounded in her chest.

She opened the next crate and what she found was even more terrifying. Rows of neatly stacked, RPG-7 shoulder-mounted rocket launchers, as well as the more advanced 9K333 Verba surface-to-air launchers.

Either of them was more than capable of taking down a forty-year-old forestry biplane.

In the next crate was a stack of papers in a sealed, plastic document sleeve. In the sleeve was a twenty-five-thousand-to-one scale map of the border region around Ziguri.

She couldn't help but notice that the Latvian border surveillance posts were marked on the map with red crosses. Those were the same positions that, according to the men back in Ziguri, were at this very moment being vacated.

She also noticed that these maps were an order of magnitude more detailed than anything she'd ever seen before. The roads, including the tracks she'd just driven in on, and which had not been marked on her car's GPS system, were laid out in such detail that special markings showed where trees were too close together to allow a three-meter-wide vehicle to pass.

Bridges were shown with codes for the material from which they were made, their official weight capacity, and their probability of carrying a fifty-five-ton vehicle.

Agata was only too aware that the new Russian T-14 Armata happened to weigh exactly fifty-five tons and had a width of exactly three meters. A test batch of a hundred tanks had been delivered to the Second Guards Tamanskaya Motor Rifle Division, based in the town of Kalininets, south-west of Moscow.

The Taman Division was the most decorated formation in Soviet military history, and the most elite unit in the First Guards Tank Army of Russia's Western Military District.

In countless war game scenarios, the Latvian military had concluded that if Russia was ever going to launch a lightning ground invasion, that was the unit they were most likely to deploy. Even with the assistance of regional NATO forces, the T-14's would be unstoppable and would overwhelm Latvian defenses.

They could be in Riga in a matter of hours if the bridges weren't destroyed.

Everyone in Agata's division took the threat of a Russian invasion seriously. They treated it as an imminent threat. They memorized railway time tables, route probabilities, bridge carrying capacities, unit formations, and equipment measurements.

They knew what a Russian ground invasion would look like in perhaps even more detail than the officers of the Russian High Command.

And this was it.

Agata looked out at maps, the crates, the camouflage netting above the structure, and she knew exactly what she was looking at.

This was an advance cache.

She didn't know for certain which side of the border she was on. It was nearly impossible to tell. But what she did know was that, either way, if Arturs Alda had accidentally flown a little too close to one of these caches, that would explain exactly what had happened to him.

She stuffed the map and some of the other documents into her pocket and pulled out her phone. She was about to take photos of the crates, when she felt the darkness of a shadow cross her from behind.

She ducked, just in time to avoid three bullets right overhead. They lodged into the pine crate, sending splinters of wood into her face.

She pulled out her gun and fired instinctively in the direction the gunfire had come from, not taking time to aim.

More bullets, definitely from an automatic weapon, came at her, shattering the side of the crate. She dove for cover behind it. Laying prone on the ground, she looked up through the gap between the crates and tried to see where the bullets were coming from.

She scanned the tree line and saw the flash of a muzzle as the next volley came her way.

As far as she could tell, there was only one gunman.

"State Police," she called out. "Hold your fire."

Her warning was met with another burst of fire. She waited, then rose up and fired six shots consecutively at the precise spot she'd seen the muzzle flash.

She dropped back down, but no more shots were fired.

She thought she'd hit him but couldn't be certain. Maybe he was trying to lure her out into the open.

She waited behind the crate, watching through the gap for any sign of movement. She watched for about five minutes, and would have watched a good deal longer were it not for the sound of a chopper flying in from the east. From the sound of it, she could tell it was a few miles out, but she didn't want to still be there when it arrived.

She got to her feet, took a breath, then ran for it. Keeping as low as possible, she made a mad dash for the trees.

No one fired at her, and she climbed up the slope and down the other side, slipping and falling and ripping her coat as she went. Just before she reached her car, she saw an off-road, four-wheeler with extra-wide tires painted a military green.

She recognized it too as Russian.

She kept running through the last stretch of trees and onto the muddy track she'd driven in on. She reached her car, got in, and revved the engine. Reversing expertly, she got all the way back down the track until the first fork, where she put her foot down hard on the brake and swung the car around to face forward.

Then she really put her foot down, sliding and skidding through the mud until she reached the paved road by the old factory.

She didn't slow down or look back once, not even when she got onto the main road back toward Riga.

She didn't realize that her badge, which she'd left on the dashboard, was gone.

7

J acob Kirov looked out the window of the cab and shivered. His plane had been delayed by four hours because of a blizzard, and he was severely jet-lagged. He was also drunk. The bar on the private jet carried the best of everything, and he'd gotten into the scotch.

"First time in Saint Petersburg?" the driver asked, his thick, uneducated accent bringing Kirov immediately back to his boyhood.

"I grew up here."

The driver nodded. He had no idea who Kirov was but had noticed the expensive coat, the diamond-encrusted Piaget chronograph, the Louis Vuitton luggage. He worked for tips, after all.

"Welcome home, then."

Kirov was not happy to be home. As Russian Consul-General in New York, he'd grown accustomed to certain luxuries that were, let's just say, difficult to acquire in other cities of the world. He'd heard recently that New York had more Russian-born prostitutes than Moscow, and he knew from personal experience it was true.

It was the greatest city in the world, as far as he was concerned. And America, which allowed all that vice to prosper while maintaining an air of pristine Protestant puritanism, was the greatest country.

A country's greatness, Kirov believed, rested entirely on its ability to conjure a narrative, a false reality, in which men could do all the things they lusted to do, while telling themselves they were doing God's work.

It had been that way in every great empire in history.

And it was the one feature the USSR had so gravely lacked.

After all, what was the point in fighting for universal brotherhood and the good of one's fellow man when no one up above was watching?

Life became futile.

It was like playing and not keeping score.

It had been many years since Kirov had returned to the city of his birth, and the view through the window brought a strange mix of emotions. Memories of cabbage soup and walking to school in torrential rain. Memories of his mother's face, and his grammar teacher's silky white hands.

The man had later been charged with molestation, not of Kirov but other children. No conviction was ever secured.

Not to worry.

Kirov had taken it upon himself to track the man down. Even though he was well into his eighties, Kirov's assassin, following careful instructions, cut off the man's balls and forced him to eat them. He recorded it on video, the old man's mouth moving up and down like a marionette as the assassin's gloved hands opened and closed his jaw forcibly.

A disgusting affair.

The footage was locked away in a safe in the New York consulate.

"There used to be a very good fish restaurant on this street," Kirov said. He had memories of dining on sturgeon and caviar to the point of vomiting, and following that up with the very finest cognac and Gurkha cigars. "Looks like it's gone," he added.

The driver nodded.

They rounded the corner of the square, and high above them, the towering façade of Saint Isaac's Cathedral rose toward the sky like the peak of a mountain. Kirov strained to see the top, the snow whipping around its spires like little demons.

Directly across the square from it was the former German Imperial Embassy. From the days when Saint Petersburg, and not Moscow, was the capital.

Kirov had always thought the placement of the buildings was appropriate.

God on one side, the Germans on the other.

"The Astoria Hotel, sir," the driver announced, pulling up in front of a grand, six-story tall, Neoclassical building that stretched the length of the square's eastern side. "Allow me to bring in the luggage."

"No," Kirov said, "the bellhop will do it."

They waited in the car until the luggage had been removed and loaded onto a brass cart by the bellhop, then Kirov pulled up the collar of his coat and stepped out into the cold.

He hurried up the steps and through the hotel's ornate revolving doors.

Everything was exactly as he remembered. The chandeliers, the marble, the enormous palms at the foot of the staircase. To his left was the legendary bar where Mikhail Bulgakov scratched out the first draft of his most famous novel.

Kirov was staying in the hotel as a guest of the president, and as such, was escorted directly to the expansive penthouse suite overlooking the square. He had a view straight down the Malaya Morskaya, to the house where Dostoyevsky wrote *White Nights*.

It was writers everywhere in Saint Petersburg. The city cherished them the way other cities valued their sports teams.

He waited for the bellhop to bring his luggage, tipped him, then locked the door. He looked around the room. It was the epitome of classical European luxury. It might not have had the amenities of a New York hotel, but what it lacked in function, it made up for in effort. Everything oozed effort. The wallpaper, the four-posted bed, the marble fireplaces and extravagantly gilded candelabra. It exuded a sense of opulence that was so self-conscious it was almost smothering.

Vladimir Lenin had once stayed in the suite.

As had Elton John.

Kirov looked at his watch and then went to the minibar. He wanted a drink but thought better of it. He grabbed a Heineken and opened it against the corner of the marble mantle above the fireplace.

Then he lit a cigar.

At some point, he fell asleep. It was dark when he woke, and a mess of ash lay on the carpet beneath his arm.

The only light came from the embers in the fireplace and the streetlights outside the window. He switched on a lamp and checked the time.

He had a shower.

By the time he'd shaved and dressed in a Canali velvet tuxedo jacket and matching pants, it was time to leave.

He put on his coat and gloves and walked out to the corridor. Two men in suits were standing outside his door.

"Federal security service, sir," one of them said.

Kirov nodded. It was normal. They were for the president's protection, not his.

"We're going to the Trocadéro," Kirov said.

"We know where you're going, sir."

The agents called the elevator, and when it arrived, they got in with him. They escorted him through the lobby and out to the street where a state limousine was waiting.

Kirov got in the backseat.

He'd been told he was meeting the president at one of the city's most famous restaurants, a place that looked out across the Neva River at the spectacular Peter and Paul Fortress, but the car drove right past it, out of the city center along the Palace Embankment and past Summer Garden.

The further they went, the more Kirov grew nervous.

It would have been an elaborate way to get rid of him, to bring him all the way to Saint Petersburg and have him check into one of the world's most expensive hotels, but the president was known to do stranger things.

He was a character.

He always injected flair into his dealings.

He liked to keep people on their toes.

It worked. Kirov had watched him retain power for more than two decades by deftly playing rival against rival, keeping them constantly off-balance, provoking responses that looked disastrous, but in the end, always served to cement his power.

He knew how to gamble, and he always raised the stakes.

The car turned away from the river and entered the

Smolninskoye District, coming to a halt on Suvorovskiy Prospekt.

"What's this?" Kirov said to the driver.

"This is where you're meeting him," the driver said, nodding out the window at a nondescript, unassuming building.

"Good thing I dressed up," Kirov said.

There was a restaurant, an old-style Italian place, and he walked to the door slowly. A security agent with an earpiece opened it for him. Another took his coat and gloves, then patted him down.

The restaurant was warm, decorated in traditional Italian fashion with candles on the tables in little red bowls and a worn leather banquette along the wall. Behind the banquette were aged mirrors, and opposite was a well-stocked bar.

Apart from the two security agents at the door, the only other person present was the bartender, who stood behind the bar, dressed in a white shirt and bow tie.

Peasant music played from a small speaker in the ceiling.

"Where are we?" Kirov said to one of the agents.

"President's favorite restaurant," the guard said.

"The food's that good?"

"It's better than good," the agent said, the expression on his face as serious as if he was giving testimony.

The bartender looked up from the glass he was polishing and said, "What'll it be?"

Kirov squinted at the bottles behind the bar, it was all top-notch stuff, and said, "surprise me."

He took a seat at the table across from the bar, it was the only one set, and lit a cigar.

A moment later, the bartender came over and placed a

crystal glass on a napkin in front of him. "This is a thirty-year-old Port Ellen."

"They told you what I like," Kirov said.

"They filled me in."

Kirov sat back and took a sip. It was potent stuff, viscous, almost like tar, as if it had been aged in barrels used to store diesel fuel.

He coughed.

"Is it all right?" the bartender said.

"It tastes like gasoline."

"Very good, sir," the bartender said and left him to enjoy it.

Kirov was about to take another sip when the door at the front of the restaurant opened.

It was the president.

He was dressed head to toe in a flamboyant, brown velvet suit that made him look more like an extra from a John Travolta film than the leader of one of the most powerful nations on the planet.

Nothing about Vladimir Molotov fit the mold, not the flashy clothing, not the carefully crafted mannerisms, and certainly not the diamond-encrusted, solid gold sunglasses he removed and placed on the table in front of Kirov.

Kirov stood in greeting, and the president motioned extravagantly for him to sit back down.

"Bartender," he shouted. "Champagne. I haven't seen this man in, what's it been?"

"Too long, Mr. President."

"Too long," the president barked.

The president was famous for being loud. For being the life of the party. He caused no end of *faux pas* at international summits and had insulted virtually every leader on the world stage.

But Kirov had known him before. Back when he was still just a lowly KGB agent finding his way in the world, learning his craft. He'd been a fairly ordinary guy back then, but within a few years, had managed to transform every aspect of his personality. He worshipped Don Corleone and practiced every mannerism, every gesture, every inflection of his voice, for hours in front of a mirror.

None of what Kirov saw now, not the bravado, not the machismo, was innate to the man.

It was all an act.

A persona.

A conscious choice.

It was as if the Devil himself had one night spoken to Vladimir Molotov, and told him he could be the most powerful man on the planet, a man with absolute power, who would make nations cower and presidents quiver in their boots.

He could become a God.

And all he had to do to get it was play the part.

Speak the lines.

Not balk when things got bloody.

The waiter came over with the champagne and poured two glasses. Then he brought the president a Cohiba cigar and a gold lighter.

The president began lighting his cigar, and between puffs, he said to Kirov, "I hope you brought your appetite because they have the best food in the world here. All the secret recipes."

Kirov nodded, and they clinked glasses.

The president seemed relaxed, happy to be there, like he was in no hurry, but Kirov knew something big was on the horizon. He hadn't just crossed the Atlantic to discuss recipes.

He waited until the president's cigar was burning, then lit one for himself.

"Do you know why you're here?" the president said after draining his glass.

"I assume it has something to do with the embassy bombings," Kirov said.

"It has everything to do with the bombings. They proved what I've been telling you for thirty years."

"That they're weaker than they look," Kirov said.

"They're not just weak, Kirov. They're made of straw. We could do anything right now and get away with it."

"Anything, sir?"

"Within reason."

"We don't have the deterrent we once had," Kirov said. "They no longer think of us as an existential threat."

"That's where they're making a mistake," the president said, sucking on his cigar so that smoke billowed from his mouth in opaque puffs of cloud. "They're at war, they're locked in a struggle for their very lives, a struggle that can have only one outcome, one victor, and they're too up their own assholes to realize it."

"They live in a dream world, sir."

"Did you see what's on the front page of *The Post* this morning?"

"I did not, sir."

"A National Park," the president said derisively. "Montgomery wants to create a new one. He wants to protect birds, Kirov."

"He's obsessed with petty interests, sir."

"Birds," the president exclaimed, slapping the table. "I just fucking blew up the Moscow Embassy, killed his diplomats. Marines' corpses were strewn all over the street. And this pussy is talking about a bird sanctuary."

"Their news cycle is incapable of remaining focused."

"Kirov," the president said, his eyes flashing brightly. "We're going to hit them again. And this time, we're hitting hard."

"How hard, sir?"

"We're taking back what's ours."

The waiter came over with a plate containing what Kirov immediately recognized to be *casu martzu*. He'd seen the dish before, a traditional sheep's cheese from Sardinia, but had never tasted it. During the fermentation process, the cheese was allowed to quite literally decompose, to the point that fly larvae grew in its pungent fats and began crawling around in it. According to the Sardinians, the larvae were what gave it its flavor. They also claimed it had to be eaten while they were still alive.

Kirov could see them now, tiny translucent worms that wriggled around on the skin of the cheese and fell off onto the plate.

The president ran his finger around the edge of the plate, crushing them, and then putting it in his mouth.

Kirov took a sip of his wine and tried not to let the revulsion show on his face.

"You eat it like this," the president said, cutting into the cheese and revealing a veritable metropolis that squirmed and writhed with life. It brought to Kirov's mind a rancid, infested wound.

White puss quite literally seeped from pores in the cheese crust, and the president said, "They call those teardrops."

"I thought this cheese was banned," Kirov said, watching in horror as the president scooped it up with a spoon and put it in his mouth.

The president shrugged. "It's a tradition," he said. "It's a way of life. The bureaucrats will never understand that they can't stop people from simply living their lives."

Kirov knew better than to skip the course. Everything was a test.

He put his spoon into the opening in the crust. When it emerged, worms wriggled and writhed and fell from it, leaving a trail across the table back to Kirov's plate.

Kirov put the cheese in his mouth and swallowed without chewing. He followed it with a large gulp of champagne.

"Tell me," the president said, putting more of the cheese into his mouth, "how you would describe the situation of our western frontier."

Kirov answered without missing a beat. "Our entire European border is the front in a new Cold War, sir."

The president smiled. It was what he wanted to hear. It was also what Kirov truly believed, which was why he'd been allowed to prosper while so many of his peers had found themselves, *sleeping with the fishes,* as the Corleones would say.

"It's an Iron Curtain," the president said. "It always has been. It never collapsed. It never fucking collapsed."

Kirov nodded, serving himself another scoop of the cheese, only this time allowing himself to taste the squirming larvae in his mouth. His life had been a progression in acquiring difficult tastes. Strange, expensive delicacies, pungent single malts, why not a rancid, maggot-ridden cheese? It was nothing compared to the taste of blood, and he'd grown quite accustomed to that.

"We've been aggressive," the president said, "and it's paid off. Just look at the Ukraine and Georgia."

"So now, we take the next step," Kirov said.

The president smiled. "And what do you think that step should be, Kirov?"

"Sir?"

The president smiled. "Go on. Take a guess."

"I'm sure I don't know, sir."

"Don't be a pussy, Kirov."

Kirov swallowed. He had no idea what the next step was, and he didn't want to offend the president by guessing incorrectly. All he knew was that he wanted to be a part of it.

"Well, sir," he said, "we're meeting in Saint Petersburg. That would suggest something involving the Western Military District command."

"You see," the president said. "That's why you're my best lieutenant. We understand each other, you and I."

"I believe we do, sir."

"I want to take back Latvia."

Kirov nodded thoughtfully, trying to look impressed while avoiding giving any hint of skepticism."

"I think your timing is impeccable, sir."

The president smiled. "I didn't just call you here to congratulate me, Kirov. I want to know what you think."

"Of course, sir."

"I want to know what risks you foresee."

There was a moment's pause while Kirov fed on the larvae and tried to savor their texture. It wasn't easy.

"Well, sir," he said once he managed to swallow the cheese, "Latvia is not Ukraine. This won't be like our occupation of the Crimea or South Ossetia. The world will take notice."

The president nodded. "I know Latvia is a NATO member," Kirov. "I know what that means. I know it's an EU member. I've been there. I've spent Euros there."

"The Americans are bound by international law to step

in and defend Latvian sovereignty. Any attack must, by law, be treated as an attack on American soil."

"We'll see about that," the president said.

"Do you think the US is ready to abandon its NATO obligations?"

"I think," the president said, dangling his spoon over the cheese, "I think that times change, Kirov. When you and I were young men, Latvia was an integral part of the USSR. They spent rubles. The Soviet military had bases."

"That's true, sir."

"And times changed."

"Yes, they did, sir."

"And if they changed once. They can change again."

"It's a risk, sir."

"If we're going to regain our position in the world, Kirov, we're going to have to take risks. Latvia is the first of many. It's a domino. The first step. It's precisely because it's a NATO member that I want it. I want to show the world that we can take anything we want. That no one's safe."

"You said the world would take notice."

"Yes, sir."

"I want them to take notice, Kirov. I want nothing more than for them to take notice. I want our military on the screen of every cable news channel in the world. I want those maps where the color red flows from Russia and spreads over Europe like spilled ink."

"Or blood," Kirov added.

The president smiled. "What appetite is there in America to stop this, Kirov?" he said.

"Sir?"

"Come on. You live there. I've been to your apartment on Fifth Avenue. I've seen the way you live. You're among them,

Kirov. You see what they see. You eat what they eat. You smell what they smell."

"I'm not sure that qualifies me to predict...", Kirov said.

"I'm not asking you to predict. I'm just asking for your opinion."

"My opinion?"

"Latvia is a NATO member. NATO is the most important, the most powerful defensive alliance in the history of the planet."

"Yes, it is."

"If I take Latvia, does Ingram Montgomery have the appetite for war? Does he have the balls?"

"Sir, well, frankly, it depends."

"I don't want to hear that, Kirov. Yes or no."

"Sir," Kirov said, taking a sip from his glass. He felt as if the temperature in the room was getting steadily hotter. "Sir, if we do this, if we want to get in clean, we're going to have to be fast. If we catch them by surprise, the president, he won't have the balls to pull the trigger."

"You're sure of that?"

"As long as we're quick, I think I can say yes. Americans care about NATO, but they care about other things more. And to be honest, I don't think you'd be able to find a single random person anywhere who could point out Riga to you on a map."

"You're quite sure, Kirov? Don't tell me what I want to hear. Tell me the truth on this."

"Sir, they're tired of these endless wars in far-flung places for people they've never heard of, places they've never heard of. Do you know how many lives they lost fighting in Afghanistan?"

"I do, actually," the president said.

"So do they, sir. So do the people. And they're tired of it."

"But we have to be fast, you say."

"Well, it won't only be the president who makes this decision."

"Who will it be?"

"The cabinet. The Joint Chiefs."

"They'll follow the president."

"They understand the strategic importance of NATO. They know that if Latvia falls, that Lithuania will be next, and then Poland, and then Germany. If they have enough time to persuade the president, he'll follow their advice."

"So we'll be fast," the president said.

"We'll need to be very fast," Kirov said. "We'll need to be in Riga before the president or anyone else in the cabinet has time to digest what's happening."

"How fast?" the president said.

"Lightning fast," Kirov said.

The president nodded.

"And then," Kirov said, his voice growing hesitant, "there's Levi Roth."

"Roth," the president spat.

"He'll be for war, sir. I can promise you that. He'll be out for our blood, whether the rest of the cabinet approves it or not."

"Levi Roth is a spent force, Kirov. He was for war when I went into the Ukraine. He was for war when I bombed the embassy. What good has it done him?"

"He's not a spent force entirely, sir," Kirov said, and his eye met the president's.

The president knew what he was referring to. The asset. Spector. He was a danger entirely in a class of his own. He'd been inside the Kremlin. He'd been inside the president's estate at Novo-Ogaryovo. He didn't play by the rules, and he was a threat not just to the interests of the state but to the regime itself. To the president personally. To Kirov. The top players.

"Spector," the president said. "What can you do about him?"

"I could have him killed," Kirov said, but even as the words left his mouth, he knew they rang hollow.

"If you could do that, you'd have done it already."

"I've got agents on hand," Kirov said.

"Do you have someone you'd be willing to bet your life on?"

Kirov shook his head.

"Do you have someone you'd be willing to bet *my* life on?"

Any attempt to kill a man like Lance Spector had to succeed. You only got one shot against a man like that. And you didn't take it unless you were guaranteed a hit. A miss, and that's it. Game over. He would come for you, and there wasn't a place on the planet you'd be safe.

"I think I've got a better approach," Kirov said. "Something ... *safer*."

"Safer for who?"

"Us."

The president bit his lip. This was a critical detail. Whatever else he had planned, he had to know that this assassin wasn't going to come looking for him.

"Spector's got a weakness," Kirov said.

"What kind of weakness?"

"What kind do you think?"

The president smiled. "A girl."

Kirov nodded.

"If you lay a finger on her," the president said.

"No," Kirov said. "Not that."

"What then?"

"All we need to do is make sure Spector is distracted. This operation is going to be so fast that as long as we can guarantee he's not personally involved, it will be over before Roth activates him."

"You're going to distract Lance Spector?"

"Just leave it to me, sir. I know what to do. It will be effective."

"And it will be...".

"*Safe,* sir, yes. You have my word."

The waiter came over and removed their plates. He asked if they wanted something else to drink. They'd made it through the first course, and the bottle was empty.

The president looked at him. "The next course is?"

"Songbirds, sir, served with polenta."

"Delicious," the president said. "How about the Didier Dagueneau?"

"Very good choice, sir."

The waiter left and returned with a bottle of Sauvignon Blanc. He opened the cork carefully and offered the president a taste. The president passed the glass to Kirov, and Kirov picked it up and inhaled deeply before taking a sip and swishing it around his mouth. He tasted grapefruit peel and minerals.

He nodded, and the waiter poured them each a glass.

Kirov reached for his, and somehow, by some curse of fate, he knocked it over.

The glass rolled across the table and was about to fall off the edge when the president caught it.

He looked at Kirov.

"So sorry, sir. I don't know what I was thinking."

"Three thousand dollars a bottle," the president said.

"I know, sir."

The president looked at him very intently. He looked ferocious. Angry. Then a smile crept across his lips.

"Relax, Kirov."

"Yes, sir," Kirov said.

"You're shitting your pants."

"This is a big risk, what we're talking about."

"You're worried about Spector?"

"I'm worried about NATO, sir. What if I'm wrong? What if the alliance isn't as decayed and atrophied as I just said?"

"Well," the president said, "I'm willing to gamble against this US president. He lacks nerve. I just leveled his embassy, the whole world saw it, the whole world knew it had to be me, and he did nothing."

"There's talk of sanctions."

The president waved his hand in the air. "Parking tickets," he said.

Kirov nodded. He took a deep breath. The waiter returned with a fresh glass and refilled it. When he left, the president said, "Kirov, I need you to listen very carefully."

Kirov had picked up the glass, but he put it back down without taking a drink.

"The best type of war to be in," the president continued, "is the war the other side doesn't see."

Kirov nodded.

"Do you follow my meaning?"

"I think so, sir."

"The Americans are not ready for this. Given time, I know the generals would get the president to the right response. They'd walk him like a child through the steps and coddle him to the conclusion that the time for war had come. I know that. But we're not going to give them time. We're going to strike like an arrow, and we'll be in Riga before they even know we crossed the border. It will be a *fait accompli.* Any talk of a response will be too late. They'll have no choice but to accept the reality on the ground."

"Sir, what if we can't move fast enough?"

"How fast do we need to be?"

"Every minute after we cross the border, those generals will be working on the president. We don't need to be as fast as an arrow. We need to be as fast as lightning."

"I can be in Riga in six hours," the president said.

"Who told you that?"

"Zhukovsky."

"Oleg Zhukovsky?"

"That's correct."

"Sir, Oleg, he's loyal."

"He's GRU overseer for the Western Military District."

"Quite so, sir. Yes. But there are concerns...".

"Concerns?"

"I mean, sir," Kirov said, backtracking. It wasn't his job to tell the president about rumors he'd surely already heard. "Sir, six hours. That's basically the time it would take a T-14 to get from the border to Riga."

"That's right."

"Assuming no delays. No blown bridges."

"They won't have time for that."

"We hope."

"Zhukovsky says it can be done."

"Sir," Kirov said hesitantly. "I'm not certain even six hours is going to be fast enough."

"Well," the president said, "how do you propose we get there faster? Aircraft?"

"NATO's air defenses," Kirov said. "That's their most developed capability."

"Race cars?"

"Sir, we're going to need ... *contingencies.*"

"Contingencies?" the president said.

"We're going to need to cover our tracks. Blind the enemy. Confuse the public."

"All right."

"Sir, execution will be extremely complex."

"That's why I've got you, Kirov."

Kirov smiled thinly. He feared it might come across more as a snarl and brought his napkin to his mouth.

"Don't be modest, Kirov," the president said.

"I'm not, sir."

"This is going to be the singular achievement of our lives."

"Of course, sir."

"If we can restore Russia to the greatness of the Soviet Union, they'll be talking about us for centuries."

"You're right, sir."

"And if anyone can get the job done, it's you."

"I'm going to need full command over Zhukovsky. Tell the Western Military District they answer to me now. Zhukovsky answers to me."

"Very well," the president said.

"I need to be able to authorize ... *anything.*"

"Anything?" the president said.

The food arrived, a large silver platter containing a dozen whole birds, each about six inches in length. In France, they were known as Ortolan, and they had to be illegally trapped in nets before their annual migration south.

"They keep them in dark boxes," the president said.

Kirov looked at him blankly.

"When they catch them," the president said.

"*Them*, sir?"

"The birds."

"Oh," Kirov said.

"The birds think it's winter and that they've failed to make it south."

"I see," Kirov said, watching in horror as the president picked one of the birds up by the head.

The waiter then handed the president a large, cloth napkin, which the president put over his head. Then, beneath the napkin, he put the bird in his mouth whole, including its feet and head, and then removed the napkin.

Kirov watched as the president spit the larger bones onto a side plate.

The waiter then handed a similar napkin to Kirov.

"Thank you," Kirov said weakly.

"Go ahead," the president said. "It's tradition to use the napkin."

"How curious," Kirov said, eyeing the beak on the president's side plate.

"According to legend, the practice started when French priests, to hide from God the fact they were doing something so cruel, put a cloth over their heads as they ate the birds."

"I don't see how it's any more disgraceful than eating other birds," Kirov said, praying he didn't throw up on the table.

"Well," the president said, "the birds, in the darkness of their little boxes, they don't know what to do. They think their migration has failed. They think winter has caught them. They eat compulsively. They can't stop."

"I see," Kirov said.

"They feed them millet, and they eat almost to the point that it kills them."

Kirov thought he was about to find out what that felt like.

"They double in size in a matter of weeks, Kirov."

Kirov nodded, looking at them. The beak, the eyes, the feet. He couldn't imagine putting all that in his mouth at once.

"When they're ready to cook," the president said, "they're drowned in Armagnac."

"At least they've been plucked," Kirov said, unfolding the napkin, which was almost as large as a pillowcase, and putting it on his head.

"Go on," the president said again.

Kirov picked up one of the birds by the head, just as the president had done, covered his face, and inserted it into his mouth. He chewed, spitting out the larger bones, and as the waiter topped up his wine, Jacob Kirov knew that this could be the biggest opportunity of his career.

He would have the most powerful part of the Russian army answering to him. As GRU overseer, every officer in the Western Military District's would be terrified of him. He could have them disappeared at the drop of a hat. He could have their families disappeared. His power over those men would be absolute.

It might even be the opportunity he'd been waiting for.

If he was risking nuclear war, nuclear annihilation, not just for Russia, but perhaps for the entire planet, then why not risk a coup.

Maybe it was his turn to wear the crown, to sit on the throne.

Then he could choose the menu at dinner, and other people would have to stomach his tastes.

They took turns eating the birds, and Kirov wondered if he'd ever be able to enjoy the taste of Armagnac again.

When the last of them were finally gone, the president beckoned the waiter back over and ordered a bottle of an exceedingly expensive Bordeaux to accompany the meat course.

Then he put another cigar in his mouth.

"Kirov," he said, sucking noisily to get the cigar lit. "The strike must be like a ballet."

Kirov could see that the alcohol was beginning to have its effect, and that the serious business of the evening would soon give way to the hard-drinking debauchery the president was famous for.

In fact, Kirov was surprised no women had been brought in to the restaurant yet.

He clinked his glass against the president's.

"I want you to overwhelm them with everything we've got. Nothing's off the table to you, Kirov. Nothing."

"I appreciate that, Mr. President. It may be necessary that I cross a few lines."

"Cross them all," the president said. "I don't give a flying fuck about the lines you cross, so long as you deliver. Sow fear. Sow confusion. But get me that prize."

"Sir," Kirov said, looking over his shoulder before saying more. "The new Kosmos weapon? Is it operational?"

The president smiled. "You see," he said, slapping his hand on the table loudly. "You see. That's why you're my number one, Kirov. That's why you're my top lieutenant. Because you think on your feet. You show initiative."

Kirov nodded. "I want to blind the eye of the cyclops."

"Blind everything," the president said. "Internet, radio, cable, satellite, all of it."

The waiter came over with the Bordeaux and two fresh glasses.

"I think we can dispense with the tasting this time," the president said.

The waiter nodded and poured the wine. Then he said, "Are you ready for the meat course, sir?"

The president examined his cigar. "Give us a few minutes," he said.

The waiter left, and the president let about two inches of ash fall to the floor.

"Sir," Kirov said, leaning in closer to him, "would it be possible to clear the room for a moment."

The president was feeling increasingly celebratory. He stood up and said to the guards, "Give us a moment alone, gentlemen."

The two guards looked at each other, then bowed slightly and backed out of the restaurant. The waiter had already gone to the kitchen, and it was just the two of them in the room.

The president brought his attention back to Kirov. "What are you planning, you sly fox?"

"The *coup de grâce,* sir. The thing that justifies everything that follows."

"And what would that look like?"

Kirov glanced toward the door, checking that they were still alone. Then he said, "An old fashioned false flag operation."

"A false flag operation?"

Kirov checked the room again.

"You're nervous," the president said.

"Sir," Kirov said, his heart was pounding, "not just any false flag operation. But I'm thinking, if we really want to avoid a war with the Americans, we're going to need to give ourselves a rock-solid pretext for this invasion."

The president nodded.

"This would have to be something that would shock the world."

"All right," the president said.

"It would have to be a massacre, sir."

"A massacre."

"A massacre of ethnic Russians by Latvian soldiers."

Very slowly, a smile spread across the president's face. Then he clapped Kirov's shoulder. "That's perfect," he said quietly. "That's perfect."

Kirov smiled.

The waiter re-emerged, carrying a silver tray. On it were two plates, and when placed on the table, Kirov almost threw up.

"La pajata," the waiter said with a flourish.

The president clapped his hands. He was positively ebullient.

"Now leave us," he said to the waiter.

Kirov dug his fork into the pile of intestines and put the food in his mouth before the president could tell him what it was.

"Tender, aren't they?" the president said.

Kirov nodded as he chewed.

"Intestines," the president said. "Taken from calves before they're weaned from their mother's milk. That's why they're so succulent. They've never eaten solid food."

Kirov nodded and put more of it into his mouth. He had to get through it as quickly as possible before he lost his nerve.

"That cheese texture," the president continued.

"Ricotta?" Kirov managed to say.

"No. Mother's milk. In the calf's intestine when it died. The enzymes cause it to curdle like that."

Kirov stopped himself from grimacing as he shoveled another forkful into his mouth.

The president filled his mouth with a large helping of intestine and then took a gulp of wine.

"What's wrong?" he said. "You look pale, Kirov."

"No, no," Kirov protested, putting another forkful into his mouth. "It's delicious."

The president's eyes remained on him as he chewed. He forced himself to swallow.

"I think you like it," the president said, smiling.

Kirov nodded and ate more. The president watched him clean the entire plate, and when he was finally done, the president stood up.

"Bravo, Kirov. You've done very well."

Kirov nodded. His stomach felt like a revolving ball. His eyes were watering. He'd done it.

The president was looking down at him. He hadn't touched his own food.

"Me," the president said, "personally, I find this dish difficult to stomach."

Kirov nodded.

"But you, you ate every last bite."

"I have a strong stomach, sir."

"I see that," the president said, and he picked up his plate and put it on top of Kirov's, right in front of his face.

"Sir," Kirov said. "That's not necessary."

"Nonsense, my boy," the president said. "Eat."

8

Laurel hadn't spoken to Lance since the day before.

She was avoiding him.

The truth was, she didn't know what to say.

How did you talk to someone who said what he'd said?

Who'd done what he'd done?

How did you follow that?

It was unnatural.

Inhuman maybe.

It wasn't tragic. Tragedy was a human condition. What he'd done, killing the pregnant mother of his own child, that wasn't human. It wasn't even bestial. No wild beast did a thing like that.

She was standing at the stove, waiting for the kettle to boil.

She heard him approach from behind and turned around.

"These are the passports?" he said.

An open package was on the table, and he rifled through its contents.

"They were couriered during the night," she said. "Straight from the State Department."

Lance nodded and picked one up. He leafed through it and stopped at the photo.

"They made me look like a choir boy."

"It wouldn't kill you to run a comb through your hair once in a while."

"When I start taking fashion tips from the federal government, that's when you know I've gone off the deep end," he said.

Laurel tried to smile but couldn't. She couldn't treat him the same way any more. As far as she was concerned, he'd gone off the deep end a long time ago.

Before she'd ever met him.

Before she'd allowed Roth to alter her appearance so that she would look like Clarice. A woman he'd murdered.

She couldn't blame him for everything that had happened. He'd been straight with her the very first time they met.

He'd warned her in no uncertain terms that there were things about him she didn't know. Things she didn't want to know.

He told her he had reasons not to come back.

He told her to find someone else.

He told her he'd done things that no man could ever atone for.

That he was damaged goods.

That'd he'd crossed the line.

Now, she realized, he wasn't feeling sorry for himself. He'd been telling the truth.

He wasn't fit to serve his country.

He wasn't worthy.

She watched him put the passport in his inside coat pocket.

"At least you get to go home," she said.

He nodded.

"That girl's still there, right?"

"Sam. I think so."

"I hope she is," Laurel said.

She bit her lip. There was nothing so sad, she thought, as looking at a man you'd respected, a man you'd even loved, and not seeing it any longer.

She'd had to work hard to persuade the president to sign off on his passport. Hers was easy, but Lance, the president saw him as a liability.

It seemed that the more Lance did to protect the country, the less people trusted him.

The less they wanted to see him.

Laurel was no different.

It was like he reminded them of the things that had to be done that they knew were indefensible, unconscionable even.

Everyone knew that in order to protect the country, bad things had to happen. Ugly things. Violent things.

They knew it, they understood it, but they sure didn't like being reminded of it.

And that was what Lance was.

A reminder of all the ugly things that had to happen for a country with enemies to remain safe.

And no one could forgive him for it.

Not the president.

Not the director of the NSA.

And now, not even Laurel.

There was an irony there. A paradox. The only reason she even knew his name was because she'd been assigned to recruit him back to the CIA. He'd wanted to quit, he'd wanted to stop being an assassin, and she'd put every ounce of herself into convincing him to kill again.

And now, the sin he'd confessed to her, the sin that she hated him for, that made it difficult now even for her to stand there and look at him, was that he'd obeyed an order.

He'd done what he was told.

Because it was necessary.

Because someone had to do it.

She'd been a traitor.

But she was carrying his child. If her actions made her a traitor, what did his make him?

Only Roth, he was the only one who didn't despise Lance Spector. He was the only one who ever stuck his neck out for him. He was the only one who looked at him, who knew the things he'd done for his country, and didn't turn away in disgust.

Laurel looked into his eyes, it looked like he was about to say something to her, but before he could, the kettle on the stove came to a boil. It whistled loudly, and Laurel turned around and took it off the heat.

Whatever it was he was going to say, she didn't want to hear it. She focused on making the coffee.

"I guess this is it then," Lance said.

There was resignation in his voice. Acceptance. He knew she was finally going to do what he'd wanted all along. She was going to leave him alone.

And it was breaking his heart.

"I'm going to leave first thing tomorrow," she said.

"Back to Langley?"

"Heading up the Special Operations Group, it's important. I can't turn that down."

"Of course."

She looked at him closely, trying to detect any hint of cynicism in his voice. Even now, she couldn't help seek some sort of approval from him.

"Of course you want the job. It makes sense for you."

"It's not the power," she said.

"I know, Laurel. I was you once. Not so very long ago."

She smiled thinly. "I know you were."

"It all turned to ashes for me, but believe me when I say I hope for you it's different."

"Thank you, Lance."

The coffee was ready, and she poured herself a cup.

"You want some?" she said.

He shook his head, turned to leave.

"I'm leaving at dawn. Roth will have a plane waiting in Galveston."

Lance nodded.

"Come with me," she said.

The words startled her. She didn't know why she'd said them.

Was it pity?

Or did she mean it?

She knew it didn't matter. He wasn't coming back. He looked into her eyes for a second but said nothing.

The last sight she had of him was from her bedroom window. He was sitting out on the pier, lighting one of his Mexican cigars, looking out at the moon.

"Goodbye, Lance Spector," she said quietly.

When she woke in the morning, he was gone.

She prayed she would never see him again.

9

Agata didn't feel safe until she was on the main highway back toward the capital. She kept looking in her rearview mirror, half expecting to see a chopper, but no one was following her.

She was looking in the mirror when she had to swerve around a slow-moving motorcycle. The driver careened to avoid her, and she realized she could have killed him.

She needed to calm down.

She told herself she was safe, but she knew what the Russian military was capable of. She wasn't being paranoid.

If she'd just seen what she thought, a weapons cache belonging to the Russian army, then there was no limit to the danger she was in.

She tried calling Kuzis, but it went straight to voicemail. She didn't leave a message. She was too afraid of who else might be listening.

She kept driving, thinking about what she'd seen, wondering if the man she'd shot had called in her license plate, wondering if there were cameras watching over the cache.

The Sunday traffic was light, and she made good time. The sun was setting, and she was just an hour from the city when Kuzis finally called her back.

"Agata," he said, his voice distressed. "Nine missed calls. What the hell's going on?"

"Why didn't you pick up?"

"I was at the dacha."

"I had to check up on a lead."

"I got your message from yesterday. Something about a missing plane?"

"Yes," she said. "It went down right on the border. I wanted to look into it, so I went out there."

"To Ziguri?"

"Yes."

"And?"

"Well," she said, then her voice trailed off.

"Did you find the plane?"

"Not exactly," she said, "but...", she stopped herself talking.

"What was it, Agata?"

"I don't want to say on the phone. Meet me at the office. I'll be there in an hour."

"Tonight?"

"Yes, tonight, Kuzis."

"Agata. What did you find?"

"One hour," she said and hung up.

When she got to the office, there was no one there but the night watchman. He nodded as she passed, and she went straight up to the fourth floor.

Kuzis wasn't there, and she made herself some coffee and put some change in the snack machine. She hadn't eaten since breakfast at the hotel, and she was feeling faint.

She stood there, staring at the snacks, while the machine waited for her to make her selection.

"Agata," a voice said from behind her.

It was Kuzis, standing by the elevator in a pair of tan slacks and a polo shirt that stretched taut over his belly.

"Kuzis."

"What's going on, Agata?"

"I'm sorry to interrupt your weekend."

"Don't worry about that," he said, leading the way to his office.

She pressed a button on the snack machine, and some chips fell off their shelf. She grabbed them and followed him.

"So," he said, shutting the door behind her. "I take it from the sound of your voice that you found something important."

"My voice?"

"Agata, I've never heard you so frantic."

She took a deep breath.

"Sit," he said.

She sat down. She looked around the office as if someone might have been there listening. It was just her and Kuzis.

"You look pale," he said.

"I should eat something," she said, opening the chips.

"Let me get something to calm you down," he said, opening a compartment in his desk. He bent down and reemerged with a bottle of Swedish Aquavit and two glasses.

He raised an eyebrow, and Agata nodded. He poured them each a measure of the alcohol and handed her a glass.

She knocked back the entire thing.

"Okay?" Kuzis said.

"It's good. Thank you."

"You look like you've seen a ghost."

"I think I'm still processing what I saw."

"Which was?"

"Well, you heard my message from yesterday, right?"

"A forestry plane," Kuzis said.

"I spoke to the officer who filed the report. He said he saw it explode."

"Explode?"

"Like it was shot out of the sky, Kuzis."

Kuzis looked alarmed. He knew better than anyone what was at stake on the Russian border.

"Let's slow down for a minute, Agata. You know what we always say about those provincial police reports. They see bogeymen beneath every bed."

Agata sighed. They screened hundreds of reports every year. They were about as reliable as palm readings.

But this was different.

"This was no bogeyman. Unless bogeymen have learned to shoot guns."

"What are you talking about?"

"I tried to find the crash site."

"And someone opened fire at you?"

She nodded her head.

Kuzis's eyes widened.

"A farmer with a shotgun?" he said.

"No, sir. Not a farmer with a shotgun."

"Who then?" he said.

She had his full attention now.

"I don't know. I ran before getting a look at the body."

"Body?"

"I think I might have shot him."

"Agata, what are you telling me?"

"I found something in the woods, Kuzis."

"Something?"

"I found weapons, Kuzis. Russian weapons."

"How do you know they were Russian?"

"AK-12s, AK-74s, rocket launchers, surface-to-air missile launchers."

"Well," Kuzis said, desperately seeking an explanation. "You were close to the border. Are you certain you didn't cross over to the Russian side?"

"What if I did? Why would they have a cache out there at all? Why would they have maps of Latvian roads and bridges?"

"Lots of reasons."

"Why would they try to kill me, Kuzis?"

"All I'm saying," Kuzis said, "is that we need to remain calm. We need to think this through."

"I have been thinking it through," she said. "I've been thinking it through for the past six hours. This is an advance drop."

"In advance of what, Agata?"

Agata lowered her voice. She checked that the door was still shut, which of course it was, and said, "In advance of an invasion, Kuzis. That's what."

"Agata," Kuzis hissed. "Please."

"Please what?"

"You have to be careful what you say."

She knew he was right. If the Russians were planning something, they'd know by now that someone had been snooping around their cache, and they'd be searching for her. Every year, dozens of people across Europe died in suspicious circumstances. They'd have a car crash, or a freak boating accident, or a sudden heart attack brought on by some Cold War-era poison.

The victims could always be traced back to Russia.

Outspoken critics of the regime.

Whistleblowers.

Journalists.

Activists.

The Kremlin didn't care.

Molotov wanted the world to know it was him.

It was a message.

Get in my way, and this is what happens.

And what Agata had just seen, assuming it was what she thought it was, put her squarely in the bracket of getting in Vladimir Molotov's way.

"Well," she said. "What do we do about this?"

"If you really saw what you think you saw," he said.

"I know what I saw, Kuzis."

"Then we have to be discrete, Agata."

"We have to warn High Command."

"Yes," Kuzis agreed, "but we have to be smart about how we do it."

"What does that mean?"

"It means, leave it to me."

"What are you going to do?"

"I'm going to get them the message, but anonymously."

"They won't believe it," Agata said.

She knew what she'd seen, but looking at it now, under the harsh, fluorescent lights of State Police Headquarters, she could see how far-fetched it seemed.

"Did you get anything else?" Kuzis said. "Anything concrete?"

"Proof?"

He nodded.

She reached into her pocket and pulled out the map and other documents she'd taken from the crates.

The map spoke for itself, but it was one of the other documents that really caught Kuzis's attention.

It looked like a Russian military pamphlet. Something that would be distributed among troops on active operations. The paper had a waxy sheen to it for weatherproofing, and the Cyrillic letters looked foreign and menacing, a throwback to the Soviet days when the Russian army was not some distant threat but a daily reality.

Kuzis took the document from her hands and looked at it closely. Agata watched him. His face remained as blank and expressionless as a stone, but his eyes were wide with fright. He knew what he was looking at.

"There's a table here detailing the composition of Latvian forests," he said. "Birch, white alder, aspen."

Agata hadn't looked at it in detail.

"Look here," he said, pointing to a graph filled with numbers.

"What's that?"

"Estimates," he said.

"Estimates of what?"

He turned the page. "Lots of things. This estimates the distance sound travels through birch and alder forests in January."

"Kuzis," Agata said.

"A snapping twig, eighty meters," he said. "Troops on foot, three-hundred meters. An idling T-14, one kilometer."

"This is an invasion plan," she said.

Kuzis's head nodded slowly. He was transfixed by the brochure like it was an artifact from another planet.

"The rifles I saw," Agata said, " they were the new AK-12s."

"You're sure?"

"I know the difference," she said. "And the rocket launchers were SA-25s."

"That's what happened to your pilot."

She nodded.

It was terrifying. The Russians were coming. They were really coming. The Russians wouldn't have issued those weapons for a training mission. They were preparing for real combat.

But somehow, Agata found herself letting out a long sigh of relief. It was as if, now that she'd passed on the warning, a huge weight had just been lifted from her chest.

She could breathe now.

Kuzis was on it.

He'd get the message up the chain of command.

He'd do his duty.

10

The Russian railway network was one of the wonders of the industrial age. It connected some of the most far-flung inhabited outposts on the planet, stretching from the remote borders of China and Mongolia and North Korea, to the very doorstep of Europe.

Of the earth's twenty-four time zones, the Russian railway stretched across eleven of them.

The distance from Port Nakhodka, east of Vladivostok at the head of the Sea of Japan, to somewhere like Pskov, just inside the Latvian border, was greater than the distance from New York City to Honolulu.

The railway lines were unimaginably vast, unimaginably lonely. There were times when the train passengers were the only human beings within literally hundreds of square miles of territory. The lines crossed eighty mountain ranges. Of the one hundred longest rivers in the world, they spanned twenty-five.

Calling them a wonder was no exaggeration.

And they were achieved at a human cost that was almost beyond reckoning.

The cost in terms of human life made the Russian rail network one of the deadliest industrial undertakings in history.

There were wars that had cost fewer lives.

And there is one word that made it all possible.

Slavery.

That singularly dark blot on the history of mankind.

And Russia was not alone in utilizing it.

The briefest of surveys would show that the absence of slavery was, in fact, far rarer than its presence.

And no one was aware of the fact more than Joseph Stalin.

He boasted that he had more slaves than were used in the Egyptian Fourth Dynasty to erect the pyramids.

"Pharaoh had a quarter-million," he would say, and laugh.

In the United States census of 1860, the last one conducted before the Civil War, there were four million men, women and children enslaved in America.

In 1944, when the Nazi forced-labor system was at its height, and the Reich kept detailed receipts of the payments made by German corporations for the use of slave labor, the tally came to six-and-a-half-million.

Stalin loved statistics. They drove his enormous, ruthless Five Year Plans. He had a statistic for everything. And he was proud of them above all else.

He knew how many people were dying under his regime. And he also knew the tonnage for steel production, coal mining, grain production, and rail construction.

Everything had a number.

And privately, one of his favorites was the Soviet slave count. On that metric, he had outstripped every other nation and empire on the planet, whether of the past or of the present.

Under the Gulag system, Stalin secretly bragged that he owned more slaves than all documented past regimes combined. For most of his rule, there were over thirty-thousand forced-labor camps across the Soviet Union, with the largest of them holding more than twenty-five thousand inmates.

Those inmates worked on many projects, but laying rail was the biggest.

Projects such as the Baikal-Amur Mainline, the Krasnoyarsk-Yeniseysk Mainline, the Amur Railway, the Primorsky Railway, the Sevzheldorlag Northern Railway, and the Eastern Railway could never have been completed without them.

Just one of those projects, the Tayshet to Bratsk portion of the Baikal-Amur line, would have taken, it was estimated, over two hundred years if voluntary labor, paid a regular wage, was used.

On the infamous Trans-Polar Mainline, three-hundred thousand enslaved dissidents worked ceaselessly on a thousand-mile stretch of rail to link the far-north outpost of Salekhard, on the Arctic Ocean Gulf of Ob, to the remote town of Igarka, a hundred miles north of the Arctic Circle.

The workers, men and women, slept in canvas tents on the track and worked in temperatures below negative fifty degrees Celsius. Over a hundred thousand died, hauling ballast and laying steel on the line that would never be completed.

Never used.

A hundred thousand lives, lost for a line that went, quite literally, nowhere.

The guards, to maintain order and, presumably, pass the

time, came up with some of the cruelest punishments on record.

One of their favorites was to tie a prisoner naked to a post and leave him. In the winter, death came mercifully quickly, but in summer, the prisoner died by being devoured by the millions of voracious, over-sized mosquitoes that hatched in the marshes.

A man could be transformed into a clean, chalk-white skeleton in a matter of days.

Another line, one that was actually completed, was the line from Moscow to Archangel. That thousand-mile stretch traveled due north from Moscow's famed Belorusskaia Station, with one departure per week making the twenty-three-hour journey through Yaroslavl, Vologda, and some of the remotest territory in the country. About two hours before the train arrives at Archangel, a strategically important port on the Arctic Ocean, it passes a port of a different kind.

In 1957, at a site called Plesetsk, two-hundred kilometers south of Archangel, the Soviets built an intercontinental ballistic missile launch site. By 1961, four fully functional R-7 missile complexes were combat-ready at the location. The missiles were designed to carry a five-megaton payload, using rockets fueled by liquid oxygen and kerosene. It could hit targets five and a half thousand miles away with an accuracy of about three miles.

The closest they ever got to being fired was during the Cuban Missile Crisis in 1962, when one of the rockets was fully fueled and loaded with a live warhead. The missile was then wheeled to launchpad 41/1, where a single mechanical trigger would have sent it on a non-recallable, one-way flight to Minot Air Force Base in Ward County, North

Dakota, where the new US Minuteman ICBMs were stationed.

For the time the missile sat on the pad, when a spark from the flint of a Zippo lighter would have been sufficient to send it on its way, it was, and remains to this day, the nearest the planet has ever come to nuclear war.

On the day that Arturs Alda's plane was shot down over the Latvian border, pad 41/1 was used for an entirely new type of launch.

The launch was immediately picked up and tracked by an analyst at the Tenth Space Warning Squadron at Cavalier Air Force Station in North Dakota. Ironically, the concrete bunker he was sitting in would have been within the blast radius of the fueled R-7 that was almost launched in 1962.

The analyst was using the new Enhanced Perimeter Acquisition Radar Attack Characterization System that had just been installed as part of a new Space Force appropriations package passed by congress the year earlier. If it were not for the upgrades to the system, the launch would have remained undetected.

Which, as it happened, it might as well have, because there was nothing the analyst, or anyone else at the Tenth Space Warning Squadron, could do about the behavior it exhibited.

The analyst tracked it diligently, and every day, more people came by his console to look over his shoulder at what it was he was tracking.

He wasn't used to being a celebrity. He was an overweight former linebacker from New Hampshire, and during Canadian football season, he drove weekly to Winnipeg to catch the Blue Bombers games.

At first, the launch didn't appear to be anything out of the ordinary. A Soyuz rocket, the workhorse of the Russian space program, took off from pad 41/1 at just before dawn local time.

The launch was given the identifier Cosmos 2542, and it gave no indication of ever being anything more than a number on a spreadsheet, one of the countless objects tracked diligently, but unremarkably, by Space Command.

About five hours after its launch, however, it did something that no Russian satellite, or indeed, any satellite from any nation, had ever done before.

It split in two.

The same analyst, with a Boston Cream donut in one hand and a cup of coffee in the other, dropped both immediately and called his superior.

"Sir, I've got something you're going to want to see," he said.

"What is it, Harper?"

"Russian launch 2542."

"I see it."

"Well, sir, it just split in two."

"It did what now?"

"Split in two, sir."

"You mean it broke apart?"

"No, sir," Harper said, staring at his screen as intently as if he'd just found proof of extraterrestrial life. "I mean, the main satellite opened up, and a smaller satellite came out of it."

"That's not possible," the officer said.

"Well, sir, someone better tell the Russians that."

And that was how, two days later, Harper found himself in a secure conference room at the federal building in Bismarck with his boss, the head of the National Reconnaissance Office, and CIA Director Levi Roth.

"One satellite came out of the other?" Roth said when Harper concluded his presentation.

"Like one of those Russian dolls, sir," Harper said. "I gave it a separate tag. Cosmos 2543."

"But that wasn't the last strange thing it did?" Roth said, looking through the printout Harper had prepared.

"No, sir. After emerging from the mothercraft, Cosmos 2543 proceeded to put itself on an orbital path startlingly close to KH-11."

Everyone in the room knew what KH-11 was. A very sensitive, very valuable American satellite.

"How close?" Roth said.

"Let's just say," Harper told him, "it was close enough that the proximity sensors on KH-11, the ones intended solely for use during takeoff, were triggered."

It was at that point that the NRO Director spoke up. "I'm sure no one in the capital needs to be reminded of the importance of the KH-class satellites."

Roth shrugged. "You'd be surprised how much reminding tends to be necessary," he said.

"Well then," the director said, "remind them that we operate Keyhole for the Department of Defense. We use them to fly drones. To guide missiles. To communicate with units in the field."

Roth nodded.

"KH is not just any class of satellite," Harper reiterated for emphasis. "If aliens ever arrive, KH is what they'll notice."

KH or Keyhole/CRYSTAL-class, was not just the most valuable, but also the most technically advanced, object ever put into space. Its specifications remained classified, but Harper knew more than most.

There were four of them, each located at a constant

polar orbit, spread evenly over the planet. In combination, they were what allowed the US military to observe the surface of the planet, anywhere, at any time, in higher resolution than what other nations could even imagine.

Each satellite was about the size of a school bus, and cost as much to build as the Hubble Space Telescope. In fact, they shared so many of the same components, from the same contractors, that it was a more or less open secret that they were basically military-purposed replicas of Hubble, but pointed downward rather than out to space.

The imagery was so clear that US intelligence agencies had been able to read the headlines of the New York Times from a satellite two-hundred-fifty kilometers above.

"I understand," Levi Roth said, "That Cosmos 2543 is so close that the slightest adjustment to its orbit, or the release of some shrapnel, could utterly destroy KH-11."

"For all we know," the NRO Director said, "they've equipped it with an energy weapon."

Harper didn't think that was likely, but he didn't say so. The Russian satellite was doing what it was doing for a reason. And that reason was not friendly.

"Sir," he said, clearing his throat.

"Speak up, Harper," Roth said. "You're the reason we're here."

"It could hurt us, certainly. It could ram us, it could release debris into our path, but even if it does nothing at all, its position, and its ability to track our orbit this closely, is extremely dangerous. From where they are now, they can look at the positioning of our scopes and see where they're pointed."

"So they can see what we're looking at?"

"Yes, sir. And that's not all."

"What else?" Roth said.

"They can listen in on the ultra-high-frequency channel."

"That channel is encrypted," the NRO Director said.

"Yes, sir," Harper said. "Of course. But even just listening is a threat. It means it can be recorded, sent back to earth, run through Russian decryption technologies."

"Will they be able to crack the encryption?" Roth said.

"Not likely," the NRO Director said, "at least in theory."

"UHF is the secure protocol used by the CIA, the DoD, the NSA, the Defense Intelligence Agency, and US Strategic Command," Harper said. "Even if the Russians don't decrypt them, this is a huge risk. They could try to corrupt them. Confuse our systems. Redirect guidance systems."

"Launch missiles?" Roth said.

"This is all theoretical," the NRO Director said, "but I agree with Harper, letting the Russians get within a million miles of those transmissions is an unacceptable breach."

"If the president wanted to go to war," Harper said, "the orders transmitted from Washington to our units in the field, to our nuclear subs, to our unmanned drones, to our guidance satellites, would all be sent by UHF."

"What's the bottom line on this?" Roth said to Harper.

"Bottom line," Harper said, "is that Cosmos 2543 is the first time we have identified a direct threat to our fighting ability from a foreign space weapon."

"You don't mean the first time ever," Roth said.

"Yes, I do, sir," Harper said. "This is it. This is the opening shot on a whole new front. This launch is Russia's way of saying space is open for business."

"And by business, you mean...".

"I mean warfare, sir."

"It wasn't open for *business* already?"

"No, sir," Harper said. "Not like this. This capability. This tracking of our orbit. It's an entirely new threat, and we need to get ahead of it."

"So let me get this very clear," Roth said, "because I'm going to have to explain all this to a lot of very skeptical people. The Keyhole satellites are the most sensitive, most valuable communications machine ever built by the hands of man."

"And Russia is now capable of ramming them out of the sky," Harper said, finishing his sentence for him.

"If that doesn't get their attention, I don't know what will," Roth said.

"You tell the people in Washington," Harper said, "that the Russians can knock out our secure comms, military GPS systems, guidance systems, targeting platforms."

"Basically anything with the word 'smart' in its name," the NRO Director said.

"They could put us back to the nineteen-forties," Harper said. "At least temporarily."

Roth let out a long sigh.

"Well gentlemen," he said, preparing to leave, "I'm going to take this back to Washington, but if this satellite does anything new, if it so much as beeps funny, or flashes its little lights in a way you don't like, I need to know about it immediately."

11

L ance crossed the border into the US at Brownsville, Texas.

The border patrol agent looked up from his passport and said, "Do I know you?"

Lance shook his head. "I don't think so."

The agent scanned the passport and said, "What were you doing in Mexico?"

"I was with a girl," Lance said.

The agent raised an eyebrow. "Is that what you call it?"

"That's what I call it," Lance said.

"Well then," the agent said, "Welcome home, mister... Smith."

"Thanks," Lance said.

He caught a flight from Corpus Christi to Missoula with a brief layover in Dallas. In Missoula, he rented a car and headed into the mountains.

Home was Deweyville, Montana, a town in the Rockies of about a thousand people that had changed little since the days when miners and frontiersmen founded it. It was in a deep mountain valley, nine miles south of the Canadian border, and was less touched by visitors and tourists than similar towns further south.

It was a good place for Lance to be.

Out of the way.

Off the beaten track.

Peaceful.

People hunted up there. They carried guns. They owned dogs and pickup trucks. It was remote enough that they could forget about the news, the politics, the economy, all the things that stressed and vexed the rest of the nation.

Driving into town, past the trapping store, the tobacco store, the old headquarters of the Farmers and Merchants Bank, Lance felt that he was home.

He drove through the town beneath a cold, blue sky and continued north along a road that wound upward into the mountains. About two miles out, perched on an outcrop of volcanic granite, high above the steep, forested valley, was his house. It had a large balcony wrapping the second floor and high, solid walls he'd built himself from hand-hewn logs.

He pulled into the driveway and walked up the front steps. His dog was already scratching at the door, barking for him.

And then the door opened.

Samantha was standing there, wrapped in a towel.

"Lance," she said, "you're back."

Lance stood on the porch awkwardly, as if it wasn't his house, and she had to tell him to come in before he moved.

Samantha was his guest, and he hadn't known if she'd still be there when he got back.

He was glad she was.

That in itself was a victory.

She'd been messing around with a bad crowd when he found her. He'd walked up to her in a bar, beat up her good-for-nothing, drug-dealing boyfriend, and brought her home more or less against her will.

"How was your... *trip*?" she said as he hung up his coat.

She knew he'd been doing something for the CIA.

The dog was very excited to see him, he'd never left her alone before, and he held out his hand for her to lick.

"Cold," Lance said.

He looked at her. Her eyes were clear. There were no fresh track marks on her arms. The house was tidy. It was warm.

She'd been staying out of trouble.

"You should get dressed," he said.

She looked down at the towel as if she'd forgotten she was wearing it.

"Right," she said, turning to go upstairs.

Lance glanced around the room. She'd made herself at home. There was a yoga mat by the fireplace. There was a blanket strewn on the sofa next to the TV controller. On the island in the kitchen was a tabloid magazine with someone from the British royal family on the cover.

He filled the kettle and put it on the stove. When it whistled, he made coffee and sat at the counter drinking it. One entire side of the house was made of glass, and outside, an eagle floated on air currents above the valley as effortlessly as if it was weightless.

It felt good to be back.

It was good Sam was still there. That she was happy.

Lance barely knew her, but he'd spent a good portion of the past few years thinking about her. He'd served with her father, and he still remembered his last words. He'd just taken a bullet that was meant for Lance, he was dying in Lance's arms, and struggling to utter each word, he said, "Watch out for my girl."

Lance promised he would.

Sam was fourteen then, and Lance knew he'd waited too long to keep the promise.

Sam had sent her father away to serve in the army, and when he came home, it was in a pine box.

That was all she knew of war. All she knew of fathers.

And that was when she'd needed Lance to step in.

But he'd been doing other things.

Soon after her father's funeral, her mother died in a car accident. She had a blood-alcohol level of point three. The coroner said it was the highest he'd seen. The other driver died too.

"Are you making coffee?" Sam called from upstairs.

"Yes," he said, pouring her a cup.

She came downstairs in fresh clothes and wet hair, went to the refrigerator, and took out a homemade cobbler.

"I baked," she said, placing it in front of Lance like a cat bringing home a fresh kill.

"You made this?" Lance said, scooping it into a bowl.

She nodded.

He offered her some, but she shook her head. Instead, she watched him eat.

"It's good," he said.

"Thank you."

"Peach?"

"Yup."

He finished it and poured more coffee.

"You seem different," Sam said.

"In what way?"

"I don't know," she said. "Just... you know."

"Different," he said.

"Different," she said again.

Lance thought about it, then scooped another helping of cobbler.

12

By the time Agata got back to her apartment, she was utterly exhausted. She felt like she'd lived a lifetime since waking up the morning before, slightly hungover, next to the varsity swimmer.

He'd left her a little note on the counter, which she glanced at briefly.

Last night was amazing.

She threw it in the garbage and stumbled into the bedroom, where she collapsed onto the bed fully-clothed. She was asleep in seconds.

When she woke, it was the middle of the night.

She reached instinctively for her phone and looked at the screen. It was three AM.

She felt a cool breeze pass over her and realized a window must be open. That was strange. It was a modern building with climate control, and she rarely used the windows at all.

It must have been the swimmer, she thought, then froze.

Her thoughts crystalized.

A sound had woken her.

A window was open.

A Russian soldier had just tried to kill her in the forest.

Her instincts kicked in, and she rolled to her left, falling off the side of the bed as the distinctive chirp of suppressed pistol fire filled the room. Three bullets hit her mattress, and a fourth hit the wall behind the bed.

As the gunman entered the room, Agata rolled under the bed. She'd never been the type to keep a gun down there, but she did have a cheap Ikea toolset, and as the gunman came closer, she pulled out the hammer and slammed it right into his knee.

He yelped in pain and stumbled backward.

Agata climbed out from under the bed and hit him again. He was wearing body armor, but she kept pummeling him in a frenzy of panic until he doubled over in pain. She raised the hammer above her head and was about to bring it down on the back of the man's skull when she caught a glimpse of herself in the mirror.

The look on her own face frightened her.

She took a breath and then pushed the injured man onto the bed, where he writhed in pain, clutching his leg.

He was dressed in black, with a jacket and leather gloves, and Agata bent down to the ground and picked up his gun.

She pointed it at him.

"Who are you?" she said.

"Go fuck yourself."

She'd been expecting Russian, but he spoke Latvian. He had a Riga accent. She looked at him more closely.

"Who sent you?" she said.

"No one sent me."

Her hand was trembling, and she didn't have time for playing his games. She stepped forward and slammed the hammer down on his thigh. She could feel the flesh give way beneath it, and the way he howled almost made her pity him.

"Who the fuck sent you? I'll pound you to a pulp, I swear to God."

She took another step toward him, brandishing the hammer.

"I work for the Police Special Branch," he said.

"The police?"

He nodded, clutching his leg pitifully.

"Latvian police?"

"Yes," he grunted.

Agata couldn't believe it. "Bullshit," she said, waving the hammer.

He reached for the zipper on his jacket, and she pointed the gun. "Don't move."

"I've got ID," he said. "I work for the Special Branch. It's the truth."

"The police don't send assassins in the middle of the night to kill other cops."

The man looked at her sadly and nodded his head. "Yes, they do," he said.

He moved his hand very slowly to his jacket, opened the zip, and pulled out a leather badge. He threw it to her, and she caught it.

It was as he'd said. Special Branch.

He was telling the truth.

"Why?" she stammered.

"Why do you think?"

"Because...".

"Because of what you saw."

"What I saw? I reported it directly to...".

She couldn't say it. He'd sold her out. Betrayed her.

"Alfreds Kuzis," the man said.

"I..." Agata stammered, "I don't understand."

"What you saw. It has to remain secret."

"But Kuzis. He's on our side. It's his job to protect us."

"There are winners and losers in everything. Even in an invasion. It was like that last time the Russians came, and it will be like that this time too."

"There's not going to be a *this* time."

The man shook his head.

"What do you think is going to happen after the Russians move in? It's going to be the biggest free-for-all since the collapse of the Soviet Union. Someone's going to win big. Someone's going to be top dog."

"And Kuzis thinks it's going to be him?"

The man was losing a lot of blood. In a few more minutes, he'd be unconscious.

"Hey," Agata said, snapping her fingers. "How high does this go?"

The man looked in her eyes, then down at her chest.

She followed his gaze and saw a red laser dot. She leaped aside, and in the same instant, the window shattered as a bullet from a high-powered sniper rifle slammed into the wall, right where she'd just been standing.

She didn't waste another second.

Keeping as low as she could, she scrambled through the apartment, grabbing her coat and purse as bullets continued to fly through the bedroom window.

She made it to the door and opened it without thinking.

Thankfully, the corridor was clear.

The elevator was to her right, but instead, she went left, letting herself into the emergency stairwell.

She dashed down five flights of stairs and, when she got to the ground floor, looked through the small window in the fire door to the lobby. Two armed men with earpieces were standing by the elevator. One of them raised his hand to his ear, then looked directly at Agata.

She stared right back at him, the thin glass of the window the only thing separating them.

He raised his gun and fired three shots.

Agata leaped down the next flight of stairs and was in the basement by the time the guards reached the door above. She sprinted for her car, desperately searching for the key in her purse as she ran.

Her fingers found the key, and she pressed the button. The car flashed and the doors unlocked with a loud chirp that echoed through the underground lot. She opened the door and got into the driver's seat right as the two men from the lobby burst out into the lot.

She hadn't started the engine, and she ducked down below the dashboard, carefully shutting the door and praying some feature on the car didn't beep or flash or otherwise give away her presence.

The parking lot was about half full, and she knew it wouldn't take them long to find her if she stayed where she was. She was still holding the pistol, and she rose her head up slowly to peek out over the dash.

The men were walking purposefully along the rows of cars, searching the gaps behind them, beneath them, looking for her.

She pressed the button to open the passenger window and then aimed the gun at the nearest of the two men.

She fired four shots.

Glass shattered, the alarms in the cars around him sounded, and in the confusion, Agata turned her ignition and jolted her vehicle out of its spot.

The second man ran out in front of her and raised his gun.

She slammed right into him before he could get a shot off, and he rolled up over her windshield, over the roof, and onto the ground behind her.

He was about to get up when she jammed her brakes, then flung the car into reverse.

The car made a gruesome sound as it rolled over him.

The other man rose up from between two cars to her right and opened fire. Webs of shattered glass stretched across the windshield, and the loud clang of bullets on steel filled her ears.

She jammed the car into drive and lurched forward, her tires screeching on the smooth concrete as they struggled for purchase. As she passed the man's position, she reached out and fired through her open passenger window.

She had no idea if she'd hit him or not and didn't slow down to check. She had to go around the row of cars and then turn back toward him on the next aisle before exiting the lot. As she passed his position, the back windshield shattered. She ducked as three bullets struck it.

She turned sharply onto the ramp, and the car's under-carriage sparked as it scraped on the concrete. She sped out onto the deserted street without checking to see if there was any oncoming traffic.

She sped to the first set of lights and drove right through them, then the next, then turned onto a side street. She sped along it as the sound of police sirens closed in from all directions.

She turned into an alley between two large office buildings and jammed the car behind a large dumpster. Then she killed the engine.

She got out of the car and, using the edge of a nail file, removed the license plates from the front and back of the vehicle.

Above her, a police helicopter flew in and began scanning the area.

She looked at her watch.

The police sirens were getting louder.

She didn't know what to do. If she couldn't trust Kuzis, if she couldn't trust the police, then she didn't know where to turn.

Who could she go to?

Who would listen?

Then she thought of her. Her ally. The one person she might be able to trust.

She straightened herself up, wiped the blood from her hands, and walked down the alley toward the street. On her way, she powered off her phone and threw it in a dumpster. She made her way to the Central Railway Station a few blocks away and checked the international departures. There was a train leaving for Warsaw in twenty minutes.

13

When Laurel's flight landed in Dulles, she wasn't sure what to do with herself. She had an apartment of her own, a barren place full of dead plants and an empty goldfish bowl.

She hadn't been there in a while and didn't relish the thought of going back to it.

Roth had been in the process of moving her and Tatyana into a fancy townhouse in Georgetown, a place he'd been planning to set up as the new headquarters of the Special Operations Group, but it had been infiltrated. The Russians had managed to find out where it was and had attacked.

That made it useless now as a base of operation, and Laurel had already listed it for sale with a high-end Georgetown realtor.

She pulled her cell from her pocket and dialed Roth's number.

"Are you back?" Roth said, dispensing with small talk.

"I'm at Dulles. I'll come to you now."

"You can't. I'm in Bismarck, North Dakota."

"What are you doing out there?"

"You don't want to know."

"All right," Laurel said. "I guess I'll take a cab to Langley."

"No, don't go there. I'm going to keep you completely off the grid this time. No leaks. No infiltrations. Just you and the few people you choose personally to work with."

"And do you have a place in mind for us to work out of?"

"A few, but I'm open to suggestions."

"I might have one or two."

"All right," he said. "Why don't you go home, freshen up, and meet me tonight at the Saint Royal. I feel like I owe you dinner."

Laurel hung up and looked at her watch. It was noon. She left the terminal in search of a cab. It was a gloomy, gray day, and she pulled her coat tightly around her neck.

"Where to?" the driver said.

Langley, Virginia, was where she should have lived. It was a leafy suburb within easy driving distance of the city. But instead, she'd chosen to pay twice as much to live in a downtown loft. It was worth it to be close to the action.

"U Street," she said.

Sitting in the back of the cab, watching the dreary DC streets pass by, a feeling of melancholy began to drift over her. January in DC had never been her favorite season, but this was more than that.

Since her first day with the agency, she'd always known her goal. She'd had one mission, and that was to recruit Lance Spector, to lure him back into the fold, to take over as his handler.

Now, he was gone.

Gone for good.

And not just physically.

The position he'd occupied in her mind, the symbol of

strength, the sense of purpose he'd given her, all of that was gone too.

And it left her strangely empty.

The cab pulled up outside her apartment, and she got out. She rummaged through her bag for her keys, it had been so long since she'd used them, and unlocked the double bolts on the steel door. She let herself into the apartment, and if she'd felt depressed before, she felt doubly so now.

The apartment was cold. She had one of those smart thermostats that could tell when you were away, and it had saved her money by letting the temperature drop to that of a morgue.

She put it up to eighty and switched on the lights.

It was a nice loft, airy, with that restored industrial look that was so fashionable, but looking around it now, it felt barren and vacant.

There were some potted plants by the windows, all dead. There was a goldfish bowl on the kitchen counter, empty. She'd flushed its dead inhabitant down the toilet last time she'd returned from a mission.

She put a pod in her coffee machine and brewed a frothy americano. Then she turned on the TV and watched the headlines while sipping it.

The news had moved on from the attacks in Moscow and Beijing. Lance's name had been cleared. The story of the day was a big national park the president was dedicating.

It was truly incredible how quickly the public's attention could be drawn to new things.

The embassies in Moscow and Beijing were still smoldering, anyone with half a brain and a modicum of imagination knew the Russian and Chinese governments had to have been behind the attacks, and yet, all of Washington had bent over backward to avoid casting blame.

They'd kept the peace.

Kept things stable.

And shown their adversaries that they were too scared to stand up to a challenge.

Maybe Lance had the right idea. Get out now, while he still could.

Everyone said Washington was a swamp, filled with self-interested politicians who passed legislation only at the behest of their wealthy corporate donors and special interest groups.

It wasn't about governance.

It wasn't about helping people.

It was *quid pro quo* on a scale to rival ancient Rome.

She shook her head.

She didn't believe that.

She wasn't that cynical.

Not yet.

Maybe the day would come when she lost all faith in the system, when she was as jaded as Lance, but that day had yet to come.

She still believed America was a beacon of light, a bastion of democracy, a protector of the rule of law in a world that skewed increasingly toward the opposite poles of authoritarianism and anarchy.

It wasn't easy.

It didn't always feel good.

The work was dirty and, when the end came, there would be more blood on her hands than she could probably even imagine.

But she believed in it.

And she was still willing to give her life for it.

She went into the bathroom and ran a hot bath. Then she poured herself a glass of wine and climbed in. She lay there for an hour, up to her neck in suds and bath salts, and when she lay down on the bed afterward, she fell into a deep sleep.

14

Kirov looked out the window of his hotel room and blew cigar smoke against the pane. It was night, and Saint Isaac's Square, lit by tall electric street lights, glowed with an unnatural bluish tint. Snow swirled around the lights like angry moths and swept around the enormous base of the Tsar Nicholas the First monument.

The enormous statue, a bronze Nicholas on horseback, loomed fifty feet above the square like Goliath. When it was unveiled in 1859, it had been lauded as a technical marvel because of the amount of weight the engineers had managed to support from the prancing horse's two hind hooves.

Those two narrow ankles were the sole reason the statue still stood.

The Soviet government, which pulled down countless other monuments to the Russian aristocracy, allowed this one to remain because of its technical merit.

Kirov had a cigar in one hand and a phone in the other. The phone was a landline, solidly built of brass and thick, black plastic, and weighed a full five pounds. He held it by the nook beneath the receiver and waited for the GRU's military exchange to connect him to Oleg Zhukovsky.

He was in the field. Out there at the border overseeing military preparations. It was his job to make sure the officers involved kept their mouths shut about what was being planned.

Kirov knew Zhukovsky was more than capable of keeping them in line. He was a sadist. Cruel. They were terrified of him.

They'd all heard the rumors.

Zhukovsky was a weirdo. A freak. He tortured things. The police had found animals in his basement, dogs, cats, raccoons. A veritable zoo of mangy, suffering creatures. Rows of cages that were kept in the dark twenty-three hours a day.

The officer who found it had been responding to a complaint from a neighbor. He didn't know who Zhukovsky was, but he learned soon enough. So did the neighbor. They were found in a meatpacking plant, suspended by their ankles, a gallon and a half of blood in a pool beneath each of them.

Zhukovsky had bled them.

He'd made a point.

And he'd kept his job.

Kirov pictured him now, out there in the wilds of the frontier country, schlepping around a muddy field, barking orders at a bunch of pimply-faced recruits who had more experience peeling potatoes than war-fighting.

Zhukovsky terrified people, but physically, he was frail. He'd fallen into the hands of the Mujahideen in Afghanistan in a war that ended over thirty years ago, but he still bore the scars. The things they'd done to him would haunt him to his grave, and one of those things was that he couldn't stand the cold. It made him ache.

Ordinarily, he did his work from an office, an extremely warm office, at GRU headquarters. It had been specially adapted to his needs.

Which was why it amused Kirov to think of him out on the Latvian border in the middle of January.

Kirov looked at his watch.

It was three in the morning.

He was hungover and had a thumping headache. His mouth tasted like something had died in it.

After his return from dinner, he'd spent two hours throwing up, holding onto the porcelain toilet bowl until he thought he was going to bring up an organ.

The thought of a cow's milk curdling in the intestines of her calf, mixing with the maggots from the cheese and the six whole songbirds he'd been forced to ingest, was too much.

When his stomach finally settled, he'd called for some tea to be brought up, and sat in the bed dozing and sipping it when the phone rang.

It was a call from GRU headquarters in Moscow telling him to get hold of Zhukovsky urgently.

He rubbed his eyes and slumped into the armchair by the window. He was wearing the plush, brown robe supplied by the hotel but still felt a chill.

When Zhukovsky's voice came on the line, Kirov recognized its harsh and dry tones immediately.

"Jacob Kirov," Zhukovsky said. "Sorry to have made you wait. This close to the border, the communications protocols are very strict."

"I received a call from Moscow," Kirov said, purposefully neglecting to greet him. "I take it there's a problem."

"There's a problem, sir. Yes."

"And are you going to make me guess what it is?"

"One of their caches has been found," Zhukovsky said.

"Caches?"

"They've committed to delivering Riga within six hours of the invasion," Zhukovsky said. "In order to make that happen, they need provisions in place close to the border."

"And someone found them?" Kirov said.

"That's correct, sir. I've already had the officer responsible taken into custody."

"I bet you have, Zhukovsky."

"It appears to have been a Latvian police officer who saw the cache."

"So kill him," Kirov said.

"It's a her, sir, and we tried."

"What do you mean, you tried?"

"She's with the national security division. She must have some special training. A team was sent to her apartment thirty minutes ago, but somehow she bested them."

"A woman police officer bested a GRU team?"

"It wasn't one of our teams, sir. Her commanding officer is on my payroll. He sent his own men."

"So she's on the run?"

"That's correct."

"And she knows what we're up to."

"She knows enough, sir."

Kirov said nothing, letting a silence fill the air. He was always distracted when speaking to Zhukovsky, picturing him in the basement with the animals, wondering what on earth it was that he was doing to them.

"Well, Zhukovsky," he said, "I don't think I need to explain to you what's at stake here. If you don't put a lid on her, it will be both our heads."

"I'm already on it, sir. I've activated every asset in the region. When she pops up, I'll have someone ready to get her."

"Hopefully it's someone more competent than last time."

"These are GRU assets, Kirov. They're very competent."

15

Mikhail Smolov was in bed with a Warsaw prostitute when his phone rang.

He didn't pick up immediately. He finished what he was doing.

Then, he laid some money on the dresser and told her he had to leave.

She remained in the bed, watching him dress disinterestedly.

"Maybe I'll come back in an hour or two," he said.

She shrugged.

The elevator in her building never worked, and he ran down the four flights of stairs. He didn't call Zhukovsky until he was a block away.

"Where the fuck have you been?" Zhukovsky said.

"I was doing something."

"Well, I've got something for you to do. I'm sending a picture now."

Smolov pulled the phone from his ear to look at the picture."

"Pretty. Who is she?"

"A Latvian police corporal."

"Shame."

"This is very important," Zhukovsky said. "Do not fuck it up."

"I think I can handle her."

"Don't underestimate her. She's had training. She took out a team in Riga."

Smolov was a trained GRU assassin. Whatever training the Latvian police had, he was confident it was nothing compared to what he was capable of.

"Where's she located?"

"She's arriving on the Riga train in thirty minutes. Can you get there?"

"I can get there," Smolov said, looking up and down the street for a cab. "Is she alone?"

"Yes," Zhukovsky said, "and as I said, don't fuck this up."

Smolov hung up and lit a cigarette.

It was frigidly cold, even by Warsaw standards, and there were no taxis. He pulled up the collar on his coat and began walking at a brisk pace toward Warszawa Centralna.

Apart from the snowplows, the streets were empty. The wind whipped around him bitterly, and he opened and closed his hands in his pockets to keep his fingers from going numb.

He didn't have a gun with him, and there wasn't time to get one, but he could operate without one.

He crossed the wide, concrete plaza in front of the cultural palace and entered the station through the main entrance.

Above the concourse, on a large digital display, the international arrivals were listed. The train from Riga was running right on schedule, arriving in ten minutes.

The central station was one of the few places in the city

that truly operated around the clock, and he went up to a kiosk and ordered a cup of hot tea. The lady behind the stall, wrapped in layer upon layer of scarves, pressed a button on a machine and handed him the little plastic cup that came out.

Smolov held it in his hands, letting the warmth bring his fingers back to life, then took a sip. It tasted like lemon water with sugar.

Behind the kiosk was a drug store, and he went inside, sipping the tea while he browsed the aisles. He was looking for the dental section, and when he found it, grabbed two packs of floss. Without a gun, he had to be creative.

He paid for the floss and made his way to the platform. There was no one else on the platform. This was the end of the line for this service.

There was a newspaper stand, and he picked up a copy of the free paper, then sat on a bench facing the tracks and waited.

He knew it didn't look right.

The platform was beneath the main concourse of the station, sheltered from the elements but still very cold. No one would be out there, at the terminal stop of a middle of the night express service, reading a newspaper.

The target was a cop.

She was on the run.

She had her guard up.

All of which meant she would be attuned to anything that seemed out of place.

He reached into his pocket and took out a pack of cigarettes. As the train rushed into the station, he lit one and stood up as if waiting to meet someone.

About fifty people got off the train, and he would have recognized his target if she'd been among them.

She was slender, in her late twenties, with sensible hair that came down around her face about as far as her shoulders. From the picture, she dressed well, in clothing perhaps a tad too expensive for someone on a Latvian police officer's salary.

He knew what he was looking for.

She was just his type.

As the crowd thinned, he had no choice but to leave the platform with the last of them. If she'd waited onboard the train, his lingering would have alerted her.

He walked to the end of the platform and then stopped and looked back at the train. Stepping off it, in an elegant, camel-colored coat, was a blonde with a cropped haircut. She was holding a black purse.

It was her.

She looked up and down the platform and lit a cigarette. Then she started walking in Smolov's direction.

Smolov had to keep moving.

There was a rickety old escalator leading up to the main concourse, and he got on it.

At the top, he went back to the kiosk he'd bought the tea at and asked for another.

"You again," the old woman said.

He nodded and took a bill from his wallet, watching the escalator.

At this hour, the station was close to empty. Even the passengers from the target's train had all but cleared the concourse by the time she got to the top of the escalator.

She was biding her time.

The fewer people around, the fewer potential dangers.

He took his tea and then asked the old lady what cigarettes she carried. She began rattling off a list of brands, and

Smolov put the tea on the counter and reached into his pocket.

He would have to make his move now, in the concourse. He wouldn't be able to follow her out of the station and get her somewhere quieter. There was too little cover.

He'd expected her to start walking for the exit. That was where the taxis and streetcars were waiting. It was the way the other passengers had gone, the last of them now just standing in the doorway, looking out into the street, perhaps waiting for a ride.

The target didn't go that way.

Instead, she crossed the concourse toward a Bank Polski ATM, it's blue and white lights creating a glow that illuminated the smoke from her cigarette.

He reached into his pocket and pulled out one of the floss containers. He pulled about three feet of floss from the roll and wrapped it repeatedly around the cuff of his coat at his wrists, as well as around his hands over the knuckles, the way a boxer would wrap tape.

"Thank you," he said to the woman behind the kiosk, leaving her and leaving his tea.

He walked directly toward the target.

16

There was too much adrenaline flowing through Agata's veins to allow her to sleep on the train. She sat, with her head resting against the cold glass of the window, trying not to think that every bump and creak of the carriage was someone coming to kill her.

She knew she was in trouble.

She knew she was out of her depth.

The train station in Riga was one of the most heavily monitored places in the city. There were CCTV cameras everywhere. And foolishly, in a moment of panic, she'd used her credit card to purchase her ticket.

She tried to put it all from her head.

To relax.

If she remained calm, she would get through this.

But the thought that kept coming back to her was that Kuzis, the one person she should have been able to trust, had betrayed her.

He'd sent killers after her.

What did that mean?

What did it mean for her country?

She knew what it meant. It meant that what she'd seen in the forest, what she'd thought she'd seen, was real.

And the Russians were coming.

And there was nothing she could do about it. Not now. She had her hands full just trying to stay alive.

She knew she needed to get off the grid. That meant dumping her bank cards. They'd be able to track her as far as Warsaw, but she would make sure the next ticket she bought, she'd pay for in cash.

Her plan was simple. Get to an ATM and get as much cash out as she possibly could. Then get the hell out of Warsaw.

She would go to Berlin. It was near. It was a NATO member. The long tentacles of the GRU would be less free there to root her out.

She watched the platform as the train pulled in from the station. Instantly, she knew something wasn't right. There was a man there, muscular, with black stubble and a brown leather bag. He was sitting on a bench reading, it must have been ten degrees below zero, and as the train pulled in, he stood.

Everything in her training told her to trust her instincts.

This guy was off.

She watched him from the window of the carriage while the rest of the passengers disembarked. He waited as long as he could, but as they made their way toward the exits, he knew he couldn't stay on the platform alone.

He followed them, and Agata got off the train and followed him. If he'd come for her, then her one advantage was that she was behind him and could see where he was.

She made her way up the escalator, fully expecting to see him waiting. When she reached the top, there he was.

He was making a purchase at a kiosk, and she walked

right by him, making sure he got a good view of her. There was a bank across the concourse, and the walls around the ATM's were of mirrored steel.

She walked toward them, watching him in the reflection as he followed her. While she walked, she reached into her coat and undid the safety on her gun. She was still carrying the gun she'd taken from the man in her room, it was the same model as her own, a Glock 17.

As she reached the ATM, he quickened his pace to gain on her. He reached out with both his hands as if about to hug her, and she turned around.

He was surprised.

He hadn't expected it.

He'd seen the blonde hair and expensive coat and assumed she was a deer in headlights.

She fired twice, striking him both times in the chest. He stared into her eyes and shook his head very slowly from side to side.

Then he dropped to his knees.

Agata looked around the terminal. She knew she was being filmed by a dozen security cameras. Her face would be all over every Polish news networks within the hour. Whoever was chasing her would see exactly what she'd done.

There was nothing she could do about any of that now.

Across the concourse, a smattering of passengers looked in her direction. They'd heard the two gunshots and were still processing what had happened.

Agata decided there was no point trying to hide it now.

The assassin was still on his knees, kneeling in front of her, blood pulsing from the wounds in his chest.

She took a single step toward him and raised her gun. She pressed it against the center of his forehead.

The people in the concourse turned and ran.

"Tell me who sent you," she said.

She fully expected the man to lie. She knew the game. He would try to waste her time. Every cop in a ten-mile radius was on his way.

She only had seconds.

But he didn't lie. He didn't swear.

He said, in the perfect Russian accent of a Saint Petersburg native, "Lady, you don't know how fucked you are."

She took a step back away from him, she didn't have time to wash blood splatter from her clothes, and pulled the trigger. His head yanked back and then came forward, and the man slumped to the ground.

Agata stooped down and wiped the back of her hand on his jacket, then took his wallet from his inside pocket.

gata looked frantically around the terminal as the wail of a hundred police sirens closed in on her.

The concourse was empty.

Everyone had run.

It was just her and the body of the man.

In less than a minute, police would storm through the front entrance, guns blazing

She looked down at her coat, her hands. A few drops of blood, but nothing that would give her away at a glance.

She stood, turned back in the direction of the platforms, and ran. She leaped down the escalators, sliding on the steel bank that separated the two, and when she got to the platform, jumped down onto the track.

She ran until she was out of the station. The track led her into a long tunnel that was illuminated periodically by orange LED emergency lights. She followed the lights until she reached one that was green and saw that it marked the location of a ladder.

She climbed the ladder, gripping it's thick, sooty rungs as if her life depended on it. At the top was a cast iron manhole cover, about two feet in diameter, and she put her shoulder against it and heaved. It was extremely heavy. The ladder groaned under the weight of it.

She pushed, and eventually, it budged. It moved only slightly, but once it had, it was unstuck, and she was able to create enough of a gap to pry her fingers through.

Slowly, she was able to nudge it bit by bit, gradually inching it out of her way, and as soon as she'd created an opening wide enough, squeezed through it.

She found herself in an open lot. It looked like a storage depot for the railway, and had been cleared of snow. At one end of it were large coils of copper wire on wooden spools, and around all of it was a chainlink fence, about six feet high, with no razor wire on top.

Agata ducked behind the spools of wire for cover as more and more police cars sped by, lights flashing, sirens wailing.

When the coast was clear, she climbed onto the wire and over the fence. It wasn't too difficult, but on her way over the top, her coat caught on the fence and ripped.

She examined the tear and swore under her breath. The coat was one of her favorites. Then, as the wail of yet another siren approached, she made her way down the street in the direction away from the train station.

At the first intersection, she crossed the street, then turned down an alley and walked through a park.

The sun would be rising soon, and she needed to get as far from the train station as possible before dawn.

There was an ATM up ahead, and she decided it was as good a time as any to use her cards and get all the cash she could.

She went up to the machine and withdrew the maximum amount from her checking, her savings, and all of her credit cards. Then she broke each of the cards in half and put them into the slot beneath the machine.

The streets were beginning to come to life, and she got onto a passing streetcar without knowing where it would take her. It brought her down a wide boulevard, away from the rising sun, and as the first rays of light poured down the street, she saw up ahead an enormous sign for the city's second train station, Warszawa Zachodnia.

She wasn't far from the place she'd shot the assassin, and entering the station was a risk, but she needed to get out of the city. Every passing minute let her pursuers zero in closer, cutting off routes of escape.

Whatever she'd seen, there could be no doubt now that some very powerful people in both Latvia and Russia didn't want it getting out.

She got off the streetcar and walked up the steps to the train station, keeping her gaze down and avoiding eye contact. Four policemen stood at the top of the steps, just in front of the entrance, and she hurried past without looking up. There were security cameras everywhere, but there was nothing she could do.

Once in the concourse, she scanned the stores and saw one that sold women's clothing. It wasn't open yet, but the proprietor was out in front of it, scrubbing the floor with a mop and bucket.

Agata walked up to her and offered to pay double for a long, black trench coat in the window. The woman let her into the store, and she exchanged her coat for the new one.

She went back out to the concourse and was relieved to see that it was filling up with early morning commuters.

She found the public washrooms and had to pay an attendant to be let in. Inside, she checked herself carefully in the mirror. She looked a fright. It was a miracle no one had stopped her on the train from Riga. Her makeup was a mess, her hair looked like it had been backcombed for a Halloween costume, and she saw a faint splatter of blood on the collar of her shirt. She didn't know whose blood it was, but did up the buttons on the coat and raised the collar.

She also washed her hands and face, scrubbing furiously with the cheap soap and cold water.

Then, she took out her compact and quickly daubed on some makeup, trying to adjust her appearance as much as she could.

She left the washroom and made her way to the closest platform. More and more people were arriving at the station. They were moving in the opposite direction to Agata, but she stayed as close to crowds as possible and never once looked up. Her eyes were glued to the floor as if she was searching for something she'd lost.

The first escalator led down to a commuter platform, and she was about to descend when she noticed six police officers standing in the center of it, large guns slung across their chests.

She turned abruptly and took the escalator to the adjacent platform. It was for express trains.

When she reached the platform, she saw that there were quite a few people on it, and she was able to blend in among them easily. A train glided into the station, and she saw from the sign it was headed for Berlin Hauptbahnhof.

That was good.

What was less good was that there would almost certainly be police on board. So soon after the shooting at Warszawa Centralna, it was inevitable. They'd be checking all the international trains. They wouldn't have a very clear image of who they were looking for, but they would have a description.

Woman with short blonde hair. Long coat.

Something like that.

She would be able to slip through if she kept her cool, but she would have to be careful. She might be questioned. She could speak both Polish and German with near fluent accents but would need a story.

She decided she would be a history teacher at the University of Poznań. The train would be passing through that city.

As she waited, the group of police officers on the other platform ascended the escalator and disappeared from view. A moment later, they appeared at the top of the escalator to her platform and began making their way down.

The train had stopped, and the people were ready to board, but the doors had not opened.

The police officers began mulling through the passengers. When they reached a blonde woman, they asked where she was going, where she'd come from, what business she had in Berlin.

Agata moved closer to a man in a heavy coat holding a briefcase, trying to make it look like she was with him, and it must have worked because the police walked past her to another solo female traveler.

The doors opened with a pneumatic hiss, and she got on board and found a seat by a window facing the direction of travel. The train wasn't crowded, at about fifty percent capacity, and she had four seats and a little table to herself.

She sat down and looked out the window. On the platform, the policemen were lighting cigarettes.

18

Oleg Zhukovsky sat in his tent with his feet in two buckets of hot water. He was getting too old for this. His body ached. Old wounds burned as hotly as the day they'd been inflicted.

When he tried to sleep, memories came back to him of wars so far in the past that the world they'd been fought in no longer existed.

What had he fought for as a young man?

What had been the Soviet objective?

What did he hope to win, and from whom?

Today, such questions were so long forgotten that even the historians rarely dusted off the old tomes that dealt with them.

But for Zhukovsky, every time he shut his eyes, he saw the faces of the men he'd killed. The men he'd tortured. The Mujahideen called him the flayer. He'd been an expert at removing a man's skin without killing him.

And when they caught him, they made him pay in kind.

The forests of eastern Latvia were not the coldest place he'd ever been, where he lived in Moscow was colder, but it was a different cold. There was a dampness here, a misty, foggy, marshy stench, that infected your bones.

His camp was close to a village called Ostrov, just a few miles inside Russian territory, and the cadets from the GRU training facility in Saint Petersburg had just arrived.

Initially, he'd been told to oversee a military action, a full-scale ground invasion by the Western Military District, and he'd been able to oversee the army personnel from the comfort of a local hotel.

But Kirov had given him a new mission.

An *action,* he called it.

And it was not to be carried out by soldiers, but by fresh GRU recruits, straight from the training farm.

"They were more *impressionable,*" Kirov said.

And impressionability was certainly something that they were going to need to pull this off.

They were arriving now, and Zhukovsky dried his feet and pulled on the coarse, woolen socks he'd borrowed from the army commander. They were horrid things, with a texture closer to that of a Brillo pad than anything resembling a textile.

But they were warm.

He left his tent, and the cadets, as they got off the bus, stood at attention in a row, awaiting his inspection.

What a waste, Zhukovsky thought when he saw them. They were the cream of the crop. The best of the best. Hand-selected from all over the country to be trained as special-action GRU assets.

Men that could, and more importantly, *would* do anything for their country.

"So young," he said when the last of them had joined the line. "So very young. Like lambs in spring."

The men stood deathly still. They were trained killers

all. And all had at least one kill on his file. It had been a criterion for selection.

They were not kills in action.

They had been performed in training, in front of superiors, usually of a hooded prisoner from some far-off battlefield.

The recruit didn't know who he was killing.

He didn't know why.

But he did it. And that was what counted. It was what separated men like these, Recruit-Classification-Red, from those who failed the test, Recruit-Classification-Green.

"By the time I'm done with you," Zhukovsky barked, "no one will ever question your readiness again, do you hear me. This is your initiation, gentlemen. This is your ticket to the big leagues."

Zhukovsky had never been one for pep talks, but this mission was going to require a lot of things that ordinarily he would have dispensed with.

He had to prepare them for one of the most important and difficult missions there was.

He had to prepare them for a close-range, face-to-face massacre of civilians. The reason it had to be close-combat was that it was going to be recorded. It was a false-flag operation, and there had to be a record of it. It was to form the pretext for the entire invasion that was to follow and, in Kirov's view, was essential to avoiding a war with NATO immediately following the occupation of Riga.

"If all we get out of this is a war we can't win," Kirov had said, "then we'd be better to pack up now and go home."

Packing up and going home was probably the smart thing to do, but that wasn't an option. The president had set his sights on the Baltic, on reclaiming all the glory lost by his predecessors, and so, this action was essential.

On paper, it was simple enough, Kirov had sold it on the basis of its simplicity, but Zhukovsky foresaw a number of technical challenges. These men were young. They were, despite their Recruit-Classifications, as green as they came. And they were going to be marched into a small village, not unlike the towns most of them had grown up in, and kill people who looked exactly like the people most of them had grown up with. The villagers they were to kill were all ethnic Russians

That was what, in Kirov's view, made it such a compelling pretext.

But that meant their screams, their pleas for mercy, the tears of mothers clutching their children, would be in Russian.

Getting this batch of recruits to carry out such an operation, to pull it off without a hitch, to get in and out according to Kirov's extremely strict schedule, was going to require preparation.

He would have to pull these men into an alternate universe, a universe in which all the laws of God and man ceased to exist.

There was a sound of barking in the distance, the preparations for Zhukovsky's first training exercise, and he continued his speech.

"In a moment," he said, "some soldiers are going to bring up a pack of dogs. Nice dogs. Good dogs. These dogs are not rabid. They are not diseased. They have done nothing wrong."

He looked at the men.

"And we're going to do something extremely painful to them. Something that some of you might object to. But I want you to swallow those objections. There's a part of you that will revolt to what we're going to do, and I want you to let that part of yourselves die, here and now, in this forest, today."

The men were not going to be told the nature of the operation that awaited them until much closer to the time. For now, all they needed to know was that it was important. Gradually, they would realize that it was a false-flag operation. They would be issued Latvian army uniforms and told to try them on. Then they would be shown maps of the village of Ziguri and told to study them. Gradually, as the training proceeded, it would dawn on them what was going to be done, and by then, it would be too late for them to do anything about it.

Of course, there would be some who rejected the mission. It was not every recruit who could go through with orders like these. It was only to be expected.

But, if Zhukovsky did his job properly, enough of them would do as ordered that the mission would be a success.

Three soldiers walked into the clearing, leading a pack of about twenty trained army service dogs. The dogs yelped and barked and jumped playfully.

Zhukovsky watched the men. This operation was like the old days.

The very old days.

Days that predated even Zhukovsky.

They'd been conducted before. These very forests had seen such operations before. World War Two had been lost and won for Russia in these forests. Rounding up villages, evacuating ghettos, lining up families, and shooting every man, woman, and child, all of it had been done before.

And if it had been done before, it could be done again.

It would be done.

And it would be caught on tape for the whole world to see.

"You," Zhukovsky said to the first man in the row.

The man stood at attention, and Zhukovsky stepped up to him and handed him a twelve-inch hunting knife. The man took the knife.

"What you're going to do," Zhukovsky said, and he figured he might as well just shock the men now.

If any of them balked, he would have them killed in front of the others. If they were to descend into hell, then the sooner it started, the better.

Before they had time to get their bearings.

"You're going to choose a dog, and you're going to skin it alive."

The man's eyes flicked to Zhukovsky, just for the briefest of seconds, just to see if what he was saying was serious, then returned to looking directly in front.

"The things we're going to do here, gentlemen, they may seem *barbaric*, but I assure you, it is not the first time Russian soldiers have been asked to do such things. And it surely will not be the last."

He watched as the man stepped forward with the knife. He walked to the dogs and grabbed one of them by the collar.

Zhukovsky knew he was crossing a Rubicon, but missions like this required extreme measures.

And the truth was, the hardest part of it all, the most dastardly, if that was the correct word, was not the job that would be given to these men, but the part Kirov had hoisted onto Zhukovsky himself.

"The men," Kirov had said, "as soon as the mission is complete, must be liquidated also."

"Kirov," Zhukovsky had said, his objection purely a reflex.

"Accept it, Oleg," Kirov had said, using a phrase they

both remembered all too well from their days in Soviet special forces. "It's a thing that must be done. It's a thing that will be done."

Oleg Zhukovsky was a confirmed atheist. It had been a requirement of becoming an officer in the Soviet Army, of course, but had come naturally to him. His grandmother had prayed. He remembered watching her as a boy, watching her gnarled old fingers fumbling over a necklace of knots while she muttered the prayers her grandmother had taught her.

And there was a piece of Oleg that knew, or rather felt, that what she'd been doing was important, more real than he liked to think.

But other than that, he never thought of God. He never thought of heaven. He never thought of hell.

Until, that was, he'd been ordered to carry out this operation.

A massacre was always tough to swallow, but killing his own men just to ensure their silence, that was pushing it, even for him.

He'd only just started planning the details of their deaths. It required care. He couldn't just pass it down the chain as a normal order. The Army wouldn't carry it out. And besides, these men were trained GRU killers. It could get messy.

The solution he was looking at wasn't quite Zyklon B, but it might as well have been.

For a man like Oleg Zhukovsky, indeed for anyone his age who'd grown up in post-war Saint Petersburg, a city that had survived years of famine and siege at the hands of the Nazi Army, the things Hitler had done were the epitome of evil.

They were the ultimate abyss of depravity.

They were, in a word, Satanic.

And now, Kirov had ordered him to plumb those depths himself.

He would do it.

He knew what would happen to him if he didn't. But also, in truth, there was a part of him that had always yearned to push the envelope. To go beyond the pale. To indulge, so to speak, in the Satanic.

There would be no atonement for this.

There would be no redemption.

But the president said it had to be done, Kirov said it had to be done, and so, it would be.

Zhukovsky went through the group, one by one, and forced each of them to carry out his grisly order. Out of the thirty-six men assembled, only twenty-seven of them were able to do it. Only they could skin a live dog.

Some of them threw up. Some of them simply got back on the bus and took their seats. There would be consequences for them. They would be punished. For Zhukovsky, they were of no more use than the quivering, whimpering dogs that were huddled behind a fence at the far end of the camp, waiting for death.

The last man had just finished his task, and Zhukovsky was about to leave them with some parting words, but an orderly approached.

"Sir," he said, "there's an urgent call for you."

"From Saint Petersburg?" Zhukovsky said.

"Riga, sir."

Zhukovsky went back into his tent and saw the light flashing above the phone on his desk. He sighed and slumped down into his chair. He knew it would be Kuzis, calling to confirm that their little problem had been taken care of. He looked at the phone and then reached into his pocket and pulled out a pack of cigarettes.

Let him wait, he thought.

He put a cigarette in his mouth and lit it with a match. There was an old heater by the desk, fed by a twenty-pound propane tank, and he pressed the button to light the pilot. The damn thing didn't start, and he had to get up and check the tank. It was empty.

"Fuck this place," he muttered.

The light was still flashing.

He sighed and picked up the receiver.

"Zhukovsky," he growled into the receiver.

"Sir," Kuzis said, his voice frantic, "there's a problem."

"Don't tell me we have a problem, Kuzis."

"The assassin in Warsaw."

"Smolov."

"He's dead."

Zhukovsky said nothing. He brought the cigarette to his mouth absently and sucked on it, allowing the news to sink in. "This is not good," he said.

"No, sir," Kuzis said.

"How did he die?"

"She executed him. Shot him through the forehead in the middle of the Warsaw train station."

"I see."

"I'm sorry, sir."

"It will be on the news then," Zhukovsky said.

"It will, sir."

"I better call Kirov."

"We think she got on a train to Berlin Hauptbahnhof," Kuzis said.

"Has the train arrived?"

"Not yet."

Zhukovsky sighed. "I don't think I need to remind you what happens if this gets out."

"Of course not, sir."

Zhukovsky hung up the phone and then dialed the secure line at Kirov's hotel.

It was scarcely dawn, but Kirov picked up instantly.

"Oleg," he said. "Is it done?"

Zhukovsky swallowed before speaking. "She got away, sir."

"Again?"

"Yes, sir."

"Who did you send?"

"Smolov, sir."

"Mikhail Smolov?"

"Yes, sir."

"What the fuck happened?"

"He's dead, sir."

"You're telling me this Latvian police officer, a woman, killed Mikhail Smolov?"

"There may be more to her than what we've been told, sir."

Kirov was silent a moment, then said, "Do we know where she's headed now?"

"She's on a train to Berlin, sir."

"All right."

"I can activate my assets in Berlin," Zhukovsky said.

"No," Kirov said. "You've done quite enough."

"What are you going to do, sir?"

"Fuck," Kirov snapped.

"Sir," Zhukovsky said, his voice sounding increasingly panicked.

"Shut up, Zhukovsky. Just shut up. I'm calling in my personal asset list. It's time we called in the professionals."

19

As the Warsaw suburbs thinned and gave way to open fields, Agata felt her pulse slow.

She'd been watching the door of the carriage like a hawk, waiting in dread for police officers to file in and arrest her at any moment.

That hadn't happened. Not when the train pulled out of the central station, and not when it stopped at the few suburban stations on its way out of the city. It was now at full speed, flying across the Polish countryside toward the German border, and once they crossed that, she felt she'd be able to breathe easier.

She needed a plan. That much was clear. Kuzis, or the Russians, or someone, had made it very clear they were trying to kill her. They were trying to keep their secret, and until she passed what she knew to someone powerful enough to do something about it, she knew she wouldn't be safe.

Sitting on the train, she went over in her head everything that had just happened in Warsaw.

The assassin had been waiting for her.

Buying the ticket with a credit card had been a mistake, but she hadn't expected Kuzis, or whoever he was feeding information to, to have real-time access to secure financial data.

She had a sinking feeling that she was on the Kremlin's high-priority radar. She'd seen it before. She knew what her chances were. When the Kremlin decided to kill someone, there was no outrunning the assassins.

She kicked herself for not seeing Kuzis for what he was. Thinking back, there'd been signs. He was blatant about his wealth, living well beyond the means of a man in his position. The lake house alone was worth millions. Because he was so open about it, Agata had just taken it for granted. She'd assumed, without ever looking into it, that his family was wealthy.

That, and she'd been distracted by his sexual advances.

The truth had been right in front of her eyes all along. Of course, the Russians were laying the groundwork for an invasion. Paying off people like Kuzis was probably the tip of the iceberg. For all she knew, they could have members of parliament, judges, the Latvian president himself on their payroll.

Russia was a country that was two-hundred-sixty times the size of Latvia. How could any country hope to maintain its independence in the face of such an overwhelming foe?

She had to accept that there was no one, at least no one in Latvia, who she could trust.

The train passed through Konin and Poznań before crossing the border into Germany at the Oder River.

In the town of Fürstenwalde, about twenty miles outside central Berlin, she disembarked.

It was a clear, crisp morning, and she looked up and

down the platform carefully before proceeding into the terminal.

The station was clean and orderly in the typical German-style, and she bought a coffee in the concourse. Then, she left the station by the main entrance and got in a cab.

"Where to?" the driver said in German.

He had on a thick, blue duffel coat, like a sailor, and Agata found herself gauging whether or not there was anything suspicious about him.

She'd decided to get off the train at the very last minute, and as far as she was aware, even the Kremlin couldn't yet read minds, so they couldn't have known she'd be here, at this station, getting in this cab.

She told herself that, but after what had already happened, it was hard not to be paranoid.

"The Brandenburg Gate," she said to the driver.

It was close to the American Embassy, and if there was one place she should be able to deliver her information, it was there. The Latvian embassy was out of the question, and she didn't know who she could trust in the German government.

The Americans, though, did have one person she believed she could trust. She didn't know how she'd get a message to that person specifically, it wouldn't be straight-forward, but if she could reach her, she was certain she wouldn't be sold out.

It wasn't that she was a friend, exactly.

But there was a trust.

They shared a common enemy.

As the cab made its way through the city traffic, Agata thought of the woman she'd met in a bar in Riga all those months before. Never in a million years would she have thought she'd be calling on her so soon.

She'd been out on a date. She'd felt it was going well, some guy who seemed to be the full package. According to his dating profile, he'd never been married, had a good job, was handsome even.

Very handsome.

He had an air of vulnerability about him, like something bad had happened in his past, but that he hadn't let it get the better of him.

The dating game in Riga was no cakewalk, Agata knew that from experience. She should have known the second he entered the room that he was too good to be true.

She'd had a glass of wine, then an appetizer of shrimp drizzled in butter, then a second glass of wine, and as she made her way to the lady's room to touch up her makeup, she was fairly certain she was going home with him.

She remembered what happened next very clearly.

She'd been looking at herself in the mirror, trying to clear her mind of any potential pitfalls the guy might have been hiding.

She knew he might be married.

She knew he might be a womanizer.

She knew he could have any number of weird sexual fetishes and that if she went home with him, she might not realize something was off until it was too late.

As she reapplied her lipstick and gave herself a last look in the mirror, she told herself to quit worrying. Every guy was a risk. Any of them could break her heart. Any of them could hurt her. At least she was taking a leap with someone she was attracted to.

She was about to leave when the woman standing next to her, an attractive woman about her own age, with dark hair that was so smooth it looked almost translucent, spoke to her.

"If you're thinking he's too good to be true," the woman said, "you'd be right."

Agata looked at the woman in surprise. "Excuse me?" she said.

The woman looked around the bathroom to make sure they were alone, then leaned closer.

"Trust me on this," she said. "From one girl to another, you do not want to go home with that man."

Agata was taken aback. She didn't know what to say. Who did this woman think she was, in her expensive Burberry coat and Hermes scarf?

Agata was about to protest when the woman left.

When Agata got back out to her table, she scanned the room for the woman but didn't see her.

She finished her meal with the man, and when it came time to decide if she was going to let him take her home, at the last minute, she decided not to go with him.

It wasn't until a few months later that she saw his picture on the police database. His body had been found by the Riga dockyards in what looked like a textbook Russian assassination. He'd been poisoned by Novichok, a binary chemical agent that was known to have been developed by the Russian State Chemical Research Institute. It was practically a signature for assassinations carried out by the Kremlin.

Agata pulled up the rest of the file and saw that the man had actually been under Latvian state surveillance. He was suspected of being a handler for the GRU, and had obtained kompromat on a number of female members of the Latvian intelligence community.

Because of what that woman in the bathroom had said

to her, it looked like Agata had just narrowly escaped becoming one of those women.

Agata looked through the rest of the file and found that it contained video footage. The area where the body was found was monitored by CCTV. While the murder itself hadn't been caught on camera, there was footage of the suspected killer leaving the scene.

As Agata watched the footage, she knocked over her coffee cup in shock. She had no doubt what she was seeing.

A woman in a long, Burberry coat, with what looked a lot like an Hermes scarf pulled up around her face.

It was the woman from the lady's room in the restaurant. Agata was certain of it.

And that's where she thought the story would have ended, but for the fact that the woman approached her a second time. This time, just like the first, it happened in the lady's room of a high-end Riga restaurant.

"We really have to stop meeting like this," the woman said.

Agata was floored.

"You're a GRU agent," she said. "I saw footage from the dockyard."

The woman nodded.

Agata didn't understand. "Why would you let me know that. If I tell anyone, your cover's blown. Your life will be in danger."

"I don't think you're going to tell anyone," the woman said.

Agata shook her head. "You're wasting your time," she said. "If you think I'm going to sell out my country, you're sorely mistaken."

"I'm not trying to recruit you," the woman said.

"Then what are you trying to do?"

"I've been watching you," the woman said. "You're on a GRU list."

"Everyone's on a GRU list," Agata said.

The woman nodded. They were both looking in the mirror, and the woman looked Agata directly in the eye. "I thought..." she said, then hesitated.

"You thought?"

"I thought maybe, that you and I had something in common."

"Oh, you did?"

"Yes, I did."

"This is a trap," Agata said.

"If I wanted to trap you, I would have let that creep take you to bed. He had more cameras in his bedroom than a porn production company."

Agata didn't know what to say. It didn't make sense. This woman was a Russian, and yet, she'd gone out on a limb, putting herself at risk, just to protect her from another Russian spy.

"What's really going on here?" Agata said.

"I thought we could be...".

"*Yes*?"

"Basically...".

"Basically what?"

"I thought we could be friends," the woman said.

Agata looked at her, the vulnerability, the hint of blush on her cheeks.

"You must be out of your mind," Agata said.

The woman arched an eyebrow. "Am I?" she said.

"Friends? What do you think this is? High school."

"You tell me what the real battle is here," the woman said. "What's the real war we're fighting."

"The same war we've always been fighting."

"Exactly," the woman said. "The oldest war of them all."

"You're not talking about the Cold War, are you?"

The woman shook her head. "Adam and Eve, sweetie. That's the real way we're going to get fucked. You mark my words."

"So, you're saying...".

"I'm just saying, sometimes, it's beneficial to have someone looking out for you."

"So..." Agata said, "what you're proposing...",

"I'm not asking you to do anything," the woman said. "I'm just saying, I'm in your country illegally. I have no diplomatic cover. I receive orders from an anonymous safety deposit box in a bank, and then I seduce powerful men and blackmail them. It's only a matter of time before I get into trouble."

"I'm not supposed to be having this conversation," Agata said.

The woman nodded. "You're not supposed to be having this conversation," she said. "I'm not supposed to even exist."

"What are you asking of me?" Agata said.

"I don't know," the woman said. "I just know, it doesn't hurt to have a friend. I'm not asking you to betray your country for me. I'm just saying, in my line of work, it could be helpful for me if you didn't betray your sex either."

"My sex?"

"Us girls..." the woman said.

"Have to stick together," Agata said quietly.

The woman spritzed herself with perfume. She didn't look weak. She didn't look afraid. If anything, she looked fierce.

But Agata understood what she was saying. She felt isolated enough at times, and she was in her own country, working for her own government, doing what she was supposed to be doing.

This woman really was all alone.

"Look," the woman said. "You've already seen how I could help you. I didn't sell you state secrets. I didn't change the course of global geopolitics. I just...".

"Had my back."

The woman nodded.

Agata didn't know what she was doing at the time. She never in a million years would have thought about getting into an arrangement like this, especially not with a GRU agent.

But the woman had a point.

Which side was she really on? Truly? When all was said and done?

Which side was almost guaranteed to get fucked, eventually, by the other?

"How do I know I can trust you?"

"Because," the woman said, "I'm going to give you something you could use to kill me if you ever wanted to."

Agata looked at her skeptically. "And what might that be?"

"My name."

Agata had never needed to use that name. She'd never called on the woman for help, and the woman had never called on her.

But it felt good knowing she had it.

That was until she saw on a NATO national security bulletin that a GRU agent with the name Tatyana Aleksandrova had defected to the American side.

Good for her, Agata had thought to herself, thinking that was the end of the story.

She thought she'd never hear the name again after that.

The woman was gone. Hiding out somewhere in Iowa, or Idaho, or Ohio, under a new identity, a new name.

She looked out the window of the cab. They were on the Unter den Linden, and ahead she could see the enormous Brandenburg Gate.

"This will do," she said to the driver, handing him some cash.

He pulled over, and she got out.

She walked the last few blocks to the American embassy on her own, picking up a newspaper on the way.

Tatyana Aleksandrova was the one name on the planet she could be virtually certain would not sell her out to the Russians.

20

Maksim Mironov realized he wasn't the only asset on the job. He'd been at the Hauptbahnhof waiting for the target, but she never showed. Another asset, Prochnow, a German, was there too, and the two men recognized each other on the platform.

They both waited, one at either end of the train until the last of the passengers disembarked.

The target was not among them.

Maksim waited at the door while Prochnow boarded the train and searched every carriage.

He came out a few minutes later and shook his head.

"We're going to be blamed for this," he said.

"Did you search the toilets?" Maksim said.

"Of course I searched the toilets."

"Were any locked?"

"I searched all of them. I looked below the seats. I checked the luggage compartments."

"She's definitely not on this train?"

"Do you want to do the search?" Prochnow said.

Maksim looked at him. "You don't talk to me like that."

Prochnow looked away.

"Hey, I'm talking to you," Maksim said, leaning in closer.

"I heard you," Prochnow said.

"You show respect, or I'll have you strung up like a pig."

Prochnow gritted his teeth but said nothing. There was nothing he could say. He was Maksim's inferior. Maksim would be the one issuing the orders. If this went south and someone had to be blamed, Maksim would get to decide which of them took the fall.

Prochnow's father had worked for the Stasi, the East German version of the KGB, during Communism. If anyone knew how to run a police state, it was the Germans. Some of the things they'd done shocked even their KGB overseers, the very ones who'd told them to do it. There was a thoroughness about how they carried out orders, an absolutism, that was wholly unknown in Russia. When the KGB told them to monitor the population, the Stasi didn't just open a few files, they built an archive building in Berlin that could hold rows of filing cabinets one-hundred-and-eleven kilometers long. Not only that, but they hired over a quarter-of-a-million clerks and recruited almost two hundred-thousand informers. By the time the Berlin Wall came down, they had files open on 5.6 million East German citizens, nearly a third of the total population. They even opened files on children, and recruited other children to report on the political statements of their classmates, their teachers, even their own parents.

That was the thing about the Germans, Maksim thought. They took everything to the extreme.

Prochnow was a prime example. While Maksim, and virtually all of the other GRU assets he'd met, paid lip service to the ideologies of the Kremlin, Prochnow was a true believer.

He didn't have to work for the GRU.

He could have had a nice, western life.

Men like Maksim did what they had to do to survive.

But Prochnow was there by choice.

The Tourist, some of the other assets called him, but not to his face.

He'd gone out of his way to get the attention of the GRU. Somehow, he'd persuaded the recruiters in Moscow that he was loyal to the Kremlin, his father's career in the Stasi had no doubt helped, and they'd taken him in and trained him. When he returned to Germany a few years later, just in time for his military service, or *Wehrpflicht,* he was a trained assassin and GRU sleeper agent,

Maksim had always thought there was something nause-ating about the whole thing.

If he, who'd spent his entire life in Russia, who had a Russian mother and a Russian father, couldn't bring himself to genuinely love his country, then how could someone like Prochnow possibly do it?

That said, even Maksim could admit that Prochnow delivered the goods. He really did seem to practice what he preached. He never balked at a mission. Maksim had seen him kill a German girl as young as seventeen without knowing anything about her other than that her name was on a list.

She'd been pretty too.

Maksim had appreciated Prochnow's fanaticism that day. It had spared him from pulling the trigger himself. He'd killed women before, but he hated doing it.

He did the job because it was what he'd been trained to do. It was expected of him. It paid well.

He didn't do it because he *believed.*

"I'm going to do a second sweep," Maksim said. "You call Zhukovsky and tell him we have a problem."

Maksim went up and down the train a second time, searching every inch of it, including the areas not open to passengers. He searched the storage areas. He pulled his gun on an engineer and gained access to the locomotive. He checked the roof and undercarriage.

"What did Zhukovsky say?" he said when he got back to Prochnow.

"He wasn't happy."

"You're a master at understatement," Maksim said.

"We're to await fresh orders."

Maksim sighed. He lit a cigarette. Prochnow did the same.

21

Kirov was in his hotel room when Zhukovsky called. He'd been tense all morning. There were many moving parts to this operation, but if they didn't manage to clean up the issue of the policewoman from Riga, then all his other plans would be for naught.

And someone would pay. He'd do his best to make sure it wasn't his head on the block when the guillotine came down, he would do his utmost to make sure Zhukovsky bore the full brunt of the president's ire, but he couldn't guarantee there would be no blowback.

Not this time.

The stakes were too high.

"Is it done?" he said as soon as he picked up the receiver.

"Sir," Zhukovsky said, his tremulous voice conveying to Kirov all he needed to know, "she never got off the train."

"What the fuck does that mean, Zhukovsky? She never got off the train? Is she still on it?"

"The train arrived at Berlin Hauptbahnhof as expected, but she wasn't on it."

"Did you search it?"

"The train?"

"Yes, the train, Zhukovsky. The train. How do you know she wasn't on it?"

"The train terminated in Berlin, sir. Both your assets were on the platform. They searched it from front to back. She wasn't on it."

"How do you explain the police footage showing her getting on it in Warsaw?"

"Sir, she must have gotten off early, sir. The train had stops. We're accessing what footage there is from those stations, but there will be gaps."

"So she's gone?" Kirov said. "On the loose? In the wind?"

"I have the assets on standby in Berlin. We're combing the Polish and German police networks. The moment I find something, I'll give it to them."

"How the fuck am I going to tell this to the president?"

"Sir," Zhukovsky said, "what do we know for certain about what she saw in the forest? It could be that she has no idea what's really going on."

"Zhukovsky, you fucking piece of shit. It's too late to downplay this now. You're the one who told me she was a problem."

"I'm sorry, sir."

"You're sorry?"

"We have to call Moscow."

"I know what we have to fucking do, Zhukovsky."

Kirov slammed down the receiver with such force he almost broke it.

He looked out the window. It was bright now. People were milling around the square, old women going in and out of Saint Isaac's Cathedral, clutching their coats and prayer beads. Three-hundred feet above, an electrotype, cast-iron dome, one of the biggest in the world, blazed in the morning sun. The gold had been obtained by melting down imperial rubles.

During the war, the entire dome had been painted gray to avoid giving Nazi bombers and artillery units a marker.

Kirov looked up at it and wondered would such a time come again.

He didn't doubt it.

Whatever the past had seen, the future would see. Nothing could be taken for granted.

Not peace.

Not prosperity.

Not life.

In his own lifetime, he'd seen machines built to asphyxiate entire cities. He'd seen labs that did nothing but enhance the lethality of history's greatest scourges.

He knew life was fickle.

And he knew the call he was about to make might be his last.

He dialed his operator and told her he needed to speak to the president.

"There's no call scheduled," she said.

"No, there's not," he said.

The operator paused, uncertain what he wanted her to do. "I need you to connect me anyway," he said. "Directly."

"I see," she said, and a moment later, he had a dial tone.

He hadn't been expecting the president himself to pick up the phone, but there was no mistaking the voice on the other end of the line.

"You fucking piece of shit," the president said, as cold and callous as if the two men didn't know each other from Adam.

"Sir," Kirov said. "It is my duty to inform you...".

"Don't hide behind that language, Mikhail. This is game

over. You know that, don't you? This whore is going to blow up the whole fucking operation."

"I've got multiple assets scouring Berlin, sir. If she's there, we'll find her."

"You *had* her, you half-wit."

"I was informed she was an ordinary policewoman, sir. I allocated the best resources...".

"*Resources* Kirov? Really? You sound like a fucking functionary from the ministry of coal."

"She,,,," Kirov stammered, "I don't know what to say, sir."

"She slipped through your fingers, that's what."

"Yes, she did, sir."

"And now, for all we know, she's in the chancellor's office, spelling out our entire fucking plan."

"My most valuable asset...".

"I don't give a fuck who's looking for her. What do you expect to happen? That she'll just happen to cross paths with them in the street?"

Kirov said nothing. Mass must have just ended. People were streaming out of the cathedral.

"If the Americans find out about this," the president said.

"The Americans are in disarray, sir."

"Don't underestimate them, Kirov."

"The Special Operations Group has practically been wiped out."

"As long as Roth is in charge," the president said, "we can't let our guard down."

"We killed all but one of their assets," Kirov said.

He knew he was clutching at straws. Under ordinary circumstances, he wouldn't have allowed himself to go out on such a limb.

"You sound like a fool, Kirov. A fool trying to save his own skin."

"Maybe she'll go to the Latvian embassy, sir. If she does, our people will get to her before she does any more damage."

"She's not going to the Latvian embassy, Kirov. That's not why she fled all the way to Berlin. And she's not going to the Germans either."

"No, sir," Kirov said.

"I want your assets on the Unter den Linden immediately," the president said. "If she goes anywhere near the US embassy, I want them waiting for her."

22

Maksim's phone buzzed, and he looked at the screen. When he saw the call was directly from the Prime Directorate, he answered immediately.

"Sir," he said.

"Maksim, you need to find this bitch," Kirov spat. "Find her, or it's your neck."

"Of course, sir," Maksim stammered.

"This is coming from the very top, you hear me? The *very* top."

Maksim had no doubts who that referred to.

"We were told she was on the train, sir."

"How many of you are there."

"How many, sir?"

"Assets?"

"Two of us, sir. Me and the German."

"If you don't stop her, you might as well pack your bags."

"Sir?"

"You heard me. Now listen closely. She needs to make

contact with the Americans. We think she'll try the embassy."

"In person, sir?"

"You better hope so."

"I understand, sir."

"And if you fuck this up, don't report back to me, Maksim. Tell that to your German friend too."

"Sir?"

Kirov hung up.

Maksim looked at the phone, stunned.

"Who was it?" Prochnow said.

"That was the Prime Directorate."

"This has gone over Zhukovsky's pay grade."

Maksim nodded. "They think she's going to the American Embassy."

"That's right across the river. How much time do we have?"

Maksim shook his head.

"You look pale, Maksim," Prochnow said.

There was a smugness about him, as if they weren't both in the shit together.

"Fuck you, Prochnow. If we don't get her before she gets to the Americans, they're going to cut us both loose."

The men split up, each running in a different direction. Prochnow went for Wilhelmstraße so that he could approach the embassy from behind, and Maksim crossed the Moltkebrücke over the river, past the German Chancellery and the Platz der Republik. From there, it was a short distance through the park before he emerged at the Brandenburg Gate.

The embassy was directly in front of him, an ultra-modern building that looked more like it housed a pricey law firm or tech company than anything related to a government.

It had multiple service entrances, but the main consulate was accessed through a single glass lobby facing the Pariser Platz.

There were security barriers in front of it, but because the area was pedestrianized, the concrete barriers that would usually be present weren't necessary.

Twenty yards from the front steps, metal crowd-control gates funneled visitors to the consulate section and split them into orderly lines depending on which department they needed to access. It was the part of the embassy where ordinary citizens could get help with passports, visa applications, and similar issues.

Right before the glass entrance, a dozen marines armed with pistols in holsters screened the visitors and shepherded them through metal detectors and a futuristic x-ray scanner. Inside, there were more marines, armed with M27 automatic rifles.

Maksim walked up to the crowd-control gates and pulled out his phone. It was a pleasant enough morning, a little cold, but there was no shortage of tourists in the square.

He leaned on the gate and lit a cigarette with his back to the embassy.

He scanned the faces of the people in the square, paying particular attention to anyone approaching the embassy.

The target was smart. She was cautious. She'd made it this far.

He removed his earpiece and began taking photos of the Brandenburg Gate on his phone. He acted preoccupied while continuing to scan anyone who approached the embassy. When an attractive woman in a long black coat and dark hair approached from the direction of the Reichstag, he recognized her from a hundred yards out.

There was no doubt it was her.

She'd made some attempt at disguise, with a scarf on her hair and some oversized sunglasses.

In one hand, she carried a newspaper and in the other, a cigarette, which she seemed in a hurry to finish before reaching the entrance to the embassy.

Maksim pulled a cigarette from his pack and walked toward her.

"Excuse me, miss," he said in Russian. "Do you have a light?"

She stopped dead.

"Don't run," he said. "There are snipers watching."

She glanced around the square. There was no shortage of buildings for them to be watching from.

"You're going to need to come with me," Maksim said.

She looked uncertain, as if she still might bolt. She glanced toward the marines at the embassy, then down at the newspaper in her hand.

"Don't run," he said, as if doing her a favor. "Please."

He nodded at the nearest rooftop, as if warning her where the bullet would come from.

"GRU?" she said.

He nodded. There was no use denying that.

"Then I'm as good as dead already."

"Not if you can be of use to them."

"I'm not going to switch allegiances."

Maksim shrugged. "Well, we can't stay here," he said, showing her the barrel of an OTs-38 Stechkin silent revolver.

It was a small gun with a long list of shortcomings.

Chambered for the silent 7.62 x 42mm SP-4, it had an extremely short effective range. Thirty feet, maybe.

But that was more than enough to kill Agata where she stood. She would fall to her knees, and the passersby would think she'd stooped to pick something up. By the time they realized she was hurt, Maksim would be half-way across the square.

He preferred, however, to get her out of view of the marines in front of the embassy.

His training taught him not to allow time for a target to think, and he said, "Come on, speak to my commanding offi cer. His offer might not be as unpalatable as you fear."

His words weren't meant to convince her, but she allowed him to take her arm and lead her toward the Brandenburg Gate. Just beyond it was the Tiergarten, and its manicured lawns and pruned trees would provide ample cover for what Maksim needed to do. He clutched her arm tightly as they crossed the street. As soon as they entered the park, he would pull the trigger.

There would be witnesses, sure, but at least they wouldn't be armed marines.

He was about to pull the gun from his coat when Agata dropped the newspaper she'd been carrying into a trash can.

He stopped, he knew the paper was important, and in that split second of indecision, she reached into her coat and pulled a gun of her own.

He grabbed her arm as she pulled the trigger and her shot missed him by an inch. At the same time, her knee rose up and caught him in the groin.

He doubled over, and Agata was off like a rabbit, sprinting back into the traffic of Ebertstraße.

She narrowly avoided being hit by a city bus, and

Maksim ran after her, moving to cut her off from the Pariser Platz and the safety of the embassy.

He fired two shots, both of which struck the windshields of oncoming cars, and she darted and dodged along the median of the street, ducking every time he fired a shot.

She was running in the direction of the Holocaust Memorial, an enormous maze of thousands of concrete slabs, and Maksim dropped his gun and pulled out a far more capable Star Firestar, single-action, semi-automatic pistol.

He stopped running and raised it up, taking aim.

He pulled the trigger, and the bullet struck her in her back. She stumbled and struggled to continue running for a few more steps, then fell to the ground.

gata felt as if something jumped up from the ground and bit her. The bullet hit her in the back, but the pain came in her gut. She stumbled and fell, reaching out to break her fall. She hit the ground so hard the flesh on her palms ripped open, and she lost hold of her gun. It slid into a traffic lane, and without thinking, she rolled into the traffic and grabbed it.

Cars slammed on their brakes, horns blaring and tires screeching, and narrowly avoided hitting her. She raised her gun and fired two shots directly at the Russian.

By some miracle, both hit their mark, the first in his left shoulder and the other in his arm. He dropped his gun and fell to one knee, a strange look of surprise on his face.

Agata could feel the blood warming her back, soaking her coat.

She didn't have much time.

She turned and pushed herself up from the ground with all her strength. Traffic in the street had come to a standstill, and the pedestrians stopped in their tracks and stared at her as she ran past.

She stumbled onto the sidewalk and grabbed onto a lamp post for support.

She looked back at the street, and to her horror, the man she'd shot was struggling to get back to his feet. She pointed her gun at him, but there were too many cars in the way.

Half-stumbling, she ran further down the street while the windows of the building behind her shattered and crashed in sheets. She thought of commandeering a vehicle, but the man was too close, the traffic too tightly woven.

She kept running, and when she came to the Holocaust Memorial, she scrambled into it. The memorial consisted of over twenty-seven-hundred concrete slabs, each approximately the size of a grave. Some of them rose only a few inches from the ground, but others were fifteen feet high. The narrow passageways between them created a maze where she might be able to lose her pursuer.

She wanted to lie down, but she forced herself to keep moving.

She felt faint.

Somewhere beneath the memorial, three million names had been inscribed. In a daze, she wondered if hers would be added to the list.

The Russian fired another shot, and it hit one of the slabs, sending chips of concrete flying. She somehow kept moving, ducking behind the taller slabs and weaving among the horizontal and vertical passageways, trying to lose the Russian. She was about to stop behind one of the larger slabs and return fire when she felt the sting of a second bullet biting into her elbow.

She cried out as she fell to the ground, and from around the corner, she could hear his footsteps on the cobbles as he approached.

"You can't escape," he cried out, his voice faltering.

Agata dragged herself around the slab and crossed to the next.

"Once the Kremlin gets you in its sights," he said, "neither God nor man can stop what's coming."

Agata struggled along a few more slabs and waited for him to speak again. He couldn't be more than twenty feet away.

She listened for his feet, and when she heard the scuff of his limp, she rose up and took aim. He must have been waiting for her because without turning his head, he fired a shot in her direction. The bullet struck the slab about six inches in front of her face.

She fired back. Her shots rang out in the air like two sharp cracks of a whip. He looked at her, his skin the pallid color of death, then ducked away behind the concrete.

Police sirens were approaching from all directions. It sounded like dozens of cars. Overhead, two police helicopters were honing in on their position, hovering low.

If she could hold off the man for a few more minutes, the police would arrive.

She listened for his feet, moved two slabs over, then rose up and fired. Her bullet missed his head by an inch, and he turned toward her.

She crouched, and then, instead of moving as she'd done before, rose back up from the same position and fired.

He wasn't there.

She'd made a mistake.

She never heard his gun, but she felt it. She spun around and tried to dive for cover, but her body failed her. Her muscles could no longer obey her commands.

She fell to the ground hard, unable to break her fall.

The man fired again, and his bullet hit the ground just

inches from her head. Chips of stone flew at her painfully, and she shut her eyes.

Without looking where she was shooting, she reached out and fired. The bullet hit home, landing in his chest. She fired again, and this time hit his shoulder. Her third shot hit him in the belly.

"Drop the gun," someone yelled from behind her.

It was the Berlin city police.

"Please," she cried. "I need to get to the embassy."

"Drop the gun," they yelled again.

Why were they yelling at her? She didn't understand.

She'd been shot three times and was close to losing consciousness.

"I need to get to the embassy," she cried out again before realizing she was speaking Latvian and not German.

Her vision blurred. She'd dropped her gun.

The policemen were crouching over her in an instant, examining her wounds, trying to keep her from losing consciousness. She could feel the blood flowing from her body, soaking into the ground beneath her, and looking up at the sky, the concrete slabs of the monument appeared to close in around her, as if she was descending into the ground, deeper and deeper.

Her vision began to dim.

Their voices faded away.

Everything grew darker.

And she realized, as if remembering something from a long time ago, that she was dying.

One of the policemen was pumping her chest. The other was doing something with her arm. They didn't know she'd been hit in the back.

"She's not breathing," one of them said.

"I had a message," she said.

"What's she talking about?"

"I think she's Russian."

"The newspaper," she said. "The note is in the paper. He put it in his pocket."

She could feel the life leaving her body. Everything was fading. She shut her eyes.

Then bang.

Bang again.

The sound of fresh gunfire.

———————

24

Christoph Prochnow was a child of Berlin. Not the Berlin of his father's time. Not the conquered, vanquished city that had been divided by the Allies and brutally repressed by the Soviets.

That city was gone by the time of Prochnow's birth.

Consigned to the ash heap of history, as Ronald Reagan put it.

That was a world that, apart from the traces it left on the landscape, the deep lines on the faces of the elderly, the industrial detritus of half a century of toil, might never have existed at all.

The children of Prochnow's generation grew up watching Superman, drinking Coca-Cola, listening to Bruce Springsteen and Michael Jackson.

They lived in a twilight world.

An aftermath.

A war had been lost.

And another.

And another.

A century of disgrace, of humiliation, of loss.

He was like a child in a bunker after nuclear war.

Every picture in every book he read, every story he heard, every hero, every artifact, came from a world that had been lost. That had been destroyed.

The political climate may not have affected everyone the way it affected him. For Prochnow, it came to define every facet of his personality.

His father had been a hardliner, a supporter of the GDR, of the Warsaw Pact, of Moscow. He worked for the Stasi.

The *Staatssicherheitsdienst.*

State Security Service.

He fought tooth and nail against the forces of reform and democratization. Where others saw freedom fighters, he saw terrorists who threatened to tear down the entire world.

When the Wall came down, he joked that if the new German government sought to replicate the Nuremberg trials, he would be the first to hang.

Prochnow didn't get the joke, but he laughed. And then he read about the trials. The Allied trial of the Nazi leadership.

The judges were British, French, American, and Russian.

The defendants were German.

They included some of the most evil men known to history.

Hans Frank, Governor-General of occupied Poland.

Hanged.

Hermann Göring, Reichsmarschall and original head of the Gestapo.

Suicide in his cell.

Alfred Jodl, Wehrmacht Generaloberst.

Hanged.

Wilhelm Frick, Reich Protector of Bohemia and Moravia.

Hanged.

Ernst Kaltenbrunner, Commander of the Einsatz-gruppen.

Hanged.

Wilhelm Keitel, Head of the OKW.

Hanged.

Joachim von Ribbentrop, Minister of Foreign Affairs.

Hanged.

And on, and on, and on.

As the old man grew older, he developed Alzheimer's. It was then that he really started talking about the things he'd done. The atrocities he'd committed.

He talked about identifying students in the schools and universities who would one day become a threat to the regime. They weren't a threat yet, they were teenagers writing essays, making jokes, but Prochnow's father's team developed the techniques that headed them off before they ever had a chance to metastasize.

Predictive correction, they called it.

They would falsify their health records, have them forcibly committed to asylums, then subject them to experimental forms of psychiatric corrective therapy.

They operated a prison, Hohenschönhausen, which never officially existed. The area it occupied in East Berlin was blacked out on all maps right up until the 1990s. At its peak, it had over four thousand inmates.

Not even the government knew the full extent of their suffering.

Prochnow's father, however, did, and in the addled state of his waning years, he shared muddled tidbits from those years increasingly freely.

Thousands died there under his watch.

They were kept in windowless, underground cells that the inmates themselves had been forced to construct with shovels, cement, and cinderblock.

"The Nazi regime never ended," he would whisper. "Once darkness has been released into the world, it cannot be put back in its bottle. We continued what they had begun. Sure, the political slogans had changed. We had a new flag. We had a new *ideology*. But the methods, down to the finest detail, came straight out of the Nazi playbook. What Hitler's henchmen did, that's what we did."

Prochnow wasn't sure what to do with this information.

"What they did," his father told him, "I did. If they hung, I should hang."

Prochnow listened to every word his father said, and as the man grew older and more senile, Prochnow spent more and more time with him. By the time he was twenty, he knew as much about Stasi torture chambers and methods as anyone alive.

And he realized, at some point, that his father's boasts, his jokes, were not bravado. His father wasn't bragging.

He was confessing.

He knew what he'd done was evil, and he was preparing, in his own way, to meet his Maker.

Prochnow watched it all happen. His father's decline from a man who turned heads when he entered a room, to a blabbering, incontinent fool.

And the month he died, he decided to go to Russia and join the GRU. It was the closest he could come to honoring a man that the rest of the world could only curse.

His father was right.

If the new government had conducted trials, he'd have hung from the gallows.

And Prochnow decided if that fate was good enough for his father, it was good enough for him.

When he returned to Germany, he was sworn to the service of the Kremlin. He didn't care what they asked him to do. He didn't care one whit about the politics. The ideology.

What he did, he did because his father had done it.

There could be no loyalty more fundamental than that.

When he heard the gunfire, he ran around the embassy as fast as he could, and by the time he reached the Holocaust Memorial, Berlin Police were already in control of the scene. He could see four cars from where he stood, and the lights of more on the far side of the river flashed in a long procession toward the bridge. Overhead, police helicopters were scanning the surrounding streets for anything related to the shooting.

Prochnow had two Heckler & Koch semi-automatic pistols, both silenced, and without hesitating, drew them and began walking toward the memorial.

The memorial was large, its thousands of concrete slabs spread across multiple city blocks.

Two police officers told him to stop as he entered, and he raised his guns and unceremoniously shot them.

Then he climbed on top of a concrete slab and made his way quickly across the maze, leaping from slab to slab until he was looking down at two police officers who were administering CPR to a woman who was lying on her back.

He was behind them, but she was looking up at him, and in the hazy euphoria of the final seconds before her death, they locked eyes.

She'd been speaking to the officers, telling them something, but she was speaking Latvian. In her delirium, she told them about a note Maksim had taken from her. It was in a newspaper, and he'd put it in his pocket.

Prochnow stood with his legs spread over the passageway on two separate slabs and fired two shots into the back of each officer's skull.

They slumped onto her.

Prochnow jumped to the ground and walked over.

Her breathing was very weak. She was almost there, almost in the hands of her Maker. She'd be dead in a matter of minutes.

He didn't need to do what followed.

But he stood over her, one foot on either side of her head, pointed down at her face, and fired a bullet straight into the center of her forehead.

He took her purse and searched her pockets for any identifying items. She had a passport in her coat, which he took, along with her watch, a necklace, and two silver rings.

Her body would be in the Berlin police morgue for a week before anyone identified the body.

Then he went to Maksim's body and checked for a pulse.

He was alive but barely.

There was no way Prochnow was going to get him out of there without being spotted. There was also no way he was leaving him there alive to be questioned by the police.

They both knew it, but only one of them had accepted it.

He leaned down close to him and put his gun to his temple.

"No," Maksim said.

"Goodbye, old friend," Prochnow said and pulled the trigger.

The top of Maksim's head came off like the cap of a hard-boiled egg, spattering blood and bone and brain onto the concrete wall of the nearest slab.

Prochnow reached into Maksim's jacket pocket and found the newspaper.

He put it inside his own jacket and then made his way to the east end of the memorial, where he was able to get onto a quiet street called Cora-Berliner. It was lined with cafés, the customers sitting outside under umbrellas and propane patio heaters, sipping hot toddies and mulled wine and fancy coffees.

Prochnow wiped some blood from his hand and walked calmly across the street. He put two fingers in his mouth and whistled. A cab at the corner pulled into the street and stopped right in front of him. He got into the back and told the driver to take him to an address in Kreuzberg.

25

Prochnow took careful evasive measures to make sure he wasn't followed. He took the cab to Alexanderplatz and switched at the station to another cab, which he took to Friedrichstraße. There, he took the U-Bahn to the natural history museum, where he disembarked with crowds of day-tripping school children.

He caught another cab outside the museum and had it drop him off three blocks from the apartment in Kreuzberg.

At the apartment, he had a storage locker in the underground parking lot. He passed through the lobby and took an elevator down.

The locker was about the size of a king-sized bed, and inside he had a change of clothes, a hat and gloves, black leather boots, and two fresh Heckler & Koch pistols. He changed his clothes, put on the hat, then got into a white Range Rover with blacked-out windows.

He drove the Range Rover across town to another underground parking lot. The lot was connected by a pedestrian tunnel to the Gesundbrunnen U-Bahn station.

He caught the westbound train to Westhafen, where he switched lines to Osloer Straße.

From there, he caught a cab to a nondescript nearby apartment on the Residenzstraße.

He entered the apartment, which was as spartan as they came, and turned on the heat. It had been empty for some time.

On the kitchen counter was a coffee maker, a carton of Marlboro cigarettes, and a selection of protein bars. He opened the cigarettes and lit one.

In the next room, two wooden chairs faced a window overlooking the street outside, and next to them, there was an electric space heater.

The entire apartment was devoid of all personal effects, all identifying objects.

He took the guns from his coat, checked them, and placed them on the kitchen counter.

Then he went to the coffee machine and inserted one of the little metallic capsules. A shot of espresso poured into a cup, and he carried it to the window.

He sat on one of the chairs, turned on the heater, and drank the coffee. He used the empty cup as an ashtray.

He shut his eyes for a minute, took a few deep breaths, then opened them and removed the newspaper he'd taken from Maksim's coat and opened it up.

He flicked through it. On one of the pages, someone had circled an advertisement for a bar and written a brief note by hand with a ballpoint pen.

Tell Roth that Tatyana Aleksandrova's friend from Riga needs to talk.

Prochnow smiled. He lit another cigarette and leaned back in the chair.

This was big. If he played it correctly, this was going to be a step up for him.

He reached into his pocket, pulled out his phone, and called his operator.

"This is fourteen," he said when she picked up.

"Status?" she said.

"Two hundred."

"And oovon?"

"Four hundred."

"Thank you," she said and was about to hang up when he cleared his throat.

He spoke up, saying something he'd never said to any operator before in his entire career. He said, "I need to speak to the Prime Directorate."

The woman hesitated, only for a second.

"Hello?" Prochnow said.

"You said your status code was two hundred."

"I know what I said."

The woman hung up, and Prochnow took a long draw from his cigarette. He tapped it against the rim of the espresso cup.

Outside, snow was falling slowly onto the street below.

This was risky. He was sticking his neck out. Asking for attention.

Showing ambition.

When his phone rang, he stubbed out his cigarette and answered in Russian.

"This is Prochnow."

"Christoph Prochnow," a voice rasped from the other end of the line. The sound of it brought to mind a lizard.

"This is Jacob Kirov. I've been told your mission was a success."

"Yes, sir. It's done."

"The woman is dead?"

"Yes, sir."

"You're quite certain?"

"I shot her in the forehead from point-blank range."

"Of course you did," the voice said, sounding very pleased.

"I also shot Maksim."

"Out of necessity?"

"Yes, sir. Of course."

"Only asking, my boy," Kirov said with a chuckle.

"He was hurt. I had no choice."

"Relax, Prochnow. I'm more interested in the fact that you asked to speak to me."

"Yes, sir."

"I'm flattered," Kirov said.

"Sir," Prochnow said, his heart pounding, "the woman was trying to make contact with the US embassy."

"That's correct, Prochnow."

"I have the message she was going to pass them."

"I see," Kirov said. "You're showing all kinds of initiative today, aren't you, Prochnow."

"Sir," Prochnow said, uncertain how to respond.

"That's the thing about you Germans. Always so industrious."

Prochnow said nothing. He detected a hint of suspicion in Kirov's voice. As a German working for the GRU, it was something he was used to, but he couldn't afford to let it hold him back.

"You came to Moscow when you were eighteen," Kirov said.

"Sir, my father served in the Stasi for decades."

"I can read, Prochnow. I can read."

"I've got forty-seven kills under my belt."

Kirov said nothing. Prochnow wondered what he was doing. Reading his file, maybe.

He lit another cigarette.

"So, what did you want to speak to me about?" Kirov said at last.

"The message, sir."

"You see, Mr. Prochnow," Kirov said. "I'm sitting here in my bathrobe and slippers, sitting by this fire, and I'm thinking, who is this man who asked to speak to me? I don't know him. I don't know his father."

"He served...".

"In the Stasi, yes," Kirov said, cutting him off. "You mentioned that."

"My service, sir, has been impeccable. My handler will vouch for that."

"I'm more interested in what Maksim Mironov would have had to say."

"Sir."

"But I can't ask him, can I, Mr. Prochnow, because you put a bullet in his head."

Prochnow swallowed. This wasn't going as he'd planned. He'd expected them to give him a medal for what he'd found. Now, he wasn't sure Kirov would even let him read its contents to him.

"I don't think I need to warn you what will happen if I so much as get a whiff of deception from your direction, Prochnow."

"Of course not, sir."

"This message you found, you should have passed it on to your handler."

"Yes, sir. And if you tell me to do so, I will."

"But now, you have me intrigued, Prochnow, don't you."

"Sir, I only meant to...".

"To what, Prochnow? To what?"

"To put myself on your radar," Prochnow said with a gulp.

"And on it, you are, Mr. Prochnow. On it, you are."

"Do you want me to give the note to my handler then, sir?"

Kirov laughed again. There was no joy in his laugh. He did it merely as an affectation, a method of expressing a certain disdain.

"Tell me what it says," Kirov said.

"It's written inside a newspaper, sir. It says, 'Tell Roth that Tatyana Aleksandrova's friend from Riga needs to talk'."

"Tatyana Aleksandrova?" Kirov said.

"That's right, sir."

"Does that name mean anything to you, Mr. Prochnow?"

"I don't think so, sir."

"Of course it doesn't," Kirov said. "You're just the messenger, aren't you?"

"Sir?"

Kirov said nothing.

Prochnow waited so long he wondered if the connection might have dropped.

"Sir?" he said again.

"I'm here," Kirov said.

"She also circled a specific advertisement, sir."

"Oh, she did?"

"An advertisement for a bar in Kreuzberg. There's a happy hour every Thursday at five. Two-for-one cocktails."

"Thursday at five?"

"Yes, sir."

Kirov let out a long sigh. Prochnow knew he had his attention. The only question was whether the old man's curiosity would outweigh his caution.

"Where are you now?" Kirov said.

Prochnow said nothing.

Kirov let out another of his hollow laughs. "Now who's being the suspicious one?" he said.

"Sir, I'm sorry."

"Don't apologize, Prochnow. It comes with the territory."

"I'm at the safe house in Residenzstraße. My handler knows where it is."

"All right," Kirov said, his voice changing tone. "I'm going to be straight with you, Mr. Prochnow. I don't want there to be any misunderstandings between us."

"Okay, sir."

"I'm going to send someone to pick up the message."

"I see," Prochnow said.

"If I find out you're up to something, I'm going to get Zhukovsky to flay you alive. Do you know what that means? Flay? I know Russian is not your first language."

"I know what it is, sir."

"You've heard the things they say about Zhukovsky?"

"I'm not lying to you, sir."

"Time will tell, Mr. Prochnow."

Kirov hung up.

Prochnow realized he'd been holding his breath. He hadn't moved a muscle in minutes. He took a breath. The cigarette between his fingers had burned to the filter and, when he moved, the long tube of ash fell to the floor.

26

"We're a little early, boss," the driver said to Levi Roth as they approached the Saint Royal Hotel. "You want me to circle the block?"

Roth nodded.

He was distracted.

Someone had dropped off a message at the embassy in Berlin, and he didn't think he could simply ignore it.

He didn't like it, though. Not one bit.

He smelled a rat.

Security in Berlin had scanned it for toxins before sending it on to Langley for his attention. The physical copy, an edition of that morning's *Berliner Zeitung*, Berlin's largest daily newspaper, was still in transit.

What he was looking at was a digital scan.

Written on one of the pages was a disturbing message:

Tell Roth that Tatyana Aleksandrova's friend from Riga needs to talk.

He'd seen messages like it before.

It could be a warning, something critical that ended up preventing a catastrophic attack and saving countless lives.

It could be something mundane that had little effect.

Or, it could be a trap, and he'd send someone right into it, costing them their life.

The Russians obviously wanted Tatyana back. They couldn't bear to allow a defector to get away without paying the price.

But he'd also distributed a national security bulletin informing the NATO allies of her defection. Such bulletins served a number of purposes, but they also created risks. And they meant when a message like this came in, there was no way of knowing who it had come from.

There was a chance it had come from another GRU agent who was ready to defect. Possibly someone posted in Riga, although it would be difficult to know without speaking to Tatyana directly.

There was a far greater chance that it had come from some two-bit Russian counter-intelligence officer who wanted to impress his boss by reeling in a defector.

Roth looked at the handwriting, the curves, the slant of the pen. He wasn't a big believer in reading deep meaning into something like a person's handwriting, and in any case, if it was a trap, the GRU would have doctored every detail of it to draw him in, but it certainly looked like a woman's cursive. It was written in English, but the letter formation was consistent with a Latvian or other Eastern European.

The driver circled the block, then pulled up to the front of the hotel, where the valet opened the door for him.

"I'll call you when I'm ready," he said to the driver as he stepped out.

"Aye aye, captain," the driver said.

The driver was new, Roth liked him, but he couldn't help feel guilt over the death of his predecessor.

He walked up the steps of the hotel and through the brass, rotating doors. The Saint Royal, located on Sixteenth Street just two blocks from the White House and three from the Washington Post, was one of the most sumptuous on the planet. It was the kind of place where the ushers wore top hats and tails, and the concierge remembered your name.

Roth scanned the lobby for any familiar faces. The bar was a favorite haunt for the Washington elite, but it was quiet tonight.

"Mr. Roth," the host said, stepping forward to take his coat. "Your table is waiting, and I hope you don't mind, I took the liberty of having a bottle of the eighty-eight Bordeaux opened for you. Compliments of the house."

"Thank you," Roth said, following the man to his table.

"Can I pour you some wine while you await your company," the host said.

Roth nodded and went through the song and dance of tasting the wine. "I'm not going to turn down a free bottle," he said.

The host poured him a glass and left.

On the table, there was bread in a basket and a pat of butter with rock salt crushed on it.

He ate some while he waited. Laurel had no trouble being on time for work, but for this, she left him waiting a precise fifteen minutes.

He looked at the images of the newspaper again. Read the message.

Needs to talk.

It could be referring to anything, but what got his attention was the reference to Riga. From what the analyst at Cavalier had told him, the DoD's satellite coverage of the Baltic was one of the most critical capabilities threatened by the new Russian satellite.

It was too early, of course, to conclude that this note had anything to do with that satellite, but Roth didn't like coincidences, and this had the smell of one.

He sighed.

The GRU knew about the satellite too. They could be using it to entice him.

He knew he needed to ask Tatyana. The only problem with that idea was, he still hadn't managed to track her down. She'd dropped off the grid, taken her sister and the other Russian with her. He'd find her eventually, he wasn't worried about that, but this made that search more urgent.

When Laurel entered the restaurant, every man in the place turned to look at her. She was stunning, in a black dress that contrasted with her blonde hair, and a sensual yet demure neckline that revealed just a hint of cleavage. Around her neck was a small, gold pendant.

"Wow," Roth said when she reached the table.

"Don't," she said.

He wasn't foolish enough to think she'd made the effort all for him, but it still took his breath away. He stood and pulled a chair out for her.

"Laurel, you look beautiful."

She said nothing.

"I don't think I've ever seen you so dressed up before."

"Well, if you hadn't picked the fanciest place in fifty miles...".

"I'm trying to compliment you."

She looked at him. She was flustered. She wasn't sure what this meant. This dinner.

This place.

"I just wanted to meet you here to tell you how sorry I am about how you were treated. What happened, the way the president turned on Lance, you getting caught up in it, that wasn't right."

"It's all right, Levi."

"You deserve better," he said.

He poured her some wine, and they clinked glasses.

"To the future," she said. "May it treat us exactly as we deserve."

They drank, and Roth said, "I hope you don't mean that as a threat."

Laurel smiled.

A waiter came over and asked if they wanted anything else to drink. They both stuck with the wine, so he ran through the features and left them with menus.

"How about some caviar and oysters to start?" Roth said over the top of his menu.

"You really don't have to do this, Levi. No one would take this job for the perks."

He beckoned the waiter and ordered a selection of the most expensive appetizers on the menu. He then suggested they try the chef's tasting menu.

Laurel agreed, and they handed the menus back to the waiter.

"So," Roth said after the waiter left, "you said goodbye to Lance?"

"Yes, I did."

Roth knew it was a delicate topic, and he spoke carefully. "I just want to say one thing about him, and then I'll change the subject."

"All right," Laurel said.

"You mustn't believe everything he says to you."

"Are you calling him a liar?"

Roth shook his head. "I'm just saying, sometimes, the truth depends on whose perspective you're looking through."

Laurel nodded.

Roth knew there was more to what had happened between him and Lance than he knew. The ugly business with Clarice Snow.

He regretted it, and he understood that he might never know the whole story.

He looked at Laurel and wondered if Lance had told her anything.

"I'm sure you didn't bring me here just to talk about Lance Spector," Laurel said.

Roth looked at her carefully. She had good instincts. She was the right person for the role he'd set out for her.

And it was no small role.

He'd chosen her, in effect, to be his successor.

He'd spent decades building up the Special Operations Group. It was the nation's most elite intelligence unit and building it had been his life's work.

Laurel was young, she had a lot to learn, but when the president named him CIA Director, Roth knew there was no one else for the role. It had to be her. The president hadn't been so sure, but Roth insisted.

"She'll grow into the role, sir," Roth had said. "Mark my words. Long after you and I have been put out to pasture, she'll be giving the Kremlin, Beijing, the whole lot of them, a run for their money."

He felt for her.

He knew the toll the job would take.

She would never have the type of life other people took for granted. She wouldn't have children. Marriages, she might try them, but they wouldn't work out.

She would be doing a job that most people, even people inside the intelligence community, were ashamed to admit existed.

They hated that it was necessary.

And they'd hold it against her.

She'd get used to commanding death, to saying a name, and then seeing a photo of the person she'd named with a bullet through his head. And there'd be mistakes. There would be collateral damage. The intelligence would be wrong, or the wrong person would get in front of a bullet. There would be times when she'd make orders, knowing there'd be civilian casualties.

All of that had an effect on a person.

It changed them.

He looked at her now, sitting in that beautiful room, in that beautiful dress, the sparkle in her eyes utterly intoxicating.

She was as beautiful as any woman he'd ever seen.

And all of that beauty was going to be destroyed because of the job he'd given her.

The waiter brought them cutlery and a tray of a dozen oysters on a bed of crushed ice.

Laurel wasn't shy. She picked up a shell and poured the contents into her mouth without any horseradish or even lemon juice. He liked that about her. She wasn't afraid of things for what they were.

And what these were, was expensive mouthfuls of seawater.

He followed her lead and embarrassed himself by slurping.

"Have you given any more thought to where we should work out of?" Laurel said.

"I thought you had some ideas."

"As it happens," she said, "I do."

"And?"

"I think we should operate out of a hotel suite."

Roth thought about that. It would have its advantages. A special agreement with the right hotel would be needed. Special equipment would have to be installed. But it would certainly be easy for her and her team to come and go without drawing attention to a specific location. And they could switch locations at the drop of a hat.

"I can see that working," he said.

"There'd be some practicalities to iron out."

"I'm sure you'd manage to get what you wanted."

Laurel fixed him in her gaze. Her eyes glittered with the chandelier's reflected light. "Are you suggesting something?"

Roth was going to respond, say something witty, but his voice caught.

"Are you all right?" Laurel said as he cleared his throat.

"I'm fine."

She handed him his water glass, and he drained it.

She eyed him carefully.

He felt he'd never dined with a creature quite so intoxicating.

The waiter brought them over the next course, an *amuse-bouche* made out of foamed sea urchin.

Laurel examined it with the tip of her fork, and Roth said, "I've got something to show you."

He took his phone from his pocket and pulled up the images of the newspaper from Berlin.

"What's this?" Laurel said.

He handed her the phone.

She zoomed in on the message and read it aloud.

"Tell Roth that Tatyana Aleksandrova's friend from Riga needs to talk."

She looked up at him.

"What do you make of it?" he said.

"It's a trap."

He smiled. Everything's black and white for you, isn't it?

"It's a trap, Roth," she said again. "You know it is."

He said nothing.

"You're not seriously thinking of sending her in?"

"I'm thinking of speaking to her about it."

"They want her back, Roth. They're livid that she's on our side. If you put her on a plane, they're going to kill her."

Roth put the amuse-bouche in his mouth. It tasted like seaweed. He forced himself to swallow.

"We received it a few hours ago."

"Where?"

"The embassy in Berlin."

"Look at it," Laurel said. "Happy hour? If you send her into that bar, that's the last we'll see of her."

"We can't ignore it, Laurel."

"Why not? If someone wants to speak to Tatyana, they can give us more than that."

"There are other factors in play."

"What are you talking about?"

"The Baltic. Latvia in particular. I'm worried about it."

"Send me," Laurel said impetuously.

"Absolutely not, Laurel."

"Why not?"

"You're the head of the Special Operations Group."

"Right now, it's a group of just one person."

"It will grow."

"If this is a trap, I'll sniff it out."

"I can't," Roth said. "It's too great a risk."

"Look," she said. "I've got no intention of being one of those spies who sits behind a desk here in Washington while other people get their hands dirty. If that's what you think, you can find someone else to run your precious group."

Roth looked at her and sighed. "There'll be plenty of chances to get dirt on your hands, Laurel. Believe me."

27

Alex Sherbakov was the type of man people forgot even while they were still looking at him. He left no impression in the mind. That was what made him so dangerous.

He was out of shape, in his mid-forties, not handsome but not shockingly ugly, with a jowly face that caused his neck to slump slightly over the collars of his cheap button-up shirts. He had a faint Long Island drawl, and bought his coffee, which he pronounced *cawfee,* every morning at Dunkin' Donuts. He took it with three creams, three sugars, and most days, with an accompanying French cruller.

For fifteen years, he'd stubbornly refused to sell the house in Bethpage where he'd grown up, and commuted every day from Long Island, all the way to his job as a technical analyst on Wall Street. The traffic was brutal. To this day, he blamed sitting in traffic on the I-495 for almost two hours, every day, each way, for his obesity.

He was a creature of habit.

Change, novelty, anything out of the ordinary, he regarded as a threat.

He'd tried everything to stay in that house.

The I-495 to the Queens Midtown Tunnel.

The Brooklyn Queens expressway to the Williamsburg Bridge.

Even the Throgs Neck Bridge north through the Bronx and down FDR Drive.

Nothing made a difference.

The traffic only got worse.

Unless someone bought him a helicopter, he was going to have to either change jobs or move closer to the city.

The commute simply ate up too much of his life. It hijacked every attempt he made to get more exercise, to lose the extra weight around his gut.

It would have made any kind of social life next to impossible, were it not for the fact that he'd waived his right to a social life a long time ago.

Alex Sherbakov was the last person in the world anyone would expect of being a Russian illegal. He was part of an SVR program that was so secretive, it was run out of a Cold War nuclear bunker two miles beneath the Kremlin.

As far as his handler was concerned, the fewer people Alex knew, the fewer women he slept with, the less risk there was of a breach.

That said, it was his handler who'd finally ordered him to move closer to his job.

"You work on Wall Street," the handler said. "You make good money. Get yourself an apartment, something with a view. Maybe in a building with a gym."

Alex did as he was told. He chose a building with a great gym. And according to his condominium-issued security pass, he had accessed it twice in the last thirty-six months.

He was the ultimate 'Average Joe,' and that was how the SVR liked it.

Born on Long Island, he knew the name of every Islanders player of the 1980s. As a child, he had a poster of Butch Goring on his wall and would have been able to recognize the faces of Ray Ferraro and Pat LaFontaine far better than those of Nikita Khrushchev or Mikhail Gorbachev.

He didn't know what people in Moscow ate when they went to a movie theater.

He didn't know how the Communist Party elected its leaders.

If he'd been asked to name the members of the Warsaw Pact, he'd have had to guess blindly.

His favorite music was a metal band from the eighties called Tesla, and his favorite movie was Top Gun.

His favorite food was medium chicken wings with ranch. He wouldn't touch the carrots or celery sticks.

His parents moved from Moscow to Calgary under a secret Sleeper Program then administered by Leonid Brezhnev, but initiated by Stalin himself. They moved on to Long Island as soon as they'd acquired Canadian citizenship.

That meant, despite all appearances to the contrary, Alex Sherbakov was a weapon decades in the making. He was the payoff for more than half a century of Soviet intrigue and planning, an asset cultivated and maintained through the most profound political developments and regime changes.

Governments rose and fell, agencies were constituted and reconstituted, Alex's handlers retired, or died, or were replaced. Not a few of them found themselves, at one point or another, in the dungeon beneath the Lubyanka.

Sherbakov remained on the books through all of it.

Of course, he didn't know what he was when he was born. It was not until the night before his eighteenth birthday that he learned that little bombshell. And bomb-shell it was. Until that night, he'd fully believed he was an ordinary American boy, an Islanders fan, a Def Leppard fan.

People sometimes said there was a job they were *born to do.* For Sherbakov, that was quite literally the case. Even his parents' marriage was part of the legend, typed out on the KGB's unusually thin office paper, and put into a file in the Lubyanka in 1955. At that point, they hadn't even met. The fact of his mother's pregnancy, even the desired dates, was all in there.

The file even told his parents how to name him, with "an ordinary American name," and that he, or she, was to be given "as ordinary an American childhood as possible."

And that was exactly what happened.

It was ordained. Some secretary at the KGB typed it up, and as surely as if it had been written by God, it came to pass.

Alex absorbed the information. He took it in the same way someone might when told they were adopted. He real-ized the relationship with his parents, while still *valid,* while still *something,* wasn't quite what he'd thought it was.

There was something *professional* about it.

He was part of their job, their service to their country.

From that day onwards, they treated him more as a colleague than a son. He began a training regime. He learned the secrets of the trade. How to communicate with Moscow. How to work with a handler. How to take on things he scarcely understood, things he could in no way relate to, and live as if they were the most important things in his life.

He realized that he was expected to live and die for a Motherland he'd never seen.

To risk his life for missions and objectives he didn't understand.

But mostly, he learned to wait.

He wasn't a physical asset. He couldn't run fast. He couldn't control his heart rate. He could barely hit a paper target at twenty feet with the aid of a laser sight.

But that didn't matter.

He was just one asset. Out of how many, no one knew.

Truly, no one knew.

Their handling was segregated.

They were operated out of autonomous cells.

Someone in Moscow knew about Alex. But that same person didn't know who else was out there, waiting, sleeping, *available* for activation.

He was in his apartment in Brooklyn on a lazy Saturday morning, watching a black and white western movie, when the door buzzed.

He looked through the peephole and saw a delivery guy in a brown uniform.

"Package for Sherbakov," the guy said.

Sherbakov opened the door and received the package. It was nothing out of the ordinary. He was no stranger to online shopping, to deliveries. He brought the package to the sofa and opened it.

That was when he realized he'd just been activated.

28

A lex's apartment was in Brooklyn's Brighton Beach neighborhood. It was an area that had declined during the seventies and eighties but got a new lease of life after the collapse of the Soviet Union and the steady stream of Russian and Ukrainian immigrants that followed.

There were so many Russians there that everyone called it Little Odessa. Russian could be heard in the streets and in the dozens of ethnic groceries and restaurants. Eventually, the money arrived, and a property consortium funded by Russian oligarchs built an enormous luxury condominium complex known as the Oceanic.

Suddenly, chauffeur-driven Bentleys could be seen double-parked outside luxury stores selling everything from beluga caviar to diamond-encrusted Cartier watches.

Like Russia itself, it exhibited that same jarring mix of hardy Slavic thrift, juxtaposed with the most extreme displays of opulence and wealth.

Deli counters selling pierogies, smoked fish, and fried cabbage rubbed shoulders with the trendiest designer boutiques in the city. Within a hundred yards of his building, Sherbakov could buy kielbasa, fur hats, illegal Cuban cigars, and thousand-dollar sneakers.

The GRU had expressly forbidden him from visiting Russia, they said it would needlessly attract attention, but Sherbakov felt the neighborhood gave him a good taste of what it was like there.

The delivery had contained a note giving him precise instructions, and he walked past the bakeries and kiosks until he got to a little café on the corner of Twelfth and Ocean View called Red Square.

Outside the café, he picked up a copy of the *Daily News* and brought it inside with him.

It wasn't far from his apartment, but he'd never been to that particular café before.

"Just me," he said to the waitress, who was busy making coffees for some customers at the counter.

The note had been very explicit on what he needed to say and do.

"Sit anywhere," she said without looking up.

Sherbakov sat at a table at the far right of the counter, facing the cash register, with his back to the window. If the table had been occupied, he would have left and come back later.

The girl was stretched thin, it was just her, and a steady stream of customers demanded her attention. Coffee to go, sandwiches to go, it was that kind of place. Everyone had a specific way they wanted their coffee prepared. Steamed milk. Frothed milk. Hot milk. Cold milk.

He waited, reading the newspaper, and as soon as the customers cleared, she came over to him.

"What can I get you?" she said.

"How are the *plyushka* this morning?"

The girl looked up from her notebook at him. "The *plyushka*?"

Alex nodded. He'd been told to order the pastries but didn't know what exactly to expect in response.

"They're good," the girl said, almost suspiciously.

She looked around the café. There was no one there but them.

"I hear your grandmother makes them," Alex said.

The girl nodded.

"Can I speak to her?"

She looked at him closely, then said, "Follow me."

She led him behind the counter and through a curtain to the private staff area. There were a few chairs, the strewn personal effects of the staff members, a desk with a computer, some dirty coffee cups, and a full ashtray on it.

"Have a seat," she said.

He sat at the desk, and she brought him an old-style landline telephone, the cord dangling behind her. It looked like something Perry Mason would have used, big and black with a metal chime built into the body.

"You know her number?" the girl said.

Alex nodded.

She disappeared behind the curtain, leaving him alone in the room.

He looked at the phone for a moment, then dialed the number. It was a thirteen digit number with a double-zero prefix, and when he dialed it, he heard a series of clicks and buzzes before a woman's voice answered.

"Hello," she said in Russian.

Alex cleared his throat. He spoke Russian, but with the fluency of a high school student.

"This is Alex Sherbakov," he said. He hesitated then, unsure of himself. He felt as if he was playing a role in an old spy movie. It didn't feel real. Then he added, "Reporting for duty."

He was scared. He'd never been asked to do anything before. He had no idea what to expect. He trusted that the GRU knew what he was capable of, how inept he was with a firearm, how utterly unsuited to the role of breaking into buildings or jumping out of airplanes. He prayed they weren't expecting him to be like the Russians in the movies.

Sherbakov was good with numbers, but that was it. He wasn't athletic. He had few friends. He was physically inept.

And as for social graces, he was about as charming as a bowl of porridge.

The seminal experience of his life hadn't been the revelation of what he was, but something that followed from it. The GRU needed his loyalty. They needed to know that, when the time came, he would do what they asked of him.

They might have tried bribing him, but money proved a poor motivator for Sherbakov. They might have tried threatening him, but his psyche profile suggested that was more likely to paralyze him.

And, in the absence of a suitable carrot, or an effective stick, they turned instead to honey.

They'd sent a woman.

He was sure she'd been sent, although he had no evidence of it. He'd heard that the GRU made use of highly-trained, highly-sophisticated honeytraps. They were, if the rumors were true, women who could make blood flow from a stone.

And that was exactly what this woman had done. She'd played the role perfectly. Almost too perfectly. She said she was all alone in America, abandoned by the people who'd brought her there, and needed desperately for someone to step in and save her. It was like the fantasy of a thirteen-year-old boy.

And on Sherbakov's undeveloped romantic mind, it worked. In the space of a month, he was so deeply in love that he would have died for her.

He knew she was out of his league.

He knew she was too good to be true.

She had GRU written all over her.

But he didn't care.

For one month, she spent every waking moment with him. She cried for him. She laughed for him. They made love over and over. He woke up in the morning to her loving gaze and fell asleep, exhausted, with her head resting on his panting chest.

She was his angel.

Too perfect.

Too innocent.

Too beautiful.

And then, one morning, she was gone.

She'd slipped out in the night, leaving only a phone number for him on the kitchen counter. He called the number and was connected to a man named Igor Aralov at the GRU's Main Directorate in Moscow.

Aralov explained that the woman Sherbakov had just spent the last month falling in love with was an agent in a GRU program known as Black Widow. He called her the crown jewel of the whole thing, the very best agent in his stable. He said that the name Sherbakov knew her as was false, and that her real name was Tatyana Alexandrova. And he said that one day soon, someone from the Russian government would call on him to do something very important.

When that call came, Sherbakov would have to make a

choice. Either he would do as was asked of him, fulfill his duty to the Motherland, and everything would be fine.

Or, he could choose to do things the hard way, and whatever happened to him, worse would happen to her. She would suffer a fate so brutal, so hideous, so barbaric, that tears were falling down Sherbakov's face by the time the call ended.

He was on hold for a few minutes, and when a voice finally came on the line, it was so raspy, so dry, that just listening to it made Sherbakov thirsty.

"My name is Jacob Kirov," the man said. "I think you know what this is about."

Sherbakov's hand was trembling. He had to clear his throat and try twice before managing to say, "I think so."

The man was Russian but spoke English as if his accent had been cultivated at an expensive British boarding school.

"The time has come for you to fulfill your duty to the Motherland, Sherbakov."

Sherbakov said nothing.

He thought of Tatyana. She'd told him her name was Anya. It wasn't so far from the truth. Maybe the rest of their month together hadn't been so far from the truth either.

He should have known better.

He did know better.

She'd been sent to tempt him. It had all been a lie.

But what his mind knew with certainty, his heart was utterly incapable of accepting.

All that mattered to him was seeing her again, and somewhere in the words Aralov had said to him, there'd been an implicit promise, a hook, a lure, that maybe, if he did exactly as he was told, he would get her back.

"You were promised something by my colleague, Aralov, were you not?"

Sherbakov stammered so badly he barely managed a response. "I was, sir."

"He said you could win back your whore."

"Sir," Sherbakov said. "She wasn't...".

"She wasn't what?"

"I mean... yes, I want her back."

"Well, I'm afraid there's been a little, how should I put this, *change of plan*."

"What are you talking about?" Sherbakov cried. "I'm ready to do my duty, sir."

"Oh, if only it were that simple."

"But it is that simple," Sherbakov stammered. "I'll do anything you ask. I'll do my duty for the Motherland."

"Sherbakov," Kirov said, his voice sickly sweet, toying with him, "you've never even set foot in the Motherland, have you?"

"You know I haven't, sir."

"And your physical performance? How would you describe it?"

"It's," Sherbakov said, looking down at his lap, "it's an embarrassment, sir."

"You can barely hold a gun, Sherbakov. How am I to give you a mission when you have proven yourself to be so utterly inept?"

"I don't," Sherbakov stammered, "I don't know, sir."

"You're soft, Sherbakov. You're a slob. You know what I think?"

Sherbakov didn't know what to say. He couldn't see why they would get him to call in if all they were going to do was humiliate him.

"I think you're more American than you are Russian."

"I assure you, sir, I swear to you, I'm loyal to the Motherland."

"You want to see her again, don't you?"

"Sir," Sherbakov said, and his voice failed him.

There it was. The lure. The bait. The one thing they knew he wanted.

"You want her back, Sherbakov. Am I right?"

"Aralov said I would be asked to do something."

"Aralov's dead, Alex."

"What?"

"Your little whore double-crossed him."

Sherbakov couldn't believe his ears. "Sir?"

"That's right, Alex. Your sweet little Tatyana. She defected. Betrayed all of us."

"No," Alex said, shaking his head. "She wouldn't do that."

"Oh, because you knew her so well?" Kirov taunted. "What did you think? That she was sitting by a window somewhere just waiting for you? Pining?"

"No, of course not."

"You thought you were her way out?" Kirov said, laughing a dry, wheezy cackle. "You didn't even know her name, Alex."

"She was...".

"She was a whore, Sherbakov. Plain and simple."

Sherbakov had gone over in his head a million times the last night he'd spent with her. The inflections of her voice. The look in her eyes. The rhythm of her breathing when she fell asleep.

He was more than another job to her.

He had to be.

"No," he said.

"A whore, Alex."

"She wouldn't," Sherbakov said, raising his voice.

Kirov went silent. He was letting the news sink in. He was waiting to see what Sherbakov would do about it.

"What happens to her now?" Sherbakov said.

"Don't ask me that."

"Tell me."

"You know what happens to her, Alex."

"You can't."

"There's nothing I can do about it."

"You wouldn't have called me if there was nothing that could be done."

"Her name's on a list, Alex. The list has been stamped and signed and sent up the chain. You betray the Motherland, the Motherland hunts you down and kills you like the dog you are."

"There must be something, some way...".

"There's no way."

"If she defected, the Americans, they'll protect her."

"They can't protect her. Not forever. Not when she's being hunted by someone with as much *patience*. You of all people, Alex, know how long we're willing to wait for something we want."

Sherbakov's hand was shaking so badly he could barely take his cigarettes from his pocket. Eventually he managed, and even got it lit. He put it in his mouth and took a long draw.

"How will she die?"

Kirov let out a hollow laugh. "How? Who knows? Who cares?"

Sherbakov pictured her alone in some alley, her head on a concrete pavement, a bullet in her skull, and a halo of blood around it.

"I care," he stammered, "you know that. That's why you're speaking to me."

"You're an interesting case, Alex. I'll give you that."

"What are you talking about?"

"Well, you're *unique,* aren't you?"

"What do you mean?"

"You're certainly not the GRU type."

"What type is that?"

"You don't look like one of us."

"I wouldn't know what a GRU agent looks like."

"No," Kirov said. "I suppose you wouldn't. But I do."

"And I'm not it."

"There's somewhere I want to send you, Alex Sherbakov. If you're willing to go."

"What are you talking about?"

"You'll have to have your wits about you. No fuck ups. Do you hear me?"

"Are you saying?"

"I'm saying, this never gets back to me. It never comes back on the GRU. No Russian involvement whatsoever."

"What is the mission?" Sherbakov said.

"There's a man. A CIA asset. Highly professional. Highly trained. Used to watching his back."

"I'll go after anyone," Sherbakov said, "if you can promise me...".

"He knows how to recognize a GRU agent from a mile away," Kirov said, cutting him off. "I don't know what it is about us. The diet, maybe. Perhaps it gives us a distinctive odor."

"Sir, if you're saying...".

"I think it's the training. The muscle development, the gait, the posture, we all become ... you know...".

"I don't know."

"The same, Alex. We all become the same."

Alex sucked on his cigarette.

"But not you, Alex. You're different. You've never been anywhere near a GRU facility. Our *stench,* it never got on you."

"Sir, what are you saying?"

"I'm saying you're a fat, lazy, American couch potato. You couldn't shoot someone if your life depended on it. One look at you, and he'd know that."

"So you have a mission for me? Something else?"

"To be honest, I haven't decided yet, Alex."

"Sir, if you, if you spare   "

"Tatyana? It's too late for that, Alex. The wheels are already in motion. I'm reeling her in as we speak."

"Don't do it, sir. I beg of you."

"Tell me, Alex, are you a gambling man?"

"I'm not sure I follow."

"There's something you could do that might be useful to me, Alex, but I need to make sure you hold up your end of the bargain. I need an ironclad guarantee that if you fuck up, if you get caught, that there's absolutely zero chance of it blowing back on me."

"Sir, I swear."

"You're lucky, Alex. There's not a lot of men I could ask to do this, but you, you have a legend. You have cover. Real cover."

"I do, sir."

"You were born on Long Island. Just another American slob. You talk like one. You walk like one. That means you *are* one, Alex. Do you understand what I'm saying? You're a, how do they say it, a regular Joe Schmo."

"I am, sir."

"That might be your ticket, Alex. That might be how you save your whore."

"Sir, I won't let you down."

"If I send you in, Alex, I need a guarantee. Something rock solid. I need you to put something on the line too."

"Tatyana's life is on the line."

"Tatyana's life was already on the line, Alex."

"Sir, I don't know what else I could offer. I assure you I'll take my secret to the grave."

"Alex, I'm going to throw you a little bit of a curveball here."

"Sir?"

"Have you ever heard the name Oleg Zhukovsky?"

"I have not, sir."

"He's a friend of mine. Well, *friend* is too strong a term. He's a colleague. Works for the First Directorate."

"I see, sir."

"To be honest with you, Alex, he's a bit of an odd duck. Always has been. He's one of those creeps that does things to animals."

"What kinds of things?"

"He flays them, Alex. Skins them alive. Does it by the dozen. Cats, dogs, rabbits, foxes. Apparently, it's some kind of fetish."

Sherbakov swallowed.

"It's truly disturbing, if you ask me," Kirov said. "Truly disturbing. The animals, he knows how to get their pelts off them without killing them. It's quite a feat. But the pain of it, Alex. Can you even begin to imagine what that's like?"

"Mr. Kirov, please, sir."

"But that's not even the worst part of it, Alex. You want to know what I recently learned? He's not just down there, playing with the animals aimlessly. It turns out there's an objective to it all. He's got some sort of plan."

"A plan, sir?

"Apparently, he's got some medical training. Don't ask

me where he got it. Probably some quack on the internet. But somehow, he got this idea that he can graft the pelt of a furry animal onto a living woman."

Sherbakov had dropped the phone. He flung himself across the room to the trash can and immediately began throwing up. He heaved so violently he thought he was going to lose an organ. When he eventually finished, he wiped his mouth and went back to the phone.

"Sherbakov," Kirov was saying. "Are you there?"

"I'm here," he said weakly.

"Apparently, that's where the fetish goes," Kirov said. "He takes the skin from the animal alive, and then stitches it onto a flayed woman so that her blood vessels begin feeding the pelt, and it stays alive."

"Please, Mr. Kirov."

"Apparently, it's no more complicated than the kinds of things they do to reconstruct burn victims, although if you ask me, I think they botch a lot of those operations too."

"Sir, I've heard enough."

"He's creating his own pet, I suppose you would say. Sick, but quite fascinating. I wonder if I'll ever get to see how it turns out."

"Please, Mr. Kirov," Sherbakov begged. "If you were trying to get my attention, you have succeeded."

Kirov's tone changed. "What I'm saying, Sherbakov, is that if you let out so much as a single peep about your GRU involvement, or any kind of Russian involvement whatsoever, then Zhukovsky gets your whore. Do you hear me?"

"I hear you, sir."

"Very good, Alex. Very good. So are you ready to hear what I want you to do?"

29

Lance and Sam were sitting at the dining table in front of a log fire. The lights were dimmed, and candles had been lit. There was a pizza on the table and a bottle of wine.

Life was good, Lance thought.

At least for tonight.

And that was something he knew not to take for granted.

He looked across the table at her. She looked like her father.

It brought to mind the first time he'd met the man. The two hadn't thought all that much of each other. There'd been some rivalry in the unit in those days. Some jockeying for position.

Lance certainly wouldn't have guessed he was looking at a man who would one day take a bullet for him.

"What are you looking at?" Sam said.

She was pouring wine into a glass, and the look on her face said she wasn't worried about anything at all.

That wasn't how she'd been when he'd found her.

And maybe, just maybe, he'd stepped in early enough to set things on the right track.

Maybe, he'd managed to keep his promise after all and had looked out for a friend's kid.

That might not sound like a lot to most men, but to Lance, it was everything.

He'd spent so much of his time putting people in the ground that he felt that if he could help just one person up off it, it might make all the difference in the world.

Sam's life hadn't been a walk in the park, but maybe life wasn't a thing you were supposed to get through and walk out clean on the other side.

Maybe no one came out clean.

That was the thing the priests never said.

They talked about the Pearly Gates, and those unsullied, who'd never put a foot out of place, breezing right on through.

But maybe there were no unsullied, and anyone who passed, if they passed at all, did so through mercy.

"You're quiet," Sam said.

"Oh," Lance said, picking up his glass, "I was thinking about something."

"Oh yeah?"

"About your father."

She looked away, it wasn't a subject she liked talking about, but there was one thing he needed to say to her, and then he'd let her be.

"He'd be proud of you, Sam."

She looked back at him. "How do you know that?"

"Because if you were my kid, I would be," he said.

She looked uncomfortable.

"Sorry," he said. "I'll stop talking now."

She shook her head. "It's all right," she said. "It's just, no one's ever talked to me like that."

"Well, I just wanted to make sure I said that to you, just that one time."

She nodded and took a long sip from her glass.

He served her some pizza, then took some for himself. They ate quietly, neither saying much and when they were done, he got up and took her plate into the kitchen.

"That was delicious," he said.

"Thank you," she said.

"What for? Ordering it?"

"That, and what you said."

He put on the coffee and went back to the table with an ashtray. Already, they were settling into an after-dinner routine of sorts. He liked coffee and a cigar. She liked another glass of wine.

He had something for her upstairs, and he said to her, "I'll be back in one second."

"Where are you going?"

"Just wait here."

He went to his bedroom and opened the safe he'd installed into the stone chimney stack of the house.

It contained passports, documents, some guns and ammo, cash in various currencies. He looked beneath the papers and found what he was looking for.

A necklace.

It was a man's necklace, a gold crucifix on a simple chain, and he brought it back downstairs with him.

"Here," he said, handing the chain awkwardly to Sam.

He wasn't sure if she'd recognize it, but when he saw her eyes, he knew.

"This was his?" she said.

"He told me once his father gave it to him."

She nodded and put it around her neck, turning to let Lance close the clasp at the back.

The backs of his fingers grazed her neck as he did it. He could smell her hair. He shut his eyes.

"Tomorrow's the anniversary," Sam said.

She turned and looked up at him. Her eyes seemed larger.

He cleared his throat and poured the coffee.

This was his friend's daughter, he told himself. He was old enough himself to be her father.

He was no choir boy.

He'd done things he couldn't say he was proud of, and he didn't tend to dwell on them. Most of them anyway.

But this was different.

He'd made a promise.

He would protect her.

If he couldn't keep his word on that, he didn't know what kind of man he was.

He sat down and lit his cigar, and when he looked up at her, she was looking at him again, with those enormous doe eyes.

"He'd want us to celebrate," she said. "He'd want me to live my life."

Lance didn't move a muscle, and Sam stood up and took a step so that she was right in front of him.

She was about to reach out. She was about to touch him. Lance saw it happen before it happened, and then he destroyed the moment.

"Dinner then," he blurted.

He stood suddenly, pushing back his chair and getting to his feet as quickly as he could. Clumsily, he knocked over the chair, and it fell to the ground behind him.

"Dinner," he said again, like an idiot, and bent down to

pick up the chair. "I'll book a table at the Eureka. Seven o'clock."

"All right," Sam said, a bemused smile on her face.

Lance backed away from the table toward the stairs. From the look on her face, she knew exactly what temperature of shower he was going to take.

"Get a table by the fire," she said. "Something with candles."

"All right," Lance said.

"And make sure they have champagne. If we're going to commemorate my father, we're going to do it right."

lex didn't sleep a wink. Over and over in his head, all he could think about was what Kirov had told him. Every time he thought of some GRU lunatic in a dungeon in Russia trying to graft animal fur onto Tatyana, he gagged. More than once, he had to run to the bathroom to spill his guts.

The rest of the conversation with Kirov was a blur. There was a man in Montana, a CIA asset.

"Call him an old friend," Kirov had said.

Alex said, "You want me to kill him."

That caused Kirov to fall into a fit of laughter, as if he'd never heard anything so ludicrous in his life.

Alex sucked down one cigarette after the next while Kirov explained to him that this was a man he could not kill.

"You said he wouldn't see me coming," Alex said.

"He'd see if you tried to kill him," Kirov said and burst into another fit of laughter. Then he said, "As you're only too aware yourself, Alex, all men have a weakness."

"A woman?" Alex said.

"She's just a girl, really," Kirov said. "Just a girl."

"And you want me to kill her?"

Kirov laughed again. "Heavens, Sherbakov. Enough with the killing. We're not psychopaths."

Kirov had been very clear. Under no circumstances was he to kill the girl.

"I need to distract this man," he said. "Not set him off on a rampage. If you kill the girl, this man will find us, Sherbakov. He'll find you. He'll find me. He'll find my colleagues. He'll find our families. He'll burn down the world if he has to. Heaven and earth won't be able to stop him. He'll kill everyone, and if he does that, then there'll be no one left to stop Zhukovsky from putting your slut into one of his cages."

Essentially, what Kirov needed, was for the CIA man to be distracted but not enraged.

Like poking a bear.

But gently.

Alex was to steer clear of the man and only approach the girl when she was alone.

Kirov knew things about her, about her personal life, that he would be able to use to draw her in.

"What do you want me to do with her?" Alex said. He genuinely didn't know.

"Nothing you'll enjoy," had been Kirov's answer. "I've got your psyche profiles here, Alex. I've got a lifetime's worth of assessments. There's really nothing in your record that suggests this will come naturally to you."

"Just tell me what it is," Alex said.

"I just want to make sure you're up for the task, Alex. I wouldn't want to send you into something you aren't ready for."

And it had been at that point that Alex found his voice.

"Don't underestimate me, Kirov," he said. "You forget

that I've been groomed for this job since before birth. I'm ready."

He'd thought that would bring out Kirov's anger, but he liked it. "That's good, Alex," he said. "That's good. Don't forget that. Don't forget who you are. That's Russian blood in your veins."

Then Kirov said something about maybe, if everything went according to plan, both of them being recalled to Moscow.

"Don't lie to me," Alex said.

"I'm just saying, Alex, this is an important mission. If you pull it off, well, who knows what the reward might be. The whore is a traitor. I can't fix that. But if you keep a tight leash on her, who'll object to you having a little pet of your own?"

Alex knew it was bait. He knew he wasn't going to end up happily ever after with Tatyana.

It was a dream.

But a dream he found himself incapable of shrugging off.

"What do you want me to do with the girl?" he said.

"I want you to *upset* her, Alex."

"*Upset* her?"

"That's right."

"What does that mean?"

"Don't worry about that now. You'll know when the time comes."

"And that's it?"

"And then you'll have to run, Alex. This man. Her protector. He's going to be looking for you. And the more you upset her, the harder he'll look. So you don't want to go too far."

"So you want me to upset her just enough to get his attention?"

"Like I said, you'll have all the information you need when the time comes."

Before he hung up, Kirov gave him the details of a charter flight out of Teterboro, New Jersey the following morning. When he got to the airport, he found a fully fueled jet on the tarmac, ready to go.

"You're the guy going to Montana?" the pilot said when Alex entered the hangar.

"Yeah," Alex said, feeling out of his depth.

"Glacier Park," the pilot said. "We had to bring you in a larger plane. The Learjet originally requested by the consulate doesn't quite have the range you're looking for."

"I see," Alex said.

"This puppy will get you there in one piece, though," the pilot said. "Shouldn't be much more than four hours flight time."

"All right," Alex said, wondering if the pilot would be blabbing all the way.

Onboard, the plane was more luxurious than anything he'd ever seen. There were six enormous cream-colored leather seats, configured so that four of them faced each other. The other two were off to one side, facing a television screen. The leather was quilted in a crosshatch pattern, and around it, the burnished mahogany was so smooth it felt like glass.

There was a stewardess and two pilots, and even before they took off, the stewardess saw to his needs, offering him drinks and hinting that she might be able to provide more *sensual* diversions if that was what interested him.

She assumed he was from the consulate and spoke to him in Russian. Alex played along, and as he sank into one of the chairs, allowed himself the indulgence of a scotch on the rocks.

Her hand brushed his when she delivered his drink.

He took a gulp and realized that for the time he was on this flight, he could have *whatever* he wanted.

That, he supposed, was how men ended up working for an agency like the GRU. He'd never really thought about it, but now that he was there, he could see the appeal.

The stewardess took her seat, and Alex watched her as the plane prepared for takeoff.

She was facing him, and the way she crossed her legs revealed the tops of her thigh-high stockings. The plane accelerated down the runway, and before the wheels even broke contact with the tarmac, she was opening the buttons on her blouse.

Alex wanted her.

Of course he did.

But Tatyana was the only woman he'd ever been with.

He turned away from her, looking out the window at the New Jersey sprawl. When they broke through the clouds, sunlight filled the cabin.

"You don't want to play?" the stewardess said.

Through the open blouse, he could see her bra, an intricate patch of black lace that only very barely concealed her nipples. He didn't know what to say.

He drained the scotch in his glass, and the stewardess reached behind her back and unhooked the clasp of her bra, letting it fall away from her breasts.

By the time the plane landed, she had become the second woman Alex had ever had sex with.

He didn't know how he felt about it.

He disembarked, and the pilots stood at the bottom of the steps, thanking him as if he'd personally paid the bill for the flight. The stewardess stood next to them, and Alex avoided making eye contact with her.

There was a local cab waiting in the hangar, and he got into it. It brought him to the Deweyville EconoLodge, where a ninety-nine dollar-a-night room with two double beds and satellite television was waiting for him.

He sat on the side of the bed and stared at the television, which was off. After a few minutes, he lay back, fully-clothed and with his shoes on, and shut his eyes.

His dreams were an unsettling mix of the stewardess, Tatyana, and Kirov's raspy, grating voice.

"Everything and everyone we ever loved will turn to ash," Kirov said in the dream.

He rolled over and looked at the clock by the bed. It was mid-afternoon, and he'd been told to check in with his handler as soon as he arrived.

He picked up the room phone and dialed the front desk. "I need some aspirin," he said.

The kid who'd checked him in arrived with water and a bottle of aspirin. Alex thanked him, took four pills, then sat on the side of the bed and rubbed his temples in a circular motion.

He went into the bathroom and rinsed his mouth at the sink.

Then he went back to the bed and dialed the number he'd been given.

A female voice, Russian but speaking English, answered.

"You're late. You were supposed to check-in hours ago."

"I know," Alex said.

"Do you have the case?"

He did have it, a leather briefcase that had been couriered to his apartment from the consulate the night before, and he lay it on the bed and opened it.

Inside, it contained a small, concealable earpiece, a Makarov pistol, and two clips.

"You're ready then?"

Alex sighed. He had no idea what he was doing. He had no idea what his life had become. He was obeying the orders that were given to him on autopilot.

He felt that if he could just get through the next few hours, everything else would take care of itself.

"I'm ready," he said.

31

Alex rented a car from the front desk of the hotel and had to wait about thirty minutes for it to arrive. He tipped the kid at the front desk and the kid who delivered it. It was a dark blue Chevy sedan, and he called his contact again from the driver's seat.

"This is Sherbakov," he said.

"All right, Alex," the operator said. "We've got visual. You're in the rental."

He glanced at the sky. He could see nothing, but something was up there, a drone, or a satellite.

Something.

It was scary what they were capable of.

"Have you put in your earpiece?"

He took the earpiece from his pocket, pressed a tiny button on the side of it, and put it in his ear. Then he paired it with the cell phone.

"All right," he said.

"Put the phone somewhere safe."

"The glovebox?"

"No, somewhere on your person."

He put it in an inside pocket of his coat and zipped it shut.

"Okay," he said. "Done."

"And the gun?" the operator said. "You've got the gun?"

"I'm not an imbecile."

"Just confirm you have it, Mr. Sherbakov."

"I've got it."

"Good," she said. "Now, the street in front of you. Turn right toward town. There's a bar on Main called the Eureka."

"All right," Alex said, pulling out of the hotel lot.

It took less than a minute to reach the Eureka, an old-style bar that looked like it had been there since the days of the gold rush. He pulled up right outside.

"Not there," the operator said.

"Excuse me?"

"Don't park there."

"Where should I park?"

"Park across the street with your back to the bar. You can watch through your rearview, and try not to draw any attention."

Alex rolled his eyes, then reversed from his spot and pulled into the one directly across the street.

"All right," he said again.

"Sit tight," the operator said. "She's inside the bar."

"Alone?"

"Just sit tight, Alex."

He waited about ten minutes, the engine running, the heat on. He'd thought it had been cold in New York. The temperature here was twenty degrees lower.

He opened his window a crack and lit a cigarette.

Eventually, an attractive girl, about twenty years old, dressed in a black turtleneck sweater and white ski jacket, came out of the bar. She wouldn't have been out of place in

Aspen or Vail, and she walked up to a pickup truck and opened the door.

"Follow her?" Alex said.

"Just sit tight, Alex. We'll tell you when to move."

She reached into the truck and pulled something out, it looked like two bottles of Veuve Clicquot champagne, and brought them back into the bar.

She came back out of the bar a minute later and got in the truck.

She fired up the engine and pulled out into the street.

"Follow now?" Alex said.

"Just stay where you are, Sherbakov. Hold back. You're not going to lose her."

He watched her drive down the street and around a corner, and then the operator said, "Now you can follow her, but take your time. It's not a race."

He pulled into the street and drove after her, stopping at every stop sign, being courteous to the other vehicles. He'd lost visual on the truck, but the operator guided him.

"Not too fast," she kept reminding him every thirty seconds or so.

"You want me to go slower than this?" he said.

She ignored him and directed him to the parking lot of a large grocery store. There were plenty of other cars in the lot, and he saw the pickup parked next to one of those bays for shopping carts.

"Park next to the passenger side of the truck," the operator said.

He did so, and she said, "Have the gun ready."

"Ready for what?"

"You're going to get into the passenger side of her truck and stay low to the ground beneath the seat. You're wearing a black coat. Use that to conceal yourself as much as possible. She shouldn't see you until she's inside the truck."

"She'll see me as soon as she opens the door."

There was a pause on the other end of the line, like she was consulting with someone, then she said, "No, she won't see you until she's in the truck. Then all you have to do is tell her to drive."

"Drive where?"

"Don't worry about that, and don't let her know you've got an earpiece. This has got to look like just some random attack by a local guy."

"What if she tries to run?"

"Try not to let her run. The point of this is to scare her, upset her, and you can do that better if you get her out of town."

"But if she runs, what do I do? Shoot her?"

"Absolutely do not pull that trigger, Sherbakov. If she runs, you let her go. You get in your car, and you drive straight back to the airport, you hear me?"

"I hear you," he said.

"We're just giving her a little fright here. Something to distract her protector. That's it."

"Got it," Alex said.

"Okay then, go. Get in her truck."

"What if it's locked?"

"Would we tell you to get in a locked vehicle?"

Alex sighed.

"And Sherbakov."

"Yes."

"Don't forget the phone."

He patted his coat pocket to make sure the phone was still there, then opened the door and, acting as naturally as possible, got out of his car, opened the door to the girl's truck, and climbed inside.

"Stay low, Sherbakov. Hide beneath your coat."

He crouched down low in the area in front of the passenger seat and saw that, in all likelihood, the girl probably would not see him until she was already driving. He opened the zip on his coat and pulled it up over his head as an extra precaution.

"I'm in position," he said.

"Sit tight, Alex. She's coming out of the store now. Just stay calm and do what we discussed. Tell her to drive the truck. It doesn't matter where she goes so long as she gets the vehicle moving."

About thirty seconds later, the door opened, and the girl put a cake box on the seat and hurried to get in from the snow.

She started the engine.

Alex waited until the truck was moving, he let her drive out of the parking lot and get on the road, before revealing himself to her.

"Keep driving," he said, pulling aside the coat and pointing the gun right at her.

He scared the living daylights out of her. She screamed, stopped, then screamed briefly a second time.

In her shock, she'd slammed the brakes, and he said, "Drive, or I'm going to shoot."

She looked at him, paralyzed with fear, then looked around at the surrounding streets.

"Get her moving," the operator said in his ear.

He jammed the gun into her thigh and said, "Don't make me do this. Just drive and no one has to get hurt."

Her hands were shaking. Her voice was quivering.

"Just take your foot off the brake and get us moving," he

said, pressing the gun firmly against her leg. "Come on. Deep breaths."

She took two deep breaths, and it seemed, after the initial shock of seeing him there, she was able to calm down enough to control herself.

"Who are you?" she said, her voice on the edge of tears.

"That doesn't matter. Just keep us moving."

There was a car behind them, and it honked impatiently before driving around them, horn blaring.

The girl looked in her rearview mirror, then began driving slowly.

"Where do you want me to go?" she said.

"Get her to drive out of town," the operator said in Alex's ear.

"Just drive," Alex said. "Get us out of town. It doesn't matter where."

From where he was, Alex couldn't actually see where they were going, but the operator was following their every movement.

"Tell her to turn right," she said, and Alex passed on the instruction.

"Tell her to slow down."

"Tell her to keep going."

"Tell her to turn off here."

Alex passed on the instructions, remaining on the floor with the gun pressed against her thigh.

After a few minutes, the operator told Alex to tell her to stop, and he did.

She pulled over, and Alex got up into the seat.

They were on a clearing off a small side road. It was a secluded spot with nothing but trees as far as they could see in every direction.

"All right, Alex," the operator said. "This is what you're

going to do. You're going to tell her to take off her coat and throw it out of the window."

Alex thought that was strange, but he couldn't question the operator in front of the girl.

"Take off your coat," he said.

The girl started to cry. It was the first time since he'd initially terrorized her that she was beginning to let her emotions get the best of her.

"Please," she said to him.

"Just do as I say," Alex said.

Slowly, reluctantly, she began to take off her coat. Tears were streaming down her face, and she was looking right into his eyes. Alex looked away, ashamed of what he was doing but also feeling strangely aroused.

He suddenly felt as if he had absolute control over this girl, as if he could get her to do anything he could think of.

"Please don't do this," the girl said.

"Take off the sweater," Alex said.

"Alex," the operator said. "What are you doing? We only want to frighten her."

"Go on," he said again to the girl, ignoring the voice of the operator.

"Please," the girl begged.

He pointed the gun in her face, and slowly, reluctantly, she began to pull off the turtleneck sweater.

"Alex," the operator said. "That's enough. Tell her to get out of the truck and leave her there. You've done enough."

Alex took the earpiece from his ear and threw it on the floor, shutting up the operator for good.

The girl had removed her sweater, and tears were streaming down her cheeks. She looked around outside the vehicle, growing increasingly frantic, increasingly desperate.

She still had on a white undershirt, and Alex told her to take that off next.

"No," she said defiantly. "I won't do it."

"Do it, or I'm going to pull this trigger," Alex said, pressing the gun against her chest.

She shook her head and tried to say something, but no sound came from her.

She was crying, but silently.

Alex had never seen anguish so extreme, emotion so intense, and he'd never felt so aroused in all his life. All those psyche evaluations, all those checks, they'd clearly missed something. He'd clearly missed something. This was a facet of himself he'd never realized existed. Perhaps he never would have realized it existed were it not for the extreme pressures of the past twenty-four hours, but somehow, something had awakened this in him.

He laughed, quietly at first, then hysterically. Kirov should have seen this coming, he thought. He'd said this was something Alex might balk at, something he wouldn't enjoy, but after the childhood Alex had had, the relationship he'd had with his parents, the realization that his entire life had been a ploy by a distant, foreign government, someone should have known there'd be a few cracks in the plaster.

There was a creature inside Alex, a twisted, corrupted creature, and once out of its box, no one would be able to put it back in.

The girl was still shaking her head. "I won't do it," she said again. "You're going to have to pull that trigger because I'm not doing it."

Alex wasn't about to let her spoil this for him. He grabbed at her shirt, and she pushed his hand away. He grabbed again, tearing at the shirt, causing it to rip, and she clawed at his face ferociously.

"Bitch," he growled and smacked her in the face.

She grabbed the hand that was holding the gun and tried to take it from him.

He smacked her again, and again, and then jammed the gun into her stomach, and before he knew it, he'd pulled the trigger.

The shot rang out deafeningly in the enclosed cabin, and the look on the girl's face said she knew her life was over.

But something strange was happening. She was breathing. Her eyes remained focused.

At the same time, they both looked down at her stomach, at the white shirt that Alex had been tearing at so aggressively, and there wasn't a drop of blood.

The penny dropped for her first, and moving like a panther, she opened her door and was out in the snow, sprinting across the clearing and into the trees at the far end.

Alex watched her run. One second passed. And another. And another.

Kirov had given him a gun loaded with blanks. Of course he had. Kirov had no intention of seeing this girl killed and had made sure Alex didn't screw up and fire the gun accidentally.

Something about that, the insult of it, the humiliation, enraged Alex. It was like Kirov, and the operator, and this girl, and Tatyana, every one of them, was conspiring behind his back to completely and utterly castrate him. To remove him of all potency and power.

And it was about to end.

He grabbed the keys for the truck and put them in his

pocket. Then he slid across to the driver's seat and climbed out.

The girl was running, sprinting, like a terrified rabbit.

Alex didn't run. He followed the trail she left in the snow with wide, powerful strides, as if proving to himself, to the world, that he was not impotent.

It would be getting dark soon, and the light was already beginning to fade, but following the girl was as easy as walking in the deep footsteps she'd left in the fresh snow.

Alex saw where she'd fallen. He saw where, in her panic, she'd slipped at the top of a hill and rolled down it. A tree at the bottom of the hill had stopped her, but there was a scarlet bloodstain in the snow.

"There's no use running," Alex called. "I'm going to find you, and when I do, you're going to do exactly what I say."

He followed her over a brook and back up another small hill on the other side of it.

And that was where he found her, on her knees, her back to him, panting and gasping for breath.

The wound was serious. There'd been no blood on her shirt before, but there was now.

She turned to face him.

"Why are you doing this?"

He looked at her. He walked up to her. He put his two large hands on her frail neck, and he began squeezing.

She struggled, but the strength was gone from her.

He looked into her face, and as it began to distort from asphyxiation, as her eyes bulged and her tongue lolled, he said to her, "I don't know, my dear."

32

I t was a crisp, clear night, and Lance felt good entering the Eureka. An enormous fire was burning in the hearth, and when he saw the table, with a candelabra holding three tall candles, and a silver ice bucket with a fancy bottle of champagne sitting in it, he felt as if he'd walked into the life of another man.

It couldn't have looked more inviting.

He'd lent his truck to Sam earlier, she hadn't told him what it was for, but now he saw what she'd been up to. The Eureka didn't stock champagne, it didn't have silver ice buckets, it didn't serve candlelit dinners like this.

The owner, a burly guy named Stodder, stood behind the bar in a plaid shirt and leather boots.

"Still snowing out there?" he said.

Lance nodded. He looked at the table and raised an eyebrow.

"She's been busy all afternoon," Stodder said. "If I didn't know better, I'd say she's fixing to get her heart set on something."

"She's not setting her heart on anything."

"I don't know, Lance. You might have signed yourself up for something here."

"She could be my daughter," Lance said.

"That never stopped you before."

Lance said nothing. He'd slept with Stodder's daughter. He didn't know if Stodder knew that or not but thought it wise to steer the topic to another subject.

"I served with her father," he said.

"I heard the story."

"Then you heard he's the reason I'm alive."

Stodder nodded.

"And I'm the reason he's dead."

"You're not the reason he's dead."

Lance was a little early and took a seat at the bar.

The bartender put a bottle of beer in front of him.

"It's the anniversary of his death today," Lance said. "That's why we're having dinner."

"We'll see," Stodder said.

Lance took a sip of his beer. He prayed he had the good sense not to prove Stodder right. He knew himself. If anything happened between him and Sam, there was only one way it would end.

"Can you do me a favor tonight," Lance said.

Stodder was polishing a glass and looked up.

"Don't let me get drunk."

"I'll see what I can do," Stodder said.

Lance looked at his watch.

Sam was running late.

He finished his beer, and she still hadn't arrived.

"I'm going to have a smoke," he said, getting up.

He went out to the front of the bar and lit a cigar.

It was a perfect night, the air so still he could see tiny

crystals of frozen vapor floating in it. It made the atmosphere shimmer in the moonlight.

He sat on the wooden bench by the door and watched the moon over the jagged silhouette of Dodge Summit. Between the town and the mountains were the icy waters of Lake Koocanusa, which straddled the Canadian border a few miles to the north.

He finished the cigar and looked at his watch again.

She was forty minutes late. He checked to see if she'd left any messages. There were none.

He went into the bar and said, "Did she call?"

Stodder shook his head.

"Did she say anything about where she was going?"

"She dropped off the champagne earlier. Said she needed to pick up a cake."

"When was that?"

He looked at his watch. "Three hours, maybe."

Lance tried giving her a call, but she didn't pick up.

Stodder offered him another beer.

Lance shook his head. "How about some coffee?"

Stodder brought him over a cup. Lance sipped the coffee and, after fifteen minutes, tried calling her again. The phone rang a few times then forwarded to voicemail.

He hung up without leaving a message.

"Something ain't right," he said, getting up.

"You don't want to go jumping to conclusions."

"She's had trouble before," Lance said. "I took her from a mean son of a bitch in Beulah. He was mixed up in all sorts of things."

"I heard what you did to that man," Stodder said. "I don't think he'd be in a hurry for more of that medicine."

Lance shook his head. "Maybe I should have killed him."

Stodder said nothing. People in the town sort of knew

things about Lance, without really knowing what it was exactly that they knew.

What Stodder did know was that if Lance said he should have killed a man, it wasn't just a turn of phrase.

Lance tried calling again, and again was forwarded to voicemail.

"Something's definitely not right," he said.

He went back outside and looked up and down the street. He didn't know what to do and was about to go back inside when his phone started to ring.

His heart flooded with relief, but when he looked at the screen, he saw that it wasn't Sam calling, it was the sheriff's department in Libby.

"This is Lance Spector," he said, his heart pounding.

"Lance, this is Mac at the sheriff's office."

"What is it, Mac?"

"I wanted to check in with you, see that you're all right."

"I'm all right, Mac. What is this about?"

"They found your truck, Lance, crashed in a ditch up by Stahl Peak."

33

L ance went back inside the bar and said to Stodder, "I need to borrow your car."

Stodder took one look at him and threw him the keys.

He drove out to Stahl Peak as if his life depended on it, careening around corners, sending snow and gravel flying. He didn't slow down until he saw the flashing lights of a police cruiser ahead of him, then jammed on the brakes, skidding to a halt.

"What the hell was she doing out here?" he muttered as he got out of his car.

It was a place of startling natural beauty in the daytime, but in the darkness of night, the spindly pine trees seemed to close in on the road like the legs of spiders.

There was no way a young girl would have been out there alone by choice.

Lance's truck had been coming down from further up the mountain and had clearly been going too fast. At the corner, it had skidded across both lanes and crashed into the ditch.

"Where is she?" Lance said to the deputy.

The deputy was over by the truck, shining a flashlight into the cab, and Lance recognized him. A young guy, pretty new to the force, his name was McCaffrey.

"Lance," McCaffrey said.

"Where is she?" Lance said again.

"Who are you talking about, Lance?"

"Sam. The girl."

"You weren't driving?" McCaffrey said.

"Would I have driven it into a ditch?" Lance said.

"Who's Sam?"

"She's staying with me."

"Female?"

"Female. About twenty. She had my truck today."

McCaffrey's tone turned more serious, and he said, "Is there any reason you can think of why she would have been driving up the side of a mountain?"

Lance shook his head.

McCaffrey looked at him a moment, uncertain what to do.

"Is she here?" Lance said. "Is Sam here?"

"No one's here," McCaffrey said.

"She wasn't here when you got here?"

"No one was here when the truck was called in."

"Then she's missing," Lance said.

McCaffrey nodded.

"Call it in," Lance said.

McCaffrey picked up his radio. "This is McCaffrey out at Stahl Peak. I've got Lance Spector here, and he says he wasn't driving the vehicle when it went in the ditch."

There was a pause, then dispatch said, "Who was driving?"

McCaffrey looked at Lance then back at the truck. "Female. Twenty years old," he said, then to Lance, "White?"

Lance nodded.

"White," McCaffrey said.

"And she's unaccounted for?"

"That's correct," McCaffrey said.

There was a pause, then the dispatch said, "All right, sheriff's on his way."

McCaffrey attached the radio to a clip on his vest.

Lance stepped toward the truck, and McCaffrey said, "Sir, I wouldn't...".

"Don't sir me," Lance said, looking into the truck.

As clear as day, right on the passenger seat, was a Russian Makarov pistol. On the steering wheel and on the seat leather was smudged blood.

"What does this look like to you?" Lance said.

"I'd say it looks like a crime scene."

Lance nodded. "Give me that flashlight," he said.

McCaffrey handed him the flashlight, and Lance did a quick search of the cab. There was a cake box on the ground in front of the passenger seat, and Lance opened it. Inside was an unharmed cake with white frosting and glazed strawberries on top.

He looked around the floor and saw something small and white, like a pebble. He picked it up and looked at it closely.

"What have you got there, Lance?"

"This," Lance said, "is an earpiece."

"An earpiece?"

Lance stepped away from the truck. His chest was thumping, and he was finding it difficult to breathe.

"Sam?" he called out into the forest.

He crossed the road and began shining the flashlight

down the slopes of the mountain. He couldn't see more than ten yards into the dense forest. He shone the light at the ground, looking for tracks or footprints.

There were none.

"Someone walked away from this truck," Lance said, turning back toward McCaffrey. "And by the looks of things, they kept to the road."

"I'd say that's a fair assessment," McCaffrey said.

"We're looking for one man."

"With a girl?"

"He's not with the girl," Lance said.

"Now, we don't know that, Mr. Spector."

"If he still had the girl, he'd have brought his gun with him," Lance said.

Lance felt numb.

He knew what he was looking at.

He knew who used Makarov pistols and small white earpieces that looked like pebbles.

He knew what he was going to find.

He strode over to his car and got in.

"Mr. Spector, where are you going?"

He fired up the engine and pulled into the road, continuing on up the mountain.

McCaffrey yelled, "What about my flashlight?" as Lance drove by.

Lance didn't have far to go until he reached the clearing. It was a sort of lookout point where high schoolers brought their girlfriends to make out in summer.

He got out of the car and saw, near the center of the clearing, Sam's white ski jacket.

Beyond it across the clearing, going down the slope into the forest, were two sets of footprints.

The prints told him everything, the smaller set, running,

tripping, stumbling, and the larger set, following calmly, deliberately. He saw where Sam had slipped down a hill, he saw a bloodstain, he saw where she'd scrambled up the other side of a stream bank, and then, he saw something that stopped him in his tracks.

He couldn't believe his eyes.

He fell to his knees.

What he was looking at didn't make any sense.

In fact, if God had created a world in which the scene before his eyes could take place, then the universe itself made no sense.

Sam hadn't just been murdered.

She'd been mutilated.

It was as if she'd been ravaged by a pack of wolves, but even wolves wouldn't have done the things that had been done to her. Her body was naked, laying on its back in the snow, stretched out spread-eagle as if someone had posed her.

Between her legs was a pool of blood.

All the strength went out of Lance's body, and he let out a sound like a child's whimper.

He stumbled up to the body and, about three feet from it, collapsed to his knees and stared, blankly, at Sam's body.

This wasn't the cold, methodical work of a professional assassin.

This was the work of a monster.

34

Tatyana Aleksandrova sat on the balcony of a cheap motel in Miami, Florida, and lit a cigarette. In her hand was a note, handwritten by the girl at the front desk in purple ink with a smiley face in place of a period.

Your uncle wants you to call.

She hadn't answered the girl's knock, and the girl had taped it to the door.

She turned it over and over, fidgeting like a schoolgirl with a love note, then held her lighter to it and lit it on fire. The wind took it, the flame lifting it upward as it floated away.

There was one problem with the message.

It didn't specify *which* uncle.

Was it one of her scary uncles in Moscow who wanted to

slit her throat, string her up by the ankles, and leave her to bleed out?

She supposed that was her answer.

If the Kremlin had found her, they wouldn't have left a note.

She flicked her cigarette off the balcony and went inside.

Svetlana and Larissa were sitting on one of the beds watching Jerry Springer reruns.

"It's good for her English," Larissa said, looking up.

The motel accepted cash payment and overlooked an Interstate highway that seemed to get louder after the sun went down. None of them had gotten a good night's sleep in a week.

Three women, two beds, one shower.

Tatyana had already made up her mind. If Roth made her an offer, she'd cut a deal. All she wanted was a guarantee of protection for her sister and Svetlana.

It seemed it was her fate to be a spy.

She'd done it for the GRU.

Now she would do it for the CIA.

She dialed Roth's number from the motel room's phone and waited.

"I wasn't sure you'd call," Roth said when he picked up.

"Uncle?" Tatyana said. "Is that how you see yourself?"

She made a sign for Larissa to turn down the TV, and she muted it.

Roth wasn't like her bosses in Moscow. Those men took liberties. They pushed boundaries. They touched what they had no right to touch.

And now, they were all dead.

It wasn't like that with Roth. There was never that feeling of *quid pro quo* that seemed to govern all relationships in Moscow. There were no insinuations.

No lewd looks.

No abuse of position.

"How did you find us?" she said.

"I'm the director of the CIA," Roth said. "It wouldn't say much about my abilities if I couldn't."

"I take it this isn't a social call," she said.

"No," Roth said. "It's not, I'm afraid."

Tatyana lit a cigarette and prepared to negotiate. Larissa was her sister, or half-sister rather. Svetlana had risked her life to help them in Moscow. She didn't think it would be too difficult to get them protection.

"Laurel's back," Roth said.

"That was fast."

"She was always going to come back."

"She's not bothered that the president is trying to blame everything that happened on Lance?"

"Lance's record has been wiped. He's back in Montana."

"Fresh starts all round," Tatyana said.

"Quite," Roth said, "and I was hoping to get the same for you."

Tatyana said nothing. She'd learned long ago to keep her mouth shut in moments like this. The less she said, the better the deal she would get.

"You'll be worried for your sister," Roth continued.

Tatyana remained silent. He'd called her. She could afford to be coy.

"I don't have to explain to you that there's no such thing as complete safety," Roth said. "Not for someone like your sister. Not after what she's done."

"I know that," Tatyana said.

"Even with the protection of the US government, a Russian defector has to spend the rest of her life looking over her back."

"I don't need you to explain to me what the Russian government is capable of."

"No," Roth said, "I guess you don't."

Crossing the Kremlin always came with a price.

Vladimir Molotov allocated a disproportionate amount of attention to making sure that price was as high as possible. Entire divisions of the Russian intelligence apparatus had been built with the sole purpose of hunting down defectors and killing them. Sometimes, the murders were flagrant, specifically designed to attract the attention of the global media. Sometimes, they were quiet, behind the scenes, so no one, not even the police officers investigating the case, ever suspected the slightest trace of Russian involvement.

Everyone in the Russian intelligence community knew the risks. They knew what would happen if they switched sides.

That, after all, was the point.

"I want her in your top protection program, Roth. A complete new identity. Full US citizenship. A relocation budget. A cosmetics budget."

She didn't know if Larissa would be interested in cosmetic alterations. They could range from something as simple as voice and accent coaching to more dramatic surgical procedures that would completely alter the way she looked.

"I've been authorized by the president to give you whatever you ask for," Roth said.

"That's it," Tatyana said. "Citizenship and protection. For both of them."

"For both of them," Roth said.

"You agree?"

"Yes, I do."

"All right," she said. "Let's talk."

35

A government car, black with black windows, came to the motel to pick up Tatyana. She said her goodbyes to Larissa and Svetlana, uncertain how long it would be before she saw them again, and got in the back seat.

"Good morning, ma'am," the driver said, looking back at her over her shoulder. "We're headed to Homestead Air Reserve Base today."

"All right," Tatyana said.

She looked out the window one last time at Larissa and Svetlana."

From Homestead, she got on a military flight to Andrews Air Force Base just outside DC.

Laurel was waiting for her at the hangar, looking quite out of place among the Air Force mechanics in a red wool coat and thousand-dollar Prada pumps.

"Wow," Tatyana said, descending the steps. "It really must be urgent if they sent you down in person."

Laurel smiled. "I just wanted to be the first to welcome you back."

Laurel had an upgraded Cadillac Escalade waiting for them, and Tatyana was glad to get in. Coming from Miami, the cold was a shock.

"You look like you landed on your feet," Tatyana said, indicating the vehicle, which was of the type reserved only for the most important government officials.

"I think we could say we both did," Laurel said.

"As good as a couple of girls like us could expect," Tatyana said.

The vehicle had a retractable divider between them and the driver to allow them to speak confidentially.

As they made their way through the traffic, Laurel opened her briefcase and showed Tatyana a crumpled newspaper.

"This is the reason Roth wanted you to come in," she said.

Tatyana looked at the paper, a copy of *Berliner Zeitung*, and Laurel opened it to a page with a handwritten message.

Tell Roth that Tatyana Aleksandrova's friend from Riga needs to talk.

"Where did this come from?" Tatyana said.

"It was passed to the embassy in Berlin."

"By who?"

Laurel smiled. "That's what we were hoping you'd be able to fill us in on."

Tatyana thought. "Friend from Riga," she said. "I was in Riga a lot. The Baltic zone is a high priority for the GRU."

"That's why Roth's worried," Laurel said.

Tatyana looked at her. "You don't share that fear?"

"I think it's a trap," Laurel said. "Look at it. It's the oldest trick in the book. How stupid do they think we are?"

"They know the reference to Riga is too big to ignore," Tatyana said.

"Exactly."

"And they're right," Tatyana said. "Laurel, we can't ignore this. What if it's real?"

"Is it real?"

"I don't know," Tatyana said.

"Do you have a friend in Riga?" Laurel said. "We can at least start with that much."

Tatyana nodded.

There was someone that came to mind, someone she could conceivably call a *friend*, but she was a police officer. She didn't handle the kind of information that would be of interest to the Director of the CIA, and in any case, Latvia was a NATO ally. If she'd stumbled across something, she would have handed it up the chain.

"I have a contact in Riga."

"A Latvian?"

"Yes. From the national security division."

"A source?"

"Not a source. More like, well, a *friend*."

"What does that mean?"

"Laurel," Tatyana said, "you know how it is. If you're a woman in this business, it can sometimes feel like there are a lot of sharks in the water. Over there, the sharks are Russian."

"I see."

"She never sold me Latvian secrets. I never asked her to."

"But you had each other's backs?"

"We'll see," Tatyana said.

"What do you mean?"

"If I show up in Berlin, then yes."

"Okay," Laurel said.

Tatyana had known she would understand.

"The thing is," Laurel said. "Would she pass a message like this?"

Tatyana shrugged. "I don't know, Laurel. She never did anything like this before. It's strange for her to start now. But everything about this message is strange."

Laurel sighed. She shook her head.

"What's wrong?"

"He's going to send you in," she said.

"He has to, Laurel."

"I know," Laurel said, "but I don't have to like it."

"The president's response to the bombings is the biggest show of weakness in a generation," Tatyana said. "If Molotov was going to make a move, now would be the moment."

"And Latvia would be the place?"

"It might be," Tatyana said. "He's desperate to show the world that NATO is just a piece of paper. That it doesn't *decide the issue*."

"Decide the issue?"

"Latvia is afraid of Russia," Tatyana said. "That's the reason they're in NATO. Everyone knows it. Riga, Washington, Moscow. The Latvian government said so publicly. And they said NATO membership meant Russia could never attack them again. They said it *decided the issue*."

They were passing the Lincoln Memorial, and Laurel, looking out at it, said, "You know you don't have to go, don't you?"

"I made a deal with Roth."

"Not for this. That was to come back to the Group. He won't force you to go to Berlin."

"He doesn't have to force me."

"If this note is from the Kremlin."

"If it's from the Kremlin, I'll know how to look out for myself."

"I'm going to need more than that," Laurel said.

"What more can I give you?"

"I want a plan, a real one, to get you out if you get into trouble."

"Nothing I say to you will make this completely safe," Tatyana said.

"Well, I want something," Laurel said. "I'm head of the Group, and I'm pulling rank. Unless you come up with some sort of feasible extraction plan, something you can fall back on if this note turns out to be a trap, I'm not letting you go."

Tatyana thought for a moment, then said, "I'll tell you what. If you promise to look out for Larissa and Svetlana while I'm gone, I'll give you a name?"

"A name?"

"The name of someone very important to me. Someone I can rely on if things go south."

"Just a name?"

"Not just any name," Tatyana said. "It's a name I'm sure you've heard before."

Laurel looked at her. "What is it?"

"The Clockmaker of Berlin."

36

Tatyana looked out as the car pulled up to the opulent Saint Royal Hotel. She knew the place well.

"What are we doing here?" she said.

"This is where we're meeting Roth."

"In public?"

"In a suite upstairs," Laurel said. "I'm arranging to make it our permanent base of operations."

Tatyana smiled.

"What?" Laurel said.

"Making some changes now that you're in charge."

"It's the perfect place for us to work," Laurel said.

"Of course it is," Tatyana said, as an usher in a top hat held the door for her.

Through polished brass doors, they entered the sumptuously decorated lobby, with marble floors and crystal chandeliers hanging on long chains from the ceiling. Another usher escorted them to the elevators, entering with them and pushing the button for the top floor.

"This is a private elevator," he said. "No one but you has access."

Laurel glanced at Tatyana before nodding to the usher and thanking him.

The elevators opened into a wide hallway, and they followed the usher through a set of french doors into a high-ceilinged rotunda. It was hexagonally shaped, with a wooden bench and a hat stand between each of three sets of doors.

"There are three suites," the usher said, indicating the doors. "As per your agreement with the hotel ownership, no one will proceed beyond this rotunda without advance permission, and as I understand it, you will be having your own locks installed."

"Thank you," Laurel said.

The man gave them a slight nod and said, "Mr. Roth has requested that a meal be served in the center suite. May I show you in."

"Thank you," Laurel said.

They followed him through the middle set of doors into a stunning dining room with a checkered marble floor. High windows, draped in floor-to-ceiling curtains of red velvet, looked out over Lafayette Square.

In the center of the room was an antique wooden table, exquisitely set for a formal lunch and surrounded by high-backed, formal dining chairs.

Tatyana and Laurel looked at each other as they were shown to their seats.

"Mr. Roth will be with you shortly," the usher said before leaving them alone.

"Laurel," Tatyana said in a mock scolding tone, "you've turned Roth's precious Group into a re-enactment of Versailles."

"I didn't know it would be this...".

"Nice?" Tatyana said.

"Formal," Laurel said.

Tatyana looked around the room. Everything, down to the finest detail, was exquisite.

"The hotel's letting you install your own security?" she said.

Laurel nodded.

"And there'll be non-disclosure agreements?"

"Roth negotiated the whole thing," Laurel said. "We'll be installing our own communications lines, our own secure entry system, our own hardware in a special service shed on the roof."

"If you think about it," Tatyana said, "it's the perfect cover."

"Like hiding in plain sight," Laurel said.

A waiter in a black suit and bow tie knocked on a side door and entered the room.

"Mr Roth called to say he will be here very shortly," the waiter said.

He was holding an expensive-looking bottle of red wine, which he opened in front of them.

"May I?" he said to each of them before filling their glasses.

The two women were seated too far apart to touch glasses, but they raised them to each other, and Tatyana said, "To the good life."

Laurel smiled. "It's a tough job," she said, "but someone's got to do it."

They each took a sip of the wine, which was excellent, and Laurel said, "Before Roth gets here, I want to talk more about this extraction plan of yours."

"The Clockmaker," Tatyana said with a smile. "I had a feeling that would get your attention."

"You know who he is?"

Tatyana nodded.

"The man's a legend," Laurel said. "I don't even think Roth knows much about him, other than rumors."

"Well, maybe we should wait for him before I tell you about it."

"Tell me about what?" Roth said, walking into the room and pulling off a pair of black leather gloves.

"Levi," Laurel said, standing up.

"Don't get up," Roth said, joining them at the table. "I'm so sorry I'm late. Something interesting arrived on my desk right as I was about to leave."

"How interesting?" Laurel said.

"Well, that depends on Tatyana," he said.

"How so?" Tatyana said.

Roth motioned for the waiter to fill his glass and then waited for him to leave the room.

"I take it Laurel showed you the message."

"Yes," Tatyana said. "I've seen it."

"Do you know who it's from?"

"I think so," Tatyana said. "There was a woman in Riga that I would refer to as a friend. She's a corporal in the State Police, National Security Division."

"I knew it," Roth said, pulling a grainy, black and white printout of a photo from his coat pocket and handing it to Tatyana.

"What's this?"

"Look closely," Roth said.

The picture looked like it had come from a surveillance camera overlooking the main concourse of a train station.

From the writing on some of the signs, it had to have been in Poland.

"Warsaw Central train station," Tatyana said.

"What about the two people?" Roth said.

"They look like they're talking to each other."

Roth was looking smug. He was enjoying this.

"Who are they, Roth?"

"One of them is your friend, Agata Zarina, a twenty-nine-year-old policewoman from Riga."

"And the other?"

"A Kremlin assassin named Mikhail Smolov."

"Smolov?" Tatyana said.

"You know him?" Roth said.

"Not well," Tatyana said. "Is Agata Zarina okay?"

"She killed that assassin. Left him in the center of the train station. According to our friends in Poland, she fled the scene on a train to Berlin soon after."

"So the message is from her?"

"I'd say it appears that way, wouldn't you?" Roth said

Tatyana handed the printout to Laurel.

"I hope the image they made the ID with was higher res than this," Laurel said.

"That's just what I could print on my way out," Roth said. "I've got a four-page report from the Polish Intelligence Agency."

"I see," Laurel said.

"You don't seem very pleased," Roth said.

Laurel sighed. The waiter came back in and asked Roth if he should begin serving the meal.

Roth deferred to Laurel. "Ask her," he said. "This is hers now."

"Please begin serving," Laurel said and waited until he

was gone before saying, "If the Kremlin's chasing her with assassins, how do we even know she's still alive?"

"Other than the note?" Roth said.

They both looked at Tatyana.

Roth said, "Is there anything about the note that suggests Agata Zarina was not the author?"

Tatyana looked at Laurel while answering. "I take it the meet is meant for this bar in Kreuzberg?" she said.

"That's how it looks," Laurel said.

"Well, the first time I met her was at a cocktail happy hour like that. A bar in Riga. There's no way anyone else could know that."

"So you think it's legit?" Roth said.

Tatyana nodded.

"And you're willing to go?"

She nodded again.

Roth turned to Laurel triumphantly. "I'll have a plane readied at Andrews immediately."

"Before we send her into God knows what," Laurel said, "could we at least get our plan straight for what happens if it turns out it's a trap."

"There's no time to send in an advance team," Roth said.

"I'm not talking about a team," Laurel said. "Tatyana's got a friend in Berlin."

Roth looked at her. "It seems you make friends wherever you go."

"What can I say?" Tatyana said. "It must be my bubbly personality."

"She was about to tell me all about him."

Roth was intrigued, they both were, and they looked at her expectantly.

"I think you know him as the Clockmaker of Berlin."

37

"Coffee," Lance said to the waitress.

"Anything to eat?" she said, eyeing him warily.

He shook his head, and she left. He was at a table by the window, and the sun still hadn't broken above the horizon. The sky had turned though, a startling orange to the east as if someone had smeared cadmium pigment across it.

He looked at his hands. He was in shock.

He'd seen more death than most, he'd dealt it at his own hand, but something about this, what had happened to Sam, the way it had been done, it wasn't right.

The Russians could be ruthless, but there was an orderliness to their work. They meted out death with the same bureaucratic disdain they doled out everything else.

What Lance had seen in the forest was not that.

It was not orderly.

It was not bureaucratic.

Someone had gone off the deep end.

And it shook him to the core.

The waitress returned with a cup of black coffee and put it on the table in front of him.

"You okay, Lance?"

He hadn't noticed she was there. He looked up.

"You look like you've seen a ghost."

He looked around the diner as if realizing where he was for the first time. He'd walked in thirty minutes ago and couldn't even remember doing that.

"I am a ghost," he said.

She looked at him more closely. He knew her. Not well, but enough to know her name.

"What does that mean?" she said.

"Everything I touch turns to ash. Do they have a name for that?"

She shook her head. "Lance, did you go home last night?"

"Did I go home?"

"You were out there again, weren't you? You're going to catch your death of cold, if you don't get arrested first."

"It's still there, Hetty. Just sitting there. No one's coming for it."

She shook her head. "You need to go home and get some sleep."

"The snowplow goes around it every night."

"Please go home, Lance. Your body needs rest."

He looked down at his coffee cup.

She stood there a minute, then sighed and left.

He looked at his watch. It was almost six.

He left some cash on the table and walked out of the diner. Across the street was the office of the Herz car rental company. It opened every morning at six.

A kid was just unlocking the door, and Lance said, "Who

rented the navy Chevrolet that's been sitting in front of the grocery store for the last three nights."

"Excuse me, sir?"

"The grocery store parking lot. It's one of yours. Got your sticker inside the windshield."

The kid looked at Lance, and from the expression on his face, knew not to mess with him.

"I took down the plate number," Lance said. "Now you're going to go on your computer and tell me who signed it out. Are we clear?"

"Mister," the kid said nervously. "I can't give out that kind of information."

"I know that," Lance said, "but you're going to do it anyway."

"It'll mean my job."

"You just tell them some madman threatened to kill you. If they don't believe you, go across the street and ask for Hetty. She'll back you up."

The kid opened the door and went inside. Lance stayed close behind him.

"You wouldn't, though, right?" the kid said. "You were just saying that to give me an alibi."

Lance was looking at the computer, impatient for the kid to log in and pull up the information.

"Enter your password," he said.

The kid typed his password and opened the database. Then he looked at Lance.

"What's the license plate?"

Lance told him what it was, and he typed it in.

"The renter of that vehicle is Ben Edelberg."

"Who's Ben Edelberg?"

"He works at the reception of the hotel."

"The Econolodge?"

"Yes, sir."

"Why would he rent a car?"

"For a guest," the kid said.

"Don't you have to get a copy of the license?"

"Looks like they took Edelberg's license."

"All right," Lance said and left.

Lance walked down the street to the Econolodge. Behind the desk, a woman with graying hair leaned back precariously in her swivel chair. Her mouth was open, and she snored intermittently.

"Wake up," Lance said.

She leaped and almost knocked over her chair. When she saw Lance standing there, a look of alarm crossed her face.

"I've got some questions, and you have to answer them," Lance said.

Lance looked rough. He hadn't shaved in days. His eyes were bloodshot. The woman was terrified.

"All right," she stammered.

"Why would Ben Edelberg rent a car from Herz?"

"What?"

"You heard what I said."

"He'd rent a car for a customer."

"Is that allowed?"

"If the tip's right."

"Do you have his number?"

"Ben's?"

"Yes."

"I'm not allowed to give that out."

"You give him a call and find out who the blue sedan he rented three days ago was for."

"I'm not sure I'll be able to reach him at this time of night."

"Either you get him on the phone, or I'll pay him a visit in person," Lance said.

The lady picked up the phone and dialed a number.

A moment later she said, "Ben, this is Aggie, at work."

She waited and told him she was sorry for waking him. Then she asked him who the car was for.

"The Russian in 404," Aggie said to Lance.

"Is he still in there?" Lance said.

She hung up the phone and typed on her computer keyboard.

"He hasn't checked out."

Lance walked past her to the corridor and found the stairs.

"You can't just go up there," she called out behind him.

He went to the fourth floor and found room 404, stood in front of it, and in a single motion, brought the heel of his foot down against the base of the door. It flew open with a crash.

Before he even had the lights on, he knew the room was empty. There was nothing in it, not a person, not a person's belongings, nothing.

He did a sweep of the room to see if anything had been left behind. He checked the sheets, the wardrobe, the side tables, the safe. Nothing.

He went back down to the lobby and said, "What was the guest's name?"

The woman looked uncomfortable. "I called the police," she said.

"What was his name?" Lance said.

"I don't have a name," she said.

"Do you have an address?"

She typed into her computer and shook her head. "It

was a client account. I'd have to call corporate to find out the name on the booking."

"What did he look like?"

The woman shook her head. "I wasn't here."

Lance turned to leave, then stopped. He looked back at her one last time.

The fear on her face was palpable.

"One more thing," Lance said. "Why wasn't his room made up for three days?"

"What do you mean?"

"The bed. It was ruffled."

She glanced at her computer. "He indicated no turn-down service."

Lance was about to leave, then turned back again.

"Please leave," she begged.

"Call Edelweiss again," Lance said.

"His name's Edelberg."

"Call him."

Reluctantly, she picked up the phone and made the call.

"Ask him to describe the guest."

She asked Edelberg and then said, "He was overweight. Forty or fifty. Dark hair."

"What about his accent?"

"What about it?"

"Where was he from?"

"New York, maybe."

"He didn't sound like a foreigner?"

She asked Edelberg and shook her head.

"How did he arrive?"

"What do you mean?"

"If Edelweiss rented him a car, then how did he get here?"

She asked Edelberg and shook her head again. "Please," she said. "He doesn't remember."

"A cab?"

"We don't know."

"Do you have security cameras?"

"Please, sir."

"Show me to the security cameras," Lance said.

"The police are coming."

"I don't care."

38

Tatyana's plane landed at the US Air Force facility near Berlin Tempelhof.

She'd tried to sleep on the plane but couldn't. Something was bothering her.

Why hadn't Agata been recorded at the embassy? Roth had a team go over every camera, every angle, and they hadn't found a single trace of her.

It was impossible to enter the US embassy in Berlin without having your face recorded. Not only did all visitors have to show ID, but the entire building was heavily monitored by multiple high-resolution cameras. The system had, in fact, been installed by a defense contractor who usually installed targeting systems in fighter jets.

The cameras were capable of tracking the heat signatures of aircraft traveling faster than the speed of sound. Running the Pentagon's facial tracking and recognition algorithms was child's play in comparison.

And yet, the message had been delivered completely anonymously.

It was found on the night watchman's desk at the end of

his shift, and despite all those cameras and the most advanced monitoring equipment in the world, no one had an answer for how it got there.

One thing was clear, however. Whoever had put that message on the desk had taken serious steps to remain concealed.

It made sense that Agata would be cautious. If Kremlin assassins were on her tail, there was no end to the steps she might take to remain hidden.

Roth was also looking into a local police report of another shooting close to her apartment in Riga the night before she fled the city.

He'd contacted her commanding officer to find out what she was working on immediately before she fled the city but hadn't heard back.

But it was beginning to look like she'd been tailed from Riga to Warsaw and that an attempt had been made on her life in both cities. If that were the case, then it only made sense that she would be taking every precaution possible to remain concealed in Berlin.

Still, it nagged at Tatyana. Some kind of visual confirmation from embassy security that the message had been delivered in person by Agata would have done a lot to put her mind at ease.

Roth had also received local media accounts of a shooting at the Holocaust Memorial in Berlin, just one block south of the Brandenburg Gate and within a stone's throw of the embassy. Roth was looking into that too, but the Germans were notoriously protective of their police records. The sharing protocol between the CIA and the German intelligence service still required manual approval by a political appointee at the Chancellor's office, as well as a federal judge in Berlin. It wasn't unusual for a request to take twenty-four, or even forty-eight hours, to come back.

Laurel had been right to be cautious.

There was definitely more going on than met the eye.

The only thing that made Tatyana willing to walk into it, was the certainty that Agata was in danger. Of that, there could be no doubt.

And loyalty had to stand for something.

She was the one who'd approached Agata.

She'd told her she'd have her back.

She said it paid to have friends.

And now, Agata was being hunted across Europe and had asked for Tatyana by name.

Things in Tatyana's life hadn't exactly gone to plan. She was being hunted by the GRU herself as a traitor to the Motherland. Before that, she'd used sex to entrap hundreds of men all over the world so that the GRU could blackmail them.

In some ways, she'd betrayed everything and everyone she'd ever gotten close to.

But this, she was not willing to turn her back on.

This was a promise she intended to keep.

She caught a cab from the airport to a hotel near the embassy. She had time for a quick shower and change of clothes before heading to the bar mentioned in Agata's message.

She wore a long Burberry trench coat, and in the inside pocket, she had the Browning handgun that Lance had given her when they first met.

"It will save your life one day," he'd said.

That felt like a lifetime ago, but she still clung to those words. They hadn't let her down so far.

The bar was a hip, lively place in the trendy district of Kreuzberg, abuzz with hipsters and young professionals. Tatyana peered at it from the back of the cab, trying to get some bearings. She couldn't see Agata inside, which made sense.

Agata would be watching from somewhere else.

Waiting.

Tatyana looked around at the surrounding buildings and tried to determine where she might be watching from.

"You going to sit here all night?" the cab driver said impatiently.

Tatyana paid him and stepped out into the January air. It was cold in Berlin, colder even than it had been in DC, and she hadn't had time to pack properly.

She hurried across the sidewalk, went inside, and found a seat at the bar.

It was a bar like a million others. Modern light fixtures over a bar of white quartz. Lots of glass and mirrors and burnished brass accents. Behind the bar, strings of LED lights were intertwined with bottles of expensive liquor.

Tatyana looked around, making note of the exits, trying to gauge the weight and fighting ability of every man she could see. She'd chosen her seat for the sight lines it afforded and instantly saw why Agata had selected the place. The front of the bar was completely taken up by a large, floor to ceiling window, and from the high-rise offices across the street, you could see clearly to every corner of the bar.

That's where Agata would be.

One of those offices.

Peering in with a pair of binoculars.

Tatyana turned toward the window, showing her face clearly.

Agata would be cautious. She'd wait to see if Tatyana had come alone.

She was doing a good job, Tatyana thought. She hadn't been trained for something like this. She was a police officer, but that didn't include training in how to stay off the grid, how to disappear, how to live off the grid while the most dangerous men on the planet hunted her.

Tatyana felt for her.

She was out in the cold.

She'd probably come across something she wasn't supposed to. And now, some very powerful men were not going to rest until she was dead.

39

L ance was still in the motel office, scrolling through security camera footage when McCaffrey arrived.

"Come on, Spector," he said. "You know you can't be back here."

Lance was staring intently at the screen. He'd just found what he was looking for, or thought he had. A middle aged, overweight man with dark hair stepping out of an orange and green taxicab.

"McCaffrey, I knew your daddy. He was a good man, but I swear to God if you don't let me finish what I'm doing, I'm going to send you up to join him."

McCaffrey was taken aback.

"That's it, Lance," he said. "Let's go."

He strode toward Lance, and Lance raised his hand, two fingers, as if in beatification. McCaffrey stopped.

Lance zoomed in as far as he could, but the resolution wasn't good enough to get more than an impression.

"This," he said to McCaffrey, indicating the image on the screen, "is the man who killed Sam."

McCaffrey leaned over the desk to take a look, then turned to Lance.

"Really?"

Lance nodded.

"How do you know?"

"I know."

"Do you know who he is?"

"I do not," Lance said.

"The hotel doesn't have a record?"

"Not here. He stayed on a corporate account."

"They're required to check the ID of all guests."

"And the car rental company is required to check the driver's license. Doesn't mean they did it."

"I'll get Darlene to call the cab company," McCaffrey said.

Lance nodded. McCaffrey called in the request, and the two of them went out to his cruiser and sat in the car.

"Do you mind if I smoke?" Lance said, opening his window a crack.

"There's no smoking in these vehicles, Lance."

Lance nodded. He hadn't smoked cigarettes in a long time. That was, until three days ago when he'd returned to them with a vengeance.

He leaned back in his seat and closed his eyes.

He must have nodded off because thirty minutes had passed when McCaffrey tapped his shoulder and told him Darlene had come back.

"What did she say?"

"She said the cab company had a record of dropping one person to this motel that day."

"Where'd they pick him up?"

"Glacier Park Airport."

"Let's go then."

"I'm not a taxi service, Lance."

"You want me to drive myself?"

"What are you going to do there?"

"Find out who flew in."

"That will be hundreds of passengers, Lance. Thousands maybe."

"It'll be one man," Lance said. "And he's a dead man walking."

McCaffrey pulled out of the parking lot and said, "If I drive you to this place, you're not going to do something stupid, are you?"

"If he was there," Lance said, "I'd kill him, I swear to God."

"But he won't be there."

"No, he won't," Lance said.

"So you won't kill anyone."

Lance said nothing.

They drove at the speed limit the forty miles to the airport and parked right outside the terminal. Inside, they went to the information desk, where a blonde with a Starbucks in her hand sat behind a set of three computer screens.

"I need a list of every arrival this week," Lance said.

She looked from Lance to the cop and then back to Lance.

"It's public record," Lance said, smiling stiffly. He was so out of it, so disheveled that it only made her look away uncomfortably.

"Yes, sir, it is," she said, looking at her computer screen. She typed something and printed out a sheet for him.

It wasn't a long list, and Lance scanned it.

"What's this?" he said, pointing to the charter flight from Teterboro, an Embraer Phenom 300. "Who was on that?"

"I'm sorry, sir," she said. "That information is going to require more than a wink and a smile."

"Can you access passenger information?" McCaffrey said.

She shook her head. "Not even if I wanted to."

"Can you tell me if that plane's ever landed here before?" Lance said.

"That, I can do," she said and did some more typing. "There's no record of that plane ever having landed here, or any other airport in Montana for that matter."

"Where was its flight before here?"

"I'm sorry," she said. "That, I don't have."

"Do you know where it's been since?"

"No, but I'm sure the FAA could help you with that sort of request."

Lance looked back at the sheet. "What about the N-number. Can you look that up for me?"

She pulled up a new database and typed in the search, then printed the result and handed it to them.

The plane was registered to a numbered corporation registered in Delaware.

"I'm sorry," she said, "but in my experience, you're going to need a team of lawyers to find out the real owner. A Delaware corp will be owned by a Cayman Islands corp, and that will be owned by a numbered account in Luxembourg, and that will be administered by a law firm in Iceland, and on and on."

Lance nodded.

"I'll tell you what," Lance said. "How about you put me on the next flight you have to Teterboro?"

It turned out there was no flight to Teterboro, and Lance had to settle for a commercial flight from Kalispell to Newark Liberty.

McCaffrey drove him to the airport, and on the flight, he managed to snatch a few hours of sleep. At Newark, he got in a cab and told the driver to take him to Teterboro.

The cab joined the afternoon traffic northbound on the I-95, and Lance stared out the window blankly.

It was a dull, gray afternoon, about equal chances of rain or snow, and the cab trudged through the slush for twenty minutes before pulling up outside the terminal at Teterboro.

The driver talked the entire way, but Lance didn't hear a word.

He had only one thought on his mind now.

Revenge.

He would find the man who'd done this thing, and he would kill him.

But he wouldn't stop there.

Someone in Moscow had ordered this.

Of that, there could be no doubt.

What their motivation could have possibly been, what message they'd been trying to send, whether it had been intentional or some mistake, some rogue agent gone off the deep end, made no difference.

Lance was going to make them pay.

All of them.

At Teterboro, he didn't enter the terminal building. He walked straight onto the tarmac, where charter jets were fueling or taxiing, or sitting in rows like jets on the deck of a carrier.

He walked along the planes and hangars until he found a Phenom 300. He checked it's tail number and confirmed it was the plane he was looking for.

Two men were fueling the aircraft, and Lance said, "Where's the pilot?"

"Right here," a man said from the small office at the back of the hangar.

Lance went over to him, grabbed him by the lapels of his jacket, and flung him into the office, kicking the door shut behind him.

"What the hell do you think you're doing?" the pilot protested.

"Sit down," Lance said.

There were some plastic chairs in the office like the ones used in high schools, and the pilot sat down.

"Did you fly that plane to Glacier Park Airport in Montana four days ago?"

The pilot glanced around the room furtively. There was a desk, some coffee mugs with rings of old coffee caked onto them.

"I don't have time to dick around," Lance said.

"Listen," the pilot said, "why don't you tell me what this is about?"

Lance looked out the office window. The two mechanics were approaching.

Anyone who worked with the Russians, in any capacity, knew to keep their mouth shut. It was the one rule that would get you killed if you broke it. This pilot was going to need some encouragement to talk, and Lance flicked the lock on the office door before putting his foot on the pilot's chest and pushing the chair backward. He fell back on the concrete floor, hit the back of his head against it.

"Hey," the mechanics yelled, breaking into a run.

Lance bent down on the man's chest and grabbed him by the hair.

"Who chartered that flight?" he said.

"I don't know what you're talking about," the pilot said,

and Lance pulled his head forward, then slammed it back against the ground.

"Please," the man yelled.

"I do that a few more times," Lance said, "and you're going to have some serious head injury. I doubt they'll let you in the air any time soon."

He lifted the man's head again, and the pilot blurted, "Please, it was the consulate in the city. The Russian consulate. They chartered it."

"And who was the passenger?" Lance said.

"I don't know," the pilot said. "Please, I don't know. I don't ask. I never know."

"Where's the manifest?"

"On the desk," the pilot said.

The two mechanics were pounding their fists on the window of the door. Lance looked up at them, and the pilot swung a fist at Lance's face.

Lance blocked him as the door of the office burst open, and the two mechanics jumped onto Lance's back.

Lance knocked them back.

The first threw a punch, and Lance deflected it, then brought his fist up in an uppercut to the man's neck. He fell to the ground, and the second was about to attack. Lance caught his eye.

He stopped.

"Get back," Lance said, motioning to the door.

The man stepped back, and Lance rummaged through the files on the pilot's desk until he found the manifest. Under the entry for passenger, someone had written in "Alex." Beneath it, in a section marked for notes, was written, "Lousy lay and worse tipper."

40

C hristoph Prochnow sat on a park bench and chain-smoked Gauloises cigarettes. It was a cold night, but he was dressed for it, in a black cashmere turtleneck and camel duffel coat.

Inside his coat was a loaded Heckler & Koch VP9 pistol. The VP stood for *Volkspistole*, like Volkswagen, a pistol for the people. It was originally designed at the request of the Bavarian State Police and was now one of the most commonly found guns in the country. It was chambered for the 9x19 Parabellum, and Prochnow's particular gun was a sound-suppressed variant.

Not that he was planning on being subtle.

He'd been waiting for Tatyana to arrive, and when she did, he felt an innate revulsion for everything she stood for.

How could a real Russian, an actual daughter of the Motherland, betray her country the way this woman had?

A faithless, disloyal bitch.

That was what she was in his eyes.

What could the Americans ever do for her that would make up for that?

This would be an easy kill.

He had no qualms about it.

As far as he was concerned, the bitch deserved to die.

He'd been warned about her training. This woman had been a high-level operator, one of the most highly-prized and effective honey-traps in Igor Aralov's Widow Program.

She knew how to kill, and she knew how to spot a threat.

But she wouldn't see him coming. How could she?

She had her back to the door.

She was expecting a friend.

The bar was packed full of young men. Prochnow himself was dressed exactly like the patrons. He'd fit right in.

He was surprised she'd allowed herself to be so vulnerable. Maybe she wasn't as good as everyone gave her credit for.

Her true talents, he suspected, were probably more apparent when she was on her back.

And all he had to do was walk up behind her, pull out the gun, and put a bullet in the back of her skull.

There was no training in the world that allowed someone to dodge a bullet at point-blank range.

He watched her sitting at the bar for a few minutes. She ordered a drink, a glass of wine, but didn't take a sip.

She didn't look at her watch. She didn't act impatiently. She didn't look nervous or in a hurry.

She looked perfectly relaxed, fitting right in with the evening crowd. Prochnow had no doubt if he waited much longer, someone would start hitting on her.

He finished his cigarette and stubbed it out under his boot.

He crossed the street and pulled open the door of the bar.

A group of women stood by the entrance, and he had to excuse himself as he walked through them.

"Hey, stranger," one of them said.

There was a man in an expensive suit, very drunk, stumbling toward the washroom, and Prochnow let him pass.

A cocktail waitress carrying a tray of empty glasses rushed by in the other direction.

He weaved through the crowd, his hand inside his coat, gripping his gun.

When he was a foot from Tatyana, he pulled the gun, pressed it against the back of her skull, and bang.

41

Tatyana was a young operative, fresh out of the academy, the first time she was sent to Berlin.

Her target was someone on their own side, a Pole who'd been sent to West Germany decades earlier to work as a spy for the Soviets. Despite being a Pole, he was one of the most unimpeachably loyal operatives the GRU ever had. For decades he'd been feeding information back to his handlers, information that proved so valuable that legends had grown up around him.

Most of the Soviet coups in Berlin during the Cold War were attributed directly to his intel.

Everyone in the GRU had heard of him.

Even the West Germans and the Americans knew he had to exist.

And yet, no one could figure out who he was.

To all, regardless of what side they were on, he was known only as the Clockmaker of Berlin.

Apart from his handlers, only two men knew his real name, the president and Jacob Kirov. And there were even rumors that the president's precipitous rise to power had been facilitated by the Clockmaker.

Tatyana's mission, something typical of the GRU at the time, was to test his loyalty. To someone so utterly corruptible as Vladimir Molotov, anyone that honest was immediately regarded as suspect.

And Tatyana's job was to be the test.

She would attempt to bribe him in some small, insignificant way, and if he took the bait, then his integrity would be immediately regarded as compromised.

In Tatyana's opinion, the entire operation was misguided. These men, who'd literally raped the entire nation, were going to test the integrity of a highly valuable operative with a cheap trinket and then judge decades of unquestionably valuable intel on that basis. But no one asked her opinion.

She was warned in advance that he'd been in the game for a very long time. It was all he knew, and he wouldn't slip up easily. Her mission was small, but enormous subtlety and skill were required to carry it off.

He had a clock repair shop on the Kurfürstendamm, and she was to visit his shop and have him appraise a watch for her.

The watch was expensive, a forty-millimeter Rolex day-date in yellow gold. The Clockmaker would appreciate its precision self-winding chronometer with calendar and day display. He would appreciate the fine craftsmanship.

But it was not an extraordinary watch. It could be purchased at any Rolex boutique, or at any high-end airport duty-free, for about thirty-five thousand dollars.

In Russia, they were used almost as calling cards among oligarchs doing business with the party elite. In order to get anything done, it was advisable to show up with a forty-millimeter day-date, packed up nicely in its distinctive collector's box.

It was known that the president owned so many that he had a jeweler in Moscow whose sole responsibility was inscribing almost microscopic serial numbers on the inside bracelet just so he could keep track of them.

They were like an informal, untrackable currency. A Russian Bitcoin, before Bitcoin was a thing. Officials even referred to the prices of certain transactions in terms of them. Bribing a federal judge cost two forties. Getting planning permission for a major project in Moscow could cost hundreds of them.

Tatyana was to show up at the Clockmaker's shop, dressed in furs and bright lipstick, and try to unload one such watch, complete with one of the president's serial numbers.

It would be obvious there was only one way a girl like her could get her hands on a watch like that.

It would look like she'd stolen it.

The Clockmaker had been in Berlin for sixty years. According to the president, even a dog's loyalty didn't last that long.

Everyone knew the rules. If you stole so much as a kopek from the president, it would cost you your life. He took it personally. It was a matter of honor.

So Tatyana would go in with the watch. An innocent girl, relatively speaking, as far as the Clockmaker was aware. A nice girl. A Russian girl who'd done no harm to him.

And she would present this dilemma.

Maybe the Clockmaker was getting soft in his old age.

Maybe his judgment was beginning to wane.

And if it was, all the more reason to have him removed.

Would he report the watch up the chain, essentially issuing the girl a death warrant, or would he keep mum?

There couldn't be a simpler test of loyalty in the president's eyes.

But when Tatyana came into the shop and saw him there, looking at her with eyes more kindly than any she'd seen in a long time, she couldn't go through with it.

At enormous, almost reckless risk to herself and her own safety, she warned him. She tipped him off.

She did it out of nothing more than simple human affection. She didn't know the old man. She knew nothing of the story of his life, the fact he was born the same day the Germans invaded Poland, or that his mother had died as a whore to Nazi officers in the General Government, or that his father had raped his mother before that, and that he was the result of that crime.

All she knew was that he had kind eyes.

And she couldn't be the cause of his death.

As she handed over the watch, she whispered, "They sent me."

It was as simple as that.

Later she'd regretted it. She thought, what if she'd been wrong about the old man? What if the test had been of her loyalty? She was the one with something to prove, after all. What if he told his handlers what she'd said?

But he never did.

Either one of them could have caused the other's death. And neither did. It was the beginning of a profound relationship of trust.

Years later, Tatyana had been lying asleep in a hotel room in Berlin. She'd just finished a series of extremely high-level, high-risk operations and was waiting to be recalled to Moscow.

She was on the home stretch of what had been one of the most dangerous weeks of her life.

And the phone rang.

She wasn't expecting any calls but picked up. It was the hotel concierge with a message.

"Madam, your clockmaker just called."

"My clockmaker?"

"Yes, ma'am. Your alarm clock is ready."

Tatyana hung up the phone. She hadn't spoken to the Clockmaker in years and had rarely thought of him. But she got out of the room immediately.

It saved her life.

42

In the instant Prochnow pulled the trigger, Tatyana reached up over her shoulder and grabbed his wrist. The bullet flew into the enormous mirror behind the bar, shattering a wall of glass that rose twenty-feet to the ceiling. The fragments cascaded down the wall like a water-fall, and Prochnow realized, as his reflection shattered, that she'd chosen her position better than he'd given her credit for.

She spun around to face him, twisting his wrist painfully in the process, then kneed him in the groin.

He doubled over in pain, and she slammed his face against the bar, once, twice. There was a rocks glass on the bar, and she grabbed it and smashed it against the back of his head.

He reached up and grabbed her by the hair, pulling her head backward. She was fast, but he had strength on his side. With her head bent backward, he thrust out his fist and punched her in the rib cage.

The blow would have floored her, but she managed to deflect it with a manicured hand.

He punched her again, this time in the belly, and her lithe frame buckled under the pressure of the blow.

He yanked her back by the hair again and was about to fling her to the ground when her stilettoed foot flew around her and landed square in his groin.

He lost his grip on her for a split second, and that was all she needed. She knew exactly where she was going.

She moved like a cat, leaping across the bar to a fire exit at the far end of the room.

He ran after her, but it seemed suddenly like every drunken idiot in the place was in his way. He had to heave and push his way to the door, which led to a narrow alley lined with dumpsters and fire escapes.

She was already out of sight.

He drew his gun and stepped carefully into the alley. To his left was a high, brick wall.

He went right.

Thick clouds of steam came from vents in the sides of the buildings, making it hard to see. The ground was filthy, the melting snow almost black. Graffiti covered every inch of the walls.

There was some movement to his side, and he fired two bullets. It had been a cat, and the shots clanged off the steel bin harmlessly, drawing sparks.

About a hundred yards ahead, he heard the crash of a fire escape being released from its latches and hitting the ground.

He ran toward it and looked up. Three floors above, Tatyana was just reaching the roof.

He fired off two more shots and this time hit his mark.

He heard a yelp of pain as the bullet tore into her flesh.

He had her.

Tatyana leaped up the steps of the fire escape, desperately trying to make it to the roof before the assassin saw her, and just as she reached it, felt the searing pain of a bullet tearing through her right calf muscle.

She knew then that the game was up.

She'd made a mistake.

There was no way she'd outrun a trained GRU assassin now.

She should have listened to her instincts.

She'd known, sitting in the bar, that something bad was going to happen. Agata wouldn't have kept her waiting like that.

It was more than a premonition.

She'd been about to leave when she caught the reflection of the man behind her in the mirror and grabbed his wrist.

She stumbled across the roof, a flat open space punctuated by ducts and vents, and tried to keep moving. Sometimes a gunshot wasn't as bad as it felt, and you could run a surprising distance before it stopped you. But this was not one of those times. Before she'd even crossed the roof, she could tell that her leg wasn't going to hold up. She was losing too much blood, and every step she took was agony. She could feel the muscle tearing.

She reached the edge of the building and, without hesitating a second or taking the time to judge the distance and determine whether she could make it, leaped across the alley.

She was blatantly risking death, the concrete three stories below was dizzyingly real, but she knew she had no alternative. When hesitation meant certain death, there was no reason not to make the leap.

If she hadn't been hurt, she might have made the jump, but as it was, she fell short, crashing into the side of the building and only barely managing to grab the ledge.

The assassin was sprinting toward her. She didn't dare look back. She didn't have to. She knew he was coming, rushing like a freight train, and if she didn't find cover before he got to her, it would be her death.

As she pulled herself up onto the roof, she sensed, like a premonition, that she'd reached the end of the line.

A few feet in from the edge of the roof was a low cinderblock wall about two feet high. She took cover behind it just in time to dodge a bullet. It crashed into the brick, sending chips of rubble into the air.

She pulled the Browning from her coat and returned fire blindly as a dark shadow flew right above her. It was the assassin, leaping from the other building, right over her. She raised her gun and pulled the trigger, and in the same moment, the gun was kicked from her hand.

It was a fluke, a moment of pure luck for the assassin. His trailing foot struck Tatyana's hand, and the Browning was knocked from her grip. She watched helplessly as it slid twenty feet across the roof.

She had two options, and in an instant, unarmed and injured, she decided.

The assassin landed with a thud and rolled, and Tatyana flung herself back over the cinderblock wall and dropped over the edge of the building.

She hung by her fingernails to the side of the building, and from that desperate position, knew she was rapidly exhausting her options.

She looked around frantically and saw a window ledge about twelve feet below. If she could get herself onto it and through the window, it would buy her time. The assassin wouldn't follow. That much was certain.

He'd have to find his way into the building another way, and that would take time.

She looked down and could only barely see the lighter colored stone of the window ledge.

It was a bad plan.

It wasn't going to work.

"Give it up, bitch," the assassin said from above.

His feet were inches from the tips of her fingers, which could only hold onto the ledge for a few seconds longer in any case.

He spoke Russian, but with a heavy German accent.

That was all she had time to learn of him because without giving herself another moment to change her mind, she let go of the ledge.

She fell like a weight of lead.

The brick wall of the building flew by her like a rocket.

The stone ledge was gone in an instant. She never stood a chance of grabbing it. All that was left was the concrete ground below, flying up at her at terminal velocity.

And then there was nothing at all.

44

L aurel stood by the window of the suite, staring out at Lafayette Square and the broader vista of Central DC.

She felt numb.

Sick to her stomach.

Two hours earlier, soon after Tatyana left her hotel room for the bar in Kreuzberg, Laurel had lost all contact with her.

Something had happened. It was the only explanation for why she hadn't checked in.

She rested her forehead against the glass pane of the window and sighed. From where she was, she could just about make out the form of the famous Rochambeau statue, its bronze glinting in the moonlight.

There was an exact replica of it in Paris, and both bore words written by George Washington extolling "the cause of liberty."

Laurel wondered what the founding fathers would make of the work she did. And she wondered what hellish trap she'd just sent Tatyana into. If the GRU captured her alive, her fate didn't bear thinking about.

Roth had entrusted her with rebuilding the Special Operations Group from the ground up. The most prized intelligence group in the history of the nation. The most elite killing machine ever created.

And within hours of her taking control, she'd potentially just sent her first ward to a brutal, grueling, hideous death.

She shook her head. She'd been so determined to avoid the mistakes of the past.

She'd wanted to create a perfect tool.

A perfect weapon.

Where the military was a sledge hammer.

And the CIA was a dagger.

She was going to give the president a scalpel, a weapon he could use with such precision that it could cut away threats to the nation without leaving even a trace of a scar.

Complete disavowal.

Zero blowback.

Zero collateral damage.

There would be no technical staff, no specialists, no analysts.

Just her and Tatyana, pulling the strings, calling in hits, striking foes, and all from a hotel suite two blocks from the White House.

No one would ever suspect it.

And there would be no leaks.

Of that, she could be certain.

Tatyana was the one person guaranteed never to make contact with the Kremlin. They wanted her head. They were after her sister too. She could never go back to them.

And then there was Lance.

Laurel didn't know if he'd ever come back. After hearing

of what he'd done, she wasn't sure she even wanted him back.

How could you trust a man like that?

A man who'd killed his own unborn child, and the woman carrying it.

Orders be damned, that was just unnatural.

And yet, there was a bond there, not just between her and Lance, but between all four of them, Roth and Tatyana too. As if their trials and traumas had forged them together.

If something had happened to Tatyana, she wasn't sure the dynamic between the remaining three worked.

The hotel phone rang, and she picked it up. It was the concierge at the front desk.

"I have a Mr. Roth for you, ma'am."

"I'll be right down."

She took the elevator down to the lobby. Roth was waiting in his car, and the usher barely managed to open the door for her as she hurried past.

Another usher opened the door of the Cadillac, and she climbed in.

"You're in a hurry."

He looked so untroubled, sitting on his leather seat with a paper cup of coffee on the console next to him and a copy of the early edition of the *Washington Post* on his lap.

"I'm sorry to have called."

"Call me any time, Laurel. Now, what's this about?"

"I'm afraid it's going to put a damper on your spirits."

"We're going to the Capitol, Harry," Roth said to the driver, and then to Laurel, "meeting with the House Intelligence Committee."

"Sir," she said, and then her voice trailed away.

He put his hand on her knee and said, "Something's happened in Berlin."

She nodded. "How did you know?"

"I figured from the way you're acting."

"I lost contact two hours ago."

"Did you have eyes in the bar?"

"Comms were a mess. I didn't dare tell the station chief in Berlin that Tatyana was in the city for fear of a leak."

"So you relied on satellite."

She nodded.

"And the Keyhole feed was unreliable."

She nodded again. "What's going on?"

"We're looking into it, believe me, but the long and short of it is that the Russians are fucking with us."

"With Keyhole?"

"I'm afraid so."

Laurel let out a long sigh. "Keyhole's, it's...".

"I know."

"I thought it was immune from interference."

"We all did," Roth said.

Laurel gave him a look that said things were beginning to go south.

"There are reports of gunfire in Kreuzberg," she said.

"Well, maybe she'll check in with her friend, the Clockmaker."

"I hope so."

"Laurel," Roth said, "this isn't your fault. She chose to do this."

"I made the call to send her in without backup."

"To avoid a leak."

"And I lost visual."

"That wasn't your fault either."

"She could be dead, Roth," Laurel said, her eyes filling with tears.

"She'll check-in. You'll see."

Laurel looked away. Wiped her face. She was embarrassed by her show of emotion.

"What are we going to do?"

"We've got an entire field office in Berlin. I'll send word to the station chief to start searching for her."

"We can't do that. We promised her."

Tatyana had made them both swear that they would do nothing to endanger the Clockmaker. She said he'd maintained his cover in Berlin for sixty years, and she wasn't going to be responsible for blowing it.

"We have no choice."

"I can be on a plane in an hour."

"I already said that's not going to happen, Laurel."

"That was before Tatyana fell off the grid."

"You're the head of the Special Operations Group now. That means keeping under the radar. Staying out of harm's way. Delegating this type of thing to other agents."

"I don't have any other agents."

45

Prochnow never saw anything like it in his life. And he'd seen a lot. The target let go of the building and tried to catch the ledge below.

Impossible.

She fell three floors to her death.

Which, he supposed, was good for her. If she'd been taken alive, the interrogators in Moscow would have had a field day with her. They took a special interest in defectors.

He stood at the edge of the building and looked down at the body.

There was a poetic justice to it.

She was traitor trash, and she'd fallen into an open dumpster.

Already, the rats were moving in on her, sniffing at the blood, nibbling her fingertips. She'd look like a pile of chicken bones by the time they were finished with her.

Prochnow spat over the edge and watched the phlegm land on the corpse.

In the night air, he could already hear the police sirens.

It was time to leave.

He entered the building through the roof access and made his way to the ground floor. It was an apartment building with an ethnic restaurant on the ground floor selling takeout. Lebanese, it looked like.

He exited through a side door into the alley, where he went to the dumpster to confirm the kill. As he approached, a putrid, sickly-sweet stench of rotting food hit him. He reached up to the top of the dumpster and pulled himself up to look over the side.

He was ruining his expensive kid leather gloves.

Rats scattered.

The smell made him want to gag.

He rested his weight on his chest and reached into the dumpster. The target lay face-down on the garbage, and he checked her wrist for a pulse.

Nothing.

He checked her neck to make sure, and was about to drop back to the ground when he felt the faint, scarcely detectible trace of a pulse.

"Fuck," he muttered.

She wasn't dead.

That was a problem.

Kirov wanted her interrogated. If Prochnow managed to bring her in alive, it would only enhance his standing with him.

But bringing her in would be a lot of work.

It would have been a lot easier simply to put a bullet in her skull.

Prochnow looked at the dumpster and sighed. He lit a cigarette.

"Fuck it," he said and pulled himself back up the side of the dumpster. He put his gun against the target's head and was about to pull the trigger.

But he didn't.

How would it look when Kirov found out she'd been executed at point-blank range?

He dropped back to the ground and took out his phone, dialing the number of his handler.

"Why are you calling this number?" a woman's voice said in heavily accented German.

"Why don't you just speak Russian," Prochnow said. "It will be easier on both of us."

Prochnow didn't know who she was. He didn't know her name. They'd never met in person. She sounded older, maybe in her fifties, but it was difficult to tell.

She switched to Russian, saying, "What do you want?"

"I need some help."

"Did you get the target?"

"She fell from a rooftop not far from the bar."

"So she's dead?"

"No. She's breathing. I can bring her in, but the streets are crawling with cops."

"Gunshots were fired?"

"Yes."

"Where are you exactly?"

"I'm sending my location now," he said, sending her the data.

"I'm sending a team now. There's a black site in Kreuzberg. We'll bring her there."

Prochnow hung up.

He waited by the dumpster for twenty minutes, smoking cigarettes, and when someone came down the alley, he expected it to be the GRU extraction team.

But it wasn't.

It was a cook from the Lebanese restaurant with a black plastic bag filled with trash.

"Give it to me," Prochnow said to him, stepping forward and reaching out for the bag of garbage.

The cook eyed him suspiciously but gave him the bag.

"Now fuck off," Prochnow said to him.

The cook looked at him more closely. Prochnow knew if he was forced to show his gun, he would have to kill him too. Otherwise, he might call the police.

"What are you doing out here?" the cook said.

"What do you think I'm doing?" Prochnow said.

He was ready to pull the gun, he was ready to put a bullet in the cook's forehead, it was nothing to him, but it would be simpler not to. He didn't know how long the team would take, and if he killed him, someone might come looking, and then he'd have to kill him too, and so on, and it would just be simpler if the guy did what Prochnow told him to do in the first place, and just fucked off.

The cook hesitated just a second, then turned away.

46

Laurel got back to the hotel suite and immediately began packing. She threw items into a bag, more or less at random, while simultaneously sitting on hold for the Lufthansa ticket office.

She had a number of identities she could travel under, and not all of them were flagged for Roth's attention.

She couldn't just sit there while Tatyana was possibly fighting for her life. She was the one who'd sent Tatyana to Berlin, she'd sent her straight into a trap, and she would be the one to bring her back.

An agent answered the phone, and Laurel said, "What's your next flight to Berlin out of Dulles?"

The agent did some typing and said, "There's a flight leaving in three hours."

"Direct?"

"Yes, it's direct."

"I'll take it," Laurel said.

Twenty minutes later, she was in the back of a cab on her way to the airport. She'd slipped out of a side entrance at the hotel and would be halfway across the Atlantic before Roth realized she was gone.

She watched the dreary city through the window. It had rained, and the air was thick with mist.

Her phone began vibrating, and she looked at it, expecting Roth.

It was Lance.

That was a surprise. She hadn't expected to be hearing from him in a while.

"Lance?" she said. "Is everything all right?"

Lance said nothing for a moment, then said, "I'm in New York."

"Oh," Laurel said, unsure what he was saying.

"I was just..." he said, and she noticed he was slurring his words heavily.

"Lance, are you drunk?"

"Drunk?"

"You've been drinking."

"She's dead, Laurel."

Laurel immediately felt a knot in her stomach. It was the thought she'd been unwilling to admit to herself for the past three hours. Tatyana was gone.

"Lance, how do you know that?"

"They killed her, Laurel."

Laurel didn't know what to say. Why was she going to Berlin if Tatyana was definitely dead? Her head spun.

Lance was ordering a drink from a bartender. He was definitely very drunk. She wouldn't have minded joining him.

"Lance," she said into the phone. "Lance. Can you hear me?"

The line wasn't dead, but Lance was no longer listening

to her. She listened to the sounds of the bar for a minute before hanging up. She tried calling him back, but he didn't pick up.

The cab arrived at the airport, and she forced herself to put Lance's call from her mind. He was drunk. He didn't know what he was talking about. There was no way for him to know if Tatyana was dead or alive.

Laurel knew it was possible the two were in touch, she knew there was more between them than what she'd been let in on, but even that wouldn't explain how he'd know before she did if Tatyana had been killed.

She passed through check-in and airport security in a haze of her own thoughts. She didn't even care if she was flagged by Roth. She passed through the final security line, half expecting the agent to tell her to step aside.

But he didn't, and she was allowed to board the plane.

She was flying business class, and as soon as she got to her seat, she had a martini and two sleeping pills.

She didn't wake up until the plane was an hour from landing. She ate a few bites of breakfast, and as soon as the plane landed at the enormous new terminal at Berlin Brandenburg, she called Lance.

He didn't pick up, and she tried him again from the back of her taxi.

It was early, and traffic along the Karl-Marx-Allee was slow. Ahead, she could see the spire of the Fernsehturm, the two-hundred-meter-high television tower that had been built by the Communists in the sixties as a symbol of Soviet power. By design, there was no part of West Berlin from which its spire could not be seen.

Laurel felt a wave of melancholy as the taxi inched along the wide avenue. The weather was as gray as it had been in

DC, and as they entered the Friedrichshain district, they passed a long section of the Berlin Wall, perfectly preserved, covered in political graffiti from a different time.

Berlin was a strange city. The Communists, Stalin, the Cold War, the Second World War, the Nazis, Hitler, the First World War, Kaiser Wilhelm the Second. All that history lived on, like strata in an excavation, each taking its shape from the one below and imparting its own to the one above.

Everything connected.

Everything reached back.

If someone knew that history, even if they'd been kept in a cave for the past thirty years, they'd have known what was at stake for Laurel and the CIA.

"Why do they oppose us?" she'd once asked Roth. "There's nothing in this war for them. There's nothing they could possibly hope to gain from this."

It was during a mission in Afghanistan in which she'd discovered that the GRU was paying locals to take potshots at American troops.

"Why do they oppose us?" Roth had said. "You'd be as well to ask why wolves hunt. It's what they are. They have no choice. They do only what nature made them to do."

She hadn't understood, and he said, "There's no understanding today without understanding yesterday, and the day before that, and the day before that. It all is what it is, and it can't be changed. It can't be rewritten."

"But why do they oppose us on absolutely every front? Year after year. When there's nothing in it for them."

"They oppose us now because of the Cold War. And they fought us then because we beat them to the bomb."

"The atomic bomb?"

"The atomic bomb," Roth said. "The single most

destructive weapon in the long and sordid history of human weapons."

"But they have the bomb too."

"For self-defense," Roth said. "To them, their nuclear capability is a shield, completely defensive in nature. They say it doesn't threaten anyone."

"They can't possibly believe that."

"They believe it, Laurel, and their fathers believed it. And their grandfathers. Their nukes are less powerful than ours. Less capable. Their delivery methods are less reliable. Their technology is aging. Their infrastructure is rotten. They don't even know themselves which stockpiles, which systems, would still work in case of war."

"That's hardly our fault," Laurel said.

"Their arsenal came second, Laurel. It wasn't built as a challenge to the West. It was built as a response. It's not a question. It's an answer."

"Come on. They'd have built nukes first if their scientists had been able to deliver them first."

Roth shrugged. "Sure. It's hard to imagine Stalin holding back on a new weapon as powerful as the atom bomb."

"But he didn't get it first," Laurel said quietly.

"No," Roth said. "We did."

"But we were their ally."

Roth smiled. "We were their ally," he repeated. "In a war that cost them twenty-seven million souls."

"Everyone suffered losses during the war."

"Not on the same scale," Laurel. "You take all other belligerents, Britain, the US, France, Germany, Italy, Japan, the Commonwealth, dozens of countries, and not even their total loss combined comes close to twenty-seven million."

"What about the Holocaust?"

"Yes, the Holocaust. An unthinkable atrocity. Death on an industrial scale, the likes of which had never been witnessed before or since. You picture those factories, those furnaces, running twenty-four hours a day, seven days a week, with the sole mission of wiping out one entire branch of the race of men."

"Right," Laurel said.

"Now picture that happening again, and again, every nine months, for four years. Because that's what happened on the Eastern Front alone. It was a mauling on an unimaginable scale, Laurel. Imagine six Holocausts. That's what Russia went through. And just as it was ending, the United States unveiled a weapon that could deliver fresh Holocausts at will, almost without limit, in an unending inferno of death that caused even the scientists who delivered it to have nightmares."

It was only then that Laurel began to see what he was trying to say. From a wide enough perspective, from the perspective of the Russian steppe and the meat grinder of the Eastern Front, Russia's actions during the Cold War might not have been as senseless as she'd always assumed.

"To us," Roth said, "nuclear war is the stuff of nightmares. Dystopian visions of a planet in its death throes. Things imagined more often by writers of fiction and Hollywood special effects artists."

"But to Russia?"

"Russia has seen it happen. They know what twenty-seven million dead looks like. They know what a War of Annihilation looks like. They've faced it. And they know it wasn't a movie, Laurel. It was real. It happened. And everything that happened once can happen again."

"They're preparing for the next one."

"Their politics is the politics of survival, Laurel. Their fight is the fight of survival."

"So what are you saying? They'll never drop their guard. They'll never put away their weapons. All traumas, even the one they faced, fade eventually. Eventually, they have to forget."

Roth sighed. "Did you know that, even before the Nazi surrender, even before they were out of that nightmare, Britain and the United States had drawn up plans for finishing the Soviets off?"

Laurel shook her head.

"Churchill drew up plans for a surprise attack against the Russian forces occupying East Germany, and what's worse, the Russians found out about them."

"I didn't know that," Laurel said.

"We'd watched the Nazis sap their power almost to breaking point," Roth said, "and we drew up plans to destroy what was left of them. Their fear of us was well-founded. It wasn't just the paranoia of a crazed leadership, Laurel. We wanted them gone. We wanted them dead. And we'd just developed the nuke."

"But we never seriously considered using it on them, did we?"

"Oh, we did, Laurel. At the highest levels, on both sides of the Atlantic. The generals and leaders in London and Washington, and the nascent intelligence organizations of both countries, plotted in detail how to bring the Soviets utterly to their knees."

Roth's words resonated with her now, as the cab rolled past these concrete segments of the wall Russia had built between themselves and West Berlin.

After what history had shown them, she could see why they built walls that spanned continents.

They were afraid.

And they were right to be afraid.

They'd always been right to be afraid.

"It was Churchill himself," Roth told her, "who said that those who forgot the past were doomed to repeat it. The Russians can't take the risk that history will ever repeat."

P rochnow stood in a cavernous underground tunnel that the Soviet government had upgraded and secured during the decades it had been in occupation of Berlin.

According to GRU documents, the tunnel's granite walls were four feet thick and lined with metal sheets that could block all manner of modern detection methods.

The tunnel was part of a vast network built by the Nazis in preparation for Hitler's new German capital, which he'd named Germania. The city was never built, but part of the groundwork had been laid, and the current tunnel extended beneath what would have been the Avenue of Splendors, a five-kilometer long thoroughfare that would have formed the central axis of the city.

Prochnow stood on a set of steel steps that connected the chamber to the tunnel above. Below him was a chamber that had been built for drainage and ventilation equipment. The equipment had never been brought in, and large slabs of Swedish granite were piled around the walls. On one of those slabs, Tatyana Aleksandrova lay stretched out, spread-eagle, her ankles and wrists secured to iron rings in the rock.

He flicked his cigarette down onto her, and it landed next to her neck. It must have burned her because she suddenly jerked away from it with a deep gasp for air.

She tried to rise but couldn't.

Prochnow had restrained her himself. Her wounds were dressed and treated.

Kirov had made it amply clear that she was to be brought back to Russia alive. But before that happened, Prochnow was authorized to interrogate her. Kirov wanted to know exactly how much information Roth had about his plans in the Baltic. As long as Prochnow didn't kill Tatyana, he could do whatever he wanted with her.

"You're awake," Prochnow said, descending the steps.

The space had the feel of an underground quarry, or a crypt, and apart from a few Soviet-era surveyors, and the KGB and GRU agents who later took possession, no one had been down there since the final days of the war.

Much of the complex was submerged in water, although this section had been drained, and Prochnow himself had explored as much of it as was possible. He doubted there was anyone alive who knew the tunnels as well as he did. He'd even come across secret stashes of Nazi treasure, paintings, and other works of art that had been confiscated or stolen from Berlin's Jews during the war.

"Where am I?" Tatyana said.

She spoke in English, but Prochnow knew that would soon change.

In his hand was a metal briefcase, and inside the briefcase were a number of vials containing the most advanced and experimental truth serums the GRU possessed.

Once administered, it would be impossible for her to

resist his interrogation. She'd be so out of it he could tell her to kill herself, and she would obey. Torture would be unnecessary.

Prochnow walked toward her slowly and made a protracted show of opening the briefcase, removing the vials, extracting the contents of one of them with a long syringe, and lifting it up in front of the light to check its content.

"Who are you?" Tatyana said.

"Think of me," Prochnow said, "as a friend of a friend."

"What friend?" Tatyana spat.

"Why, Jacob Kirov, of course."

She turned away from him, but that was fine. They'd be talking like lovers soon enough.

He grabbed her arm and jammed the syringe deep into the bicep. She didn't react, but he knew the serum would begin to act soon enough.

She looked around the chamber, searching for ways to escape, and her movements grew heavier and less coordinated as the serum took effect. He could practically see the cogs of her mind slowing down, looking first at the steel ventilation duct, then at the staircase he'd just descended, before reaching the point where she just stared vacantly at the ceiling above her.

There was no way she was going to escape. The restraints at her ankles and wrists had been drilled into the granite during the war, apparently Prochnow wasn't the first to use this chamber as an interrogation room, and if the passage of eighty years hadn't pried them loose, Tatyana's feeble struggling wasn't going to.

"My, my," Prochnow said. "Look at you, so pretty, splayed out like that. I must admit, I've always had a fondness for a woman in shackles."

She said nothing. The serum was working its way into her nervous system, into the neurotransmitters in her brain. Before long, she'd be spewing so much unintelligible gibberish he'd want her to shut up.

He smoked a cigarette while he waited, then tried again.

"Tatyana Alexandrova," he said, walking around her so that she could see his face. "Do you remember me? I'm your friend."

She looked at him, and he could see the confusion in her eyes. It really didn't take a lot of skill to interrogate someone with these serums. She didn't believe everything he said, not yet, but she'd get there.

"You were just telling me who you were meeting at the bar in Kreuzberg," he said.

There was a look of intense concentration on her face. She was doing her best to resist him, but the human brain obeyed certain rules, and scientists at a government lab in Sverdlovsk had been looking for ways to crack interrogation resistance for decades. There was only so long she'd be able to fight back.

"I wouldn't tell you that," she said.

Prochnow smiled. He placed his hand on her neck and began to squeeze, just slightly at first, but enough that she would know what he was capable of.

"You were meeting your friend from Riga," he said.

She shook her head, and he squeezed more tightly. Fear and oxygen deprivation increased the effectiveness of the serum. His grip grew tighter and tighter, and he looked into her eyes as he squeezed.

"You were meeting your friend, Agata Zarina, the Latvian policewoman."

"I would never tell you that," she said again, gasping for air, her mind struggling to hold onto its grasp of reality.

"Yes, you would," Prochnow said, his grip growing tighter and tighter. "I'm your friend too. You need me to help her. If you don't tell me, she's going to get hurt."

"You're not my friend," she gasped.

A sneer crossed Prochnow's face. He was surprised. He'd never seen anyone show such resistance to the drug. Physically, it was working. Her pupils were so dilated that the entirety of her irises were black. Her blinking was so slow she looked like a video recording in slow motion. He checked her pulse, and it was in the thirties.

"The others are coming soon," Prochnow said. "They're coming to rescue you."

"Rescue me?" Tatyana said.

"That's right," Prochnow said. "They love you, Tatyana. They're coming to rescue you."

"Lance is coming?"

"Lance?"

"Lance Spector."

"That's right. Lance Spector is coming. And the others."

He had to be careful. Her mind was so suggestible now that anything he said to her would become a new reality. If he planted too many seeds, it would be impossible to differentiate what originated from her from what he'd planted.

"Laurel is coming too?" Tatyana said.

"That's right," Prochnow said, "to the arranged place."

"To the place?"

He said nothing. Every time he made a suggestion, it prompted her thoughts but also introduced the danger that she would begin to imagine the things he wanted her to think.

He couldn't risk contaminating this detail. He needed it to be real.

"Cedric will help them," Tatyana said.

"Cedric?" Prochnow said, leaning in closer to her.

He tightened his grip on her neck to the point that he was in danger of asphyxiating her. If he crossed the line and killed her, Kirov would not forgive him. She was gasping for air, straining desperately for breath, but he didn't allow her to get air.

She couldn't even speak if she'd wanted to.

And he felt her try, felt the movement in her throat, the struggle of her larynx and vocal cords.

"Cedric Chopin," she gasped.

The words were almost a whisper. She was on the verge of losing consciousness. For a moment, he feared he'd gone too far, then she started coughing.

He had to go all the way to the surface, along tunnel after tunnel, through cavernous sections and up flights of metal stairs, until he reached a metal doorway, like the door of a safe, that let him into part of Berlin's modern underground service tunnels. He was in a tunnel that lay beneath the Air Ministry Building, and he followed it all the way to a section of the Air Ministry's basement that was no longer in use.

He had a way of getting from there into the service hall of the Detlev Rohwedder Building, and from there, to a secret access that had been used during the Nazi years but had been concealed by the GRU after the war.

As soon as he got back out to the street, he dialed the code for Kirov's operator and waited.

"Did she talk?" Kirov said the instant he picked up the phone.

"She talked," Prochnow said.

"And?"

"She said a name. Cedric Chopin. Have you ever heard it?"

When Kirov spoke, he sounded genuinely stunned.

"She said that name?"

"Yes, she did."

"I see," Kirov said.

"You know him? You know where to find him?"

"Prochnow," Kirov said. "Have you ever heard of the Clockmaker of Berlin?"

48

The Clockmaker of Berlin was not a young man. He was not even spry, as they said. He wasn't one of those elderly men who was in good shape for his age.

Decades of indulging in fine cognacs and expensive pipe tobaccos had taken their toll, and he'd been diagnosed with cancer of the larynx and esophagus just six months earlier. He'd undergone chemotherapy and a total laryngectomy, and while the treatments had taken a huge toll on him, aging him by twenty years and turning him completely bald, and while the laryngectomy had removed his ability to speak, so that he now needed an electrolarynx machine, and sounded like a poor impression of Darth Vader, they had done nothing to put the cancer into remission.

He was a man used to being surrounded by clocks, and now, their ticking no longer marked time that had passed, but rather, time that was left.

They ticked for him.

He'd lived a long time, and he looked backward more than forward.

As his body betrayed him, one organ at a time, and as his wits began to lose their grip on reality, it was really only his memories that remained. As everything else faded, they became the last vestiges of the man he was, the man he had been, and what that man was made of.

He realized, as all men do in the end, that a man becomes his memories. The moment he loses those, is the moment he no longer exists.

Cedric Chopin was a man without family.

No wife. No children. No grandchildren.

He'd lived most of his life an orphan, and he'd spent that life not seeking to build a family but to avenge one.

Whereas others looked forward through the generations, taking joy in the children and grandchildren they were leaving to posterity, Cedric Chopin looked only back at those who had come before.

And sought revenge against them.

His forefathers were from the German nobility, that class of Pomeranian and Prussian Junkers, itself descended from Teutonic knights, who owned all the German estates and duchies east of Berlin.

It was they who furnished Hitler's army with its marshals, field marshals, and Reichsmarschalls.

Names like von Rundstedt, von Bock, von Manstein, von Bismark, von Hindenburg, von Siemens, von Moltke, von Tirpitz, von Kleist, von Papen, von Ribbentrop, and even, von Clausewitz, all came from that same Junker class.

To Cedric Chopin, it was difficult to find a tribe of men anywhere in history, more intimately entwined in the deaths of millions than those whose blood coursed through his own veins.

There were those who subscribed to the philosophy that

what was buried in the past should stay buried in the past. That the only way forward lay in moving on.

Cedric Chopin was not of that opinion. To him, in the indelible record of human events, all ledgers had to be balanced, all debts had to be settled.

In full.

And so, he'd spent his life trying to do just that, avenging the sins of his fathers while simultaneously atoning for his portion of them.

The circumstances of his birth were as strange as the circumstances of his life.

He was born in Warsaw on the first of September, 1939.

It is a day that looms large in the history of the human race.

The day Nazi bombers began bombarding Warsaw.

The day Hitler invaded Poland.

The day World War Two began, a war that would over the coming years rack up over a hundred million corpses.

Less than three weeks after the Nazi invasion from the west, the Soviets invaded from the east.

That was the substance of the Molotov-Ribbentrop Pact.

Cedric Chopin always said that the invasion of one country by another was a rape. And that what Hitler and Stalin did to his country, just as he was coming into the world, was a gang rape.

And although he did not know it until years later, he himself was the result of a rape.

And not just any rape, but the rape of a Polish woman by a German man.

The man was the descendent of a Pomeranian duke, and Chopin's mother, whose name was Kasia Szopen, the spelling was altered later when he immigrated to Germany, was a maid in his house.

The German, Chopin's father, although he never thought of him as such, owned a clock factory that made some of the finest timepieces in all of Europe.

Chopin knew nothing of the relationship between his mother and father in the early days of his life. He knew he himself was never acknowledged. And he knew that when he was less than a year old, a foreman from the factory came to his mother's house and filled out paperwork that changed his name from Szopen, as his mother spelled it, to Chopin, a more Germanic form.

Later, that piece of paperwork saved his life, though not the life of his mother.

Before the war, Hitler drew up a plan that was unusual, to say the least, from a military point of view. He ordered that the city of Warsaw be *erased*.

The erasure of a city of that size, over a million souls, had never before been contemplated, and indeed, Hitler almost achieved it. By war's end, ninety-five percent of its buildings had been destroyed, and the new government in Poland seriously considered not rebuilding it.

By that point, almost no one was left in the city.

Hitler's plan was strangest, though, not because of its scale, not because of its sheer destruction and loss of life, but because it served no objective. It wasn't necessary. It was not the byproduct of battle or strategic aerial bombardment. It was a plan based entirely on spite.

A simple act of hatred.

And it was during the years of Nazi occupation, while the plan to blot out the city was underway, that the formative events of Chopin's life occurred.

Chief among them was the death of his mother.

In Warsaw, the Nazis engaged in strange and grotesque behaviors, things that were not seen in other cities.

There was a children's game at the time the locals called *łapanka*. It was the same game American children called tag.

The Germans adapted it for their own purposes, selecting an area of the city at random, an important street, a busy market square, or a train station, and sealing it off with soldiers.

They then closed in, capturing everyone inside the cordon. If they found Jews, they were shot on the spot, and everyone else, man, woman, or child, regardless of who they were and what they'd been doing in the area, was rounded up and sent to the central train station, where they were herded into cattle cars and transported to Germany for slave labor.

To the Germans, it was a game. A way of instilling terror. A way of emphasizing the cruelty, the randomness, of the fate of the citizens of Warsaw.

Chopin was with his mother the day she was captured. She had identity documents, an *Ausweis*, as the Germans called it, that should have protected her, but no one cared.

Chopin's identity card, however, with its German spelling, saved his life. He was returned to the clock factory, where over the coming years, he learned his trade and, piecemeal, the story of his origins came to light.

When he was old enough, he signed up for the Polish Intelligence Service. They tried to place him in the Ministry of Internal Affairs, but when the Defense Minister heard his story, he had him transferred to the Second Directorate of the General Staff of the Army. From there, he was sent to Moscow for training by the KGB before being dispatched to Berlin.

He established himself as a clockmaker, and for the next

sixty years, while other agents lost faith in the Soviet system and abandoned their posts, Chopin stood firm.

He remained loyal to the Soviets far longer than anyone could have expected, not because he loved Russia, but because he felt the need to atone for the deeds of his ancestors.

And he'd been doing it too long.

He was getting old.

Soon, his life would be over.

He still went to work every day, but when he left his apartment, the cold hit him like something sharp. It got into his bones. Into his joints. It was worst in the damp.

At work, customers were taken aback by his appearance.

When he spoke with the electrolarynx machine, he frightened some. Disgusted others.

All were made uneasy.

He set out from his apartment on this particularly cold January morning in two layers of full-body underwear, well made winter clothing, and a heavy, dark green Tirol-style Loden coat, which he wore almost as a cape, with his arms free and the button on the neck the only one fastened.

He walked slowly, aided by a wooden cane, to his favorite coffee house on the Kurfürstendamm. The broad avenue, with its rows of trees, reminded him always of Paris.

He walked past the Kaiser Wilhelm Church, which still stood tall, if less proudly than it had before it was bombed. The church was struck during an air raid on the twenty-third of November, 1943, and what remained now was the part of the spire, entrance hall, altar, and baptistry that survived the bombing. They remained, unrepaired, as a reminder of the war. In the middle of the church, to this day, stood a damaged statue of Christ that had been on the altar the night of the bombing.

Chopin entered the church and looked up at the statue.

Next to it was a cross made of nails taken from the roof timbers of Coventry Cathedral, which the Germans had bombed in 1940.

He didn't pray. He was not a man who could bring himself to do that.

He simply stood, leaning on his cane, looking at the broken stone statue.

He reached into his pocket for some change and put it in the offering box. The box was for church upkeep, and it had been placed there by a group of British former bomber pilots as a sign of goodwill.

Then he turned to leave. It was time for his coffee. His whipped cream. His pastry.

The one pleasure he had left.

He shuffled toward the door just as a man in a long black coat was entering the church.

Chopin stopped. He recognized the man. They'd never met, but Chopin had seen his picture.

In a file.

He'd even assigned him missions.

He reached back into his coat pocket and pulled out his electrolarynx machine.

"You've come for me at last," he said, the synthetic voice filling the empty church with a strange, mechanical presence that was out of place.

Chopin knew nothing of Tatyana's presence in the city. She hadn't contacted him in a long time, and even now, she had no intention of drawing him into the risky operation she was engaged in. She'd given his name to Laurel and would have gone to him if she'd escaped Prochnow's attack, but that hadn't happened.

Christoph Prochnow didn't say a word. He walked up to

the old man, pressed his gun against his temple, and pulled the trigger.

The old man's body slumped slowly, as if his age and decrepitude slowed even the action of gravity. It formed a crumpled heap on the ground.

Prochnow looked around the church, then stood over the body, opened his fly, and pissed on the dying Chopin.

"You betrayed us first," he said.

49

L aurel walked along the Kurfürstendamm until she found the Clockmaker's shop. When she reached it, she kept walking.

There was a café across the street with seats and umbrellas outside, and she sat down and ordered a cappuccino.

She was nervous.

This was the place Tatyana had told her to come in case of trouble.

And trouble, there was.

She sipped her coffee and watched the shop. It was like something from another time, with a rich wooden façade, a painted sign on the window, and warm light spilling from the frosted glass of the door.

She tried to see inside, but a lace curtain and a display of expensive clocks blocked the view.

The sign on the door said the shop was open, but no one entered or left in the time she'd been watching.

In all likelihood, it would be just the proprietor, the Clockmaker himself, who was inside.

She should have checked in with Roth, he'd been trying to reach her all morning, but she couldn't face the earful he'd give her for disobeying him. It would be better to call him with good news, hopefully after she'd found Tatyana.

She felt for her gun, felt the reassurance of its cold, steel grip, then paid for her coffee and got up.

She crossed the street and pushed open the door of the shop.

Inside, it was like something from an old Victorian set. The air was musty, laden with the scent of wax polish, pipe smoke, and something that reminded her of a barbershop. The shelves and countertop were made of rich mahogany, polished over decades to a high sheen.

On the shelves, clocks of every kind ticked, and behind reinforced glass screens, some of the most expensive watches in the world were on display.

There was no one behind the counter, but there was a curtain leading to a workshop.

"Hello?" Laurel called.

And then she felt it, like a sting from a hornet, a sharp, piercing pain in her right calf muscle.

She swung around to see where it had come from. A hidden contraption had been set up beneath the counter, like a sort of miniature crossbow.

She looked down at her leg and saw a stainless steel dart, about two inches long, harpooned into her flesh.

She reached into her coat and pulled out her gun, but as she swung around, lost her balance. She lost her grip on the gun, and it fell to the ground.

The room spun, and she felt herself falling.

She hit the ground hard, banging her head painfully.

Everything began to fade.

50

Lance woke up hungover. His mouth was dry. It tasted like an ashtray.

He'd spent the night in some cheap hotel close to the Russian consulate. He barely remembered checking in.

He'd slept in his clothes, and there was a woman lying next to him, her skirt still hiked up around her waist where they'd left it the night before.

He fixed it for her, saving what dignity there was to be saved, and went to the window.

Outside, a garbage truck was emptying a dumpster.

It was just after dawn.

He'd intended to break into the Russian consulate and find out who'd killed Sam. The flight to Montana had been booked by the consulate. The Consul-General, a man named Jacob Kirov, had to know the identity of the passenger.

In fact, he was probably the one who'd sent him.

But Kirov wasn't at the consulate.

He was in Saint Petersburg.

Lance lit a cigarette and looked at the woman he'd spent the night with. He wasn't proud of himself. He doubted she would be either.

The room was disgusting, one of those cheap, rooming houses that could only be found in a city like New York.

He vaguely remembered calling Laurel from a bar.

He couldn't remember what he'd said to her, but he had no doubt it was humiliating.

She'd want nothing to do with him now, not after what he'd told her about his past.

He went into the bathroom. The bathtub had rust stains below the faucets, and he stared at the pattern they made, like piss-colored rivers, toward the drain.

He showered longer than usual.

He had no reason to hurry.

Sam was dead.

The men responsible for her death would be dead soon.

Every last one of them.

And when that was done, what then?

There would be nothing.

He could go back to Montana, but it wouldn't be the same.

He thought of the cobbler she'd made, then he shut off the water and stepped out of the shower.

The woman on the bed was stirring to life.

"Hey, stud," she said.

He pulled on his jeans and shirt. He would need some fresh clothes.

"Do I owe you money?" he said bluntly to the woman.

"Excuse me?"

"Sorry."

"What did you say?"

"I..." he stammered.

"You asked if you owed me money."

"I was just checking."

"Checking? Checking what?"

"If...".

"If I was a whore? What kind of asshole wakes up in the morning and doesn't know if the woman he fucked was a whore or not?"

"Sorry," Lance said again, putting on his jacket.

"And now you're leaving?"

"I've got to go. Last night was amazing."

"Fuck you, asshole."

He was about to leave the room when he stopped, took out his wallet, and left some cash on the sideboard by the door.

Just in case.

A shoe flew by his head and knocked a picture from the wall.

He left the hotel and walked down eighty-seventh street to the corner of Lexington. There was a pharmacy, and he went inside, bought a toothbrush, deodorant, some soap, a change of underwear, and a fresh white shirt. Then he used the pharmacy's washroom to change.

He left the used items in the washroom and went back to the counter to buy aspirin.

Then he went into a diner across the street and took a booth.

"Coffee?" the waitress said.

He nodded and pulled out his phone. He needed to buy a ticket to Saint Petersburg but as he was about to dial, it started ringing.

It was Roth.

He looked at the screen, unsure whether or not to answer.

"What is it, Roth?"

"Lance," Roth said, "don't hang up."

"I'm not hanging up," Lance said.

"We're in trouble, Lance."

"What are you talking about?"

"Tatyana's missing. I walked her into a trap. I should never have sent her."

"Slow down, Roth. You sound like you're having an anxiety attack."

Roth took some deep breaths.

"Now," Lance said, "did you just say you sent Tatyana into a trap?"

"Yes."

"Why would you do that?"

"Because she agreed to go. She knew the risk. She *wanted* to go?"

"Where is she?"

"Berlin. At least, that's where we sent her."

"She won't stay there long," Lance said. "They'll bring her back to Russia for interrogation. It won't be pretty."

"That's why I need you to go after her."

"You sure about that?"

"Lance, you're the only one I trust."

"And what does Laurel have to say about that?"

"Laurel's already there."

"What?"

"She left last night, against my express orders, and now I've lost contact with her too."

"Roth, you've lost both of them?"

"Lance...".

"If anything's happened to them, Roth, I swear to God."

"I know, Lance. That's why I'm calling you. I need you."

"Get a plane ready."

51

Prochnow had always been ambitious. He'd always wanted to rise up the ranks.

When he told Kirov what he'd achieved, he was certain he'd view him in a new light.

Not only had he brought in Tatyana Aleksandrova, the highest-level defector Roth had ever managed to turn, but, if the rumors were true, Laurel Everlane was his new protégé. She was single-handedly responsible for a string of recent breaches that had left the GRU reeling.

Together, they marked a massive blow to Roth's capabilities, and right at a time when Russia was about to make a major strike at the very heart of the CIA's mission.

Next to them, finding out the Clockmaker was involved was merely the icing on the cake.

Prochnow, with the help of the same GRU team Kirov had before, had brought Laurel to the tunnel beneath the Air Ministry Building where he was keeping Tatyana.

The GRU men had brought two dollies with them, which made moving the prisoners easier. They were heavy-duty hand-trucks with thick rubber wheels and an L-shaped steel frame.

The women stood on the steel plate at the bottom of the dolly and could be wheeled around the tunnel with ease.

Both women were unconscious, heavily drugged, and Tatyana's gunshot wound would begin to fester soon.

Prochnow had secured the women to the dollies using strong, plastic ties at their ankles, wrists, knees, and elbows. Around their waists and necks, leather straps held them so tightly against the steel frame that it was impossible for them to twist out of the position he had them in.

He'd placed the dollies at the top of the metal staircase at the entrance to the room, very close to the edge. The steps were sharp, about thirty of them, and the dollies were balanced so precipitously close to the edge that if either woman struggled or rocked her dolly too much, she would in all likelihood cause them both to fall down the stairs.

Because they were tied upright and unable to protect themselves from the fall, there was a good chance such a fall would kill them.

Prochnow wasn't authorized to kill them, but they didn't know that.

He walked up to Tatyana and jabbed a syringe of adrenaline into her neck. She regained consciousness with a gasp for air, and he had to hold her in place to stop her from falling down the steps.

When she saw where she was, she was confused. She didn't understand what was happening. She could see down the stairs, she could see that she was balanced precipitously close to the edge of the top step, but the drugs had disoriented her to the point where she couldn't remember most of what had happened since her capture.

Prochnow repeated the process with Laurel, and again,

had to hold her steady so that she didn't knock the entire dolly forward.

"Now, ladies," he said when they'd stopped struggling and were aware of the risks of too much movement. "You see where you are, don't you?"

"What is this?" Laurel said.

That was when Tatyana realized for the first time that she was not alone. She strained against the restraint at her neck and could just about see to her side that Laurel was there with her.

"Laurel?" she gasped.

"Tatyana," Laurel said.

"What happened? How did you get here?"

Laurel said nothing, and Prochnow tipped them each back on the wheels of the dolly and turned them around so that their backs were to the stairs.

"I think you've both seen what will happen if you squirm and struggle too much," he said.

"Who are you?" Laurel said.

"I'm the man who lured you here, Laurel Everlane."

"You don't know what you're messing with," she said.

He smiled at her, leaning back on the railing of the gangway. He removed a pack of cigarettes from his pocket and lit one.

"Oh, I understand perfectly well what I'm messing with," he said. "It's been almost too simple. I lured you here," he said, nodding toward Tatyana, "when I killed the cop from Riga, and I lured *you* here," he said, nodding to Laurel, "when I caught Tatyana."

"So Agata is dead?" Tatyana said.

"She put up a fight," Prochnow said, "she certainly gave us a run for our money, but we got her in the end."

Prochnow smiled. He couldn't believe what he had. Not one, but two of Kirov's most wanted prizes.

"What are you going to do with us?" Laurel said.

"Oh," Prochnow said, pulling his phone from his pocket. "I'm just an underling, really. Just a foot soldier. The real decisions are made by others."

He opened the camera on his phone and took a picture of his two captives, and sent it to Kirov.

Kirov called him back immediately.

"It seems I underestimated you," he said.

"They're in a black site, sir. The Clockmaker is dead. I think that takes care of any loose ends."

"I want them transported to Russia immediately," Kirov said.

Prochnow looked at the two women. Transportation would be a challenge. He would have to get them across Germany, into Poland, and from there, over the Russian border. That would be the hardest part.

"I see," Prochnow said.

"You don't sound pleased."

"Moving them will be difficult. The CIA will be scanning the region with everything they've got."

"You won't have to worry about that much longer."

"Sir?"

"I can't talk about it, but the CIA's ability to track movement on the surface will be severely degraded very soon."

"I see," Prochnow said.

"You're to get them to the Kaliningrad border. There's a road crossing at Mamonovo-Gronovo close to Braniewo. Do you know it?"

"I know it, sir."

"There's a logistics port in Braniewo. Just off the highway."

"I see, sir."

"On the Polish side."

"Yes, sir."

"If you get them that far, an extraction team from Moscow will take them from there."

"And the American satellites, sir? They won't see us?"

"Like I said, Prochnow, that capability will be degraded soon. I'll tell you when it's safe to move them."

52

K irov was sitting by the window in his hotel room, watching the people hurry back and forth across the square. He wondered what it would be like, just for a day, to be one of them.

To have an ordinary life.

To have a family.

To have an ounce of human warmth in his life.

He hadn't always been alone. There'd been someone, once, a very long time ago. He was dead now, of course. Everyone from those days was dead.

He was relaxed. Well, as relaxed as could be expected. Things were going according to plan. Everything was in position.

Apart from one detail.

The sleeper agent from Long Island. Kirov regretted sending him. He should never have sent someone so untested, so inept. He'd wanted to scare the girl only. To distract Spector. And he'd used Alex Sherbakov for the sole reason that he couldn't be traced back to the Kremlin.

But it had completely backfired.

Someone had broken into the airport hangar and beaten up the pilot, and apparently, there'd been inquiries at the consulate into Kirov's whereabouts.

It was a problem.

The phone rang, and he found himself grabbing for the receiver as if his life depended on it. It was the concierge down in the lobby.

Kirov needed to calm down.

"Your *guest* is here, sir," the concierge said, emphasizing guest in a way that signaled disapproval.

One of the things he hated about being back in Russia was the way certain segments of society still tiptoed around the topic of homosexuality as if they'd never met a gay man before.

"He's early," Kirov said.

"Yes, sir."

"Then keep him down there. I said not to send him up until I called."

"Very good, sir."

Kirov hung up and glanced at his watch. He was annoyed. The *guest* was early. The last thing he needed was a male prostitute hanging around in the lobby, especially as he was there on state business.

"Nothing personal," the president had said to Kirov before passing the most draconian legislation against gay rights since the Stalin-era.

"Of course not," Kirov had said.

"It plays well with the base, is all."

"I understand, sir."

"And in any case," the president said, "you've always been the epitome of discretion, Jacob."

Kirov had kept his face as blank as a white sheet of paper, but he understood perfectly that what the president was telling him was a warning. What he did behind closed doors was one thing, but in public, he had to hide who he was.

The phone rang again, and this time he actually did knock it over. He got down on his hands and knees to pick up the receiver.

"Please hold for the president," a voice said.

He waited while the connection was made, and then the president's voice came on the line, clear as a bell.

"Kirov. Update me."

"It's done, sir."

"Both of them?"

"Both of them, sir."

"Kirov, my boy, that's good news."

"Yes, sir."

"Well done."

"Thank you, sir."

"She took the bait like the rat she is."

"She did, sir."

"Who was the man you used?"

"It was the German who came through in the end. Prochnow. The Stasi agent's son."

"I see."

"And there was some collateral damage in the process, sir."

"Collateral damage?"

"The Pole. Chopin. The Clockmaker."

"He was mixed up in this?"

"His name came up. I had Prochnow look into it, and sure enough, when Everlane showed up, it was at his shop."

"So he's dead?"

"He is, sir."

"So that's it, then? Everything's going to plan."

Kirov swallowed. "There is one matter I wanted to bring up, sir."

"What's that?" the president said, his tone suddenly growing concerned.

"The operative in New York, the sleeper agent."

"What sleeper agent?"

"Alex Sherbakov."

"What's he got to do with anything?"

Kirov had planned to tell the president everything. That he'd sent Sherbakov to distract Spector by scaring his girl, but he realized now how bad that would sound. Spector had been completely out of the picture. No one was worried about him. As far as the president knew, Roth was no longer making use of him.

Kirov didn't want to have to tell the president that because of his misjudgment, and Sherbakov's fuck up, Spector was now actively trying to track him down.

"Nothing, sir. But I tried to contact him today, for another matter, unrelated."

"And?"

"And I haven't been able to reach him."

"I hardly think that's a priority right now, Kirov."

"Of course not, sir. I'll look into it myself. It's only been a few hours. I'll get someone to pay him a visit."

"We need to focus on the task at hand, Kirov. I don't need to remind you how long our nation has waited to regain this lost territory."

"I understand what's at stake, sir."

"Our nation has been operating like one of those war veterans who's lost a limb. He wakes up in the morning trying to move it, his phantom limb, thinking it's still there, and then he remembers it's no longer there. He remembers what he's lost. He remembers that he's incomplete."

"Yes, sir. I understand."

"He's incomplete, Kirov. Unformed. Lacking the wholeness even of his own body."

"Of course, sir."

"It's unnatural, Kirov. It's a searing, raging fury. And that is the fury I feel every time I look at the map."

"I understand, sir."

"The time has come for us to right this wrong, Kirov. Latvia will be brought to heel. And after she falls, so will the rest of them, like dominos."

The president hung up, and Kirov sat very still.

The Sherbakov thing was a problem. He could feel it in his bones.

Spector was engaged.

And Kirov realized that if Spector didn't find him, the president would kill him himself when he found out what he'd done.

Nothing could get in the way of his precious invasion. It was the first step in the reconstitution of the Soviet Union.

Kirov knew that if he didn't find Spector and stop him, that it was likely going to cost him his life.

He picked up the phone and dialed the concierge.

"Mr. Kirov, sir?"

"Send up my prostitute."

53

L ance flew into Berlin on a military-owned C-21A Learjet. When he boarded the plane, a CIA secure pouch was waiting for him with all the details of what Roth knew.

There was a copy of the original message handed into the Berlin embassy.

There was also a file, typed up by Laurel herself for the Group database, that detailed the extraction plan she and Tatyana had agreed on in case things went south.

It involved a Soviet intelligence asset code-named the Clockmaker, who operated a business on the Kurfürstendamm.

Lance had heard rumors of the Clockmaker and was surprised to see his name here. According to legend, he was the longest-serving and most effective assets the Soviets had in Berlin. He'd managed to remain undetected there for the entirety of the Cold War, and in the opinion of some, was nothing more than a myth.

Lance wasn't surprised that he existed. He'd seen the evidence of his handiwork more than once. In fact, Lance knew that Roth had considered him one of his most serious adversaries for a very long time.

What surprised him was that he would be helping Tatyana, a known Russian defector.

With Tatyana's information, Roth had been able to pull together a file of sorts about the Clockmaker, and Lance read it with interest. He was a Pole by the name of Cedric Chopin, who'd been stationed in Berlin since the fifties.

He was in his eighties now, but at some point, he and Tatyana had forged an alliance of sorts, and she trusted him.

Tatyana had a knack for making friends, it seemed. There was the cop in Riga, the Clockmaker in Berlin, she'd even made friends with Lance in Syria.

And it wasn't an act.

The alliances were genuine.

Lance called Roth from the plane.

"I just read this file you cobbled together."

"Can you believe it?" Roth said. "I've been hearing whispers about this guy since my first day on the job. He's been there since the very beginning, Lance. He predates all of us."

"And in all that time, he's never signaled a willingness to come over to our side?"

"Not even a hint."

"Ever?"

"Well," Roth said, "decades ago, there was a serious campaign from our side to get him to cross over. There was a meeting arranged, and then, the four men we sent to the meeting ended up dead, their bodies found floating in the River Spree."

"He killed them?"

"That was the consensus at the time," Roth said. "And nothing I've seen since has persuaded me to reassess. This guy has been loyal to the Russians since day one. Right back to the early days, Lance. The Bay of Pigs. President Kennedy. That's how far back he goes."

"And he's still loyal?"

"There's nothing in our system to suggest otherwise, that's for sure."

"Strange position for a Pole to adopt, isn't it? Considering all that's happened since the collapse of the Soviet Union."

"Some men are true believers," Roth said. "And from what I've been able to unearth, this guy has some very personal reasons to explain his position."

"What personal reasons?"

"I haven't confirmed it yet, but it looks like his mother was raped by a German."

"I see."

"So, you know, as far as he's concerned, spying for Russia is his way of ensuring the fascists never rise again."

"Then why is he helping Tatyana?"

"The only thing that explains it," Roth said, "is that he has some sort of personal relationship with her that outweighs his political allegiance."

"That's a big ask from someone with a sixty-year record, isn't it?"

"I don't know that it's that far-fetched," Roth said.

"Would you turn traitor after sixty years of service?"

"For Tatyana? I might bend a rule."

"Very funny," Lance said.

"She had a relationship with you, didn't she," Roth said.

"Of a sort, yes."

"She didn't betray her country, but you helped her, you saved her life, and she remembered that. She formed a loyalty to you that went outside the bounds of her political position. It was personal."

"So that's what she has with the Clockmaker?"

"There's certainly been opportunity for such a relationship to develop. She's been in Berlin on multiple occasions, and the GRU used her repeatedly on particularly dangerous missions. God knows, she'd have had need of an ally of some sort."

"Maybe they had it in for her," Lance said, thinking back to the position she'd been in when he first found her.

"There were some close calls in Berlin," Roth said, "but she always managed to come through intact."

"And you think it's because of the Clockmaker? Some loyalty the two of them shared that went above and beyond their loyalty to the GRU?"

"I think so, yes."

"Then where's Laurel?"

"I know what you're thinking, Lance."

"I'm thinking this Clockmaker was part of the trap."

"Maybe," Roth said, "but has Tatyana ever been wrong about someone before? She has good instincts, Lance. And she told Laurel to go to the Clockmaker."

"No one's right a hundred percent of the time," Lance said.

Roth sighed. "Just tread carefully, Lance. There are a lot of moving pieces in Berlin right now."

"There are always a lot of moving pieces in Berlin," Lance said.

Berlin was a singularly complicated city. Most cities stood clearly in one camp or the other. Washington, blue. Moscow, red. London, blue. Beijing, red.

You always knew whose territory you were operating in.

Hostile or friendly.

And it had a way of coloring every decision you made after that.

But Berlin had always been a creature of its own.

It had gone from being the capital of Hitler's Nazi empire, to one of the principal capitals of the Kremlin's Warsaw Pact, to a beacon of democratic governance and reform as part of the European Union.

Berlin was all things to all men, it seemed.

"Just tread carefully," Roth said. "I think this Clockmaker was Tatyana's friend. If something bad has happened to Laurel, I'd be willing to bet something bad has happened to him too."

54

The plane landed in Berlin, and Lance looked out the window at the dreary day that awaited.

He caught a cab into the city, and his mind focused on the task at hand. Laurel and Tatyana were in trouble, and he couldn't afford to let his own grief, his own rage, cloud his judgment.

Lance had always thought of Berlin as a city of bones.

A city of graves.

He hoped to add one more before this day was up.

The cab moved slowly through the afternoon traffic, and hot air from the car's heater blew in his face. It was so warm inside the cab that flakes of snow melted the instant they touched his window.

"Could you turn down the heat?" he said to the driver in German.

The driver nodded and turned it down a little.

"You mind if I smoke?" he said.

Lance shrugged.

As soon as they reached the Kurfürstendamm, Lance told the driver, "I'll walk from here."

He got out, and the cold air revived him.

The street was quiet, and it was beginning to get dark.

A few people went in and out of the stores, and some sat in warm coats and scarves in the street-side cafés, smoking and sipping drinks.

Lance walked on along the street and, as he approached the Clockmaker's shop, even from a distance, could tell something was not right.

Two police cruisers were parked on the pedestrianized street, their lights flashing, and access to the shop had been blocked with police tape.

A van belonging to a local television station was parked outside, and Lance approached one of the cameramen.

"What happened here?"

"Big story," the cameraman said, sucking on the last of a cigarette before flicking it away. "The murder at the Memorial Church. This was the guy's store?"

"What murder at the Memorial Church?"

"Don't you watch the news?"

"I must have missed it."

"Someone was shot at point-blank range. An old man. Right in front of the statue of Christ."

Lance shook his head.

"They're saying it might have been some religiously motivated thing."

"That's shocking," Lance said.

The cameraman sighed. "You do this job long enough, nothing will shock you after a while."

"I believe it," Lance said.

The cameraman leaned in closer to Lance and lowered his voice. "It hasn't been made public, but the body smelled like piss," he said.

"People lose muscle control when they're shot like that," Lance said.

"No," the cameraman said, shaking his head. "Not from the old man. From the shooter."

"You're not serious," Lance said.

"That's what the cops said. Whoever killed the old man went ahead and pissed on him."

"Why would someone do that?"

The cameraman shook his head.

"In front of the statue of Christ?" Lance said.

The cameraman continued shaking his head.

"What's the world coming to?" Lance said, walking away.

The Remembrance Church wasn't far, and he made his way directly to it. When he got there, he saw even more police cruisers and television people than had been at the Clockmaker's shop.

There were police guarding the church, keeping the public out, and Lance didn't think he'd be able to get in without causing a stir.

He walked once around the church, mingling among the passersby and rubberneckers who'd gathered outside the police tape.

He counted six CCTV cameras pointed at the church from different angles and was able to get close enough to five of them to read the serial numbers printed on embossed labels on their protective housing.

Then he crossed the street and entered a bustling café that overlooked the church. It was a traditional place with ornate cast iron tables and waitresses in black dresses and white aprons.

"Coffee, please," he said to his waitress, "and a glass of water."

Then he pulled out his phone and called Roth.

"What's going on?" Roth said. "What did you find?"

"Your Clockmaker's dead," Lance said.

"How?"

"It's going to be all over the news here. Executed at point-blank range," Lance said.

"Executed?"

"Inside the Kaiser Wilhelm church, two minutes from his shop."

"That means...".

"It means whoever did it has Laurel. I'm surprised your team didn't already tell you all this."

"I don't have a team on this, Lance. I'm afraid to extend the loop."

"Well, I think we're going to have to. I took down the serial numbers of some police CCTV cameras around the church."

"German police cooperation will take time."

"How much time?"

"You know how they are with civil liberties. They have the strictest privacy laws in the world. Everything requires judicial review. Civil oversight. It's a nightmare."

"So we're looking at?"

"Twelve hours at least."

"I can't wait twelve hours."

"I know that, Lance."

"Can't we hack in? Take what we need?"

"They're an ally."

"Laurel and Tatyana are out there, Roth. Grow a pair."

"If we want to follow the killer," Roth said, "I think the fastest way will be to use Keyhole satellite surveillance."

"Just get me a location," Lance said. "I don't care how you do it."

"I'll stand up a team," Roth said. "You might as well give me those serial numbers too."

Lance read out the numbers, and Roth wrote them down.

"One more thing," Lance said before letting him go. "It looks like someone took this execution personally."

"The Russians take everything personally."

"Well, this time, their man pissed on the Clockmaker's body after he'd killed him."

"Pissed on him?"

"Yes," Lance said.

"In a church?"

"That's right," Lance said.

He hung up and raised his hand for the waitress's attention. He didn't think it would take long for Roth to get back with more information.

"I'll have another coffee," he said to her. "Vienna style," he added as she hurried off.

She was back a moment later with a coffee topped with whipped cream, served in a glass.

Lance leaned back on the chair and watched the police across the street. He looked at the church, its stunted steeple, its caved-in roof.

One thing was certain.

Tatyana and Laurel were in trouble.

He lit a cigarette and sipped his coffee. An hour later, Roth was calling back.

55

Roth was talking as soon as Lance picked up the phone.

"The CCTV's been tampered with."

"What are you talking about?"

"The cameras you gave me. The NSA was able to tap into their feeds, but they've already been deleted by an XML script."

"The system wasn't secured?"

"It has the usual protocols, but it looks like these files were deleted from the inside."

"From inside Berlin police?"

"Yes."

"That's just what we need."

"There was a partial recovery of the feed from the sixth camera, but it's been severely degraded."

"Maybe your guys can clean it up."

"I don't want to get your hopes up on a facial match. But what we might be able to get is the exact time the assassin left the church."

"Get the satellite guys working on it. If they can get a

visual on the assassin, they might be able to track him all the way to his location."

"We'll see," Roth said. "The Russians have been interfering with our European Keyhole feed. It's beginning to become an issue."

"They need to figure it out," Lance said. "If we can't track this guy from the church, the trail goes cold."

Lance hung up. He knew he was being impatient. There were a lot of ways they could investigate the Clockmaker's murder. The problem was, all of them took time.

Time that he didn't have.

Laurel and Tatyana's lives were in the balance.

He finished his coffee and ordered more, chain-smoked cigarettes. It was another hour before Roth called again.

"Lance, the Keyhole guys found something. I'm patching the analyst in now."

A voice came on the line. "This is Lieutenant Harper of the Tenth Space Warning Squadron at Cavalier Air Force Station."

"What have you got for me, Harper?"

"The man leaving the church, we weren't able to get a facial."

"What were you able to get?"

"We were able to tag him. That allows the algorithm to trace his movements for as long as he remains on the surface."

"And how far were you able to track him?"

"He went from the church to the Detlev Rohwedder Building."

"What the hell is the Detlev Rohwedder Building?" Lance said.

"It's an old wing of the Air Ministry Building," Roth said. "Are you familiar with it?"

"I know it," Lance said.

When it was constructed by the Nazis, it was the largest office building in all of Europe. It was the archetype of what later became known as intimidation architecture. It was a seven-story, stone and concrete monstrosity that occupied all of the space between Wilhelmstraße, Prinz-Albrecht-Straße, and Leipziger Straße, as well as the site formerly occupied by the Prussian War Ministry. It was so large that even today, staff needed bicycles to get around its more than four miles of corridors.

It was the type of bureaucratic nightmare written about by Franz Kafka, a world unto itself that dehumanized the individual before the immense power of the nation-state, making them feel almost like insects.

Given how many acres of space it occupied, it was something of a miracle that it suffered no significant damage during the War, and as soon as the Soviets took control, Stalin had it transformed from a symbol of totalitarian Fascism to a virtually identical symbol of totalitarian Communism.

There were many rumors about the building, including that it still maintained its original tunnel connections to the underground network of bunkers built by the Nazis.

"The CIA has intel that both Stasi and KGB agents made use of the tunnel network during the Soviet era," Roth said.

"If the Russians were going to hide Laurel and Tatyana," Lance said, "an underground tunnel network would be the place."

"I'll see what I can get in terms of diagrams and maps," Roth said, "but anything I find will be very limited. Those tunnels were kept under tight wraps by everyone who ever had access to them."

The analyst spoke up again. "From what we can tell, it

looks like the target entered the Detlev Rohwedder Building off Leipziger Straße."

"All right."

"There are no doors or windows facing Leipziger," the analyst said.

"Which suggests some kind of secret entrance."

"Correct," the analyst said.

"All right, good work, Harper," Roth said. "Lance, get to Leipziger Straße, and I'll see what else I can find that may be of use to you."

Lance left some money on the table and left the café. He was able to hail a taxi from Budapester Straße, and while he was in the cab, the exact location where the target had disappeared into the building was sent to his phone.

Lance was armed with two fifth-generation Glock 17 semi-automatic pistols with sound-suppression. They'd been altered by the French military and were perfect when discretion was required.

He got out of the cab close to the location he'd been sent and waited for the taxi to drive away. The street was completely empty, and he walked up and down the wall of the building, searching for any clue as to where the assassin had gone.

The walls were of solid, chiseled limestone. Over fifty quarries had been used to supply the construction, and looking at the expanse of smooth stone in front of him, Lance could see why.

The lower three feet of the wall had a travertine façade, and etched into it was an intricate crosshatch pattern. Lance examined the lines of the pattern more closely, it was difficult to see in the dim light, but there appeared to be even finer, vertical and horizontal lines inside the coarser crosshatching.

If you knew what you were looking for, and Lance had a head start, it was almost possible to make out the very faint outline of an entryway. It wasn't a door, exactly. It was lower, rising from the concrete sidewalk upward about two feet. It almost looked like an old coal delivery chute, the kind used in the nineteenth century, but the building was too modern to require coal deliveries of that kind.

There was no way anyone looking at the building, or walking by on the street, would ever have seen it.

Lance pressed against it, and nothing happened. There was no sign of a handle or lock. He pressed against it, against each of the individual stones, then stepped back to get a look at it from a distance.

And then he saw it, embedded into the horizontal, vertical, and diagonal crosshatched lines, he could make out, inscribed in a classic serif font, the letters HG.

Hermann Göring.

He'd been head of the German Aviation Ministry when the building was originally constructed.

Beneath them was a smooth protuberance, about the size of the back of a soup spoon, and he pressed it.

Nothing happened.

He looked again, and this time, saw a foot above Göring's initials, another pattern.

AH.

Adolf Hitler.

And a second protuberance.

He tried pressing them both simultaneously and heard the sound of a mechanical latch clanking against a steel plate. He pushed the wall again, and this time, it moved.

It was heavy and suspended on heavy hinges, but it swung inward like an old letterbox.

Lance looked up and down the street, which was still completely deserted, and then slid in through the opening.

It was dark inside, and he used his cigarette lighter for light.

He was in a service tunnel, large enough for a man to walk through at a hunch. He checked his phone to see if Roth had sent any more information, but he hadn't.

He proceeded along the corridor in the direction of the oldest portion of the Air Ministry Building. The corridor remained straight for about a hundred yards, then turned to the right and connected to what appeared to be an older set of tunnels. He followed the older tunnel, which ran steadily downward, until it came to a large, steel doorway, like the door to a bank vault.

He turned a series of handles, and the door cranked open with a groan.

The tunnel beyond the door was more cavernous, wide enough to drive a vehicle in, and he followed it for a few hundred yards until it opened up into a large chamber cut out of solid rock. Lance realized he was in an underground bunker built by the Nazis.

56

Zhukovsky looked over the names of the men on his list.

They were the cream of the crop.

The very best the GRU's training facility in Saint Petersburg had to offer, and of the batch he'd been sent, he'd whittled the list down to just twenty-four men.

And those men had been utterly brutalized. He'd put them through the meat grinder. They'd been subjected to torture and humiliation. They'd been forced to torture animals and prisoners from the prison in Pskov.

He'd also made them kill prisoners.

They'd done it in a number of ways.

Holding them under water.

Slitting their throats.

Shooting them.

It was grisly work, and not all of the recruits could go through with it. And of those that could, fewer still had been able to do it to female prisoners.

Zhukovsky had considered sending for children from

the state orphanage in Ostrov, but he'd been afraid too many of them would fail that test.

Kirov had said he'd need two squads, twenty-two men. He couldn't afford to lose another dozen to weak stomachs. He was confident these men were up to the task he would set them, and was ready to tell Kirov as much.

The base was remote, deep in the forested, marshy territory that marked the border region between Russia and Latvia, and that isolation was key. It had allowed Zhukovsky to conduct his training in a way that brought the men into a world of his making.

It was a brutal place.

A dark place.

Many recruits died.

All those who chose not to continue with the training had been murdered.

The remaining men didn't know it yet, but they were about to find out.

Zhukovsky wanted there to be no doubt in their minds that the mission they were about to be given was essential. When they heard the details, they would balk. Their minds would rebel against it. They would need *encouragement.*

He went out to the courtyard in front of his tent and had them assemble.

"Men," he barked, looking at them.

They were a sullen lot now. Eyes downcast. Spirits crushed. Ready to do whatever they were told.

There was a dump truck in the clearing, and Zhukovsky drew their attention to it.

"I have an important cargo for you to see. The time for our operation is drawing near, and if any of you feel unable to carry out the orders that you are going to be given, I want you to know what the consequences look like."

Zhukovsky walked over to the truck and climbed up into the cab. He turned on the engine, then pressed the button to raise up the bed of the truck and tip out its contents. A dozen half-decomposed corpses, still in their military khakis, slid out of the truck and formed a pile on the ground.

Zhukovsky got out of the truck. The rancid stench immediately assailed him, and he had to struggle not to gag. The corpses, even in the freezing weather, had decomposed to a state where larvae could be seen crawling in the eye sockets and mouths of the dead men.

"You men continued with the regimen when these cowards opted out," Zhukovsky said. "I know it's been a difficult road, but we're almost at the end of it, and the Motherland rewards those who sacrifice in her name. I've been authorized to pay each of you a bounty of fifty-thousand rubles for each kill you rack up on our upcoming operation."

The men knew nothing of the operation yet, but the fact that there would be killing went without saying.

"Now bury the bodies," he said to them.

The ground was frozen solid, but the hard labor would do them good. He also wanted to make sure they got up close and personal with their former comrades. There could be no doubt in their minds that if they didn't go through with their mission, only death awaited.

What they didn't know was that Zhukovsky had been ordered to kill them all after the operation anyway. Kirov wanted absolutely no chance that word of the operation would leak, and that meant there could be no witnesses.

It was that matter that Zhukovsky meant to address now, and he went into his tent and told his orderly to leave him. Then he dialed Kirov's number.

"What is it, Zhukovsky? I've got enough on my mind."

"The men are ready," Zhukovsky said. "Two squads, as requested."

"They're ready to do *anything*?" Kirov said.

"Anything," Zhukovsky confirmed.

"Including women and children."

"That's correct, sir."

"Very well. Then stand by for further orders. I'll give you the go-ahead personally."

"There was one matter I wanted to bring up with you, sir, if I may," Zhukovsky said.

"What's that, Zhukovsky?"

"Liquidating the squads, sir. I think it's a waste."

"Don't tell me you've gone soft," Kirov said. "You of all people. I wouldn't believe it."

"It's not that, sir."

"You couldn't care less about the lives of these men, and don't try to tell me otherwise."

"No, sir, it's a more practical concern. I've been overseeing their training personally, and I have to report, I've never seen killing squads like this in my life. They're ready to do anything. In the right hands, they'll prove to be a very valuable tool."

"I see," Kirov said.

"Very valuable, sir."

"I'll pass your suggestion on to the president," Kirov said.

"Very good, sir."

"If there's a change in the instructions, I'll let you know."

"Thank you, sir."

"But unless you hear otherwise, Zhukovsky, the existing order stands. All men are to be liquidated on return from the operation."

"Yes, sir."

57

L ance continued along the tunnel, down a set of steel steps, and into another large chamber. There, he found a very old wooden crate that still contained old Karabiner 98k Mausers. They'd been standard issue for the German Army during the Second World War, and it was clear they'd been there since Hitler's days.

It seemed the rumors were true. The tunnels really had been kept secret from the incoming German government after reunification.

He went through the cavern, into another corridor, and down another long tunnel until he saw a faint glow in the distance. The smell of fumes filled the tunnel, and he heard a gasoline generator running.

He approached cautiously, and when he got close enough, made out the voices of men speaking German.

He crept closer and saw that one of the men was giving instructions to two others. The area was lit up with electric lights of the kind used by construction workers. There were also some large fans blowing the generator fumes down the tunnel. As Lance's eyes adjusted to the light, he saw that two people, unconscious, had been tied to two dollies the way a psychiatric patient might be tied to a bed. The dollies rested precariously at the top of a set of stairs so that if the prisoners struggled, they would be in danger of falling.

Lance didn't need to see their faces to know that the two people tied to the dollies were Tatyana and Laurel.

It looked like the men were preparing to move them.

Lance felt a flood of relief rush through his body.

He wasn't too late.

They were still alive, and they were still there.

He crouched behind some slabs of stone and drew his pistols. He wanted to question the leader of the men, so he aimed at one of the others, steadied his hand against the rock, and pulled the trigger. Even with the sound-suppression, the enclosed area amplified the sharp pulse of the gunshot.

One of the men's heads jerked to the side, and he fell in a heap to the ground.

The man next to him instantly dropped to one knee and returned fire.

Lance ducked as bullets flew all over the tunnel, ricocheting in every direction. Shards of rock flew everywhere, and the dust created a cloud.

Lance glanced over the top of the rock before ducking back down.

He was worried about the way the dollies were positioned. The slightest push from one of the men would send them over the edge, and he didn't think the women would survive the fall.

He peered around the rock and saw that one of the men was now pointing his gun at Laurel's head.

"Whoever you are," he called out, "you better come out." He spoke English, but his accent was so thick it was hard to make out what he was saying. "If you don't come out, this girl gets it."

Lance swung out from the rock, aimed for the man's chest, and pulled the trigger. The man fell to the ground and dropped his gun. He reached for it again, and Lance shot him in the arm. Then he rolled back behind the rock as a hail of fire came from the third man.

He waited for the shooting to stop before looking again.

The third man was gone.

He was running down the staircase the two dollies were at the top of, and Lance couldn't take a shot without risking hitting Laurel or Tatyana.

He ran toward the chamber, jumping down the large slabs of rock that led into it. When he reached the steel gangway, he approached the dollies carefully. He wanted to give chase to the man running, but Laurel and Tatyana looked like they were in rough shape.

The man he'd shot in the chest and arm was on the ground, still alive. Lance searched him for weapons and found some cable ties. He pulled his wrists behind his back and tied them.

"Laurel, Tatyana," he said. "It's me, Lance."

They'd been drugged, but as it dawned on them who he was, he could see the relief in their faces. He brought their dollies back from the edge of the stairs and began opening their restraints.

Tatyana was badly injured. She'd been shot in the calf, and the only treatment she'd received was a tight, cloth bandage. Lance looked at the wound and could tell the bullet was still inside.

The wound would be infected soon, if it wasn't already.

"We need to get you two out of here," he said.

"You need to go after that man," Tatyana said, slurring

her words badly. "He got information out of me. I couldn't help it. My mind wasn't clear."

Lance looked down the steps and knew she was right. There was no telling what information he'd managed to get from her, or Laurel for that matter, and from the look of Laurel, she was even more drugged than Tatyana was.

He nodded toward Laurel and said to Tatyana, "You're going to have to look after her. She's completely out of it."

Neither of them could stand, they'd been restrained in position for too long, and Lance helped them to the ground, where they sat.

"Watch that guy," he said to Tatyana, handing her one of his guns.

He wasn't comfortable leaving them, they were in bad shape, and neither of them was in possession of her faculties, but there was no time for anything else.

He ran down the steps and chased the man who'd gotten away. There were dozens of tunnels and caves, all pitch black, and he had no idea how many ways out of the complex there were. He was unlikely to catch up to the man before he disappeared completely.

He ran down the main corridor for hundreds of yards, and eventually, it opened out into an enormous cavern. It looked large enough to be an underground train terminal, and he knew it was part of Hitler's plans for a new underground city.

At the far end of the cavern was the ancient steel hull of an enormous tank. The scale of the machine was monstrous.

And Lance recognized it as a prototype for the largest tank ever built.

He'd seen a prototype just like it before, in a museum. The Kubinka Tank Museum outside Moscow contained what was thought to be the only prototype of the Panzer VIII Maus, a Nazi super tank that was one of the planned *Wunderwaffe,* or super-weapons, that would win the war for Germany.

Lance saw now that the Nazis had built at least two of the monsters.

It weighed over one-hundred-eighty tons and was armed with two main cannons. The first was a 128 millimeter Krupp gun that could take out any Allied tank at a range of over two miles. The second was a smaller, 70 millimeter gun for faster moving targets.

It was so perfectly preserved that it looked like it would be possible to fire up the engine and drive it right out of the cavern.

He looked out across the enormous space and counted eight separate tunnels leading out of it. He had no idea which way the man had fled, and in any case, was in a hurry to get back to the women.

He'd get the man another time.

58

As Lance made his way back to the women, he saw something on the ground. It was a pistol, the old Browning he'd given Tatyana a long time ago in a hotel room in Damascus.

He picked it up and, when he got back, gave it to her.

"Thank you," she said, handing him his Glock.

She looked like she was doing a little better, and Laurel's drugs seemed to be wearing off too.

"I need to get you two to some medical attention," Lance said.

"How do we get out of here?" Tatyana said.

"The same way I got here, but first, we have to decide what we're going to do with this guy."

He was standing over the captive. He'd been shot twice and would bleed out soon if he didn't receive medical attention.

"Tell me," Lance said to him. "Who do you work for?"

"You know who I work for," he said.

"The Kremlin."

"Yes," the man said.

"Didn't you hear?" Lance said, "The Soviets lost. They had their day. Now they're done."

The man spat at him, and Lance stepped back. "Feisty," he said, "for a man that's about to be left down here to bleed out alone."

"You wouldn't leave me down here."

"Sure I would," Lance said.

The man shook his head.

"What were you going to do with these two women?" Lance said.

"He came in at the end," Tatyana said. "It was the other guy, the one who got away, that was running the show."

"What were you brought in for then?" Lance said to the man.

"Go fuck yourself."

Lance pulled his cigarette lighter from his pocket and said, "Why don't I set your hair on fire? See if that jogs your memory."

"No," the man said, as Lance raised the lighter to his head. The air filled with the acrid smell of burning hair, and the man said, "No, stop. I'll talk."

"Talk, then," Lance said.

"Prochnow needed help transporting the women," he said. "He'd been ordered to get them to Russian soil."

"What Russian soil?"

"We were going to drive them to the Kaliningrad border. The Kremlin was to send a crew to meet us in Poland. Someone wanted them back in Russia. Alive."

Lance nodded.

It sounded plausible.

It would take more than one man to get the women to a vehicle and out of the city. Hence the dollies and the extra manpower.

He turned to Laurel and Tatyana. "It's time to get you two out of here."

He helped them to their feet, and the man said, "What about me?"

"What about you?" Lance said.

"I'm going to die down here."

"You might not die. Someone might find you."

"No one will find me," he said. "No one knows what's down here."

Lance shrugged. He helped Laurel and Tatyana up the rock slabs, back toward the tunnel he'd come down, as the man cried out for them not to leave him there.

"It would have been kinder to shoot him," Tatyana said as they approached the round steel door.

"I wasn't feeling kind," Lance said.

When they reached the opening back out to the street, Lance went first and made sure the coast was clear. When he was satisfied, he pulled Laurel and Tatyana out, attracting as little attention as possible. They walked down the deserted street to the corner, through the courtyard of some government buildings, and out to a busier street where Lance was able to flag down a cab.

"Where to?" the driver said, eyeing them in his mirror.

The women looked in no fit state, both had been drugged, and Tatyana's leg was drenched with blood.

The driver's eyes widened, and he said, "What's going on here?"

Lance took his wallet from one pocket and a gun from the other.

"In Colombia," he said to the driver, "they have a saying, *plata o plomo*. Silver or lead. Which do you choose?"

The driver looked Lance in the eye, then looked at the two women.

"Please," Tatyana said, "believe it or not, he's actually our friend."

The driver sighed.

"I'm going to make a call," he said to the driver, "then I'll tell you where we're going."

He called Roth.

"We're out," he said.

"All three of you?"

"All three of us. I need a safe house, and Tatyana's going to need to see a doctor."

"All right," Roth said. "I'll send you a location."

Lance hung up, and a moment later, his phone dinged with the address of an apartment in the Bergmannkiez district. He didn't give the driver the address but told him to drop them at the main train station. At the train station, they switched cabs, and the second driver didn't object to the condition the women were in. Lance told him to take them to Bergmann Straße.

They then walked the last stretch to their building, with Laurel and Lance helping Tatyana walk.

The building was an elegant tenement from the nineteenth century with a wrought iron gate in front of the door. Roth had sent a code to get inside the building, and Lance typed it into a metal keypad. From the hallway, they got into an old-style elevator that was made like a cage.

The elevator brought them to the fourth floor, and from there, they entered the apartment.

The apartment was clean, simple, with minimal décor and a marble fireplace that housed a gas insert.

Lance waited by the window, smoking and watching the street while the women washed up in the bathroom. Laurel helped Tatyana into one of the bedrooms, then joined Lance in the living room.

"When will the doctor be here?" she said.

"Not long."

They looked at each other awkwardly until Laurel said, "I'm going to make coffee."

"There isn't any," Lance said.

"You checked?"

He nodded.

That seemed to upset her, and she slumped onto the sofa. The fireplace was gas-fueled, and Lance went over to it and switched it on.

"I'll go buy some supplies," he said. "You two are going to need some fresh clothing and toiletries."

Laurel nodded.

He gave her a Glock. "Don't take your eye off the doctor."

She took the gun and leaned back on the sofa.

"And don't fall asleep," he said.

"And you quit barking orders."

"I'll be back soon."

"We'll be fine," Laurel said.

Lance left the apartment and went down to the ground floor. He had no intention of leaving the building just yet.

He trusted Roth, but the doctor could be anyone.

And besides, he had no idea how secure the Berlin safe house network was. There was always a chance the Russians knew about the place.

He found a place to hide on the ground floor and waited for the doctor to arrive. It didn't take long. The man looked like a doctor. He carried a leather bag of the type doctors carried.

He knew the code for entering the building and acted like he'd been there before. He got into the elevator, and Lance raced up the steps to keep up with it. He was on the third floor when the elevator reached the fourth, and he stopped running. He remained out of sight and waited to see what the doctor did next.

From where he was, he could see the door of the apartment. If the doctor put a foot out of step, it would be lights out.

The doctor pulled something from his pocket. Lance drew his gun and aimed at the man's head.

It was a cell phone. The doctor looked at the screen, then knocked on the door.

Lance took his finger off the trigger.

Laurel came to the door, and the man said, "I'm the doctor. Levi Roth sent me."

59

Both women were asleep when Lance returned with the supplies. The doctor had seen to Tatyana's leg, and it looked like he'd bandaged Laurel's wounds also.

Lance had picked up enough takeout from a local Chinese place to feed six people, and he made tea before waking the women.

They sat together in the living room by the fire, Tatyana laid out on the sofa and Laurel on an enormous, upholstered armchair.

They were relaxed.

At ease.

When they were done eating, Lance went to the refrigerator and took out a bottle of chardonnay he'd picked up.

He poured three glasses, and Tatyana made a toast.

"The team's all back together," she said.

Lance glanced at Laurel then away.

"The man who captured you," he said, changing the subject, "he was German."

"His name is Prochnow," Tatyana said. "Christoph Prochnow."

"Who does he work for?"

"He's GRU. I never worked with him directly, but I knew of him. Apparently, he's more loyal to the Kremlin than any Russian."

Lance raised his eyebrow.

Tatyana was looking at Laurel, then she said, "You went to see the Clockmaker, didn't you?"

Laurel nodded. "He wasn't there."

"He's dead, isn't he?"

"He's dead," Lance said.

Tatyana said nothing for a moment, then she said, "I thought maybe that was a dream. Or a nightmare."

"Whatever happened, it wasn't your fault," Laurel said.

"He drugged me. He got me to talk. I gave him up."

"It wasn't your fault, Tatyana."

"He trusted me. He put his life in my hands. He'd been operating here since long before any of us was born, and now, because of me, he's dead."

"You had no choice," Lance said. "You were drugged. You know what those serums do."

Tatyana shook her head. "There's always a choice," she said. "What I said, it killed him, as surely as if I pulled the trigger myself."

Laurel cleared her throat. "If we're making confessions," she said, "I was the one who sent you blind into a trap."

"I knew the risk I was taking," Tatyana said.

"It's all my fault," Laurel said. "I'm Group Director. I'm the one who's supposed to interpret the data. I'm the one who's supposed to call the next move. I messed up."

"You didn't mess up," Tatyana said. "We needed to know

what Agata Zarina was running from. We needed to know what information she had."

"And we still need to," Lance said.

They looked at him.

"We still don't know what message it was she was trying to get to Tatyana, but I think it's safe to say, whatever it was, it was important."

"Important enough for GRU assassins to chase her through three countries," Tatyana said.

"There's another clue," Lance said.

Both women looked at him.

"When I was trying to find you, the satellite operator said they were having problems with the Keyhole feed."

"That's right," Laurel said. "There's interference from a new Russian satellite."

"Is it affecting the entire Keyhole network?" Lance said.

"No," just one.

"The one above us."

She nodded.

"They're getting ready to make a move," Lance said. "I bet dollars to donuts they're planning an invasion."

"Of Latvia?" Laurel said. "Are they ready to run that risk?"

"Molotov's emboldened," Lance said. "He blew up the embassy, and the president did nothing."

"But an attack on NATO. That's going to lead to nuclear war."

They both looked at Tatyana. She said, "Molotov wants to reconstitute the entire USSR," she said. "It's no secret. Invading the Baltic States would be the first step."

Laurel drained her glass. "I need a cigarette," she said.

Lance handed her one and held up his lighter.

She sucked on the cigarette and exhaled. "It all leads

back to Zarina," she said. "If we knew what she'd found, we'd know what Molotov was planning."

"She was your friend?" Lance said to Tatyana.

"Not so much my *friend*," Tatyana said. "She and I had a lot in common. We were in the same boat."

"What boat?" Lance said.

"She was a woman in over her head," Tatyana said. "She was scared. And so was I."

"Could she have been mixed up with the GRU?" Lance said.

"You mean, was she a traitor?"

Lance nodded.

"She was targeted by the Kremlin," Tatyana said. "They made attempts to turn her, but I don't think they succeeded. If they had, she'd have sold me out too. And that never happened."

"Roth thought that if she found out something about Russian invasion plans, she'd have come to you," Laurel said.

Tatyana nodded. "I think he's right. And I think that's what cost her her life."

"We need to find out what she was doing before they attacked her in Riga," Lance said.

He looked at Tatyana. Tears were streaming down her face. He turned to Laurel, and the expression on his face told her it was her job to say something.

"Tatyana," Laurel said.

"Sorry," Tatyana said. "It's just... it seems that becoming my friend is a very dangerous decision."

Laurel got up and put her hand on Tatyana's shoulder.

"I'll call Roth," Lance said, taking his phone from his pocket and stepping over to the window.

"Lance," Roth said. "Are the girls all right?"

"They're fine. Your doctor patched them up."

"Tatyana's leg?"

"She'll walk."

"We're at a dead-end here," Lance said. "We're no closer to knowing what Agata Zarina found out. Like you said, it looks like the Kremlin's set its sights on Latvia, but we're just guessing."

"You remember your friend from the Tenth Space Warning Squadron?"

"Lieutenant Harper," Lance said.

"I've had him hone in on everything we knew about Zarina's movements before her death. Are Laurel and Tatyana with you?"

"They're right here."

"Put me on speaker."

Lance put Roth on speaker and went back over to the women. Tatyana had stopped crying, and the look on her face almost dared Lance to make fun of her.

"The Keyhole data's still spotty," Roth said, "but I had my guy trace as much of Zarina's movements as he could. I also had the NSA hack into the Latvian national police database."

"What did they find, Roth?"

"Well," Roth said, "this all seems to have started when a small Latvian forestry plane went down along the Russian border."

"Shot down?"

"That's what Zarina went to find out. She traveled out to the border region and then returned to the capital in a real hurry. When she got back, she reported to her superior, then went home. That night, she was attacked in her apartment."

"Did she file her report before she was attacked?" Laurel said.

"She did," Roth said, "but looking at the Latvian database, it appears as if that report has been deleted."

"Latvia's an ally," Lance said. "Why don't we just call them and ask what the hell's going on?"

"I've been trying to get in touch with the Latvians," Roth said. "Zarina was in the national security division. Her commanding officer is the man I've been trying to contact."

"And he's been dodging your calls?" Lance said.

"Looks that way."

"And he would have had access to Zarina's report? He could have had it deleted."

"Right," Roth said.

"What's his name?" Lance said.

Roth shuffled through some documents and said, "Kuzis. Alfreds Kuzis."

Tatyana repeated the name, correcting the pronunciation.

"You know him?" Roth said.

"I've heard the name," Tatyana said. "But I don't know anything specific about him. He's an important man in Riga. That's all I know."

"Roth," Lance said, "can Harper scan the border region where the plane went down? See if he can spot signs of anything suspicious on the Russian side of the border?"

"He can try," Roth said. "Like I said, Russia's been jamming the KH network."

"Jamming the UHF signals?" Lance said.

"I know," Roth said.

"How are we supposed to...".

"We're looking at workarounds, Lance."

Lance muttered under his breath, and Roth said, "What was that?"

"Signal's cutting out," Lance said. "Just get Harper to

trawl over the area again and get back to us if he finds anything."

He hung up the phone and looked at Laurel and Tatyana.

"How would you two feel about a trip to Riga?"

Kirov was lying face down on a wooden massage bed while not one but two young men in white cotton shorts and shirts dug their fingers and knuckles into the knots in his back. His face was in a leather-cushioned ring, and through the hole in the middle, he could see their feet, in plastic slippers, moving around him.

"Lower," he said, gasping in agony as they worked their way into the deepest recesses of his muscles.

He watched their feet and wondered, when he faced them, if he'd be able to tell whose feet had been whose.

He was naked, and was about to turn over so they could begin the second portion of their _service_, when his phone rang.

"Damn it," he said, grabbing the phone. He saw Prochnow's name on the screen.

"Christoph, this better be fucking good."

"It's not good, sir," Prochnow said, and Kirov could tell from his voice that he was close to panic.

"What is it?"

"They're gone, sir."

"Who's gone."

Prochnow hesitated, and Kirov said, "Both of them?"

"Yes, sir."

"How could that happen?"

"Sir, Roth's got another asset in Berlin."

Kirov thought of what would happen to him if the president found out about this and barked into the phone, "I don't need to tell you that this is a big fucking problem, do I, Christoph?"

"No, you don't, sir."

"I should have you killed for this."

There was a long pause. Kirov looked up at the two men. They were beginning to get started without him, and he watched as one of them stripped out of his shorts.

He didn't know how he was going to deal with this. It was all Sherbakov's fault. He'd sent agents to that imbecile's apartment, but it was empty.

"Can you fix this?" he said weakly to Prochnow.

"I don't know how, sir."

"Who took them?"

"A man. He found the tunnels."

"How is that possible?"

"I went straight from the church to the secret entrance."

"Why didn't you take precautions?"

"Sir, you told me the tracking satellites were degraded."

"Someone might have followed you."

"No, sir. No one followed me."

Kirov sighed. This was a problem. This was a big problem. It could cost him his life, and he knew it. He'd known it from the moment Sherbakov made his mistake.

But he had no choice.

If he was going to get out of this alive, the only way was to keep going.

"Did you get a look at the man?" he said to Prochnow.

"I did not, but I think we both know who it was."

Kirov gritted his teeth. "Yes," he said, "I think we do."

He looked at his masseurs. They were playing with each other on the bed, looking at him, oblivious to the disastrous news he'd just received.

He was waiting for Prochnow to beg. He was waiting for him to begin crying, and pleading, and apologizing.

Prochnow wasn't apologizing. He wasn't begging for his life. He could see the situation for what it was. Kirov was in as much trouble as he was.

They would both get through this or die together.

"We can't tell anyone about this," Kirov said.

"I understand, sir."

There wasn't a hint of relief in Prochnow's voice.

"I'm going to have to keep it from the president."

"I can be in Riga in a matter of hours, sir."

"Yes," Kirov said. "Get to Riga. If there's any chance of us pulling this thing off now, it will require everything we can throw at it."

61

Harper was exhausted. He'd received direct orders from Roth to scan the Latvian border with Russia and had been trawling over the region for eight hours straight, but it was useless. The Russian interference with his UHF feed was getting worse and worse. He should have been able to read the headlines in a newspaper, but at times now, his resolution was so bad he could barely tell a lake from a village.

He'd told his superiors he'd be better off switching to civilian satellite feeds, but everyone knew that would be admitting defeat. There was no way those satellites would pick up the movements Roth needed.

Harper rubbed his eyes. He needed to clock off. His relief was supposed to be there by now but still hadn't shown.

He looked at his watch. Fifteen minutes late.

His hand absently reached for the donuts, but all he found was the sugar at the bottom of the box.

He was about to call his supervisor when a red blip pulsed from Cosmos 2543. Alarm bells started ringing.

Not literally.

Harper was in a heated, steel shipping container in a remote part of North Dakota that had for decades played an over-sized role in America's system of Cold War defenses.

There were no actual alarm bells.

There were no barracks full of men in boots, ready to hit the ground running.

Apart from a small weapons room and enough weapons for the twenty-four armed personnel stationed at the base, there were no weapons.

The alarm bells were in Harper's mind.

Because the little red blip he'd just seen, if he wasn't gravely mistaken, was the equivalent of a twenty-first-century Pearl Harbor.

He began typing on his keyboard to confirm that what he'd just seen wasn't a glitch, then pinged the KH-11 Keyhole/CRYSTAL satellite.

He got no response.

His heart pounded in his chest.

Was this it?

Was this the moment space became a contested arena. Everyone knew it would happen eventually. There were treaties claiming space would never become a war zone, but they weren't worth the paper they were written on.

The US military ran on Keyhole, and as soon as the Russians and Chinese developed the capability to challenge them, the temptation would be too great not to do it.

There were four Keyhole satellites, at four opposite poles over the planet, and they were the military's eyes on the earth's surface.

When the Pentagon published detailed photographs of a North Korean nuclear plant, or an Iranian launch site, or a

Russian aircraft carrier under construction, those photos came from a Keyhole satellite.

While spy planes and drones could later go in for a closer look, the ability to scan the entire surface of the globe existed solely because of the Keyhole constellation.

The network also supplied the US military with its top-level secure communications ability, which handled the encoding for the most sensitive communications, such as strike orders, the targeting of guided weaponry, and the navigation of supersonic aircraft.

And unless Harper was grossly mistaken, one of the four Keyhole satellites had just disappeared from his screen.

He pinged it again. The response should have been near-instantaneous. The speed of light.

Instead, he got something he'd never seen before.

An animated loading spinner, as if he was waiting for a Netflix stream to buffer.

He tried a hard link to the satellite, and the message was rejected.

Then he tried to access the data stream that came from the Keyhole constellation's combined stream.

He almost fell off his chair. One-quarter of the globe, like the thick slice stretching from the north pole to the south, and from an imaginary line in the Eastern Atlantic to somewhere not too far west of Moscow, was dark.

Basically, the satellite capability over Europe and Africa was down.

He picked up his phone and called the number Levi Roth had given him in case of just this eventuality.

"Hello?" he stammered.

"Lieutenant Harper?" Roth said.

"It's happened, sir."

"I see," Roth said.

"They took out KH-11, sir. The one that Kosmos 2543 has been tracking."

"That's Europe and Africa," Roth said.

"It is, sir."

"How did they do it?"

"I have no idea, sir."

"Can you find out?"

"I could redirect the scopes on the two neighboring Keyhole satellites, sir. But that would mean the network was down for two more quadrants of the planet."

"And if we were to do that, Harper, what would it show us?"

"Debris, sir. Probably nothing more."

"I see," Roth said. "In any case, I suppose how they did it isn't really the issue."

"No, sir. There are a thousand ways they could have done it. Simply ramming us would have done it."

"What matters here is that they did it at all."

"This is the first time we've ever been attacked by another nation in space, sir."

62

The next morning, Lance, Tatyana, and Laurel were on a train to the Latvian capital of Riga. Tatyana's leg was still badly injured, but she was on antibiotics, and as long as she didn't do anything too demanding, it would heal.

The train left Berlin Hauptbahnhof before dawn, and they watched the sun rising in the east as the train crossed into Poland.

They sat on seats facing each other, and Laurel said, "What made you come back, Lance?"

Lance shrugged. "Roth said you needed me."

She nodded. "It's just, you seemed pretty adamant you were done with all of this last time we spoke."

"This is different," Lance said. "This was personal. I'm not here for the government. I'm here because I want to be."

"Because of us," Tatyana said, grinning at Laurel.

Lance smiled. He didn't tell them that someone had been sent by the GRU to kill Sam. They didn't need to know everything about his reasons for being there.

They had to change trains in Warsaw, and Lance helped Tatyana walk.

"This is the way she came," Tatyana said as they passed through the concourse.

They boarded the train to Riga and ordered breakfast from a man wheeling a cart along the aisle. Sandwiches with some kind of deli meat and three cups of coffee in paper cups.

About two hours out of Warsaw, the train slowly came to a halt, and Lance got up to see what was going on. They were in open farmland, not far from the border into Latvia, and there was no reason for the train to stop there. It was an intercity express.

He walked down the carriage until he found a conductor, and he said in Polish, "What's going on?"

"Something's wrong with the signals on the Latvian side of the border," the conductor said.

Lance knew enough to know that nothing was ever a coincidence.

A delay on the train spelled one thing.

An ambush.

He hurried back to his seat and told the others to be ready.

"Something's up with the track signals ahead," he said.

All three were armed, and even with Tatyana's injured leg, they made a formidable fighting team. Any assassin would have his hands full.

Laurel looked at her phone and said, "I don't think this is directed at our train in particular."

"What do you mean?"

"The NATO Cyber Defense Center just sent me a notification. The entire Latvian communications network is under massive attack."

"Massive attack?" Lance said.

"Network distortions on an unprecedented scale," she said, reading the message, "specifically targeting servers located in Latvia."

"What kinds of traffic distortions."

Laurel was reading from her phone. "DDoS attacks, ping floods, botnet swarms."

"Basically everything," Lance said.

"It's right out of a Russian cyberattack manual," Tatyana said. "The transportation network, the power grid, the banking system, cell phone towers, government websites, news sites, they're going to go after everything."

"She's right," Laurel said. "Even Latvia's English-language Wikipedia entries are being hacked."

"It's exactly what the Kremlin would do in preparation for an invasion," Tatyana said.

"That's exactly what the NATO Cyber Defense Center is saying too," Laurel said, still reading the message. "Threat of Russian military intervention in Latvia extremely high."

Lance looked out the window. "When did the attacks begin?"

"Thirty minutes ago. Already ATMs are down. Traffic lights are down. Medical equipment, power grids, news, it's a mess."

"This is it," Tatyana said. "The precursor to a military attack. This is what they'll use to smokescreen everything else that follows."

Lance stood up and looked out the window.

"We need to get to Riga," he said. "We need to get there fast. And this train isn't going to get us there."

A few minutes later, the train began moving slowly back in the direction it had come from.

An announcement came over the speaker from the

driver saying that the Latvian rail system was experiencing technical difficulties. He apologized and said the train company was offering bus tickets for the final leg of the journey.

The train brought them back a few miles to the Lithuanian village of Saločiai, and everyone disembarked.

"How far is it to Riga from here?" Lance asked the conductor as they descended the steps.

"Fifty kilometers," the conductor said.

At the train station, the passengers milled around, waiting for the buses the train company had arranged.

"Let's get you two inside," Lance said, helping Tatyana walk.

They waited for him on a bench while he went to the car rental desk. By some miracle, he was able to get a five-series BMW. When he got back to the women, they were drinking sweetened tea from plastic cups that a Romany woman had sold them.

Lance showed them the keys. "Come on," he said. "We're out of here."

They were able to cover most of the distance to Riga on a highway that was relatively unscathed by the cyberattack that had brought down all of Latvia's traffic systems.

Once they got closer to Riga, however, that changed.

Riga was not an enormous city by any standards, it was roughly comparable, population-wise, to Portland, Oregon, but even from the highway, Lance could tell that the traffic was going to be a battle to get through.

It wasn't just the traffic lights, which had all defaulted to a flashing red, but things like gas station pumps, toll booths, and camera activated signals were down too.

Without connectivity, nothing worked.

Some of the city's radio stations were still broadcasting,

but they were using backup, analog systems that hadn't been used in years, and the content being transmitted was a pre-recorded emergency message recorded by the government.

"This is an emergency signal," the message said in a robotic female voice. "Remain calm and obey all orders from the authorities."

Bank machines, credit card processors, cell phones, and the Internet were completely offline.

Riga was ordinarily a peaceful city, orderly, with well-maintained parks surrounding the city center, but Lance knew how quickly that could change. In an atmosphere of chaos and uncertainty, even the most peaceful city could become as dangerous as a war zone.

"I think I just saw someone break the window of an electronics store," Laurel said.

She was sitting next to Lance in the passenger seat.

Tatyana was in the back with her leg up.

"It doesn't take long for things to descend into chaos in an atmosphere like this," Tatyana said. "The GRU has entire attack plans for breaking down public order in a city like this."

"Why is it," Laurel said, looking over her shoulder at Tatyana, "that Moscow is so much better at using chaos to achieve its objectives than we are?"

"Well," Tatyana said, "the Kremlin never stopped thinking of itself as a superpower."

"Tell me about it," Lance said.

"But they lack the economic power, the military power, the technological power, to match those ambitions, so they have to be creative," Tatyana said.

"I heard Molotov was into judo in a big way," Lance said.

"Exactly," Tatyana said. "It's all about using the opponent's own size against him."

"But we do that too," Laurel said.

"It's not the same," Tatyana said. "The US is always looking for solutions. Everything about your country, everything about your education system, everything about your corporations and government institutions and universities, trains people to look for solutions. If something is broken...".

"We try to fix it," Laurel said.

"Exactly."

"And you don't do that in Russia?" Lance said.

Tatyana laughed. "Our approach is more like, if ours is broken, and yours isn't, then we have to break yours too. We learn how to break things, not fix them."

Laurel shook her head. "Always creating trouble," she said.

Tatyana nodded. "Chaos is the Kremlin's best weapon, and they know it. We know our country is weak. We know we can't make it as strong as the West."

"So you seek to make the West as weak as you," Laurel said.

Tatyana nodded.

"But how do they hope to prevail in the end?" Laurel said. "Eventually, at the end of the day, someone needs to be strong. Problems need to be fixed.

Tatyana smiled. "Laurel, that's the thing. There is no end. There's no solution. International politics, competition, human history, it never ends. As far as the Kremlin is concerned, it doesn't even change over time."

"Of course it changes," Laurel said.

"That's the difference between you and a Kremlin strategist, Laurel," Lance said. "You still think there's a happy ending to all of this. Some solution that will make things right."

"So what am I missing?" Laurel said. "Explain it to me like I'm a five-year-old."

"There are so many ways the West is vulnerable," Tatyana said. "Look at this cyber attack. How much effort did it take for the West to invent the Internet, to invent mobile phones, to invent satellite communications, and an electronically powered international payments system?"

"A lot," Laurel said.

"Exactly. And what do you think it cost Russia to tear it all down?"

"Probably a bunch of teenagers in a basement in Saint Petersburg," Lance said.

"That's right," Tatyana said. "And the more advanced Latvia's communications system becomes, the more damage those teenagers can do from their basement."

"Right," Laurel said, nodding.

"You can't even buy gasoline in this city right now," Tatyana said. "And the Kremlin didn't have to lay a finger on a single fuel depot to make that happen."

"Okay," Laurel said.

"And look at the US military. How much have they invested into advanced technology? Global positioning? Defense systems that can shoot missiles out of the sky? Guidance systems that can tell a soldier what's over the next hill? Unmanned drones and guided missiles that can fly to any spot on the planet? How difficult was it to get all of that up and running?"

"Very difficult," Laurel said.

"Trillions of dollars developing the most advanced military the world has ever known," Tatyana said. "A military that is technically capable of almost anything you can imagine."

"But there's a vulnerability," Laurel said.

"You bet there's a vulnerability. Compared to all that technology, satellites guiding bullets, guiding soldiers, guiding missiles, guiding ships and planes and drones and tanks and turning basically the entire planet into a three-dimensional model, compared to all that, what do you think it costs the Kremlin to interfere with those systems?"

"It's not like our systems aren't defended," Laurel said.

"American systems are like a Porsche," Tatyana said. "The Kremlin knows that, and their entire strategy is to make sure they're never in a race against that Porsche."

"How can they beat it then?"

"How do you beat a Porsche when all you have is a piece of shit Lada?" Tatyana said. "Ask yourself this, if you were in an argument in a parking lot, who would you rather be? The guy with the hundred-thousand-dollar Porsche, or the guy with the one-dollar brick?"

"That's what all this chaos is," Lance said, looking out at a scene of increasing disorder in the street in front of him.

"That's what all this chaos is," Tatyana said, "and it was achieved by a bunch of hackers in a basement."

"And the only reason it works," Laurel said.

"The only reason it works is because Latvia invested heavily in modernizing its society and its economy, and now everything is connected to the internet."

"We're all fucked then?" Laurel said.

"It goes deeper than you could ever realize," Tatyana said. "It's not just technological. It's about social cohesion too. Human nature. Chaos is at the root of every aspect of the Kremlin's strategy."

"What do you mean?" Laurel said.

"Well, the West says that freedom is a source of power, right? Democracy, free speech, the right to live your life how you want and pursue happiness and all that?"

"Right," Laurel said.

"Well, the Kremlin is trying to turn American freedom into a weakness. Look at the way they abuse freedom of speech norms to distort political debates. Their internet trolls can say anything on social media, and everyone in the US gives them a hearing because of their right to free speech."

"Same with the press," Lance said.

"Right. In the Kremlin, they always say that if the West didn't have a free press, they would have had to invent one for them."

"Very funny," Laurel said.

"It's not funny when the Kremlin can influence media outlets and get them to affect Western public perceptions."

"Like what?"

"Like anything. Like immigration. Immigration can be a flashpoint in any nation's politics. Do you know what proportion of the US population was born in a foreign country?"

"One in six," Laurel said.

"That right," Tatyana said. "The US, with its economy and political freedoms, is the ultimate destination for people around the world who are looking for a better life. All that freedom. All that economic prosperity. It's a good thing, right? It's a strength. Open borders. Freedom to travel. Freedom of religion. All of it. It's the reason more technology comes out of the US in a single year than has come out of Russia in the past five decades."

"But it creates a vulnerability," Laurel said.

"Of course it creates a vulnerability. It creates tensions. It creates opportunities to drive wedges between groups. To drive people against each other. People who are supposed to be neighbors."

"It was Abraham Lincoln who said it," Laurel said.

"Right," Tatyana said. "What did he say? A house...".

"A house divided against itself cannot stand."

"That's the Bible," Lance said.

"I think it was Lincoln," Tatyana said.

"Lincoln might have said it," Lance said. "But he got it from the Bible."

"I didn't peg you as a Sunday schoolboy," Laurel said.

"There's a lot of things about me you might not have pegged," Lance said.

"Well," Tatyana said, "look at it this way. The US brings in immigration, it benefits economically, people want to come. They bring their talents. They bring their scientists. All of that is supposed to be the benefit for democracy."

"Whereas in Russia?" Laurel said.

"In Russia, almost everyone is an ethnic Russian. Almost everyone was born in Russia. Almost everyone will die in Russia. They don't get to vote in free and fair elections. They don't get to travel freely to other parts of the world. They don't get to listen to a million different media outlets, telling them a million different ways to see the world."

"And that makes them stronger?" Laurel said.

"No," Tatyana said. "The Russian people are oppressed. They are deliberately kept in the dark. They are kept poor. They are kept shut off from the global economy and global information flows."

"But somehow, the Kremlin turns that into a strength," Laurel said.

"Well, if no one ever leaves. If no new people ever arrive. If every newspaper and news channel says the same thing, and if there are no political disagreements between politicians...".

"Then the house can never be divided," Lance said.

"That's the crux of it," Tatyana said. "That's the Russian way. Look at what everyone else is doing...".

"And do the opposite," Laurel said.

"And pick at weaknesses," Tatyana said.

63

By the time Lance, Laurel and Tatyana made it to the center of Riga, it was getting dark. It took them two hours to cover a distance of fewer than five miles, and with every passing hour, the mood on the streets got less stable and more dangerous.

"This is it," Tatyana said as they approached the hotel.

It was a grand, nineteenth-century building in the center of the old town, and Lance pulled up in front of the entrance.

"Wait here," he said to the women. "I'll go get us a room."

He entered the lobby with a swagger in his step, speaking loudly, trying to look and sound like an American tourist. He stepped up to the front desk and slapped his wallet on the counter.

"It's chaos out there," he said in English.

"Yes, sir," a snooty looking guy in a tight suit and black tie said, looking at Lance over the top of wire-rimmed glasses.

"I need a room," Lance said. "All the flights have been grounded."

"I'm terribly sorry, sir," the man began, but Lance reached into the wallet and put a wad of US twenty-dollar bills on the desk.

"I know your system's down," Lance said. "Everything's down. I'm as upset about it as anyone. But I've got cash, and I don't need wifi, and I don't need to book online. I just need a room, a suite if you have one."

"Without our system, sir."

"As far as I'm aware," Lance said, "the internet has no effect on beds, and bedrooms, am I right?"

The man looked around, checked behind him, and moved the cash off the desk and into his pocket.

"You're absolutely correct, sir. I do happen to have a very nicely appointed suite."

A few minutes later, Lance was in the room with Laurel and Tatyana, and directly across the square from them was the headquarters of the Latvian State Police.

"So that's where she worked?" Lance said

Tatyana nodded.

Laurel went to the minibar and took out a bottle of champagne.

There were two flutes on the counter above the bar, and she filled them.

"You didn't want any, did you?" she said to Lance. "There were only two glasses."

"I guess not," Lance said.

He was looking across the square at the police building and wondering if Agata's boss was still in there. He was the only person they knew for certain had spoken to Agata before her disappearance.

Lance was willing to bet he was mixed up with the Russians.

If anyone knew what was coming, it was him.

With the Latvian phone system completely down, there was no way for them to call Roth.

"We need a location for Zarina's boss," Lance said.

"Do you think Roth knows where he is?"

She shrugged.

"I don't know how we'd contact him to ask," Tatyana said.

"There's a satellite communications capability at the US embassy," Lance said, "but if we go there, every Russian agent in the country knows we're here."

"You're going to have to find him the old fashioned way," Laurel said.

Lance looked at her. She'd kicked off her shoes and was sipping champagne. Tatyana looked equally comfortable on the bed, her injured leg stretched out in front of her.

"I'm sorry," Lance said, "I didn't realize we'd come here for a vacation."

"Tracking down a Latvian police officer," Laurel said. "I'd say that's your job, Lance." She turned to Tatyana, "What do you think?"

"Definitely," Tatyana said. "What's the use in having you here if you can't do that much?"

Lance shook his head. "We've got an address for him, right?"

"Sure we do," Laurel said.

"I don't suppose we have a photo?"

Laurel shook her head. "Not without Internet, we don't."

Lance went to the minibar and took out a packet of nuts. He turned on the television.

All of the channels had been taken over by the same emergency broadcast signal they'd heard on the radio.

"I'm not surprised the police captain's in the Kremlin's pocket," he said. "How can a country like this defend itself against a neighbor like Russia?"

Tatyana said, "The only reason the Kremlin's not already here is the threat of US retaliation."

"And if that threat goes away?" Laurel said.

"If that threat goes away?" Tatyana said, "if it goes away completely, well, I've seen the list."

"What list?" Lance said.

"A shopping list," Tatyana said, "of territory Russia will gobble up the moment it's powerful enough to do so."

"What's on that list?"

"Over sixty million people," Tatyana said. "Most of them in Europe and Central Asia."

"What countries?"

"All the ones you'd expect," Tatyana said. "The Baltics, the Caucasus, the Central Asian republics, Belarus, Ukraine, Moldova."

"They're in most of them already," Lance said.

"Yes, they are," Tatyana said, "and the official strategy says that the moment the West is too weak to oppose them, they'll invade and annex all of them."

"That's a lot of territory," Lance said.

"It's the former USSR. The Russian military knows the terrain. They know the people. They have their claws in the national leaderships. They supply the natural resources."

"They're ready to go."

"People talk a lot about China these days," Tatyana said.

"China's a rising tsunami," Lance said.

"Sure," Tatyana said, "but what are its current territorial ambitions?"

Laurel shrugged. "A few enclaves in Bhutan," she said. "Same in Nepal. Some shoals and atolls in the South China Sea. The Paracel Islands. Scarborough Shoal. Some of its border regions with India. The Spratly Islands."

"Taiwan," Lance said.

"Add it all up," Tatyana said. "What have you got?"

"In terms of square miles."

"In any terms you like," Tatyana said.

"It's not a lot," Laurel said. "Really it's not much more than any other country their size."

"What about the Uighurs?" Lance said.

"Compare it all to what Russia has its sights on," Tatyana said.

"Which is?"

"Two million square miles of territory," Tatyana said.

"What document did you see this on?" Laurel said.

"It's a file called Sphere of Influence Fifteen, and it's been signed by every Marshal, General, and Colonel in the Russian army," Tatyana said. "I've seen a copy with my own eyes."

"How did you come to see a copy of a document like that?" Laurel said.

"The Main Directorate had me spying on three of the signatories at the time of its circulation."

"You mean, sleeping with?" Laurel said.

Tatyana's eyes flashed. "You know that's what I mean."

"Sorry," Laurel said.

Lance wasn't surprised by any of what he was hearing. Everyone knew Russia had territorial ambitions. Molotov wouldn't be satisfied until every inch of the USSR was back under his control.

Russia was like a glacier. It moved slowly, very slowly,

but in the end, it proved unstoppable. Any force, if it only moved in one direction, would reach its goal eventually.

As Lance left the hotel room, the two women were ordering room service and checking the television and their phones for any signs that the Latvian communications system was back up and running.

He went down to the lobby and had the valet bring his car around. Then he began fighting his way through the city's mangled traffic. It was getting late, traffic was lighter than it had been, but getting around was still a battle.

At one intersection, some people attacked the car in front of him. A woman was driving.

Lance got out and pointed his gun at them, and they dispersed.

"Things are getting out of control," he said to the woman. "It would be safer to get off the streets."

She nodded her head frantically and thanked him.

Kuzis's address was a well-appointed apartment in a grand, art nouveau building in the Teika district. Lance parked outside and smoked a cigarette while he waited for one of the building's residents to open the front door.

He didn't have to wait long, and as one of the residents stepped out, he stopped the door from shutting and went inside.

He was wearing black pants, a black leather jacket, and black leather gloves. In his coat were two fully-loaded, silenced pistols. He knew Kuzis had a family, and he was already preparing himself mentally for the fact that he might have to do something to this man in front of his children.

It wasn't a part of the job he relished, but he didn't get to make the rules.

He climbed three flights of stairs and found Kuzis's

apartment. The door was solid, with an iron gate in front, but when Lance checked, he found that the metal gate was unlocked.

He didn't waste time.

He raised his foot and brought it down so that his heel hit the bottom corner of the door, as far from the hinge as possible.

The wood of the door bent inward, and the air was filled with the sharp crack of snapping wood. He brought down his foot two more times before the lock gave way, and the door swung open.

Then he reached around the wall and flicked on the light in the apartment.

It was empty.

64

Lance searched the apartment efficiently, flicking through the sideboard in the hallway, looking through the top drawer closest to the kitchen, checking the calendar on the refrigerator door.

There was some mail by the phone, and it didn't take long to find the bills. There were bills for this address and for a dacha Kuzis owned in the lake country north of the city. Lance put an electricity bill for the dacha in his pocket.

He also scanned the family photo albums, which were lined up in a row on the bottom shelf of the bookcase in the living room. He still didn't know what Kuzis looked like, and found some photos of him and looked at them closely.

He was one of those smug-looking men whose wife was a lot more attractive than he was. She was slim, with smile lines around her eyes and lustrous hair that hung down over her shoulders. He could tell from the apartment that she had good taste.

Lance wondered what had made her marry a man like Kuzis.

Lance also made note of Kuzis's children and felt a pang of remorse for what was to come.

He left the apartment without taking any steps to hide the fact he'd been there other than shutting the broken door behind him. With the telephones down, he didn't have to worry about anyone warning Kuzis.

He got back in his car and made his way north out of the city. The street lights were out, the cyber attack was affecting the power grid too, and above him, the sky opened up to reveal more stars than he'd seen in some time. The cold air seemed to make them brighter.

He drove fast on the highway and exited onto a regional road that wound through dense forest. He could tell the area was popular with vacationers. The houses on the lakes were expensive, with boats and docks and swimming pools. There were few businesses on the road, but those he passed, a gas station, a local diner, catered to tourists.

Kuzis's dacha was located at the end of a long, dirt driveway, and the view over the lake would have been spectacular in the daylight. As it was, he could see a wide vista of ice that seemed to shimmer in the moonlight like Swarovksi crystal. Out across the lake, he could see the twinkling lights of a few other dachas. They were far enough away that they wouldn't hear what was about to happen.

When he saw the lights of the house up ahead, he pulled over and cut the engine, covering the last hundred yards on foot.

The dacha was built in the style of a Bavarian mountain house, with ornate wooden shutters and detailed carvings on the dark wood beneath the eaves. There was a set of steps leading to a wraparound porch on the first floor. Light glowed from some of the rooms facing the lake.

Lance climbed the steps quietly and was about to check

the front door to see if it was locked when he heard the sound of hammering coming from the lake.

He crept around the porch, ducking below windows and checking to make sure no one was looking out. When he reached the back of the house, he saw that a man was out there, about a hundred yards away, chipping at the ice with a pick.

It looked like he was making an ice-fishing hole.

Next to him, lying on the ice, was a broken hand auger, as well as some fishing rods and tackle. In his mouth, the red ember of a cigar glowed in the dark.

Lance made his way quietly to the edge of the lake and said aloud, "Alfreds Kuzis."

His voice broke the silence that hung above the lake like a crack of thunder, and Kuzis dropped the pick.

"The country's in a state of absolute turmoil," Lance said in English, "and you're out here fishing. I'd have thought the captain of the police national security division would be more concerned."

"Who are you?" Kuzis said.

"You know who I am."

Kuzis shook his head. He glanced around, looking for a way to escape, but there was nothing he could do. Out on the ice, without cover, his body creating a clear outline against the white ice in the moonlight, he was singularly vulnerable.

He hadn't prepared.

He had no weapon.

He'd thought he was safe.

"You really didn't think we'd come for you?" Lance said.

"I thought..." Kuzis stammered.

"You thought you'd get away with it."

Kuzis said nothing.

"You thought you'd serve your country up to the Kremlin on a silver platter, and no one would have anything to say about it."

"You're CIA."

"I'm CIA," Lance said.

"Where were you when we needed you?" Kuzis said. "Where were you all these past years, as the Kremlin ramped up the pressure? Where were you when they first approached me and forced me to make a decision?"

"Did you ask for help when the Russians approached you?"

Kuzis said nothing.

"Did you report it up the chain? We have a station chief in Riga. Why didn't you go to the embassy?"

"I didn't know who to trust."

"You took the money."

"I was looking for security," Kuzis said. "I was looking for safety, for my family."

"You're not safe, Kuzis. Your ass is hanging in the wind, and there's not a thing your Russian friends are going to do to save you now."

"If you lived in the world we live in," Kuzis said, "even for a minute, you'd have done the same thing."

"You live in a dangerous world, Kuzis. I'll grant you that. You're right on the doorstep of the largest and most aggressive nation on earth, Vladimir Molotov's Russia."

"Exactly," Kuzis said. "It's so easy for you Americans to come here and tell us we should stand up to them. I'd like to see how you acted in our situation."

"You were dealt a tough hand, Kuzis. I'll grant you that. But that doesn't change the fact that you still have to play it. Every man, no matter where he's from, knows that. You play the hand you were dealt."

"Easy for you to say," Kuzis said. "Your hand is nothing but aces."

"You haven't seen my hand," Lance said.

"Americans," Kuzis spat. "You have it so easy, and then you come to us and preach that we should act as you act. But we're not holding aces."

"Like I said, Kuzis, you haven't seen my hand."

"I don't need to."

"Let me tell you something," Lance said, "not that it will do you much good now, but the difference between you and me isn't that I was dealt four aces, and you weren't."

"What is it then?"

"It's that I play like I was dealt four aces."

Kuzis let out a hollow laugh. "Oh, I see. You're just bluffing your way to victory then."

"I'm saying, it isn't the same as a card game, Kuzis. You're only dealt one hand in life. One hand. And that's the hand you play."

"Now you're going to preach to me how I should have played."

"When you're only getting one hand, Kuzis, you don't play it like it is. You play it like it's aces."

Kuzis drew from his cigar, and a cloud of smoke billowed from him.

"What are you going to do to me now?" he said. "You know how I played the hand I was given. Now you get to judge me."

"I ain't judging you. You sold out your country. You killed your own officer. You left the door wide open for the Russians. You, Kuzis, judged yourself."

"So what happens now?"

"That depends."

"On what?"

"I want to know what's coming, Kuzis. What are the Russians planning? How many units? What equipment are they bringing? Where will they cross the border? And when?"

"There's nothing you can do to stop it."

"You let me be the judge of that."

"Oh, I see. American hero. Bluffing aces will only get you so far. The Russians are calling your hand."

"Like I said," Lance said, "you haven't seen my hand."

"But I know the Russians," Kuzis said. "And they're a tide. You can't hold back a tide. When it comes, it comes."

"You keep saying this invasion is inevitable, but that's just you justifying your actions."

"I don't have to justify my actions."

"You betrayed your country."

"My country?" Kuzis spat. "A country is an idea. Same as a religion. It's not real."

"Oh, you think so?"

"I know so," Kuzis said, "It's a construct. It means nothing."

"Fuck you," Lance said, and he fired a suppressed bullet at the ice at Kuzis's feet.

The sound of splitting ice filled the air as long cracks spread across the ice about three yards in every direction.

"Don't," Kuzis said.

"Don't what?" Lance said, and he fired another bullet into the ice.

Kuzis saw what was happening. The ice was thick, maybe four inches, but not so thick that it would hold up to gunfire. Enough bullets, and it would give way beneath his feet.

"Stop," he said.

"How many people do you think died so that Latvia

could be a free country?" Lance said. "They played their hand so that men like you could be free."

"All right," Kuzis said, beginning to panic. "I admit it. I sold out my country."

"The least you could have done," Lance said, "was recognize that millions of men, with cards no better than yours, fought and died so that this country could be free from Russia."

"You can say that," Kuzis said, "because you're the one holding the gun, but you know as well as I do that none of this makes any difference. Latvia is a patch of dirt. Whether the flag is red or blue or green, who gives a fuck? Whether we're part of NATO, or the EU, or the USSR, what difference does it make? What difference does it make to the farmer plowing in the field? What difference does it make to the builder laying bricks? What difference does it make to the soldier firing the bullets?"

"You start going down that path," Lance said, "and where does it end? USSR versus USA. You really think it makes no difference who wins? Nazis versus Allies? No difference? Really?"

Kuzis nodded his head. "Really," he said.

"You believe that," Lance said, "and you believe in nothing."

"I do believe in nothing," Kuzis said, "and you tell me what makes you so certain I'm wrong, and you're right."

"I'm not certain," Lance said. "Maybe you are right. But you sold out your own agent. Agata Zarina. She was under your charge. You were sworn to protect her."

"I never swore anything to her."

"You're nothing but a faithless, lowdown traitor," Lance said. "You sell out your friends. You sell out your country. That woman is dead because of what you did. And you know as well as I do that you had your reasons. You say you believe in nothing, but you believe in something, Kuzis. Everybody believes in something."

"That's bullshit," Kuzis said.

"That's bullshit?" Lance said. "You're bullshit, Kuzis. You believe in something, and you decided what it was. You decided to believe in filling your pockets with Russian money. That's what you chose. So don't tell me you believe in nothing."

Lance fired three shots into the ice, and the cracks spread out from each bullet hole like spider webs.

"Please," Kuzis said, dropping to his knees.

He began to whimper, and Lance said, "Where are the Russians going to attack?"

"I don't know," Kuzis said. "They don't tell me things like that."

"Near where that biplane came down?" Lance said. "Where Agata Zarina went looking? That's the place, isn't it?"

Kuzis nodded.

"The border region," Lance said.

"There's a village out there called Ziguri," Kuzis said. "She stayed in a hotel there. I never sent her. She just went."

"And that's where the Russian's are coming?"

"It's the most likely place. She found something she wasn't supposed to find. But I never sent her."

"What are Latvian defenses like in that region?"

Kuzis shook his head.

"Come on, Kuzis. I've seen the NATO disposition documents. You've got monitoring on the border."

"Along that stretch," Kuzis said, "our forces are nonexistent."

"Nonexistent? How is that possible?"

"I advised the military to pull them out."

"What? Why?"

"Why do you think?"

"The Russians told you to?"

Kuzis nodded.

"You actively sabotaged your own military?"

"I told them to redeploy farther south."

Lance shook his head. "How can you do that?" he said.

"I told you. None of it makes a difference. Latvia is a nation of two million people, next to a country with a hundred-forty-million, with the largest chemical, biological, and nuclear stockpiles on the planet. If they want to invade us, they're going to invade us. It's futile to resist a force like that."

"And what about NATO?"

"What about NATO?" Kuzis said. "You tell me where NATO's going to be when Russian troops cross the border. You tell me."

"The Russians wouldn't dare attack a NATO member without the help of insiders like you making it easier for them."

"This country," Kuzis said, "this land you're standing on right now, this lake, these forests, when I was a boy, this was all part of the USSR. It was then, and it will be again. It's inevitable."

"It's only inevitable if you let it be," Lance said, and he fired his gun three more times into the ice.

"No," Kuzis screamed. "Please."

"You tell me what you believe in now," Lance said, turning to walk away.

The ice around Kuzis was beginning to come apart, and Kuzis started running for shore. Lance had already decided he'd give the man a sporting chance, but it made no difference. The ice came apart at Kuzis's feet, and he disappeared into the lake.

He never broke the surface again, never fought, never came up grasping and gasping for air.

He just disappeared into the black water as if he'd never been there at all.

And from inside the house, Kuzis's wife watched without uttering so much as a word.

65

Zhukovsky pulled off his socks and rubbed his raw feet. He dried them off and held them over the propane heater next to his desk.

This weather wasn't doing him any good. His old wounds ached. A man his age, with his seniority, should have been operating out of the General Staff Building in Saint Petersburg, not living in an army tent in a marsh, eating field rations like a fresh conscript.

His men were ready to go. Two squads, as ordered, all of them dressed in Latvian army uniforms and trained so thoroughly that they were willing to carry out any atrocity.

They were sworn to secrecy and had been observing complete radio silence for weeks.

No one knew where they were.

No one knew what they were about to do.

The operation Zhukovsky was about to lead was an order of magnitude more sinister than previous Russian false flag operations. The soldiers would be disguised, to an extreme degree, as Latvian soldiers. No one, not even they themselves, knew exactly what it was they were doing, and as soon as the operation was over, they would be pulled back to Russian territory.

The entire Latvian communications network had been brought to its knees to allow Russia to control the narrative, and even US military satellites had been attacked in an unprecedented space operation that blinded the Keyhole network across one-quarter of the planet's surface.

While this operation took place, there would be no surveillance, no satellites, no news crews, no social media posts, no witnesses.

And once the invasion began, the most advanced elements of the American military would be so unreliable that the Pentagon would not be able to muster a response until it was too late.

The extreme measures were necessary.

Not only was the president planning a full-scale ground invasion of a NATO member, a Western democracy, but the false flag operation was not against the Latvian military, it was a massacre of civilians.

And what was more, the soldiers themselves, once they returned to Russia, were going to be liquidated. Zhukovsky had argued against that, not out of moral concern, but because they were an asset he'd personally trained, and would have liked to get more use out of.

But the president was adamant. There could be no evidence of what was perpetrated here. The men had to be silenced. Permanently.

There was a problem, though.

A delay.

Zhukovsky was supposed to be crossing the border any minute. Everything, down to the tiniest detail, had been painstakingly orchestrated.

The Keyhole satellite was down.

The Latvian communications system was down.

The Latvian army had been pulled out of the border region and moved south.

Zhukovsky and his men were ready, out in the cold, surrounded by swamp and forest and bitterly cold winds from the north.

Zhukovsky picked up the receiver on his satellite phone and called Kirov. Kirov had moved from his hotel to the General Staff Building in the center of the city to run the invasion. The building was the headquarters of the Western Military District and gave him direct command over all of the most advanced and elite units in the Russian military.

"Kirov, sir," Zhukovsky said when he was connected. "We're at the border."

"Zhukovsky, we have a problem."

"What problem? We're ready to go. Just give me the order."

"I can't give you the order. I haven't been able to get in touch with Kuzis."

"We gave him a satellite phone."

"He's not answering it," Kirov said irritably.

"Sir," Zhukovsky said, "we're ready to go. You need to issue the order now, or we'll miss our window."

"You've still got hours until dawn," Kirov said. "I can't take the risk something's not right. The president himself requires an update before the final order is issued."

"So what are you going to tell him? That some fat, Latvian policeman's not answering the phone?"

"Just hold your position, Zhukovsky. Do not cross the border until you hear from me. That's a direct order."

"Sir," Zhukovsky said, "we've confirmed that the Latvian monitoring equipment has been pulled out. The entire sector is clear."

"I know," Kirov said.

"Kuzis has fulfilled his usefulness."

"Just do as I said, Zhukovsky. Hold your position. I'm going to contact my asset in Riga and see if I can find out what's wrong with Kuzis."

"How long is that going to take?" Zhukovsky protested.

"It will take as long as it takes, Oleg. If you have a problem with it, take it up with the president yourself."

66

Prochnow was in the back of a white van in central Riga. He had a secure, direct satellite connection with the General Staff Building in Saint Petersburg, where the invasion was being commanded from, and he saw that a call was coming in from Kirov.

"Fuck," he muttered to the other two operatives in the van. "How much do you want to bet this isn't good news?"

The men were in Riga to provide backup to the pro-Kremlin protest movement that the GRU had orchestrated. The protests were a crucial element of the invasion and were to provide the backdrop, and pretext, for the military intervention that was to follow. Thousands of ethnic Russian protestors had been flooding into Central Riga since nightfall, and Prochnow and his men were there to make sure they made an impression.

With the Latvian communications system down, the GRU's own television crews would be the only source of information to the outside world on what was going on.

He picked up the phone as one of the other men offered him a cigarette.

"This is Prochnow," he said, lighting the cigarette.

"Prochnow, this is Kirov."

"Of course, sir."

"What's your status?"

"We're in Riga as you ordered, sir, getting ready to film the protests. Everything is proceeding like clockwork. Riots and looting have already broken out on Tērbatas Street."

"The commercial district?"

"The shops, sir, yes. The people are looting them, stealing goods, setting buildings and cars on fire. It will make for excellent footage."

"What about the political protests?"

"Yes, sir. Crowds are beginning to congregate outside the Saeima. It won't be long before they reach critical mass. Once that happens, it will only take a very little spark to ignite a fire."

"That's good," Kirov said. "Very good."

"With the weapons we've got, sir, the government will be forced to respond. Things will get bloody fast."

"Very good," Kirov said again.

Prochnow knew how important the protests were. He hadn't been briefed on what exactly was being planned by the military, although he could have made a pretty good guess. All he'd been told was that the protests were a crucial aspect of the larger operation, which Kirov would be commanding from the Western Military District headquarters.

In the Kremlin's view, Riga was a tinderbox. About a third of the city's population was ethnically Russian, and Kirov wanted every single one of them out on the streets tonight. It hadn't been too difficult to orchestrate. Many of those people had been denied citizenship and other rights under the Latvian constitution. Persuading them to rise up and protest, especially when the GRU was willing to offer them cash to do so, was easy.

Word had spread throughout the city before the communications network was taken down, and every Russian in the city knew that if he was able to provide proof afterward that he participated in the protest, he'd be able to claim a one-time electronic cryptocurrency payment equal to about five hundred dollars.

That was a lot of money to attend a protest that most of them would have agreed to anyway.

The Kremlin had also taken the time to distribute materials that would amp up the tension and effectiveness of the protests and increase the likelihood of their turning violent. Placards and banners had been distributed that did not air the usual grievances of ethnic Russians, such as better access to jobs, education, and social welfare, but instead called for the direct aid of the Russian government to intervene in their defense.

Ominously, Prochnow noticed that some of the placards called for the immediate ceasing of Latvian massacres against Russian civilians in the east.

The GRU had also distributed weapons. These included thousands of guns and ammunition, instructions and materials for making Molotov cocktails, and CS gas launchers.

The protestors would be better armed and more militant than anything the Latvian government could have possibly predicted. They would have more than enough firepower to fight back against the Latvian police and military, who would inevitably be called in to quell the disorder.

Things were going to get messy in Riga tonight.

Very messy.

And that was precisely what the Kremlin wanted.

In order to make absolutely certain that things went

according to plan, and that some last-minute political maneuvering from the Latvians didn't dispel the crowds, the GRU had also bussed hundreds of its own activists into the capital. They'd come from all over Latvia, as well as from the Russian side of the border, and had been explicitly instructed to foment unrest and ensure that the weapons that had been distributed were used.

They were the sparks that would ignite the entire city.

As far as Prochnow knew, the Kremlin had calculated that within a matter of hours, over a hundred thousand ethnic Russians would be rioting in the streets of Riga, they would be heavily armed, and they would be actively fighting back against Latvian security forces.

Their placards and banners would call not for justice but for direct intervention from Moscow.

The Kremlin had also made sure that this was the one story that was being emitted from Latvia's crippled communications network, because as well as shutting down the national communications grid, they'd also established a number of satellite uplinks for their own media outlets to transmit news on what was happening.

And what would be happening would be exactly what Moscow wanted to be happening.

The Internet would be down, social media would be down, and the only footage would be of ethnic Russian protestors fighting against the Latvian government and calling for intervention from Moscow.

It was a potent cocktail of factors, but Prochnow knew that Moscow hadn't stopped there. It was a multi-pronged attack that he concluded was designed to lay the groundwork for a full reoccupation of Latvia by the Russian Federation.

It was genius.

So simple.

And it made perfect sense.

Russia had lost the Baltic states during the collapse of the USSR, and the only way to get them back was by force.

This was an audacious move against NATO, the United States, and the European Union, but nothing important had ever been gained without risk.

Prochnow had the feeling that he would be witnessing history in the making this night, and that by morning, the entire world would be a very different place.

"Listen, Prochnow, something's come up. I need you to look into it for me."

"Of course, sir."

"A captain in the national security police there in Riga was providing me with some very sensitive information."

"I see."

"His name is Alfreds Kuzis. He was out at his dacha in the lake country near the capital. He went dark about two hours ago."

"Send me the address," Prochnow said. "I'll be at the dacha within the hour."

Prochnow took down the address and had the operatives drop him at the Russian embassy where he could get a car. Then he drove out to the lake district outside the capital. The traffic system was a mess, and the center of the city was chaotic with the mounting protests, but once he got out of the city, he made fast progress.

When he reached the address of the dacha, he saw two police cruisers were already there. There was also an ambulance, and Prochnow saw the paramedics lifting a body from the lake and placing it on a stretcher.

He went up to one of the police officers and asked in his broken Latvian what had happened.

"Went through the ice," the cop said.

"Who went through?" Prochnow said.

The officer looked over his shoulder then said, "I can't give out that information."

"Was it the captain?" Prochnow said. "It's all right. I work for him. I was supposed to meet him here."

The cop nodded.

Prochnow lit a cigarette. This wasn't good news.

"Any sign of foul play?" he said.

The cop shrugged.

It didn't matter.

Nothing was a coincidence in this game.

He knew that.

Kirov knew it.

Everyone knew it.

He went back to his car and called Kirov on his sat phone.

"I found out what happened to your police captain," he said.

"What is it?"

"He had an accident."

"What kind of accident?"

"He went through the ice at his lake."

"Fuck," Kirov said.

"I'd say someone's trying to put a wrench in our plans, sir."

67

The president's limousine was a custom, Russian-built behemoth. It weighed seven tons and was twenty-two feet long. It was descended from the Russian-made ZiL limousines that had been used to transport Communist leaders during the Soviet era.

It was one more sign the president was sending the world that the USSR was back on the rise.

The car was known as the Aurus Senat, and was a bombproof, bullet-proof tank that the president had taken a personal hand in designing. Its door openings were custom sized to allow him to step out without dirtying the leg of his pants, and the passenger compartment had been designed by him down to the last detail.

It contained the most advanced communications equipment in the world, and he was capable of running a full operational command center from it in times of crisis. Its windows were six centimeters thick, enough to withstand any high-powered sniper shot, and its ventilation system was capable of detecting even trace amounts of toxins and poisons. In the case of a chemical attack, it was equipped with an air suppression system, and the steel hull was reinforced to withstand all known improvised explosive devices. At the rear was a secret emergency exit, and even when the privacy shades were closed, digital screens on the interior showed exactly what was going on outside. Its four-liter, eight-cylinder engine was able to get the car up to a hundred kilometers an hour in under six seconds, and in the event it ran out of gas, it was equipped with a backup electric engine.

The car had been flown to Saint Petersburg in advance of his arrival, and the president sat in the back seat and sipped champagne.

He wanted to be in the city to see first hand the results of all his months of work. He'd wanted to go directly to the General Staff Building, but his security team prohibited it. Because of the building's age, his security there couldn't be guaranteed. Too many legacy issues to deal with.

Instead, he would spend the night in the Imperial Winter Palace, directly across the Palace Square from the General Staff Building, where he would host a select group of dignitaries in celebration of what he was going to announce as the rebirth of the USSR.

His cavalcade zipped through the streets of Saint Petersburg. He knew every street of that city like the back of his hand, he knew the people, and while he didn't spend much time there, he considered it, and not Moscow, as his true home.

The light on his communications panel lit up, showing an incoming call from Kirov, and he picked up.

"I hear the Latvian monitoring troops are moving south," he said into the receiver.

"That's correct, sir. It appears Kuzis was able to get all the necessary orders through."

"And the protestors are wreaking havoc in Riga. Our news crews are already sending out footage to international outlets. It's the only news coming out of the country."

"Excellent news, sir," Kirov said.

"The American systems have been crippled by our satellite attack."

"That's correct, sir."

The president looked out his window. He was just passing the General Staff Building, which was the building Kirov was calling from, and he could tell from Kirov's voice that something was wrong.

"I'm right outside," the president said.

"Already, sir."

"I'm hosting a reception at the Winter Palace," the president said. "You must come and join us once your work is done."

"I would be honored, sir."

"But first, you have to tell me why it is that you've called."

"Well, sir...".

"Spit it out, Kirov."

"There's been a slight complication, sir."

"Slight?"

"Kuzis is dead."

"What? How did that happen?"

"I don't know, sir."

"This is a problem."

"It changes nothing, sir."

"Changes nothing? It changes everything."

"It might have been accidental."

"That woman. The policewoman. She got the word out before your man got to her in Berlin."

"Impossible, sir. He got her while she was approaching the embassy. The message was still inside her coat pocket."

"Well, something's going on, Kirov."

"Give me some time to look into it, sir. I'm sure it's nothing we can't handle."

"We can't afford to make a mistake here," the president said. "If we misjudge this, it could lead to nuclear war, Kirov."

"We can still pull off this operation, sir. I've spoken to Zhukovsky. His men are ready. The American satellite system is down. The protests have begun. The Latvian monitoring units have withdrawn."

"I don't know, Kirov."

"We've come too far, sir."

The president let out a long sigh. This was a risk. A big one. One of the most dangerous of his long career. He'd been at the helm, guiding Russia back to greatness for almost two decades, and he knew how quickly things could go south.

He was confident he could outmaneuver the American president.

Presidents came and went like the changing of the seasons. He'd sat across the table from so many of them he was beginning to lose count. They were tourists. Useful idiots.

They were senators, or businessmen, or whatever they were. Then, suddenly, they won an election, and randomly, without any control or planning or forewarning, they were the president of what was supposedly the most powerful nation on earth.

A month earlier, they'd never even seen the inside of the White House.

And he was supposed to sit across the table from them as equals?

That was ridiculous.

American politicians were ridiculous.

They were like tough guys who signed up for a sheriff's department because they liked the golden star they could pin to their lapel.

The real threat from the US wasn't the politicians. It was the career men. The military and intelligence men.

The deep state.

The men who remained in place regardless of who was in the White House.

The real rival of the Russian president wasn't the man in the White House, it was Levi Roth, and he'd been playing the game longer.

He was the one Molotov needed to watch out for.

"If Roth is onto us," the president said.

"He can't be, sir. It's not possible."

"Someone's in Riga," the president said. "Someone just killed Kuzis. You're not going to tell me I imagined that."

"Of course not, sir."

The president shook his head. He was worried, but like Kirov, he felt they'd gone too far to stop now. They'd come too close. They were so close to victory he could already taste it.

He took a cigar from a leather case in the pocket of his coat and put it in his mouth.

"If we're going to play with fire, this close to Roth's face, then we need to take every precaution," the president said.

"Of course, sir."

"What assets do the Americans still have in Riga?"

"Nothing, sir."

"If they killed Kuzis, how are they operating."

"Out of the embassy, sir. That's the only place."

"And can he still communicate with the embassy?"

"The UHF system is down, sir, but there are still NATO systems. The embassy can still communicate."

"I want the US embassy completely cut off, Kirov. I want them put in the stone age."

"I can activate a team, sir. They can take out the embassy's comms."

"Do it," the president said. "If Roth's trying to fuck with us, I want him cut off."

"Consider it done, sir."

The president brought his cigar to his lips and sucked.

He felt this. In his bones, he felt it.

This was a risk.

It was a roll of the dice.

It was a mistake.

"And give Zhukovsky the order to proceed with the massacre," he said.

68

The US embassy in Riga was on a spacious compound in a leafy suburb west of the city. If it weren't for the steel fencing and guard posts at the entrances, it could have been mistaken for a local college or community center. It was a modern building with blue windows and a sandstone facade. As Lance approached the front gate, two guards from a local security contractor waved their flashlights and told him to slow down.

"The embassy is closed," one of the guards said in Latvian.

"I have to speak to the CIA station chief," Lance said. "This is an emergency."

The guards looked at each other. They were local men. They'd never seen someone ask for the CIA station chief before. This was clearly something that went above their pay grade.

One of them went back to the guard post and spoke into a radio.

"The comms are still acting up," he called out to the other guard.

"Comms are down everywhere," Lance said. "The entire country is down."

"You don't need to tell us about this country," the guard said.

"And you don't need to keep me here talking," Lance said. "I need to speak to someone who can let me into this compound, and I need you two to make it happen. Fast."

The guards consulted, then the one who'd gone to the guard post entered the compound and went to the main embassy building.

"He's going to speak to our supervisor," the other guard said.

"This is urgent," Lance said. "I really need to get inside and speak to someone."

The man looked at him and then looked back toward the building where the other guard had just gone.

"The supervisor will know what to do," the guard said.

Lance looked at his watch. An hour had passed since he'd left Kuzis's dacha. Every minute that passed brought the Russian invasion closer. He needed to get the word to Roth, and the embassy's NATO comms system was the only way he could reach him.

With enough warning, Roth might be able to find out what the Russians were planning, where they were going to strike, and could maybe even authorize a preemptive response.

Lance sat in the car for two more minutes, watching the seconds tick by, then got out and walked to the guard.

"Get back in your car," the guard said, pulling his weapon.

Lance lunged forward and knocked the gun from his hand.

The man looked at him in shock.

Lance shook his head. "Don't," he said.

From the tone of his voice, the guard knew that he wasn't kidding.

"Sir, I can't let you pass without authorization. You know that."

"Look at it this way," Lance said. "Do you really want to get in a fight with the guy who's asking to see the CIA Station Chief?"

The guard didn't say anything, and Lance didn't waste any more time. He stepped past him, grabbed a visitor's pass from the desk, and walked through the guard post to the entrance of the main building.

It was the middle of the night, and the lobby, which would usually be bustling with people, was all but deserted. There was one marine sitting at a desk close to the elevators.

Lance walked up to him and said, "Where do I find the CIA offices?"

The marine looked up at him, and his eye stopped on the visitor's pass.

"Who's asking?" he said.

"I'm not at liberty to say," Lance said. " But if there's someone with the CIA here, I need to talk to them."

"There's a CIA presence," the marine said.

"In this building?"

The marine nodded toward the front doors. "The one across the courtyard," he said.

Lance went back outside. The building across the courtyard was made of the same sandstone, low-rise, with windows that were shaped like slats. He walked through the glass doors, and inside, another marine sat at another desk.

"You need to send someone down from the CIA," Lance said.

"Who are you?"

"Just tell them it's an emergency."

The marine was smart enough to know that something was going on. The communications across the country were down, and riots were beginning to break out across the capital.

"They're on the second floor," the marine said.

"Can you let me up?"

Someone came rushing through the door. It was the guard from the front gate, breathless.

He stood awkwardly by the door, and Lance and the marine looked at him.

"He just walked in," the guard said to the marine.

"Just walked in?"

"Through the front gate," the guard said.

The marine's hand moved down to his weapon.

"Don't break my balls," Lance said. "Just get them to send someone down. It's urgent."

The marine bit his lip, thought about it for a second, then picked up the phone. As soon as he heard the dial tone, he remembered that the system was down and replaced the receiver with a sigh.

"Escort me up," Lance said.

"I'm going to regret this," the marine said.

69

Kirov felt sick. The president had almost called off the entire operation, and he didn't even know about the fuck up with Alex Sherbakov. He had no idea that Lance Spector was involved. If he knew that, he would have canceled it for sure, and it would mean Kirov's head.

He dialed Prochnow's sat phone and waited.

"Sir," Prochnow said. "What do you need?"

"Where are you?"

"Making my way back into the city, sir."

"Stop," Kirov said. "I need you to head east. There's a village near the border called Ziguri. Have you heard of it?"

"No, but I'll find it."

"I need you to go there immediately."

"Sir, you realize, don't you, that I still don't know what this operation is?"

"There are only three men alive who know what this operation entails, Prochnow, and it's going to stay that way."

"That's all well and good, sir, but if our friend is in Riga."

"Our friend?"

"Lance Spector."

"We don't know that for certain."

"Sir. It's got to be him. Who else would have gone after Kuzis?"

Kirov sighed. He knew Prochnow was right. And he knew what it meant. He was just having trouble coming to terms with it.

"Have you spoken to the president, sir?"

"Prochnow, don't forget yourself."

"I'm sorry, sir. But does he know what's going on?"

"He knows what I told him."

"Which was what?"

"That someone killed Kuzis, and that we don't know who. Which is the truth."

"He'll suspect Roth."

"He did suspect Roth."

"But he didn't call off the operation?"

"I persuaded him that we had to keep going."

"And he gave the green light?"

"Would I be telling you to go to Ziguri if he didn't?"

"I don't know what you'd be telling me, sir. I don't know what's waiting in Ziguri."

"I'm giving you an order, Prochnow. That's all you need to know."

"Sir, could Kuzis have told Spector about Ziguri?"

"Just get out there, and give me a call when you get there."

"Very well, sir."

"And if anything happens to you, you take the information you have to the grave, you hear me?"

"I hear you, sir."

70

W hen the station chief arrived, he was breathless. He knew something was going on, and even though he had no idea who Lance was, the fact that he was there, asking for him, was enough to get him to run.

He was an older guy, in his mid-fifties, a real career man in a tweed jacket and comfortable shoes. He introduced himself as Greenfeld.

"We've got an emergency," Lance said to him without wasting time on formalities.

"Mister," Greenfeld said, "I don't know who you are, and I just walked out of a top-level meeting with the ambassador to come see you."

"You ask Levi Roth who I am," Lance said.

"I'm going to need more than that," Greenfeld said.

"How about Special Operations Group security clearance Delta, Delta, Charlie, Bravo?"

"That code expired weeks ago," Greenfeld said.

"Look, do you want to get in a pissing match over technicalities, or do you want to find out what's going on? You've got riots in the streets. Protestors marching on the capital. And the entire communications network of the country is down. What do you think that is?"

"That's exactly what I was just discussing with the ambassador."

"And let me guess," Lance said. "Neither of you had the faintest idea what to make of it?"

"We're completely blind here," Greenfeld said.

"You need to get in touch with Langley," Lance said. "I have urgent information you need to get to Levi Roth."

"I already told you, the comms are down. I can't speak to Roth."

"Latvian comms networks are down," Lance said. "But you have your own satellite link, right?"

"What part of the comms being down don't you understand?" Greenfeld said.

"What are you saying to me? That the embassy's cut off from Washington? How is that possible?"

Greenfeld gave a look to the marines like maybe he thought Lance was simple. "The. Comms. Are. Down."

"Don't talk to me like I'm an idiot," Lance said. "What comms protocol do you usually have with DC?"

"Why don't you start by telling me who you are and what it is you want to say to DC?"

Lance looked at the man. He looked at the marines who were standing next to him. "Where's the rest of your department?" Lance said. "Where's your command center?"

Greenfeld laughed, as if that confirmed his concerns about Lance's intelligence. "My department? My command center? Are you kidding me? Where do you think we are? Baghdad?"

Lance shook his head. "What are you saying? It's just you here?"

"It's just me," Greenfeld said.

"I need to speak to Levi Roth right now."

"And I told you, the embassy's comms link to Washington is down."

"You're expecting me to believe that we're completely in the dark."

"Where I come from," Greenfeld said, "that's *what comms* down generally means."

Lance gave him a look that told him not to get sarcastic.

"How is it possible that an American embassy in a NATO country is completely cut off from communications with Washington?" Lance said.

"We were attacked."

"What do you mean, you were attacked?"

"Three men, less than an hour ago. They took out the satellite dish with a small explosive. We're working on getting it back up and running, but it's going to take time."

"Who made the attack?"

"We don't know," Greenfeld said.

"The Russians."

"It could be anyone."

"Just when the entire communications network of Latvia goes down, someone coincidentally takes out your satellite dish? This is a coordinated attack."

Lance sat down. He ran his hands through his hair and thought. Then he stood back up. "I need you to get a message to Langley as soon as you can. And you need all hands on deck getting those comms back up because if they don't get this message out soon, it's going to be too late."

"The ambassador's working on the comms. We're sure the Pentagon is too," Greenfeld said.

Lance turned to the two marines who were still in the room. "Do you have a fuel tank here?"

"What kind of fuel?" one of the marines said.

"Gasoline, for that car out there?"

"We do," the marine said.

"Then go get that tank filled," Lance said. "I'm not going to be able to buy gas on the road."

The two marines looked to Greenfeld, and Greenfeld nodded.

When they were gone, Lance said, "You need to tell Riuth that Russia is going to invade Latvia. That's what all this confusion is about. They're going to cross the border near a village called Ziguri."

"Are you sure about this?" Greenfeld said.

"They're coming," Lance said.

The look on Greenfeld's face said he didn't believe what he was hearing.

"I know it sounds far-fetched," Lance said.

"Far-fetched?" Greenfeld said. "It's impossible. If they did that, they'd trigger NATO's defensive pact. It would be the beginning of World War Three."

"They're gambling," Lance said.

"They wouldn't gamble on that," Greenfeld said.

"Then you explain to me what's going on right now. You've got Russians demonstrating on the streets of Riga. Our comms with Washington are down. The entire communications system of this country is down."

"Oh my God," Greenfeld suddenly said.

"What is it?" Lance said.

"I didn't put two and two together until just now, but when the comms went down, I tried our emergency protocol."

"What protocol is that?"

"We're equipped with a separate Keyhole UHF capability here."

"You've got full Keyhole comms?"

"Yes, we do. A secret satellite dish that wasn't hit in the attack. Our comms automatically switched to it as soon as the main dish was taken out."

"And?"

"It didn't work."

"What do you mean it didn't work? It's UHF. It's rock solid."

"It didn't work," Greenfeld said again.

"It must be your dish," Lance said.

"That's why I didn't connect the dots," Greenfeld said. "I figured, our dish is down, that's why our comms are down. But like I said, the UHF comes in on a completely different dish. That dish wasn't attacked."

Lance shook his head. That didn't make sense.

"Wait," he said. "Why would you have Keyhole UHF here? You don't need it."

"We're right on Russia's doorstep," Greenfeld said. "It's precisely because of a situation like you just outlined that we were equipped with it."

"But Keyhole isn't a local service," Lance said. "There are four satellites covering the globe. If your dish isn't the problem…".

He waited a moment for the meaning of his own words to sink in. Then he saw what had caused Greenfeld to go so suddenly pale.

"If Keyhole is down…" he said.

"If it's down here," Greenfeld said, "then it's down for all of Europe."

"It's down for a quarter of the globe," Lance said.

"Which means…".

Lance shook his head. "There's nothing we can do about that right now," he said. "You just focus on getting the regular comms up and running, and then you tell Roth the invasion is about to take place near the village of Ziguri."

"They're really coming," Greenfeld said.

Lance nodded. "They're really coming," he said.

71

B y the time Prochnow arrived in Ziguri, it was just a few hours before dawn. He did a circle of the village, checking to ensure there was no military presence, then drove into the village square and pulled over.

The village did not interest him in the least.

It was like a thousand other villages, in a dozen other countries. A square at the center, a church, a bar or two, a hotel.

It was late, but there were still some men gathered around the bar. They were very drunk and stumbled on the snow-covered sidewalk, wailing things at each other.

There were no women.

In the square, some geese were huddled by the fountain. Prochnow wondered if it was strange that they hadn't flown anywhere more hospitable for the winter but didn't know.

He pulled a silenced pistol from the glovebox and stepped out of the car. The snow crunched satisfyingly beneath his boot.

He looked around the square to see if anyone was paying attention to him.

They were not.

The snow on the ground was pristine, everything white and clean. There hadn't been time yet for people to leave their tracks in it.

He walked away from the square down the main village away from the bar. As the men receded into the distance, everything grew unnaturally quiet.

Kirov had filled him in on the plans for this place, and as he walked along in the snow, he imaged all that white turning to red.

All that silence turning to screams.

It wouldn't be so strange, he told himself.

Not if one took a long enough view of things.

Massacres had happened in this region before.

Not even that many years ago.

There were men alive in that village now who had witnessed what had come before.

Nothing under the sun was new. It had all been done before

And nothing Kirov had planned hadn't been done there before. It had been done by the Soviets, by the Germans, even by the Latvians themselves.

The orders he'd been given were as old as man himself.

Prochnow was a soldier. And tens of thousands of men before him, men just like him, had carried out orders just like the ones he'd been given.

"Everything that's about to happen has happened before," he said to himself as he walked up to the police station. There was a single lightbulb on above the door, and he didn't go up to it but went around to the back. "And everything that's happened before will happen again."

There were specific incidents he could point to to show that what he was doing was just more of the same. He was no different from the soldiers who'd come before. They all did the things he was about to do.

Not so far from where he stood, in a single week at the end of November 1941, Germans just like him from Einsatzgruppe A, with the help of Latvian auxiliary police from the Arajs Kommando, unloaded a thousand German Jews from trains that had arrived directly from the Reich. They marched the Jews into a forest known as the Rumbula.

That day, like today, the commanders brought in an outsider. Today, it was Prochnow.

That day, it was a man named Friedrich Jeckeln.

Both had shown themselves to be capable killers, although Jeckeln had killed more than Prochnow ever could have imagined. In a brutally efficient massacre in the Ukraine known as Babi Yar, Jeckeln, with just fifty men, had killed thirty thousand Jews without incident.

Next to that, what was to happen here in Ziguri was mere child's play.

Prochnow wasn't in charge of the massacre that was to take place here, that distinction fell to a man named Oleg Zhukovsky from the GRU's First Directorate in Moscow.

Prochnow was just there to facilitate.

To make sure that things went according to plan.

But like Jeckeln before him, Prochnow appreciated the need to pay attention to practicalities.

If the massacre was to go off without a hitch, Zhukovsky would have to arrive before dawn, before the village came to life and the people had their wits about them.

The element of surprise was needed.

As was order.

When there was order, the people would obey almost any orders.

Jeckeln had planned everything.

He knew the distance he needed to march the Jews was eight kilometers.

He knew that in Latvia in November, he would have about eight hours of daylight during which to perform his grisly work. He grouped the Jews into batches and made sure that the path they were to march along was lined with soldiers to prevent escape.

When they arrived at the forest, six large pits, mass graves sufficient to hold twenty-five thousand bodies, were already waiting for them. The pits were dug in levels, like inverted pyramids, with the broader levels at the top and a path that went down to the bottom. That way, the victims could be marched down into the pits, down to the level at which they were to be buried.

Prochnow doubted Zhukovsky had planned things down to that level, but then, he didn't need to be as tidy. His job was to create an atrocity that would attract the attention of the world. Russian television crews would follow him, filming the results of the massacre and claiming that the Latvian government had carried it out.

The people in this village were Russians.

No one would believe the Russian army had invaded Latvia to kill ethnic Russians.

It was remarkable how many people could be killed, and how easily, when everything was planned out ahead of time.

With just twelve men from the Einsatzgruppe, Jeckeln managed to kill thousands in the eight hours of daylight available to him. The twelve men were all German.

No Latvians were selected.

It was thought they lacked the necessary skill.

To save ammunition, the victims were killed with a single bullet to the back of the neck. Genickschußspezialisten, or Neck-shot Specialists, were needed to do it, and Jeckeln used men he trusted.

Twelve Germans.

That was all he wanted, and that was all he used.

The massacre was carried out using a *Sardinenpackung*, or sardine-packing, system. It was cruel because it required the victims to lie down directly on top of those killed just before them.

But it saved Jeckeln's men the heavy labor of moving the bodies into the graves after death.

To create a veneer of deniability should the mass graves ever be discovered, the final step was to spray the bodies with Russian submachine guns.

Prochnow entered the police station through the back door, and a small bell chimed above his head.

A sleepy officer in uniform looked up from his desk, roused by the sound.

"Can I help you?" he said in Latvian.

"I think you can," Prochnow said, drawing his gun.

The policeman simply looked at the gun and sighed, as if his corpulent mass had been deflated by a pin.

"What's your name?" Prochnow said.

The man shrugged, as if he didn't know the answer. "Why do you want to know my name?" he said.

He seemed resigned to his fate.

As if it didn't surprise him.

As if he knew what Prochnow knew.

That everything that had happened in the past could happen again, and indeed, would happen again.

Prochnow let out a little laugh, mostly to himself. "I guess I'm just curious," he said.

The cop let out a long, sad sigh. "My name is Baskin," he said.

"Baskin," Prochnow repeated.

"Why are you here?" Baskin said.

"You know why I'm here."

"No," Baskin said, his eyes fixed on the barrel of the gun. "I do not."

"You know," Prochnow said again.

"Your accent," Baskin said. "You're German."

"Yes," Prochnow said.

"What is a German doing here?"

"Only what's been done before."

"I see," Baskin said.

There was a certainty in his voice. As if, after a lifetime of slow, country policeman's work, he'd always known this day would come.

"You're a German," Baskin said, "but you work for the Russians."

"Yes, I do," Prochnow said.

Baskin nodded. Very sadly, he said, "You know, we're all Russians in this village. The older ones, they don't even speak Latvian."

"That's why you've been chosen," Prochnow said. "That very reason."

Baskin didn't have time to nod, to acknowledge the brutal fact of what was going to happen, because Prochnow pressed the trigger, and a bullet hit him right between the eyes.

72

It was just an hour before dawn when Zhukovsky finally received the order to proceed. He was livid that he'd been forced to waste the night.

Kirov wasn't a military man. He didn't appreciate the impact of such delays.

Zhukovsky's men had been sitting around all night, losing focus.

That could be the difference between success and failure on a mission like this.

They were the best of the best, but a butchering job like this required a particular mindset.

They were being sent across the border in false Latvian uniforms.

They were going to kill ethnic Russian civilians, their own people, women and children. They all knew it was a dishonorable mission. They knew it was a cruel mission.

Evil.

And Kirov had just given them all an entire night to sit and think about it.

If they failed to carry out the mission, it would be Kirov's fault.

He had his men assemble in front of the vehicles and prepared to address them. They stood erect in their stiff Latvian uniforms, lined up in the cold, the air from their breaths billowing in front of them.

The uniforms hadn't been easy to come by. They'd been stolen from a Latvian laundry contractor in Riga a couple of weeks previously. Kirov then ordered that the laundry facility be burned to the ground so that it would be impossible to know if any uniforms were unaccounted for.

"All right, men," Zhukovsky bellowed. "I know you're wondering what you're doing in foreign uniforms, and I'm not going to lie to you. The Hague Convention makes the wearing of false uniforms a war crime."

He looked at the men. He knew he wasn't telling them anything they didn't already know. They didn't care about the Hague Convention. After the training he'd just subjected them to, they should have been ready to break every rule of war, every law of man and God, every protocol of every statute, if he ordered them to

It was a waste.

Kirov had personally made the arrangements for after their return. There would be no celebration. No breaking out of beers and music.

They were to be gassed in the back of a helicopter.

Zhukovsky couldn't say they deserved better, they were about to commit an atrocity on a scale Europe hadn't seen in decades, but he still felt a loyalty to them.

They were his creation.

"We're going to commit a war crime today," he said. "A crime against humanity."

They'd known it was coming. Their faces didn't make the slightest response.

"When you return from this mission, you are all going to be made officers of the Main Directorate of the General Staff of the Armed Forces of the Russian Federation."

Their faces were as immovable as statues.

"And that is what I want you to concentrate on while we carry out our orders."

He paused, reaching into his pocket for a pack of cigarettes.

"You will no longer be green recruits," he said. "You will be hardened men. Tested men. The Western Military District will immediately begin to rely on you, and given the operation that we are spearheading, it is no exaggeration to say that careers will be made in the coming months, gentlemen. Heroes will be made. And fortunes will be made."

He stepped closer to them.

"What we are about to launch is the full-scale invasion of Latvia, a NATO member, and while that may seem like an action that would spark off World War Three, our leadership has determined that the West will not respond in force. What that means, for our nation, for our Motherland, is that we are about to embark on nothing less than the complete reconstitution of the USSR, in all her former glory."

He put his cigarette in his mouth and began inspecting the men from close range.

"And it is in recognition of the historic nature of this mission that I am going to do something I've never done before."

He lit the cigarette and blew out his smoke at them.

"I'm going to give you this one chance to opt-out of the mission."

They were so young. Some of them weren't even old enough to shave.

"I make no apology for this, gentlemen, but this mission will seem an ugly one. The word used in the Hague Convention is *perfidy*. Do you know what the word *perfidy* means?"

Not one of them moved a muscle.

"It means treachery, gentlemen. It means deceit. It means faithlessness."

He'd seen these men torture animals. He'd seen them execute prisoners. They didn't care about this warning, but he had to be certain.

"The military manuals of two hundred nations, including Russia," he said, "going back two centuries, call what we are about to do a War Crime."

Zhukovsky lowered his voice. "So, any man here who does not want to take part, step forward now."

No one moved.

That wasn't surprising.

He'd already shown them what happened to those who backed out. He'd unloaded a dump truck's worth of corpses in front of them.

They weren't stupid.

They knew what he was offering them.

"Last chance," Zhukovsky said. "Step forward now, or forever hold your peace."

No one moved.

"Because, gentlemen, if any of you balks once the operation has begun, the punishment will be meted out not against you, but your families at home. Your parents, your brothers and sisters, your girlfriends, everyone you've ever loved. Am I understood?"

The man he was standing in front of caught his eye.

"You look like you have something to say," Zhukovsky said.

To Zhukovsky's surprise, the man stepped forward.

Zhukovsky couldn't believe it.

"You're refusing the mission?" he said.

The man didn't make a sound, but almost imperceptibly, he nodded his head.

Zhukovsky knew this was a moment when the entire mood of the group could change. Morale was a delicate thing.

"You unpatriotic swine," Zhukovsky said, and he pulled his service weapon from his coat and shot the man in the skull.

The man slumped to his knees and then fell forward, facedown in the snow.

"Gentlemen," Zhukovsky said to the remaining men, "what you are about to do can never be undone. We are at war. Make no mistake. And the steps you take today are the beginning of Russia's journey to reclaiming all of the glory lost in the past. Now, let's roll."

73

Prochnow leaned on the side of his vehicle and inhaled deeply from a cigarette. He'd pulled over to the side of the road on a small rise overlooking a stretch of forest that extended eastward from the village of Ziguri toward the border. Through his binoculars, he could see nothing but trees, even with night vision, but he knew they would be there soon.

Zhukovsky was personally bringing two squads of men across the border, dressed in Latvian uniforms.

According to Kirov, he was a competent commander and a man who could be trusted to get the job done. With the Latvian monitoring positions abandoned and the US satellite compromised, there was nothing in Zhukovsky's way.

All communications were down across the entire country, so even if someone saw them now, there was little they could do about it. Even the village's only policeman was dead.

It was almost dawn, and a redness brushed up against the underside of the clouds to the east.

As the first beams of light began cutting through the trees, Prochnow saw something, two squads of twelve men each. They rode in GAZ Tigrs, the Russian equivalent of Humvees.

They were armed with Heckler and Koch G36 assault rifles chambered for a 5.56 NATO round. Each had two thirty-round magazines, but the men also carried one-hundred-round drum C-Mags. The guns were a compact sub-carbine variant, the same one used by Latvian ground forces.

In addition to the G36's, each man also carried a Heckler and Koch UMP, or *Universale Maschinenpistole*. It was the standard-issue submachine gun of the Latvian Army and was chambered for a 9x19mm Parabellum. Everything was designed to be traced back to the Latvian Army.

They also carried Heckler and Koch 40 millimeter grenade launchers and M2 variant Carl Gustavs, whose 84mm shell could take out any tank used by the Latvian Army. It was unlikely they'd be needed, but they were on hand if necessary.

It was not lost on Prochnow that the weapons were mostly German. The German chancellor would protest this atrocity vehemently, and yet, German factories provided the guns.

The population of the village of Ziguri was over a thousand souls. In a shockingly short time, the massacre would be complete. The pictures would then be sent to every newspaper and outlet on the planet, and Russia would have a pretext for the quickest invasion in its history.

By noon of that very day, the tanks of the Second Guards Tamanskaya Motor Rifle Division would be in central Riga. With the riots, the protests, the lack of a communications system, the country would be on its knees.

Kirov already had news crews from Moscow and Saint Petersburg waiting by the border. As soon as the massacre was complete, they would flood into Ziguri, and their version of events would be the first, indeed the only, to hit international media outlets during the critical timeframe.

Their footage would be distributed globally before any Latvian news crews were allowed on the scene. But even when the local crews arrived, they would only be able to report what the Russians had already broadcast. That hundreds of ethnic Russians had been massacred by men in Latvian uniforms.

By then, Russia would be in possession of the capital, and the president would have demonstrated to the world that he was reconstituting the USSR.

It would be the biggest *fuck you* to the West since 9/11.

The West was accustomed to victory. The defeat of Nazi Germany. The surrender of the Japanese Empire. The collapse of the Soviet Union on the day after Christmas in 1991.

The West didn't really know what defeat tasted like.

This would be their first bitter taste.

And it would be only the beginning.

Russia was rising.

China was rising.

NATO was in its twilight.

Even Americans were ready for it. They were tired of footing the bill, of providing for the security of the entire globe.

A factory worker in Michigan, a farmer in Oklahoma, what did he care about the security of Latvia, a place he would never see and couldn't find on a map?

NATO, by propping up weaker states, was an aberration against the laws of nature.

The future belonged to the strong.

The time had come for the weak to wither and die.

74

Zhukovsky and his men met Prochnow east of the village.

Zhukovsky strode up to him and saluted. The German made a half-hearted attempt at a salute back, then sucked from his cigarette.

"Everything ready?" Zhukovsky said.

The German nodded "The only cop in town is dead," he said in Russian.

Zhukovsky nodded and turned to his men. This was the moment he'd been waiting for. The moment when he would find out what they were made of.

"There are a lot of people," Zhukovsky said, "who say our nation is on the decline. They say we've been sapped of our power. They say the fire has been knocked out of our bellies."

He looked at them, he looked at their eyes, and saw nothing.

He'd spent months wearing them down.

They'd been tortured.

They'd been brutalized.

And when this mission was done, they'd be slaughtered like cattle.

They'd heard enough of his words.

The time had come to issue the order.

"All right, men," he said. "I want a thousand dead bodies in the streets of this village. Men, women, children. No quarter. Do you understand me?"

They saluted but gave no clue as to their state of mind.

"I don't care who you kill," he said. "Just rack them up. A thousand corpses."

He looked at Prochnow and realized that, now that the time had come, even he looked pale. A massacre was no simple thing. Tactically, it was like shooting fish in a barrel, but psychologically, it played games on men's minds.

Prochnow looked like he'd just seen a ghost, and the cigarette that had been hanging from his lips fell to the ground unfinished.

"Surround the town," Zhukovsky said. "Start at the outskirts and work your way toward the center. There'll be a crowd in the square by the time you get there."

He looked at the men and tried to assess their thoughts.

Would they obey the order?

Would they do it?

"Bravo, you go around the village and approach from the west. Block off the road to Liepna. No vehicles get out. Do you hear me? Use the grenade launchers to block the road if you have to. Charlie, split up and take the north and south. I want Plešova and the forestry track cut off."

He looked at the German.

"Prochnow, you and I will walk in from the east. Treat it like a sport. It will go easier on you."

Prochnow nodded weakly.

"No one move in until you hear my gunfire," he said.

The team leaders waited, ashen-faced, unflinching.

"Go," Zhukovsky said.

The men turned and began making their way down the hill toward the village on foot.

They were operating under complete radio silence, but the operation was so simple it didn't matter.

Zhukovsky watched them leave, then turned back to Prochnow.

"Prochnow," Zhukovsky said, "are you all right?"

Prochnow looked at him blankly.

"I'd have thought a German would have a stronger belly."

"It's a lot of people," Prochnow said. "I wasn't prepared."

"It's nothing," Zhukovsky said. "A drop in the bucket. In your grandfather's day, they'd have done this ten times without batting an eye."

"I guess this isn't my grandfather's day," Prochnow said.

"Nonsense," Zhukovsky said. "Every day is every other day. It makes no difference. Same sky. Same sun and moon. Same devils in the hearts of men."

"I don't know," Prochnow said. "I thought I knew, but now, this, I don't know."

"Nonsense," Zhukovsky said. "Stick with me. I'll show you how it's done."

Prochnow said nothing.

The sun was breaking over the tops of the trees, and Zhukovsky could see the village coming to life. He lit a cigarette and offered the pack to Prochnow.

Prochnow took one, and Zhukovsky lit it.

They smoked in silence.

It didn't take long for the other teams to get in position. Zhukovsky finished his cigarette and began walking down the hill toward the nearest farmhouse.

He would be the first to open fire, and his gunfire would be the signal for the killing to commence.

The whole thing wouldn't take more than thirty minutes. It was surprisingly easy to kill a thousand people when they were laid out bare for you like this.

He looked back over his shoulder and saw that Prochnow wasn't following.

"Hey, German," he shouted back.

Prochnow said nothing.

"Aren't you coming?"

75

P rochnow felt as if his feet were welded to the
ground. He knew he should follow Zhukovsky. He
knew that he would regret it forever if he didn't.

He wasn't some soldier of fortune, a mere mercenary
who fought for the highest bidder.

He was a true believer.

He believed in what was being done here this day, and
he knew that it was necessary.

He believed if it all went according to plan, that it would
change the world. Like the first uprisings of the Communist
Revolution.

Nothing ever changed without the spilling of blood. The
blood of the innocent was what watered the soil of history.

And yet, he couldn't move.

"Come on," Zhukovsky called. "I never took you for a
German coward."

Even that didn't get Prochnow to move. He was a man
who'd killed more people than he could count, but when
the sounds of the first shots broke out, he winced.

His eyes filled.

And it wasn't from the cold.

He watched what there was to watch. The men from the other teams entering the village, entering houses.

The lights had already started coming on inside the houses. The people were rising. Thin lines of smoke came out of their chimneys and up into the still sky.

Some people were already out on the roads, in the fields, or at the square at the center of town.

The gunfire began as a staccato pulse, like the sound of an old motorcycle engine being fired up.

One gun.

Zhukovsky's.

He was using the submachine gun. It sprayed nine-millimeter bullets like a garden hose spraying water.

And then the other guns started up.

And then a grenade.

And then the screaming.

At first, he heard just one lady scream. From her voice, he could tell she was older. She was in the nearest of the farmhouses. The one Zhukovsky had gone into.

And no sooner had she started than she stopped.

Her scream marked the beginning, a herald, and in a matter of seconds, hundreds more could be heard rising up from every quarter of the village. The screams and submachine gun fire were punctuated by the occasional explosion caused by a grenade launcher or, once, a Carl Gustav, which was fired at a vehicle that was trying to flee. The shell cut through the side of the car like a knife, and the occupants crawled out like napalm victims.

Between the two squads, they would have no difficulty reaching Zhukovsky's grisly quota of a thousand corpses. People ran into the streets, into the paths of the soldiers, as if they thought they would save them. They couldn't have made it simpler if they'd wanted to be shot.

Prochnow never would have guessed that such modest houses contained so many people.

He saw an entire family, man, woman, four children, go down in a single spray of fire.

He saw three men rush at one of the teams from behind. They were ten feet from the nearest soldier when he turned, almost languidly, and cut them down.

As the soldiers progressed along the main thoroughfare, it became clear that a concentration effect was taking place. Anyone who wasn't shot instantly instinctively ran for the square at the center of the village, where they thought somehow that the gathering crowd would protect them.

It did not.

That became clear as the square filled and the people realized that all routes of escape were blocked.

There were a few villagers who fought back. Some had hunting rifles, some pistols, a few shotguns, but they were no match for Zhukovsky's men.

Their ammo wasn't up to the task.

Neither was their aim.

Any resistance was quickly subdued.

By the time the squads converged on the square, most of the village was in it, cowering like sheep in a pen. Many were only partially dressed, and as they huddled together for warmth and protection, their breaths rose above them in the cold air like mist from a lake.

Prochnow watched in a rapt mix of awe and horror as Zhukovsky and his men began working through the crowd with the ruthlessness and efficiency of an Einsatzgruppe.

They were like reapers sheafing corn.

Like some monsters from another time, another war.

They fired at the outer edge of the crowd, and the people in their terror began to claw and fight at each other to get toward the middle. Those on the periphery fell to the ground, and the rest, like cornered animals, realized that whatever direction they fled was as hopeless as every other.

Prochnow watched for as long as he could, then, eventually, turned his back on the butchery of it.

It confirmed what he'd always known.

That nothing had changed since the time of his grandfathers.

Men were as easy to butcher today as they'd been in 1940.

They could be mowed down like beasts in a field.

76

L ance left the embassy in a State Department Bell UH-1 Iroquois chopper with diplomatic clearance. An hour later was closing in on the village of Ziguri. Even before he got there, he knew something wasn't right. The first thing he saw was a red glow in the sky, and as he closed in, the smell of smoke mingled with the morning mist.

He did a single pass over the village and could scarcely believe what he saw.

He was a man who'd seen it all. He'd seen Russian *Double Tap* sites in Syria that deliberately targeted rescue workers. He'd seen a civilian convoy of four hundred people blown to dust.

But this was different.

It wasn't the numbers.

He'd seen this many people killed before in airstrikes and artillery bombardments.

That was not what he was looking at.

As he landed in a clearing close to the central square, he

484 SAUL HERZOG

could see that this had been murder at close range. This had been butchery.

There were bodies everywhere. Women, children, the elderly.

He got out of the helicopter, and there was so much smoke in the air he had to rub his eyes.

He knew what he was looking at.

Someone had gone out of their way to make this massacre as bloody, as barbaric, as possible.

Gore was strewn everywhere.

Bodies were piled up in the square like a scene from a zombie movie. There were hundreds of them. Maybe a thousand. And nothing at all had been done to hide the atrocity. In fact, it had been staged to highlight the gruesomeness of it. After the bodies had been piled up, someone had shot the pile with a grenade launcher.

Lance looked at the scene and felt a weakness in his knees. He had to reach out for a lamppost just to keep himself up. And then he retched.

Europe had seen this before.

But not in a long time.

Of course, the world was still full of massacres and bloodshed. Conflicts everywhere smoldered.

Atrocities happened every day. Just because they weren't on the news didn't mean they didn't happen.

Man was a beast, and as Lance had seen in countless countries, a beast cannot change its nature.

But this?

This was different.

And as the helicopters began to fly in, civilian helicopters bearing the names and logos of television networks, Lance realized what he was looking at.

This was a showpiece.

A setup.

The news networks were Russian, all of them, and as they landed, a Russian military helicopter approached from the east.

Lance stood and watched as the first news crew unpacked its things and began to set up a camera in front of the pile of bodies.

"They're not even cold," Lance said to one of the cameramen in Russian. "The blood hasn't even dried."

"Please," the cameraman said. "We're just following orders."

"What does that mean?" Lance said, but the truth was, he already knew.

He didn't need a cameraman to tell him how the world worked. He didn't need a news crew to explain to him that this was a maneuver on the part of Russia that would have global geopolitical repercussions.

This was the beginning of a resurgence that would pull the world back into a new Cold War.

The tanks, the invasion force, was already on its way.

The news reporters, slim, attractive Russian women in neatly-tailored blazers and fur-lined leather gloves, began reporting as if they'd actually witnessed the massacre happen. They were reading from preprepared scripts, each with their own, individualized copy, and one fact was constant.

The Latvian army was responsible.

Lance stood by one of the newscasters and listened to her report.

"At dawn this morning, and in response to growing protests across the country, the Latvian government cracked down in a manner that has not been seen in these lands for eighty years. They sent a small contingent of soldiers into an ethnically Russian village close to the border, and committed atrocities that can only be described as something out of a nightmare. Behind me, the flames of the village of Ziguri still smolder, and the bodies of over a thousand ethnic Russians lie dead, their blood painting the snow with the color of a flag that once shone proudly over this land.

The Red Banner of the USSR."

Lance was about to leave when he heard crying coming from one of the farmhouses. He walked up to the door and pushed it open. The house was a wreck, the windows shattered, the wooden table and chairs in the kitchen kicked over.

He entered and waited.

Then he heard it again.

The sound of a child crying.

It was coming from upstairs, and he quietly made his way toward it.

The stairs creaked under his weight, and the crying stopped.

He reached the top and in Latvian said, "It's over. They're going to help you now."

There was no sound.

"The nurses. They're coming to help the children."

He walked into the first of the bedrooms. There was a large double bed, and on the bed were the bodies of a man and woman. Their blood had seeped through the sheets like crimson dye.

Lance went to the next room, which he could tell from the size of the bed and a porcelain doll in a pink dress, belonged to a child.

"It's all right," he said softly, sitting on the bed.

There was no sound.

"This doll needs a friend," he said, picking it up.

He heard the sound of movement under the bed and bent down. There was a little girl, about five or six years old, and he passed her the doll.

"The bad men are gone," he said to her.

77

As Lance made his way back to the helicopter, he saw that three Russian soldiers were standing in front of it. One of the men was an officer.

"Stop right there," the officer said, raising his weapon.

Lance kept walking toward them.

"What's going on?" he said. "What are Russian soldiers doing on Latvian territory? You can't be here. You're going to cause an incident."

"I think it's a bit late for that," the officer said.

Lance acted casual. "Well, what do you want?" he said.

"Whose helicopter is this?"

"It belongs to the US State Department and is protected by diplomatic credentials."

The officer looked at the two soldiers and then said to Lance, "And who are you?"

"I'm a US State Department observer," he said. "I'm here to find out what the hell's going on."

"How did you get here so quickly."

"I could ask the same of you," Lance said. "I count six

separate news crews too. It's almost as if they'd been told to be ready."

"You need to come with us," the officer said, drawing his sidearm.

Lance made like he would let them take him into custody, then ducked and jabbed the officer with a quick punch to the groin. The officer doubled over, and Lance heaved up under him, lifting him onto his shoulders.

As the other two soldiers tried to grab him, he spun around and threw the officer on top of them.

The soldier on the left ducked and grabbed Lance around the neck. Lance punched him twice in the ribs, then reached up and grabbed his head. He clamped the man's neck between his forearm and elbow and cut off his air supply. As he lost consciousness, the other two got to their feet and drew their weapons.

"What are Russian soldiers doing in Latvia?" Lance said from behind the man he was holding.

The officer fired a shot, which hit the unconscious man in the chest, and Lance pushed him forward at the other two. Then he drew his silenced pistol and killed the soldier on the left with a shot to the head.

The officer fired again but Lance kicked his arm, causing the shot to fly harmlessly in to the air.

The television crews had noticed the fight, and some of the cameramen had turned their lenses onto the action.

Lance grabbed the officer and twisted his arm behind his back until he dropped his gun. Then he jammed his gun into the man's ribs, holding him in front of him.

"Smile, you're on camera," he said.

The officer struggled, and Lance jammed the gun harder against his ribs. "Not so fast," he said. "Next bullet's for you."

"What is this?" the officer said. "What do you want?"

"Look at all those cameras," Lance said. "You're a dead man."

"Go fuck yourself," the officer said.

"Who ordered this operation here?" Lance said.

More helicopters were approaching from the east, and Lance knew they'd be carrying more soldiers.

"Come on," he said to the officer, pushing him forward toward his chopper.

"What are you doing?" the officer stammered. "Where are you taking me?"

Lance pushed him into the back of the chopper and cuffed both his wrists to the overhead handrail.

Some of the cameramen had begun to approach, and Lance turned the gun on them.

"Everyone get back," he said.

He got into the driver's seat of the chopper and powered up the engines. As the Russian choppers landed, he took off, heading east.

He'd have a few minutes head start before any of them realized what was going on.

"Where are we going?" the Russian soldier shouted from his seat in the back.

Lance could barely hear him over the noise of the engines.

Lance leaned back and said, "Who was responsible for what happened back there?"

The man didn't answer.

Lance tapped his leg with his gun. "Look out there," he said, indicating the icy forest beneath them. "You start talking, or I'm going to throw you out of this helicopter, you understand me?"

"Fuck you," the officer said.

"I doubt the fall would kill you," Lance said, "but it'll

break your legs. Then, it will either be the wolves or the cold that gets you."

"They're going to kill me anyway," the officer said.

"All right," Lance said. "So you want to jump?"

The officer could see they were headed toward Russia. He knew Lance wasn't lying.

"I don't know the whole picture," the man said. "I was as shocked by what I saw as you were. I didn't know they were going to do a thing like that. That was a Russian village. Those were Russian people."

"Who was responsible for carrying it out?" Lance said.

"I don't know," the man said.

"You better tell me something," Lance said, nodding toward the forest below.

"There's a training camp," the man said. "A secret camp. We had to transfer it to the GRU."

"Where?"

"East of the Vecumu Meži. Just across the border."

The Vecumu Meži was the forest Agata Zarina had gone to in the first place. What she'd seen, and the reason the biplane was shot down, was in that forest.

"If there was a camp that close to the border, NATO surveillance would have found it."

"No, not this camp," the officer said. "It's completely camouflaged."

"Then how do I find it?"

"I'll show you," the man said. "If you promise not to kill me."

Lance nodded. "You show me then," he said.

"They'll kill you," the man said. "They'll shoot us out of the sky."

"No, they won't," Lance said. "You'll give me plenty of warning."

They flew on for another minute or two, and the man said, "It's another mile up ahead. The camp. Over that rise in the east."

Lance scanned the forest for somewhere to land, and the man said, "What are you going to do with me?"

Lance didn't answer. He had plans for the man. The helicopter would have been tracked the moment it entered Russian airspace, and it would be convenient for Lance if it were to fly back out of Russian airspace without him on it.

"You know how to fly one of these things?" Lance said.

The man nodded. "I think so."

"Just ease up slowly. Smooth motions. This is the throttle."

The man looked at him incredulously.

"Who ran the training camp?" Lance said.

"An old-timer from the GRU. That's all I know."

"Someone senior?"

"Definitely."

"From Moscow?"

The man nodded. "From the First Directorate."

Lance landed the chopper at a small clearing in the trees and got out, leaving the engine running.

He gave the soldier the key to the handcuffs and said, "Ease up gently, and if you want to live, fly west and turn yourself in to the Latvian forces."

The officer looked at him, then said, "Zhukovsky."

"What's that?" Lance said.

"That's who you're looking for. The man who ran the camp. Oleg Zhukovsky."

78

Zhukovsky wiped spattered blood from his face as the vehicle pulled back into the camp. He felt a strange mixture of exhilaration and horror at what he'd done.

He was sitting in the back seat, and in the passenger seat in front of him was Prochnow.

They came to a halt, and Prochnow turned back to look at him. He was about to say something when he stopped himself.

"What is it, Prochnow?"

"Nothing, sir."

"No, go ahead. You can tell me."

Prochnow shook his head, saying nothing.

Zhukovsky looked at him for a moment before climbing out of the vehicle.

"Coward," he muttered as he made his way into his tent.

At the entrance, he stopped and turned back. His men were getting out of their vehicles, and were so covered in blood that they looked like extras from a horror movie.

"Men," Zhukovsky bellowed. "It's done. Go clean up. You'll be flying back to Saint Petersburg in thirty minutes."

He entered the tent and went straight to the toilet, grabbing the sink with both hands.

All of a sudden, a wave of nausea passed over him like a shadow. He gripped the sink so tightly his knuckles were white, and his entire body shivered so violently that he was in danger of pulling the sink from the wall.

He knew that he would never be able to forget the things he'd just done.

For as long as he lived, the memory would haunt him.

On his death bed, the sound of the screams would come to him.

He looked up at the mirror slowly, as if afraid of what he might see, and when his eyes focused, he saw that there was so much blood on his face he looked like an ancient warrior in war paint.

He turned on the water and began scrubbing violently at his hands and face, getting as much of the blood off his skin as possible.

He looked down at his blood-soaked uniform and began clawing at it, ripping off his jacket and yanking at the shirt so violently that the buttons were torn out.

He got off the shirt and washed his arms and chest, splashing the icy water all over his upper body, when an orderly entered the tent.

"Get out," Zhukovsky yelled.

"Sir," the orderly said, holding a phone, "there's a call from Saint Petersburg."

Zhukovsky took a deep breath and steadied his nerves, then walked over to the orderly and took the phone from him.

Zhukovsky knew who it was and took another long breath before saying, "Kirov, it's done."

He knew why he was being called. The mission had gone according to plan. It had been, despite Zhukovsky's overwhelming urge to vomit, a success.

"Oleg Zhukovsky," the voice on the other end of the line said, and to Zhukovsky's shock, it was not the voice of Kirov but of President Molotov himself.

"Mr. President," Zhukovsky gasped. "I wasn't expecting...".

"Zhukovsky," the president said, interrupting him, "I'm calling from the Winter Palace of the Czars, drinking champagne to your victory."

"Sir," Zhukovsky stammered. "We...".

"We were victorious," the president said.

The president wasn't alone. Zhukovsky could hear others in the background, drinking, and toasting and celebrating.

"We were victorious, sir."

"The work you did today," the president said, "will form the groundwork for the complete restoration of the USSR. I hope you understand that?"

Zhukovsky wasn't sure what he understood.

The president spoke in grand terms, but Zhukovsky didn't think in such terms. The words failed to hold meaning for him. He knew only what he saw with his own eyes, what he felt, what he tasted, and right then, all he could taste was the metallic viscosity of human blood.

"We are going to regain all the former power of the Soviet Union," the president said. "We never ceased being a superpower. Do you understand that?"

"I understand, sir."

"This is a signal, a clarion, a shot across the bow. The

world is on notice. What was it that Winston Churchill said?"

"I'm not sure, sir," Zhukovsky stammered.

"From the Baltic to the Adriatic, an Iron Curtain has descended across the Continent of Europe."

"I think so, sir."

"Well, Zhukovsky, you just restored that curtain. This is the first step."

"Thank you, sir," Zhukovsky said, not sure at all how to respond.

"You have gone far beyond the call of duty today, Zhukovsky. I know it wasn't easy for you to take personal command of this team."

"It was an honor, sir."

"I just issued the orders for the Tamanskaya Motor Rifle Division, the Częstochowa Tank Brigade, the 112th Guards Missile Brigade, the Warsaw Artillery Brigade, the 96th ISTAR, and the 69th Logistics, to cross the border into Latvia."

"I see," Zhukovsky said, honored to be let in on such details by the president himself.

The units the president mentioned were the most elite forces of the Western Military District, the cream of the Russian Army. This truly was the beginning of a new age of Russian aggression.

"I want you back in Saint Petersburg," the president said. "You're taking over as GRU liaison."

"Taking over? What about Kirov, sir?"

"Kirov," the president said, "is hiding something from me. I haven't figured out what it is yet, but I will."

"I'll organize transport immediately, sir."

"No need. I'm sending you one of my personal choppers. Kirov will meet you when you land."

"I'm honored, sir."

"The world may never know of the blood you spilled today, Zhukovsky, but I know, and I'm going to make sure your name goes down as a hero."

"It is an honor to serve the Motherland, sir."

"Remember this moment, Zhukovsky. This is the feeling of Russia's resurgence. This is the taste of victory."

L ance moved carefully through the forest, ducking branches and placing every step carefully. He knew exactly the type of devices that would be placed around a facility of this nature and moved along the rutted track slowly, examining every twig, every blade of grass, until he found the first tripwire.

The wire was connected to a POMZ-type fragmentation mine that had been placed on a stake twelve inches above the ground. It was a simple device, a crude sleeve containing a two-and-a-half-ounce rod of TNT. The sleeve was cut in a crosshatch pattern that ensured it would fragment into sharp shards in the event of detonation. It had a four-meter kill radius, but individual shards could easily be lethal at greater distances.

This particular mine, which was concealed in the undergrowth, had been wired to detonate on release. If someone tripped it and realized, they could remain as still as possible and call for help. If they were still enough, and the help came fast enough, there was a slim chance the explosive could be disarmed.

It was a precaution in case a friendly tripped the wire, which was far more likely than not at a camp like this.

Lance went around the tripwire and crawled the last hundred yards through the brush until he reached the edge of the camp. There was the sound of a single generator, and he could also see signs of the extensive measures that had been taken to conceal the camp from the air.

It was situated in a dip between two hills, and he was able to get an idea of its general layout by climbing a tree overlooking the site. Even from that proximity, it was difficult to make out the tents.

There were a few separate clearings, all covered with camouflage nets suspended from the trees. In each clearing was one or more army tents. One was likely a barracks, one a command tent, and there would be others for storage and equipment.

It didn't look like the camp housed more than about thirty or forty men. The generator was on but most likely wasn't used often for fear of giving away the camp to NATO surveillance drones, which monitored the area closely.

Lance watched the site for a few minutes, long enough to get an idea of the locations of the few guards on duty, and when he heard two Russian Mi-8 choppers approaching from the north, he climbed back down the tree.

The first chopper was painted in the high-gloss camouflage pattern that was standard for the Russian military, but the second bore the gray, red and blue color scheme used for the Russian president's personal fleet.

Lance was also able to identify the distinctive square windows and over-sized external fuel tanks on the second chopper that marked it as having been upgraded for VVIP, or Very Very Important Person, transportation.

For a second, he wondered if the president himself was on board.

It would have been ballsy, but the Russian president had been known to take risks like that.

A few years ago, he was filmed driving a tank over a frozen lake. He'd also once abseiled into a deep crevasse inside a Siberian glacier.

The first chopper was a troop transport, and as it approached, two squads of men came out of the barracks tent and prepared to board. Lance knew that, in all likelihood, he was looking at the men responsible for the massacre.

Lance had no intention of letting them leave. Once that chopper flew out of here, tracking down all the men involved in what had happened would become exponentially more difficult.

He checked the weapons he'd been supplied with by Greenfeld, two silenced fifth-generation Glock 17's, a Latvian-issue assault rifle with 3x optical sight, and a forty-millimeter grenade launcher.

The two choppers touched down in a small clearing outside the camp, and Lance crept through the forest toward the site.

Apart from the pilots, both choppers were empty.

They were definitely there for the extraction of the soldiers responsible for the massacre.

Lance prepared for his attack. He'd intended to wait for the soldiers to board the choppers, then hit them with a well-placed grenade once they were all packed in, but as he watched, he saw something curious take place. The pilots of both choppers, four men, got out and unloaded some equipment that looked like a large fuel tank.

They set it up next to the chopper and attached a rubber

hose from the top of the tank to a connector on the hull of the aircraft. Then they went to the main transport door and made some adjustments to the locking mechanism. Lance was about a hundred yards away, and he crawled carefully through the brush to get closer.

When he was about fifty yards away, he saw that the chopper had been altered so that the passenger cabin was sealed off from the pilots. Its windows had also been blacked out with what looked to be sheets of steel plate.

Something wasn't right.

As the first of the soldiers came out from the barracks toward the chopper, the pilots stood by the doors and helped them board.

To Lance, it looked as if they were making sure the men got on board and stayed on board.

The soldiers had a sullen look about them. Lance knew that look. They'd been through an intensive regimen, which wasn't surprising considering the task they'd just been given.

And Lance had no doubt what was about to happen to them.

Lance knew how the world worked.

He knew the inexorable logic of the Russian military.

These men were tools.

They were expendable.

And they'd performed their function.

Apart from a small group of commanders, they were the only men alive who knew for certain what happened in the village of Ziguri. With the satellites down, with Latvia's internal communications networks down, these men were the only witnesses.

There would be survivors in the village, but their accounts would be confused, chaotic. Some would have heard Russian spoken, but others would have only seen the Latvian uniforms. All, in their terror, would have been overwhelmed by the screams of the dying and the pools of blood that flowed over the cobbles in the square like rainwater.

In any case, Russia had already begun securing the village and sealing it off. Once the invasion started, any eyewitness testimony would be heavily censored.

Lance watched the men board the chopper, and when the last of them was on board, the pilots shut the door and then locked it so that it couldn't be opened from the inside. Then they went into the cockpit and fired up the engines. The engines revved, but the propellers didn't turn. Instead, the sound of screaming could be heard from inside the sealed passenger compartment.

The men must have been flinging themselves against the walls of the compartment because the entire helicopter shook from the movement.

Seconds turned to minutes, and the heaving and screaming grew louder and louder. It felt like an eternity before the men grew silent. Ten minutes had passed. The pilots checked their watches then powered down the engines.

When they opened the door, there was nothing inside but corpses. They let the air clear, then pulled the bodies out to make sure they were dead. Lance saw that the skin on the men's faces and hands was pink as ham.

80

Lance watched the pilots for a minute, then opened fire on them with the silenced pistols, killing all four.

He proceeded toward what he'd determined to be the command tent, already knowing where to expect guards. With all the men who'd committed the massacre dead already, there weren't many left to guard the place.

Two soldiers sat in a guard post by the barracks surrounded by sandbags. They were relaxed, smoking cigarettes, not paying attention. Another two stood outside the command tent in the next clearing.

Lance took a grenade from the launcher and lobbed it into the guard post. As it exploded, he darted to the next clearing and opened fire with the assault rifle on the two men stationed outside the command tent.

He kept moving, rotating around the clearings through the brush and undergrowth in an anti-clockwise direction.

Four more guards came running out of the barracks tent and Lance figured that must have been about it for men in the camp. The guards had no idea where Lance was, they had no idea if they were under attack from the air or from land, by one man or a hundred, and Lance picked off the first of them with two shots to the torso. The man fell to the ground and the other three opened fire in his direction.

Lance dropped to the ground and fired a grenade.

Then he retreated about fifty yards into the brush, past the place where he'd found the tripwire earlier. He took cover behind the trunk of a fallen tree and waited for the soldiers to approach.

The instant the lead man tripped the wire, he froze.

The others looked at him, terror on their faces.

"Don't move," one man said.

Lance rose up from his position and shot the man who'd tripped the wire. All three of them were caught in the blast.

Lance made his way back to the camp in time to see an overweight man, half-dressed, with pasty skin and a gut, running for the president's Mi-8 chopper.

"Stop," Lance called out.

The man knew his time had come. He stopped running and raised his hands. His back was to Lance, but he seemed to know who was standing behind him.

His pants were open, and with his hands in the air, they fell down around his ankles, revealing a pair of white, cotton briefs.

Unconsciously, he made to pull them up, and Lance said, "Don't move."

The man raised his hands back up.

"Turn around," Lance said.

The man turned. The front of his tunic was open, as were the buttons of his shirt, and apart from the white cotton underpants, every inch of his clothing had been spattered in blood.

"You're Oleg Zhukovsky," Lance said.

"And you're Lance Spector," Zhukovsky said.

Lance stepped closer to him. "You led those men," he said. "You did that. You killed all those people."

Zhukovsky looked Lance in the eye and sneered.

Lance could already see that he would get nothing from him.

He was a broken man.

Destroyed.

There was nothing Lance could threaten him with that compared to what he'd done already to himself.

"They were Russian," Lance said.

"That's why it had to be them we killed," the man said.

"To provide a pretext," Lance said.

The man said nothing.

Lance stepped closer to him, holding his gun out in front, ready to fire if he so much as moved.

"Who are you?" Lance said.

"You know who I am."

"I know your name," Lance said. "That's not the same."

The man didn't answer, and Lance said, "I suppose it doesn't matter. You'll be dead soon enough."

The man remained very still.

"If you're remembered at all," Lance said, "it will be as a murderer."

"Men who do things like me," Zhukovsky said, "are never remembered. No one wants to write about such things in the history books."

Lance shook his head. "Come now, Zhukovsky," he said. "I can call you that, can't I?"

"I don't care what you call me."

"You think you're a special case, don't you, Zhukovsky? You think what you did today sets you apart from other men. The truth is, there have been soldiers like you all through history. In every time. In every country. In every war. You're not special."

"I did what needed to be done," Zhukovsky said.

"You're a dog, Zhukovsky. A dog that got a taste for it."

"A taste for what?"

"A taste for blood, Zhukovsky."

Zhukovsky shrugged.

Lance knew he was wasting his time. What was there to say to a man like this?

As if to confirm the thought, Zhukovsky said, "If you're going to kill me, kill me."

"Don't you have anything left to say? Any last words."

"Do you want me to say something?"

Lance shook his head. He didn't know what he wanted.

"Those people were Russians," Zhukovsky said. "They belonged to the Motherland. And the Motherland needed them to be sacrificed."

"They didn't belong to Russia," Lance said. "They belonged to God, and to God alone. So when you killed them, Zhukovsky, when you took their lives, you took something that belonged to God."

"There is no God," Zhukovsky spat.

"You don't know that," Lance said. "No one knows."

"It's all lies," Zhukovsky said.

"And the bullet I'm about to fire into your head," Lance said, "is that a lie?"

Zhukovsky let out a quick laugh.

"Is this all amusing to you?" Lance said.

Zhukovsky cleared phlegm from his throat and spat it out. He said, "I killed those people for my country. I killed them because I was ordered to do it. And now you're going to kill me for your country. Because you were ordered to do it."

"No one ordered me to do this," Lance said.

"I know who you are, Lance Spector," Zhukovsky said. "And I know that when they order you to kill, you kill. Same as me."

"That's different," Lance said.

Zhukovsky laughed. "That's the real tragedy," he said. "You don't even know what you are. What you're becoming."

"I'm not like you."

"And you think I was always like this?" Zhukovsky said. "You think I was born a sadist. When I was your age, Lance Spector, I did what you do. I killed when they told me to kill. I told myself I was on the side of the good guys. I was just like you."

"We're not the same," Lance said.

"We're certainly not so very different as you imagine, Lance Spector."

Zhukovsky let out another long laugh, then broke into a fit of coughing and spitting.

"Look at you right now," he said, "itching to end my life. Just dying to pull that trigger. Aren't you?"

"Shut up," Lance said.

"How are we different?" Zhukovsky said. "Because I killed a thousand people today, and you did not? That's just math, Spector. I killed a number. You kill a number. Is it the number that matters, or the killing?"

"You shut up right now, or I'll blow your brains out."

"Go on," Zhukovsky taunted.

Lance didn't know what to say. Maybe they were the same. Maybe he was on a path that would end up as Zhukovsky had done. Maybe, if he wasn't a monster yet, he was on his way to becoming one.

He could feel it.

He knew what rage was.

He wanted to avenge Sam, and Clarissa, and the unborn child that died at his own hand.

"We're on the same path, you and I," Zhukovsky said. "And if you're right that there's a God, he'll curse us both to the same inferno. You mark my words."

"You know," Lance said, "you're wrong to say I'm here on orders."

"Of course you're here on orders. What other reason could there be?"

"No one ordered me to be here, Zhukovsky."

"You're here then because…".

"Because of what happened in Montana. I'm here for my own reasons. I'm not here for my country. I'm here for revenge."

"Revenge?"

"I gave my word that I would look out for someone. A girl. And now she's dead."

"I don't know what you're talking about," Zhukovsky said.

"You know what I'm talking about."

Zhukovsky shook his head. "Why would I be involved in something like that. My work was here."

"Then who ordered it?"

Zhukovsky laughed. "Shoot me, or don't shoot me, Lance Spector, but we're done talking."

"Who ordered her killed?" Lance said again.

"Why would I tell you?"

"Because you're about to die, Zhukovsky. You're going to die because of that order. And why should you die while he lives?"

Lance raised up the gun and pointed it at Zhukovsky's bare chest.

"Tell me," he said.

Zhukovsky laughed again. One last time. Then Lance fired.

The bullet struck his chest with a thud, and Zhukovsky, like the beast he was, didn't flinch at all.

He didn't make a sound. He didn't move.

He stood still for about thirty seconds, then finally, all at once, dropped to his knees.

Lance watched, then walked over to him.

"You know who had her killed, Zhukovsky."

Zhukovsky looked up at him, blood filling his mouth, "That's really the only reason you're here? A thousand innocent people were just massacred, and all you want to know is who killed your whore of a girlfriend."

Lance sighed. It was true.

All that blood.

All that talk of God.

And the only reason he was there was to get revenge.

"You're right," Lance said. "So give him to me."

"In all of this," Zhukovsky said, "the only person who really cares about those people, the only one who knows what happened to them, the only person who was there when they died, was me."

"Who ordered the hit on Sam?" Lance said.

Zhukovsky fell forward from his knees. He stopped himself, holding himself up, his hands wrist-deep in the snow, and saliva fell from his mouth to the ground, turning the snow pink.

Lance bent down.

"Tell me," he whispered into Zhukovsky's ear. "Tell me so I can kill him."

Zhukovsky looked at him. Their faces were very close to each other. Then he said, "That man you want is Jacob Kirov."

"Jacob Kirov," Lance repeated.

Zhukovsky nodded. Blood was dripping from the hole in his chest in a steady stream.

"Take the chopper to Saint Petersburg. He'll meet you at Levashovo airport. Tell him I sent you."

Lance nodded. He was about to finish Zhukovsky off when, at that very instant, the man's head exploded.

A bullet had entered the right temple and exited on the other side of his skull, causing the entire thing to blow open like a watermelon.

Lance dropped flat against the ground as a hail of gunfire came at him from the trees.

81

Lance scrambled behind Zhukovsky's headless corpse for cover and made it just in time. A hail of bullets slapped into the body, sending splatters of blood into the air.

"I've got you pinned down," someone called from the trees.

He spoke English with a heavy German accent.

Lance had the forty-millimeter grenade launcher strapped to his back. As more bullets came his way, he fired off three shots in the direction of the voice.

The moment they began to explode, he got up and ran.

He'd just made it to the tree line when bullets started pelting into the wood in every direction. The trunks of the trees splintered, and Lance dove to the ground.

He held up his rifle with one hand and gave himself some scattered covering fire, then poked his head up above the brush and tried to get a read on where he was being fired from.

He wanted to know if the man was still in the forest or if he'd moved.

He got the distinct feeling the man wanted to talk, like he had something to get off his chest, and he called out, "What's a German doing here?"

The man didn't reply.

"It's all over," Lance called out, trying to coax the man into revealing his position. "You just committed the worst atrocity Europe has seen in a generation. The entire world will hunt you down."

Still no answer.

"If you believe in God," Lance called out, "it's time to make what peace you can with Him."

That one hit the mark.

"What do you know about God?" the man called out.

His accent was definitely German, and from the direction, Lance could tell he was still in the trees across the clearing.

He picked up the grenade launcher and angled it like a mortar. He could use an old trick he'd learned from some artillerymen. From where he was, it would be very difficult to get an accurate shot on the shooter. However, if he timed the grenade to explode in the trees, the force of the explosion would send enough shrapnel of wood into the forest below that it would multiply the blast radius of the grenade by a factor of three.

He poked his head up to get one last read on the distance. A stream of bullets came at him from the opposing side of the clearing.

Then he fired the grenade up, through the clearing, high into the air. It arced perfectly and exploded the instant it fell into the trees on the other side.

He fired off two more shots, and when the explosions had passed, he heard blood-curdling screams from the man's position.

Lance left the grenade launcher where it was and made his way around the clearing through the brush. When he reached the man, he saw why he was screaming so loudly. Shards of wood had pierced through him in a number of places, in his arms and legs, his back and torso, but somehow, one piece, about the size of a butter knife, had lodged itself deep into his left eye.

The man was in agony, delirious with pain, and Lance just walked over to him, grabbed the shard of wood, and yanked it out of his eye. The eyeball came with it, plucked from its socket like a plum from a pie, and Lance flung it into the brush behind him before the man had time to realize what had happened.

He was howling in agony, screaming like a banshee, and Lance ripped a piece of cloth from his jacket and tied it around the man's head. Then he pulled the man out into the clearing.

"Take off your coat," he said to the man and then left him there, wailing like a little child.

Lance entered the commander's tent and found the first aid kit. The fentanyl citrate was in a small glass bottle, and he pierced it with a syringe and pulled the liquid up into the tube.

He went back to the man, who was still screaming and jabbed the opioid into his leg.

Instantly, the man's muscles relaxed, and he stopped screaming.

"What's your name?" Lance said, suspecting he already knew the answer.

The man was so high from the drug he could barely speak. Lance had to slap him in the face a few times, then give him a little time for the fog in his mind to clear enough to answer.

"What's your name?" Lance said again, holding up the syringe, which still contained some of the clear liquid in its tube.

"Prochnow," the man said. "Christoph Prochnow."

"The German."

The man nodded, and Lance, looking at him more closely, knew he was the man he'd seen in the bunker beneath the Air Ministry Building in Berlin.

"You took Tatyana Aleksandrova and Laurel Everlane," Lance said. "That was you."

The man said nothing. Lance doubted he even understood the question.

"You're the one who killed the cop. The Latvian. Agata Zarina."

Prochnow smiled like an imbecile, and Lance had to put some pressure on a wound in his leg to get his attention.

"You killed the Latvian," Lance said again.

Prochnow nodded.

"She got the message to us," Lance said. "That's why I'm here."

Prochnow said nothing. He was out of it. Useless.

"You killed the Clockmaker too," Lance said.

Prochnow reached out into the air in front of his face as if trying to touch something that wasn't there.

Lance shook his head. "Tell me," he said, "why do you Germans keep coming to this frozen forest to die?"

Prochnow gave him no answer, and Lance raised his pistol to the man's temple. He looked away. He pulled the trigger and grimaced as the blood splattered back on him.

Then he went inside the commander's tent and searched until he found a Russian uniform that fit him. He cleaned the blood from his hands and face, changed into the uniform, and reloaded his weapons.

Then he went to the presidential Mi-8 chopper, fired up the engine, and took off, heading north.

82

Laurel and Tatyana were in the lobby of the US embassy in Riga. Outside, across the courtyard, a team of men in brown overalls worked on the roof trying to repair the satellite communications system.

"This is insane," Tatyana said.

It had been over twenty-four hours, and the embassy was still completely cut off from Washington.

They were sitting on some corporate sofas that were arranged in an L-shape, and there was a coffee machine on the sideboard next to them.

"You want a refill?" Laurel said, getting up.

Tatyana shook her head. She had her leg up on the sofa, and it seemed to be recovering well since the doctor in Berlin had taken a look at it.

"I wouldn't mind something a little stronger," she said.

Laurel looked at her watch. It was seven AM.

"What?" Tatyana said.

"Bit early, isn't it?"

"What else are we going to do. We're trapped here. We can't communicate with DC. I can't even walk."

Laurel poured Tatyana a cup of the strong, black coffee.

"Thanks," Tatyana said.

Riga was in utter chaos. They'd seen it in the cab ride from the hotel. The phone lines were still down, cell phones, Internet, satellite comms. TV and radio were down apart from a prerecorded government message telling people to remain calm.

In addition, riots during the night had left dozens dead. In a city as peaceful as Riga, that was a calamity of epic proportions. At multiple spots, police had clashed with rioters, and as the riots grew more violent, tear gas, rubber bullets, and even live ammunition had been deployed.

Banks and department stores across the city had been looted, cars burned out, property destroyed on a grand scale.

What worried Laurel, however, was the political motivation behind the riots. She'd seen them from the hotel. The people weren't calling for the power to be turned back on. They were calling for Russia to take control of the country.

A man walked across the lobby and introduced himself.

"Ladies, my name is Greenfeld. I'm the station chief here."

"Thank you for having us here," Tatyana said, trying to bring her foot off the sofa.

"Please," Greenfeld said, "make yourself as comfortable as you can. On a day like today, I think it's best for us all to be together."

"Any update on when the comms will be re-established?" Laurel said.

"They're still working on it," Greenfeld said, "but in the next hour, we're expecting direct helicopter flights from the nearest neighboring embassies giving us updates on what's been going on."

"That's assuming those embassies aren't in the dark themselves," Tatyana said.

Greenfeld nodded.

With the Keyhole system down, the scale of the Russian operation was unknown. Maybe it extended beyond Latvia's borders. Maybe all comms across the region were down. Without getting an update, they knew nothing.

"I just got more reports from my field agents in the city," Greenfeld said. "Large protest groups are gathering at the main government buildings in Riga again today."

"This is a coordinated assault on all fronts at once," Laurel said.

Greenfeld nodded. "And there are rumors that the protests aren't just limited to Riga. They've spread to other cities across the country."

"The protests are part of the attack," Tatyana said. "They've been planned and set in motion by the Kremlin."

Greenfeld nodded. "These are the largest protests in the country since the days of the USSR," he said.

"They're the precursor to an invasion," Tatyana said. "All of this is. Cutting the power. Cutting the comms. Destabilizing the country on all fronts."

"When will the invasion come?" Greenfeld said.

Tatyana looked at both of them. "Soon," she said.

Greenfeld sat down. He looked deflated. Laurel wasn't surprised. He was the head CIA asset in-country, and he was completely cut off from Langley.

"I feel like we're sitting on a time bomb," he said.

Tatyana nodded. She leaned back in the sofa and said, "What do you think that marine over there would say if I lit a cigarette?"

Laurel smiled. "This isn't a Russian embassy, Tatyana. You can't just do whatever you like."

"Come on," Tatyana said.

Laurel stood up. "Wait a second," she said. "At least let me talk to him first."

She walked over to the marine's desk, putting a little sway in her hips. She smiled. She wasn't above using her femininity to get something when she needed to, and when she reached the guard's desk, she leaned forward, giving him a view of her cleavage.

"Hey," she said, "what are the chances we could light up a couple of cigarettes over there?"

A wide grin crossed the marine's face.

"You think it would be okay?" Laurel said.

The marine looked over at Tatyana, and Tatyana waved back.

"Lady," the marine said, "you and your friend can do whatever you want to do."

"Thank you," Laurel said.

She gave him even more hip sway on her walk back to the sofa, where Tatyana was already lighting her cigarette.

One of the men from the crew working on the roof walked into the lobby, and everyone turned to him.

"Give the comms a try," he said.

"Really?" Greenfeld said.

The guy shrugged.

There was a television above the sofa, and Greenfeld grabbed the remote. The TV was currently running the manufacturer's screensaver with a message saying 'no signal.' Greenfeld flicked through the channels and suddenly got a clear signal.

"Right there," Laurel said.

"Channel nine," Greenfeld said. "RNN."

It was the Russian, state-run news service, basically a mouthpiece for Russian government propaganda.

"Is that the only station that's working?" Laurel said.

Greenfeld ran through the rest of the channels, but they were all scrambled.

"Go back to RNN," Tatyana said, lighting another cigarette.

Laurel asked her for one.

On the screen, they saw footage of a small Latvian village. The subtitle confirmed it was Ziguri, the village Agata Zarina had gone to.

A newscaster was speaking to the camera, and clearly visible behind her, about fifty yards back, was some sort of pyre, like someone had lit an enormous bonfire in the central square of the village. It must have been fifteen feet high. The flames were gone, but smoke still rose out of it.

The newscaster spoke Russian, but a man's voice was dubbing her in heavily accented Latvian.

"This morning at dawn," the voice said, "Latvian military forces brutally crushed anti-government protests in the ethnic Russian village of Ziguri in eastern Latvia."

"What the hell?" Laurel said.

"Are those?" Tatyana said, raising her hand in front of her mouth.

"The Latvian government has bigger things to worry about than protests in a remote village," Laurel said.

"Laurel," Tatyana said, pointing at the screen. "Those...".

"What?" Laurel said.

"That pile. The fire. Those are ... *bodies*."

83

I t was another hour after the RNN news footage came through that the embassy was finally able to restore comms with Washington.

The first call the station chief made was to Langley, where he asked to be patched through directly to CIA Director Roth.

Laurel and Tatyana were in his office with him, and when Roth's voice came on the line, Greenfeld said, "Mr. Roth, thank you for taking my call."

"Taking your call? We've been worried sick about you over here."

"I'm here with Laurel Everlane and Tatyana Aleksandrova," Greenfeld said.

"Thank God you're all alright," Roth said.

"We're alright," Laurel said, "but did you see the footage they're showing on RNN?"

"That footage is playing on every news outlet on the planet," Roth said. "Not just in Latvia. It's everywhere."

"What happened?"

"The Russians are claiming Latvian soldiers opened fire on a Russian village. Killed a thousand civilians."

"That's ludicrous," Laurel said.

"Of course it is," Roth said. "The president knows it, congress knows it, our NATO allies know it."

"I hope the media is calling it what it is," Laurel said.

"There's a spectrum," Roth said.

"What? They're actually buying it?"

"Some outlets are, but that's not our biggest problem right now."

"What could be a bigger problem than a massacre?"

"Russian troops are crossing the border north and south of Ziguri as we speak, Laurel."

"They can't violate Latvian territory."

"They're saying it's necessary to protect ethnic Russians from further atrocities."

"No one's going to believe that," Laurel said.

"Some people will believe the Kremlin no matter what it says."

"But we can disprove it, can't we?"

"That's the other issue," Roth said. "Our Keyhole satellite is down, which means we had no eyes on that village when the massacre took place. If we're going to prove anything conclusively, it will take time."

"And by then, it will be too late," Laurel said.

"The Russians will be in complete control of the country by then."

"We need to hit back," Laurel said. "This is a violation of a NATO member. We need to bomb those Russian units back to wherever they came from."

"That's what I'm going to tell the president now. I'm just pulling up to the White House."

"White House? Shouldn't you be at the Pentagon?"

"The president didn't want to send the wrong signal," Roth said. "He didn't want to give the impression we were jumping to conclusions."

"Jumping to conclusions? Russia is invading our ally."

"I know, Laurel."

"We're under attack, Roth. If he's worried about impressions, he should be concerned with appearing too weak, not too aggressive."

"That's the problem," Roth said. "He already addressed the press from the White House and emphasized that *we're* not the ones under attack. Latvia is."

"But Latvia's in NATO. If we let Russia pick off our allies one by one, then it won't be long before they're at our gate."

"I know that," Roth said, his voice betraying signs of strain. "And believe me, I'll be arguing forcefully to that effect when I see the president. I'm at the security point now. I should let you go."

"You've got to make him see sense, Roth. He's got to stand up to this aggression."

"Laurel, I'll try, but the president doesn't want to be the man responsible for kicking off World War Three."

"He's not kicking it off. It's already started."

"Not in his eyes."

Laurel was furious.

She couldn't believe this was happening.

Again.

First, the president had failed to stand up to Moscow and Beijing when they attacked the embassies. Now he was letting allies be invaded. Where would it end?

"Roth, tell me what has to happen," she said, "for this president to see that the Russians are never going to stop. They're going to push, and push, and unless we start pushing back harder, they're going to unmake the entire world order we've created."

"The president has a lot to consider, Laurel. We're only seeing part of the picture."

"Part of the picture?" she said, dumbfounded. "You just told me Russia is re-invading its former Soviet Republics."

"I know," Roth said.

Their voices were both so loud they were practically shouting at each other.

Laurel knew Roth was on her side. He was one of the last hawks in Washington. But there was only so much he could do. It was the president's call.

And that terrified Laurel.

Because all she could see, more and more, was a leadership in Washington that was unwilling, and unable, to stand up to the forces that were massing against them.

From the Taiwan Strait to the Baltic, America's enemies were rattling their sabers, preparing for war, and Washington was just burrowing its head in the sand.

Roth was the only one who fought the president on the issue of defense. He told the president to his face that he was dropping his guard. That he was creating vulnerabilities.

Roth was the Watcher on the Wall.

He was the sentinel.

Laurel knew she was yelling at the wrong man.

"I'm sorry," Laurel said.

"It's all right, Laurel. I understand your fears."

"Will you at least tell the president that if he allows stronger nations to dominate weaker ones, that the world will descend into chaos."

"I'm afraid that the way the president sees it," Roth said, "we're the strong nation here."

"Only because men better than this president stood up to the dictators of the past. It's on their shoulders that he stands."

"I can't tell him that," Roth said.

"Well, tell him…, I don't know, Roth. Tell him *something*."

"I'll do my best, Laurel. But in the meantime, you have to try to get in touch with Lance. If the president doesn't listen to reason, he might be our only hope of stopping this invasion."

"I'll try to make contact," Laurel said, "Whatever brought him back, I'm sure glad it did."

"Well," Roth said, "that's another issue, but we don't need to discuss it now."

"What issue?"

"Sam, the girl in Montana he was living with, the Russians killed her."

"What?"

"That's why he's back, Laurel."

"They killed Sam?"

"Yes, they did."

"They fucked up."

"Yes, they did."

84

R oth's vehicle moved toward the White House security checkpoint, and Roth opened his window.

A guard said, "Just you tonight, Mr. Director?"

"Just me," Roth said, letting him have a look around the passenger compartment.

Outside, more guards did a quick check of the undercarriage of the vehicle before waving them through.

They drove up to the West Wing visitor entrance, and Roth was immediately escorted up to the Oval Office.

He entered the room and found the president seated by the fire. With him was the Chairman of the Joint Chiefs, Elliot Schlesinger. The room was warm, the glow of the fire imbuing it with a sense of intimacy. Outside, snow fell silently in the night.

"Mr. President," Roth said. "Elliot."

Elliot was standing by the bar, and he poured three measures of scotch into crystal glasses. He brought them to the seating area by the fire.

"Thank you," Roth said, taking a seat.

The three men sat in silence, staring at each other. Schlesinger put ice in his scotch, and the cubes clinked against the glass.

"Well, gentlemen," the president said, breaking the silence, "it looks like the day we always dreaded has arrived. We're closer to war with Russia than at any point since the Kennedy administration."

Roth was relieved by the president's tone. He appeared to be taking Russia's movements with the gravity they deserved.

"I've ordered the entire cabinet to assemble at the Pentagon."

"When, sir?" Roth said.

"Twenty minutes."

"That's good," Roth said.

"I wanted to speak to the two of you before going to the Pentagon," the president said. "You are the two most hawkish members of my cabinet, and it's important that the three of us present a united front."

"I see," Roth said, uncertain how much of what the president was saying Elliot had already heard.

"As you are both aware," he said, "I've always been a pacifist at heart. Russia has been antagonizing us every day I've been in power, and I see a large part of my job as preventing a devastating war from breaking out between us. That's what I believe to be my mission from God, if you will. The reason He placed me in this position of great power. The role Providence laid out for me."

Roth looked at Elliot uncomfortably. He prayed the president wasn't going to back down from a fight because of some *sign* he'd seen.

"Mr. President," Roth said. "I think I speak for both

myself and Elliot when I say we have the utmost respect for your beliefs."

"If I allow you two to persuade me to go to war with Russia tonight," the president said, "I may very well be taking the first step down a path that will lead to nuclear war."

"Sir," Schlesinger said, "I don't think the Russians are looking for an outcome like that."

"That may be," the president said, "but they've just committed a massacre on NATO soil, Elliot. I know we'll try to contain this conflict. I know the Russians will have parameters they're trying to remain within as well. But we'd be fooling ourselves if we pretended it couldn't get out of hand."

"Have we confirmed that Russians forces have crossed the border?" Roth said. "With Keyhole down, we haven't been able to confirm their movements through the usual means."

"We've been forced to switch to NATO SATCOM for all Pentagon systems," Schlesinger said. "That's been able to plug some of the gaps created by the attack on Keyhole."

"And what do we know?" Roth said.

"We received imagery in the last few minutes," Schlesinger said, "that suggests the mobilization of virtually the entire Western Military District."

"Good God," Roth said.

"Tank divisions are preparing to cross the border as we speak. And Russian soldiers are in the village of Ziguri, where the massacre took place."

"What time is it in Riga now?" Roth said.

"About eight AM," Schlesinger said.

"So," Roth said, "when we get to the Pentagon, what are we going to say?"

"Well, we've got Russian tanks ready to cross the border. What are our options?"

"With Keyhole down," Roth said, "our most advanced systems are crippled."

"We're moving new satellites into position," Schlesinger said. "We'll have Keyhole capability back online in the next few hours."

"Thank God for that," the president said.

"Sir," Roth said, turning to him. "The question isn't what can we do. It's what are we *willing* to do?"

"I don't want to unleash Armageddon," the president said.

"Of course not, sir. But are we willing to really go to war with Russia? Or will we be looking at supporting a lower level NATO response?"

"What do those options look like?"

"Well, sir, to put it bluntly," Schlesinger said, "what Roth's saying is, are we ready to go to war? Are we going to unleash a full-scale operation that will push Russia back, something like Desert Storm when we pushed Saddam out of Kuwait?"

"Or we could go smaller?" the president said.

"Well, sir. We could look to provide support to the Latvians to help them push back the Russians themselves."

"Would they be able to push them back themselves?"

"No," Roth said. "They wouldn't."

"But it would buy us time," Schlesinger said. "There'd be a lot of casualties. Russian and Latvian ground forces would engage face to face. And we'd do our best to prop up the Latvian side."

"While they fought, we could open a dialogue with the Kremlin," the president said.

"They won't open a dialogue until they've brought the

entire country under their control," Roth said. "And by then, it will be too late. They'll have won."

"So those are the only two options?" the president said.

"Sir," Schlesinger said, "both options are localized to the Baltic theater."

"And what if we start winning?" the president said.

"Well, that's what we want, sir."

"But won't the Russians escalate? Won't they bring in more and more forces, bigger and bigger weapons?"

"That's a risk, sir," Roth said. "But the only alternative to winning would be losing."

The president took a long drink of his scotch and sighed. He looked at his watch.

"We need to leave for the Pentagon," he said.

Roth and Schlesinger stood up and put on their coats. Schlesinger looked about to say something when the phone on the president's desk began ringing.

All three men looked at it.

"Aren't you going to answer?" Roth said to the president.

"I told them not to call unless the Russians attacked," the President said.

"I see," Roth said.

The president picked up the phone. Roth and Schlesinger listened.

"Thank you," the president said, then hung up.

Roth and Schlesinger looked at him expectantly.

"The Russians just launched cruise missiles at targets inside Latvia."

There was a machine like a computer printer on a desk by the wall, and it began printing furiously. Schlesinger went over to it and ripped the paper from the tray when it stopped printing.

"3M-54 Kalibr rockets," he said. "Launched from Kilo-class submarines in the Gulf of Finland."

"Were we able to intercept?" Roth said.

"Our systems rely on Keyhole," Schlesinger said. "But according to this, the Estonian SHORAD system shot down four missiles in their airspace."

"Four, out of how many?" the president said.

"It doesn't say how many missiles were launched, sir."

"I see," the president said.

"The local missile defense systems in Latvia and Estonia will be overwhelmed very quickly if we don't step in," Roth said.

The president looked at Roth blankly, and Roth realized that even now, with the invasion already underway, the president still hadn't made up his mind to go to war.

85

L ance got in the presidential Mi-8 chopper. He was dressed in a Russian officer's uniform. Once he was airborne, he made contact with military flight control at Siverskiy Aerodrome. They confirmed what Zhukovsky had told him, that he was cleared for a direct flight to Levashovo. Levashovo was an airbase north of Saint Petersburg that belonged to the Russian Sixth Air Army.

He made his way north, and in the forests east of Ostrov, saw the tanks of the Częstochowa Brigade lined up in vast columns.

He was so close he could see the diesel fumes from their exhausts. They were idling, waiting for the final order, and from their disposition, he knew they would be crossing the border soon.

This was it, he thought.

This was how the world ended.

War between Russia and America.

War had been fought in these lands, back and forth, for centuries. It was as regular as a tide.

Now, it would engulf the planet.

It had happened before.

And it was happening again.

There was no way around it. Not even President Ingram Montgomery, a pacifist who would have been more at home on a Nantucket fishing boat than in the White House, could stand back and allow this to happen.

There was no question.

If Russia invaded Latvia, regardless of what calculations the Russians had made, and what steps they'd taken to hide their actions and provide themselves with a pretext, the US would respond. No false flag operation could allow the US to sit back and watch this one play out without intervention.

At least, that was what Lance hoped.

What had happened in recent years in the Ukraine, and Montgomery's response to the embassy bombings, reminded him that nothing was guaranteed.

He reminded himself that it wasn't his problem, wasn't his fight. He flew on toward Saint Petersburg, and his radio channel filled with chatter. He was on a VVIP craft that was part of the president's personal fleet, and it was cleared for the highest level comms.

The Russians had launched airstrikes.

First, thirty-six 3M-54 Kalibr rockets launched from Kilo-class submarines in the Gulf of Finland north of Estonia. They flew through Estonian airspace, and Estonia's modest missile defense system took down a handful of them. Latvia's defense system took down six.

But over twenty of the missiles successfully hit their targets. The targets were all Latvian air defense installations, including Latvian Air Defense Headquarters at Adaži, and the new medium-range air-defense system that was being installed there.

Lance recognized these attacks for what they were. The precursor to Russian air supremacy.

As he approached Levashovo, he saw that the helipad had been prepared for a dignitary, with a red carpet laid out that led from the center of the pad to a black limousine with tinted windows and Russian Federation flags.

Lance lowered the visor on his helmet and made sure his pistols were loaded and ready. There were two soldiers standing at attention by the limousine.

Lance touched down, and the soldiers came to the helicopter to open the passenger doors. When they did, they saw that the compartment was empty.

They turned toward Lance, just in time for two bullets from his silenced pistols to penetrate their skulls.

Then he opened fire at the limousine, aiming for the driver. He couldn't see through the car's tinted windows, and it lurched forward. Lance kept firing at the glass, and one of his bullets must have hit its mark because the car came crawling to a halt.

The horn sounded in a constant tone, as if the driver was slumped over the wheel.

The back door opened, and a man in a suit began firing at Lance.

Lance ducked and climbed from the front of the chopper back to the passenger compartment. He took two shots out the open door. The first hit the man in the shoulder, and he dropped his gun. The second hit the man's thigh.

The man fell to the ground, but Lance knew the injuries were not life-threatening.

Lance climbed out of the chopper and walked toward the man.

The man managed to lift himself from the ground and

scramble back into his car. He tried to shut the door, but Lance caught it. Then he reached into the car and pulled the man back out.

"Don't kill me," the man begged.

Lance didn't have much time.

They were out on the tarmac in plain view of the control tower. In a matter of seconds, soldiers would pour out of the terminal building across the runway, guns blazing.

Lance pulled the man to the helicopter and shoved him into the pilot's compartment.

Then he got in next to him and took off, back into the air.

"They'll shoot us down," the man said.

"Maybe they will," Lance said, veering the chopper west over the airfield, keeping as low as possible. A few seconds later, they were out over the open waters of the Baltic.

"They'll shoot us out of the sky," Kirov said again, growing more frantic.

"Your name is Jacob Kirov," Lance said to the man.

"What?" the man said. "What are you talking about?"

"You ordered the hit."

Kirov looked at him blankly, then, all of a sudden realized what was happening.

"You're Lance Spector."

Lance removed his helmet. "Why did you kill her?" he said.

Kirov was still shaking his head, like he didn't know what Lance was asking him.

"The girl," Lance said. "The girl in Montana. What did she have to do with any of this?"

"I didn't kill her," Kirov said.

"How about for each lie you tell me," Lance said, "I gain a hundred feet in altitude."

Lance began gaining altitude, making the chopper, as Kirov was all too aware, an easier target for surface-to-air missiles.

"All right," Kirov said, his voice shrill with panic. "All right. I'll talk. Just take us down."

Lance reduced his altitude and looked at Kirov.

"It was the idiot, Sherbakov," Kirov said.

"Sherbakov?" Lance said.

"A sleeper agent. An idiot sleeper agent in New York. He's a nobody."

"What are you talking about?"

"I sent him to Montana to distract you. He wasn't supposed to kill anyone."

"Killing her was the one thing guaranteed to get my attention," Lance said.

"He was supposed to scare her. That was all. I swear to God."

"And Sherbakov went off script?"

"He completely fucking lost it," Kirov said.

"Well," Lance said, "you're going to pay for his mistake."

"Please," Kirov said. "It was an accident. There's an arrangement we can come to, you and I. I know who you are, Lance Spector. I know what you want."

"What I wanted was for that girl to stay alive."

"I can tell you what's coming next," Kirov said.

"I already know what's coming next."

"I can tell you the plans for the invasion. I've been commanding the entire thing. I know every detail."

"I don't care about any of that."

They were flying very low over the icy Baltic waters, and Kirov read Lance's intention.

"Are you ready to go for a swim?" Lance said.

"You don't have to do this," Kirov said. "I can help you.

I'll tell you everything. I know where they're running the invasion from. It's not five miles from here. I can get you in."

"I don't want your help."

"You can stop the invasion."

"I'm not here to stop the invasion. I'm here for you."

"The General Staff Building," Kirov said. "Across from the Winter Palace. I can get you inside. You can stop everything."

Lance knew the building. It had been one of the most important buildings in Russia during the days of the Czar.

"I can get you inside," Kirov said again.

Lance looked at him, then pulled a gun from his jacket.

"Get out," he said.

"Please," Kirov begged. "Let me help you. You'll need my help."

Lance shook his head.

"Get out," he said again. "Get out, or I'll put another bullet in your leg, and trust me, the less blood in the water, the better it will be for you."

Kirov looked at him, then very slowly, turned the latch that kept his door shut.

The door flew outward, and freezing air immediately filled the cockpit.

"This is for Sam," Lance said.

He raised his leg and shoved Kirov unceremoniously out the door. The man flailed in the air for a second then hit the water with a crash. Lance circled back once and saw him on the surface, frantically trying to swim as the weight of his clothing pulled him down.

With the water temperature what it was, he'd be dead in seconds.

86

As Lance flew low over the Kronstadt Naval Cathedral on Kotlin Island, two surface-to-air missiles came flying toward him. He pulled up hard on the controls and deployed the enhanced decoys that were part of the presidential defense upgrades that had been made to the chopper.

The missiles missed, but by mere feet.

He knew more would follow.

He was fast approaching the southern shore of the gulf and could make out the distinctive shape of the Peterhof formal gardens. He brought the chopper in for a hard landing in front of the enormous Fountain of Neptune, just as two more missiles flew overhead, missing their mark by less than ten feet.

More missiles flew over the chopper, confused by its laser decoys, and exploded in the air.

Lance leaped from the chopper and rolled across the ground as a missile finally made contact.

The chopper exploded in an enormous fireball that billowed into the air in a cloud of black smoke.

He was on the lawn of one of the Tsar's most famous palaces, the Russian Versailles, as it was known, built on a scale to rival any of the palaces in Europe.

Lance got to his feet and ran. He could already hear the sirens approaching and didn't intend to still be there when they arrived.

He ran past perfectly manicured rows of trees and shrubs, and some of the most intricate fountains ever made.

At the end of the lawn was a set of fourteen-foot-high wrought iron gates, painted with black and gold leaf. Lance climbed over them and dropped to the other side.

He ran into the street, forcing the traffic to swerve around him, and drew his gun. The first car to stop was an old Mercedes sedan and Lance pointed his gun at the driver.

"Get out," he said.

The driver, a man in his twenties, got out of the car.

Lance got in and gunned the engine, speeding down Saint Petersburg Prospekt, past the Aleksandriyskiy Park, and weaving his way through the morning traffic. If he stayed on the road, it would have brought him through the Krasnoselsky and Admiralteysky Districts before entering the city center, but Lance knew there was no way he'd be able to get through all that traffic without Saint Petersburg Police stopping him.

There were streetcars that ran along Stachek Prospekt, and at Leninskiy Avenue, Lance pulled over and abandoned the vehicle. He boarded a streetcar and took it in the direction of the Winter Palace. As he passed the enormous apartment buildings by the main dock railway, he counted fourteen police cruisers, lights and sirens blazing, speed by in the opposite direction.

The streetcar was about fifty percent full, and Lance sat still, making eye contact with no one. The massive apartment buildings gradually gave way to older architecture closer to the city center, and the streetcar grew more crowded. They passed the industrial zone around the Electric Depot and then the more expensive residential neighborhoods between the canals and Trotsky Prospekt.

Lance got off the streetcar on the Palace Embankment and walked the last few hundred yards along the wide Neva River. Where it forked before entering the gulf, icy wind gusted in from the coast, and Lance raised the collar of his army uniform jacket.

That stretch of the embankment brought him past some of the most imposing structures in the city. All the palaces and mansions of the aristocracy, as well as the residences and embassies of foreign governments lined the river. Across the frozen river from the Imperial Arts Academy and the Menshikov Palace was the enormous bronze statue of Peter the Great on horseback.

When he reached the buildings of the admiralty, he turned right through the Alexander Garden. The ornate, golden dome of Saint Isaac's Cathedral was visible through the barren branches of the trees, and ahead, the imposing victory column in Palace Square towered over everything.

The square was ringed by the neoclassical assemblage of buildings that housed the Hermitage and Winter Palace, and directly across from those buildings was the wide arch of the General Staff Building.

Lance stood at the edge of the park, looking over the windswept square, the flurries of snow rising in the gusts like dust devils. The square was one of the most visited spots in Russia, drawing millions of tourists every year, but today, in the bitterly cold wind, it was empty.

Lance checked his hands, they weren't exactly numb from the cold, but they weren't as dexterous as he would have liked. He needed to warm them. He looked around and saw an old-fashioned coffee house on Nevsky Avenue that overlooked the Bol'shaya Plaza. He entered it and sat by a window overlooking the plaza.

"Good evening, officer," the waitress said.

The coffee house was a fancy place, in a fancy part of town, and the patrons were well-dressed. It had a formal atmosphere, and the waitress was dressed in a French-style black dress with lace trim. She wore shoes with a slight heel, and Lance pegged her at about fifty.

He calculated that she was competent, that she would know an opportunity when she saw one, and he gave her the most charming smile he could manage.

She placed a menu in front of him and left.

From where he sat, he could see out across the plaza to the back of the General Staff Building.

Lance took off his coat and looked at the building. It was tremendously grand, like the headquarters of a London investment bank, and Lance knew that as soon as he passed through the doors, every room and corridor would be bristling with security.

The waitress returned and said, "What can I get for you?"

Lance spoke Russian fluently, he'd trained in all of the major dialects and accents, but he hoped now, here, that no nuance of pronunciation or diction would give him away as an American.

"I need to make a phone call," he said, taking out his wallet and counting out three American hundred dollar bills.

The waitress was as smart as he'd predicted and quickly threw a cloth napkin over the bills. Then she picked them up.

"I'll be right back with a phone, sir," she said.

"And I'll have some hot coffee," he added as she left.

She came back a minute later with a personal cell phone and his coffee, then left him again.

Lance then went through the routing process with the phone, calling a partially automated CIA switchboard located inside Russia. No one, not even Roth himself, knew for sure where the switchboard was located or who exactly was responsible for operating it, but it provided an extremely valuable backup system for operatives located inside Russian territory. The fact that it was manual, and built entirely on Cold War era telephony, meant that it was immune from satellite interference or modern cyber attacks.

The phone clicked and beeped, like an old modem from the nineties, and eventually, someone on the other end picked up.

"This is Lance Spector for Levi Roth," Lance said.

A female voice with a slightly British, slightly foreign accent said, "Under what authorization?"

Lance had no active authorization codes, he hadn't been sent to Russia by the CIA and had no operational codes of any kind. What he did have were older, top-level codes, complete with embedded distress flags, and he gave one of those codes to the operator. He didn't append a distress flag, but he did provide a little nod to sentimentality that he wasn't even sure Roth would notice.

"Please hold," the operator said.

Lance took another sip of the coffee, then raised his hand for the bill.

87

D eep beneath the Pentagon, in a secure conference room that was equipped with its own air and water filtration system, lead shielding, and enough communications equipment to allow for direct orders to be issued to any branch of the US military, the president's cabinet sat assembled, ready for war.

Roth sat at one end of the table, the president at the other, and around them was the president's Chief of Staff, the Chairman of the Joint Chiefs, the director of the NSA, as well as the Chiefs of Staff of the Army, the Navy, the Air force, and Space Operations. The Commandant of the Marine Corps was also present, as well as a number of other cabinet members.

On an enormous screen was a live satellite feed of Latvia and the surrounding territory. The three remaining Keyhole satellites had been reoriented to provide coverage over the region, and the National Reconnaissance Office, along with the DoD, the Defense Intelligence Agency, and the National Geospatial-Intelligence Agency, were working furiously to ensure that all of the Pentagon's advanced systems that relied on Keyhole integration were up and running.

"The question is," the president said, "do we or do we not invoke Article Five of the North Atlantic Treaty?"

Article Five was the crux of NATO's defensive alliance. It stated that an attack on one member was to be regarded as an attack on all.

Everyone sitting at the table looked at each other and at the little icons on the screen that represented Russian troops.

Schlesinger was the first to speak. "I think there's no question," he said. "This is it. This is the day we've been preparing for since the end of the Second World War."

"World War Three?" the president said.

"Well," Schlesinger said, "an attack, at any rate. We've got Russian missiles in the air. We've got Russian tanks crossing the border. As far as I'm concerned, this is game on."

"Isn't there anything we can do to get Russia to stand down?" the president said, looking directly at Roth.

"Sir," Roth said, "at this stage, I really don't see Russia standing down. They're claiming there's been a massacre of Russians on Latvian soil."

"We all know that's bullshit," Schlesinger said.

"No, we don't," the president said. "Not definitively."

"Why on earth would a country the size of Latvia do something like that?" Schlesinger said. "It would guarantee a response from the Russians. That village is less than five kilometers from the Russian border."

"Maybe someone in Latvia is trying to trick Russia into making an attack," the president said.

Everyone at the table looked down at their documents.

No one believed that.

This was an act of Russian aggression, plain and simple, and everyone but the president was ready to admit it.

Russia had been itching for decades to take back the land lost in the collapse of the USSR. Every minute that those tiny Baltic Republics were allowed to defy Moscow was an insult. Not only had they broken free of Moscow's grip, but to rub salt in the wound, they'd also become fully-fledged members of NATO.

The Kremlin had learned from the experience.

When the Ukraine tried to pull closer to NATO, Moscow stopped the process in its tracks.

And now, they were taking back what they saw as territory that was rightfully theirs.

The president let out a long sigh and looked at Roth as if he was begging him for a solution.

"Sir," Roth said, "you're right. It's not, strictly speaking, too late for something to pull us back from the brink. If we were able to get the Russians to hesitate. If we were able to get them to question their own plans. If we were able to somehow scare them back into their corner...".

"Then war might still be averted?" the president said hopefully.

"Yes," Roth said, "but it would require something extraordinary. It would require them to change course, now, when they're on the very precipice of an invasion."

"What could make them lose faith now?" the president said.

"I don't know, sir," Roth said. "And I think it would be prudent for us to get in a position for war."

"You really mean that?" the president said.

"I do, sir."

"Because you, Levi Roth, you're my last chance here. You're my *tertio optio*. If you can't find me a way to pull the plug on this, the United States is going to be at war with Russia. And we all know the unprecedented carnage that might follow from such a course."

"I understand, sir."

"You're the last line of defense, Roth."

"Sir, my recommendation is to prepare for war. I'm sorry that I can't give you advice that would be more palatable."

"If you're telling me we're out of options, Roth, then that's the end of the line. The end of diplomacy. The end of intelligence. The end of countermeasures."

"And the beginning of war, sir," Elliot Schlesinger said.

"And the beginning of war," the president repeated.

"Shall I go over our dispositions, sir?" Schlesinger said.

The president nodded sadly, looking at Roth one final time before turning away from him.

Schlesinger pressed a button on the desk, and the satellite imagery moved westward, from Latvia to the open waters of the Baltic.

"Vice Admiral Cleveland, of the US Sixth Fleet," Schlesinger said, "is already moving a destroyer squadron from its homeport in Gaeta. He has also ordered Task Force Sixty, currently assigned to Carrier Strike Group Two, to sail into the Black Sea."

"The Black Sea?" the president said. "You told me that we would be doing everything in our power to limit this conflict to the Baltic."

"Sir, we thought a full Carrier Strike Group so close to the Russian fleet at Sevastopol might give them pause."

Roth knew this was a long shot. A single carrier strike group, thousands of miles from the Baltic, while formidable, was not about to scare the Russian president back into his lair. If anything, it threatened, as the president feared, to turn a conflict in Latvia into a broader war.

"What are we threatening with this move?" the president said.

"Currently, between Novorossiysk, Sevastopol, and occupied Ukrainian facilities, the Russians have their entire Thirtieth Surface Ship Division, as well as seven improved Kilo-class diesel attack subs, four guided-missile corvettes, and a few dozen smaller ships, stationed in the Black Sea."

"So we're threatening their navy?"

Schlesinger looked around the table. "I'd say we are, sir. That strike group includes the Eisenhower, the nine squadrons of Carrier Air Wing Three, a Ticonderoga-class cruiser, three Arleigh Burkes."

"So you're proposing?" the president said.

"It's a show of force, sir."

"Sir," the Navy Chief of Staff, Frederick Winnefeld, said, "in addition to Task Force Sixty, we've got two additional carrier strike groups currently heading for the Baltic."

"That's the Ford and the Truman?"

"That's correct, sir."

"Something tells me that's not going to be enough to get the Russians to stand down," the president said.

"It might if we show that we're willing to use them, sir," Schlesinger said.

As much as Roth hated to admit it, he had to agree with the president. Russia was not some second-rate rogue state. It had been staring down the US nuclear arsenal for the better part of a century. It was used to brinkmanship. It had been gauging America's willingness to respond to aggression for a long time. First, by flagrantly breaching bioweapons treaties, then by coordinating with Beijing to blow up two high profile embassies.

In both cases, president Montgomery had backed down.

Now, they were paying the price for that failure to respond.

"Sir," Roth said, "if we don't show the Kremlin a willingness to use overwhelming force in the next hour, we're going to be looking at a full-scale invasion of Latvia. That means an invasion of a NATO member, which is tantamount to an attack on our own territory. If we don't defend Latvia, we're sending a clear signal to all our allies that they're on their own."

"I understand that, Levi," the president said.

"We need to be decisive, sir," Roth said. "We need to go to war."

Roth didn't agree with those who thought President Montgomery was weak. He understood his reservations. The prospect of war with Russia sobered the president, as it should.

It wasn't a political consideration.

It was existential.

The president brought up God when he spoke of it, not because he was a zealot, but because war with Russia threatened every man, woman, and child on the planet.

It threatened annihilation of the race.

"So we strike at their forces?" the president said.

"A mere show of force will do nothing," Roth said. "We need to strike immediately, sir. I know that's not what you want to hear, but it's the truth."

"And what targets do you propose?" the president said, turning to Schlesinger. "Surely you don't want to attack their ships in the Black Sea."

"No, sir. The forces in the south are a threat. Our actual strike should focus on the forces directly involved in the invasion. That includes the units already crossing the

Latvian border, as well as the other units that have been mobilized by the Western Military District."

"Is everyone at this table certain of this?" the president said.

Roth looked around the table. The assembled cabinet members nodded their heads in unison. The president was the only one who was hesitant.

"We need to launch now, sir," Roth said. "If we wait any longer, it will be too late. If we hit them hard enough now, we might be able to turn them around. It's the only way to end this quickly."

"They're not going to turn around, though, are they?" the president said.

"No, sir," Roth said. "They probably will not."

"And what then, Levi?"

Roth looked at the president and shook his head. He knew what they were looking at. Airstrikes would not be enough to turn the Russians around, and that would mean sending in more and more forces.

It was a path to all-out war.

And he'd just recommended to the president that they embark on it.

He didn't know what to say.

There were moments when men had no choice, when nations had no choice.

Moments when fighting, and not fighting, both led to annihilation.

He knew that if the president made this order, he would be failing to do what every American president since the Second World War had successfully done. He'd have failed to prevent the Cold War from turning into a Third World War.

Roth was about to speak, he wasn't even sure what he would say, when there was a knock on the door.

Every person around the table turned as an orderly entered the room and approached the Chairman of the Joint Chiefs.

He handed Schlesinger a note, then left.

Schlesinger read the note, then handed it to the president.

Everyone in the room waited. Then the president looked up and Roth and said, "Levi, there's a call from your man in Saint Petersburg."

Roth was surprised. "I don't have a man in Saint Petersburg, sir."

The president raised an eyebrow. "Well," he said, "it would appear that you do now."

88

L ance's call was patched through to the conference room, where it came through on a speaker in the center of the table.

"Lance," Roth said, "Nice of you to check in."

"Comms were down across Latvia," Lance said.

"Well, I should let you know," Roth said, "I have you on speaker, Lance. We're in the situation room at the Pentagon. The president and the joint chiefs are listening in."

"I see," Lance said.

"Lance Spector," the president said. "We understand you're in Saint Petersburg."

"That's correct, sir. I killed Zhukovsky and Kirov, but the Russians will just replace them."

"Zhukovsky and Kirov?" the president said.

"They were the GRU operatives responsible for laying the groundwork for this operation, sir," Lance said. "They're dead now, sir, but I think this has switched from being an intelligence operation to an all-out military assault. It's no longer the GRU we need to worry about. It's the Russian Army."

"And what do you propose, Mr. Spector?" the president said.

"Well, sir, I'm looking at the Western Military District headquarters right now."

"But that's the General Staff Building in the center of Saint Petersburg, isn't it?" Schlesinger said.

"Yes, it is," Lance said.

"That's one of the most secured facilities on the planet, Lance."

"It's got its weaknesses," Lance said.

"How could you possibly know that?" Schlesinger said.

"Because, sir," Lance said, "this is precisely the type of situation you trained me for."

Schlesinger turned to Roth. "What's he talking about?"

"You didn't train me just to be an assassin," Lance said.

"I didn't know that we trained assassins at all," Schlesinger said.

"Sure you did," Lance said. "You just didn't want to admit it."

"If you're not only an assassin," the president said, "then what else are you, Lance."

"I'm what Roth is," Lance said. "I'm the last line of defense. I'm a sentinel against the things we've always known were out there, lurking, waiting to strike."

"We're taking lessons now from this guy?" Schlesinger said to the president.

The president turned to Schlesinger and said, "Shut up, Elliot." Then he said, "And what's that, Lance? What's lurking out there?"

"Sir," Lance said, "it's not losing a war that we're afraid of. With our weapons, with Russia's weapons, with our destructive capability, it's not losing a war that will destroy us."

"Oh, please," Schlesinger said.

"If it's not losing a war that we're afraid of," the president said, "then what is it?"

"It's fighting one," Lance said.

Roth watched the president closely. He'd never heard Lance speak like this before, and he was surprised at how closely Lance's and the president's views coincided.

The president said, "So you're our last line of defense in terms of..."

"In terms of preventing a war that could destroy us, sir. Even if we win it. That's what you trained me for. That's what Roth created me for."

"You think you can prevent this war?" the president said.

"Yes, I do, sir."

"How?"

"I've studied the schematics of every known military site and command post in Russia, sir. At Roth's direction, I've memorized the location of every service entrance, every water main, every electrical box, every utility intake. I've studied every inch of this building, sir. "

"And you think you can hit it."

"I wouldn't have come to Saint Petersburg if I didn't, sir."

The president looked at Roth.

"Lance," Roth said, "you know that if you walk into the General Staff Building right now...".

"I'm not going to walk in," Lance said.

"Lance, you'll never come back out."

"That's an outcome I've considered, sir."

Roth looked at the president, and the president nodded.

"You're okay with that?" Roth said.

"Sir, you know me. You know my life."

"What does that mean?" Roth said.

"You know I've got nothing to live for, sir."

"Lance," Roth said.

"This is what I trained for," Lance said. "If war breaks out between the United States and Russia, that's on us, Roth. That's our failure. Our job is to keep that fight at bay. To push it back. To postpone it. To postpone that final reckoning for as long as possible."

"For forever," Roth said quietly.

"For forever," Lance said. "That's what I signed up for. That's what you told me the day you recruited me."

Roth remembered it. He remembered the words he'd spoken. He hadn't known until this moment that Lance had even heard them.

"You told me we were the vaccine that holds back the virus. The fighters that hold back the war."

Like a vaccine. It was true. Roth had used the analogy. He'd forgotten that.

"Lance," the president said. "Let's be explicit. You're going to take out the General Staff Building?"

"That's correct, sir. They can't launch this invasion without their command. Especially if you hit them hard at the same time."

"Can we do that?" the president said to Schlesinger. "Can we hit them with... *hard*, as Spector put it?"

"We can hit them hard, sir. We can strike the Black Sea fleet immediately, taking out a huge part of their navy. That will threaten their hold on Crimea and the Donbas regions of Ukraine. And at the same time, our two carrier strike groups in the Baltic can launch airstrikes against all their forward positions inside Latvia. In addition, we've got the entire 480th Fighter Squadron deployed and ready to scramble out of Spangdahlem, sir. Currently, we've even got F-22 Raptors available at that base."

The president reached onto the desk and put his finger

on the speaker. "Lance," he said, "I'm going to mute you for one second."

He muted the mic and looked at his cabinet.

"This is it, gentlemen. This is the moment our fathers warned us of. This is a strike against Russian targets on Russian soil, fired in anger. If anyone has any objections, speak now or forever hold your peace."

Everyone looked at each other, like the witnesses at an uncertain wedding, and no one uttered a single objection.

"We're going to hit the Russian Black Sea fleet with the Eisenhower and its strike group. We're going to hit the Russian forward positions in Latvia with the Ford and Truman strike groups. And we're going to hit mobilized forces inside Russia with the 480th Fighter Squadron out of Spangdahlem."

"And Lance is going to take out their command," Roth added.

The president nodded. He gave everyone one final opportunity to speak up, then unmuted the mic.

"Do it, Spector. Take out the building. We're going to hit them with everything we've got on our end."

"Yes, sir."

"And Lance," Roth said.

"Yes, sir."

"Godspeed."

89

L ance looked out the window of the café across the Bol'shaya Plaza at the General Staff Building.

It was a truly magnificent structure, a Five-hundred-meter long façade that arched around the Palace Square that seemed almost to embrace the Czar's Winter Palace. Its two wings were separated by an enormous triumphal arch that commemorated the Czar's victory over Napoleon in 1812. Its monumental, neoclassical style, its vast scale, its imperial aspirations all spoke to the grandeur of what was, after all, the world's largest nation.

It was a truly magnificent building, but it also had weaknesses.

For one thing, its full schematics had once fallen into the hands of the enemy.

For two years and four months, the city of Leningrad, as Saint Petersburg was known during the Second World War, stood firm in the face of the most devastating siege known to modern warfare.

For eight-hundred-seventy-two days, the Nazi army tried

to starve, freeze, bombard, and burn the city and its inhabitants into submission.

The city never surrendered.

But in all that time, many of its secrets fell into the hands of the German forces. Those secrets were later sold to the CIA, and with respect to buildings still used by the Russian military, Roth had ensured that they remained as complete and up to date as possible.

He'd also ordered all Special Operations Group assets to study them.

Lance was the only asset left, and therefore, one of the few people on the planet who had memorized the blueprints for the General Staff Building.

He knew exactly where he had to go.

And he knew how he would get there.

That there wasn't a way back out was a detail that he didn't allow himself to consider.

He still had the waitress's phone, and he made another call, this time to the embassy in Riga, where he asked to be connected to Laurel.

When she picked up, he said, "It's me."

He heard an audible gasp on the other end of the line.

"Lance," she said. "I wasn't expecting...".

"Laurel, I wanted to...".

He didn't know what he wanted to say to her.

"What is it, Lance?"

"I'm going into the General Staff Building."

"What do you mean, you're going in?"

"I told Roth I'd take out the Russian command."

"But Lance, if you go in there...".

"I'll be fine, Laurel."

"You will not be fine, Lance. You'll be...".

"I'll be all right."

"I've seen those schematics, Lance. I know where you're going. There's no way out."

"Laurel, listen. The president's ready to stand up to the Russians."

"The time to stand up to them was weeks ago," she said. "Back when the Kremlin first started rattling its sabers. Now, it's too late."

"Better late than never, Laurel."

"But Lance, you're not thinking straight. You can't mean to end it like this. There are other options. Other ways to take out the Russian command."

"None of them will be fast enough," Lance said.

"Lance," Laurel said. She was crying. "Please don't do this."

"I have to do it."

"No, you don't. This isn't even the reason you came back."

"Of course it is."

"You're only here to get revenge for what happened to Sam."

Lance made to speak but stopped. He hadn't known she knew about Sam's death.

"Laurel," he said. "That's not the only reason I came back. You know that."

Laurel was really crying. He'd never heard her like this.

"This is goodbye, isn't it?" she said. "Oh my God. That's why you called. I can't believe it."

"Laurel."

"Lance, you don't have to do this."

"You know I do," Lance said.

"If the president orders airstrikes," Laurel said, "the Russians will back down."

"No, they won't," Lance said. "You know they won't. Not if they can fight.."

"And you think...".

"I think this is the only way."

"Lance, you haven't thought this through."

"Yes, I have, Laurel."

"But...", she said, and he waited while she sobbed. "Why me?" she said. "Why did you call me."

"Because we're ...".

"We're what?"

Lance didn't say it. He didn't know how to say it. He looked around the café. The people sitting, chatting, sipping drinks, and the snow falling outside over the plaza.

"Because you know me, Laurel. You know who I am. You're the only one who knows who I really am."

90

L ance left some money on the table and walked out of the café. Directly across the street, at the corner of the plaza and Nevsky Avenue, was the Saint Petersburg branch of Privatbank Zürich, a secretive Swiss bank that the CIA maintained a relationship with because of the proximity of its branches to Russian government buildings.

Roth himself, over thirty years ago, had been the one to advocate the strategy, stating that if you couldn't beat them, then you joined them.

He recognized that, because of Switzerland's extreme bank secrecy laws, laws that put it at odds with the US government, CIA targets were extremely likely to be doing business with them. The banks offered a range of complex services that allowed secretive people with shady dealings to remain secretive, and to conduct their dealings without the interference of law enforcement agencies.

Roth told the then-president that virtually every single high-level CIA target from the previous thirty years had a relationship with at least one Swiss bank.

And so, rather than fighting the banks, as his predecessors had done, Roth began doing business with them. He set up a number of shell companies under the aegis of the Special Operations Group and used those companies to build relationships with the banks most likely to be used by terrorists, Russian oligarchs, and foreign dictators.

Roth soon learned that as well as allowing him to get closer to his targets, the services the banks offered were exceedingly useful to spies too. He was able to maintain accounts for deep-cover agents, transfer funds to foreign informants secretly, and use bank safety deposit boxes around the world as weapons caches.

Some of the banks, when they realized what he was using them for, actually went out of their way to increase their level of service to him and to his network of assassins.

As had been the case in countless other wars, the Swiss were perfectly comfortable serving both sides at the same time.

Privatbank Zürich was one of Lance's favorites precisely because of the location of its branches, as well as the nature of its safety deposit box system. Specializing in services that were of particular interest to politicians who needed to avoid the scrutiny of domestic regulators, the bank maintained elaborate facilities close to the major centers of power in Moscow, Saint Petersburg, Riyadh, Beijing, Shanghai, Hong Kong, Tehran, Damascus, and even Pyongyang. Within a kilometer of the seat of government of every major nation deemed a credible war opponent by the Pentagon, Privatbank Zürich maintained safety deposit boxes that could be used by anyone to store virtually anything.

In Lance's name, the Special Operations Group maintained a special type of contract that allowed him to access a metal box measuring seventeen-and-a-half inches by thirteen inches, at any of their forty-two branches worldwide. Inside each box was an identical, secure briefcase that always contained the same items.

The boxes were available to him at any branch, at any hour of the day or night, without the need to use a key or show any kind of documentation or identification.

Inside the briefcase was a silenced Glock pistol, ammunition for the pistol, passports containing his photo from Russia, China, Iran, Britain, France, Germany, Canada, Ireland, and the United States, a variety of vials containing chemicals that could be used as poisons or truth serums, a few hard to get medications, some illicit recreational drugs, cash in US dollars, Swiss Francs, Pounds Sterling and Euros, three radio detonators, and half-a-pound of a substance called EPX-1.

EPX-1 was a research-stage, experimental explosive compound made from pentaerythritol tetranitrate and dibutyl phthalate that had never been used publicly by the US government or any of its agencies. As such, it could not be traced back to the US government if it was ever used in a sensitive operation.

Its secrecy was valuable, but the main reason it was used by the Special Operations Group was its stability in storage, its explosive characteristics, its detonation velocity, and its thermodynamic profile.

Combined, these characteristics made it more suitable for Group use than any other military and civilian explosives available on the market.

Lance entered the bank, where a security guard escorted him to a private room and asked him to verify his identity. This was done using a retinal scan, a pre-recorded voice recognition match, and a fingerprint scan.

He was then brought into a waiting area that resembled

the lounge of an exclusive club, complete with leather furniture, a fireplace, and an assortment of the finest whiskies in the world. These were laid out in exquisite crystal decanters on a bar of finely inlaid mahogany.

Lance waited for another security guard, who escorted him to the safety deposit box room.

There, he was left alone.

He found his box and opened it, removing the case and opening it carefully.

He didn't think he would require the passports or cash, this was a one-way trip, and he'd accepted that.

The explosive was wrapped in a metal foil and was about the size of a stick of butter. He removed it from the case, as well as the detonators, the Glock, and the pistol ammo.

Then he left the bank.

91

R oth knew what Lance was going to do. He'd seen the same schematics Lance had seen. He'd analyzed the building for the same weaknesses. All buildings had weaknesses.

The thing that made the General Staff Building different was that, despite the implementation of the most advanced security upgrades available, its blueprints, down to the finest detail, had fallen into enemy hands.

Construction on the building, one of the largest and grandest in all of Czarist Russia, had begun in 1819, and even today, with all its upgrades, it had a number of vulnerabilities.

The Keyhole satellite system was back up and running, and Roth, the president, and the other members of the cabinet were seated around the table, watching the building through ultra-high-resolution, real-time surveillance footage.

"Where's he going now?" the president said as they watched Lance enter one of the buildings off the Bol'shaya Plaza.

Roth raised an eyebrow.

He wasn't sure.

He had to think for a second before remembering what was there.

"Of course," he said. "It's a bank. A Swiss bank. The Group keeps safety deposit boxes in it. It will have supplies Lance can use."

"We have a safety deposit box that close to the General Staff Building?"

"The bank was chosen specifically because of its proximity to all the main Russian government buildings."

"We use Swiss banks for weapons caches?" Schlesinger said.

"That's correct," Roth said.

Schlesinger nodded. "That's genius," he said.

They waited, and a few minutes later, Lance came out of the bank. He wasn't carrying anything extra, but Roth said, "There's an explosive compound in the safety deposit box. He must have that on him now."

"How much explosive?" the president said.

"Not enough to take down a building, sir," Roth said. "But enough to set off other explosions if you know what you're doing."

"The military command doesn't occupy the entire General Staff Building, correct?" the president said.

"That's correct, sir. As you can see, there are two wings, separated by the triumphal arch in the middle. Command of the Western Military District is in the west wing."

"What's in the east wing?" Schlesinger said.

"It's part of the Hermitage museum," Roth said.

The museum contained some of the most important works of art in all of Europe, and Roth would be sorry if it was damaged, but it was a price he was willing to pay.

Next to the screen tracking Lance's movements was another screen showing a broad satellite view over the Baltic Sea and the Gulf of Livonia. On that screen, they could see Carrier Strike Groups Ford and Truman speeding toward Latvian waters.

They made for an impressive sight, even from space, with the Nimitz-class USS Harry S. Truman flanked by a guided-missile cruiser and a squadron of five Arleigh Burke-class destroyers. A few miles to their east was the USS Gerald R. Ford, flanked by two Ticonderoga-class cruisers and over a dozen other warships. As well as the ships, the carriers had multiple squadrons of F-18 Hornets, F/A-18 Super Hornets, Boeing EA-18G Growlers, and surveillance aircraft.

The planes were visible on the decks of the ships, fueling and preparing for take-off. Their targets would be the Russian units that had already crossed the border into Latvia and which appeared to be headed directly for Riga.

Separate forces from Spangdahlem would be flying even more dangerous missions over Russian territory to attack the ground forces that had been mobilized for the second wave of the invasion.

"What's the vulnerability of those Carrier Strike Groups?" the president said to the Navy Chief of Staff.

"Once this agent blows up their command center," the admiral said, "there'll be very little risk of a coordinated attack."

"What about right now," the president said. "Don't the Russians have carrier killer missiles?"

"Sir, people throw around the term *carrier killer,* but taking down these ships requires a kill chain far more complex than simply firing off a missile. I don't think the Russians are capable of it in this theater. These ships are the largest warships ever built, sir. They're higher than a twenty-five story building.

"Doesn't their sheer size make them vulnerable?" the president said.

The admiral looked around the room for support, then said, "Sir, the sea is a big place. Even finding these ships requires more low-earth orbit satellites than the Russians can currently muster."

"But we're going to be getting a lot closer," the president said.

"We are sir, but I assure you, our anti-missile defenses are more than up to the task at hand. We can take out hundreds of targets within minutes of a Russian missile being fired, and it would take a lot more than a single missile to take down these ships."

"What about mines? And subs? The Russians have dozens of subs."

The admiral shook his head.

"Sir, these ships wouldn't have been deployed if they were vulnerable. The chance of a Russian submarine surfacing close to our position is virtually nil, and with our defenses, we'd take it out long before it got into a shooting position. And then, even if they fired off twenty torpedoes, and all of them hit their mark, the hulls of these ships are made of literally hundreds of watertight, armored compartments that prevent a single breach from becoming a serious problem."

"So they're safe?"

"Sir," Schlesinger said, interrupting, "there's nothing on the planet with the warfighting capability of these carrier strike groups. Believe me when I say that."

"Because we only have eleven of them, right?"

"Sir, these ships are the most difficult craft in the history of human navigation to bring down. This is the type of scenario they were built for."

Roth was watching the screen of the Bol'shaya Plaza and could see Lance entering the General Staff Building's main west wing entrance next to the triumphal arch. He was in the uniform of a Russian officer, and most likely carried some of the credentials of the man who'd owned the uniform.

However, the Russians knew Lance was in Saint Petersburg. They'd be expecting him.

"He's in," Roth said as Lance disappeared into the building.

"What now?" the president said.

"Now, sir, we wait."

92

L ance entered the lobby of the General Staff Building and quickly scanned for security cameras. He knew they'd be searching for him using facial recognition algorithms, and at this proximity, he had little chance of staying off their radar for more than a few minutes.

It was clear that it was an important day for the Western Military District. There were all sorts of people in the lobby. Most of them in their formal uniforms, active-duty personnel who'd been told something big was going down.

Lance couldn't have asked for a more perfect arrangement to inflict maximum damage. Everyone who was anyone was in the building.

The lobby was a large, open atrium, surprisingly spacious for a building so old. In front of him was an array of security equipment, metal detectors and x-ray scanners, and beyond those, facial recognition scanners.

To the right, a wide staircase curved up to the second floor. To his left was the main security desk, where two soldiers were sitting at computers, monitoring the feeds from the cameras and sending anything suspicious upstairs for analysis.

One of the soldiers rose from his seat and walked over to a door marked "Security Personnel Only."

Below the lobby were three basement levels. The first two contained offices and meeting rooms, and the third was the service level.

That was where Lance needed to get.

This building, he knew, was one of the locations the Russians would be expecting him to attack, and after the stunt he'd pulled with Kirov and the chopper, they certainly knew he was close by.

It was only a matter of time before they sealed off the entire district.

His face would be matched by the facial recognition system, and an entire division would be sent in to surround the building.

There'd be no possible way for him to make it out of there alive.

But that was all right because he had no intention of trying to get back out.

This was a one-way trip, and he was resigned to that fact.

"Can I help you, sir?" one of the guards said.

"I'm looking for corridor fifty," Lance said. "It's in the third basement level."

The guard gave Lance a curious look, he wasn't used to people requesting sections of the building by their blueprint designations, but Lance didn't have time to come up with a plausible cover story.

He needed to get to that basement, and he needed to get to it fast.

Outside the building, in the distance but growing closer,

he heard the distinct wailing of Saint Petersburg city police sirens.

He wondered if they were for him.

Had the facial recognition system already identified him and set off the alarm?

The lobby would be filling with soldiers any second if it had.

The soldier standing next to Lance hadn't noticed the police sirens, but his radio beeped, and he put his hand to his ear. He listened to a message for about five seconds, then turned toward Lance and looked at him as if seeing him for the first time.

Lance waited for him to reach for the assault rifle slung across his chest, then drew his Glock and pressed it against the soldier's stomach. He pulled the trigger twice, and two silenced pulses sank into the man. Lance let go of him, and he slumped to the ground.

Lance bent down and picked up his gun, an AK-12 assault rifle chambered with live 5.45x39 enhanced penetration rounds, and opened fire on the lobby, spraying the entire place with bullets.

There were two guards at the main security desk, twelve others operating the security screening equipment, and besides them, every single other person who happened to be in the lobby, about twenty people in all, were armed active-service military personnel.

Behind Lance, outside on the street, police cruisers were screeching to a halt, and armed police officers were getting out of their cars, their guns trained on the entrance of the building.

Lance ran forward and dove for cover behind one of the security scanners, just as bullets began to come at him from every direction. The building's alarm system went off, and

Lance could see from the lights above the elevators that they'd been disabled.

There were two armed soldiers firing at him from the direction of the entrance, and he took them both out with shots to their torsos. Then he rose up from behind the scanner and took out two more guards on the stairs.

He ran across the lobby, keeping low, as guards and soldiers opened fire from all directions. He gave himself blind covering fire and had to slide across the polished floor to the wooden doors leading out to the service staircase.

He descended the stairs, leaping down entire flights, and was at the bottom of the third level when more gunfire came from above.

He gave a few shots in return, then slammed through a set of steel doors into the service level.

Assuming the building's layout hadn't changed in the eighty years since the Nazis acquired the blueprints, Lance knew exactly where he needed to go. The building was heated by natural gas, and there was a twelve-inch, municipal-grade gas transmission pipeline, laid over a hundred years ago, and operating at a pressure of four-hundred-pounds-per-square-inch.

That was an extremely high pressure for a single building, even one as large as this, and had been identified by both the Nazis, and later by the CIA, as a potential flaw in the building's design that could be exploited.

Lance rushed past a dozen thick steel doors, like the doors on ships, and turned right into a side corridor, then immediately left into another. Behind him, he could hear soldiers running around, searching for him. At the end of the corridor was a door unlike the others. It was heavy and steel, but round, like the door of a bank vault.

Lance ran up to it and began desperately turning the

handle. It unlocked with a loud, ratcheting clank that the soldiers definitely would have heard, and Lance swung it open.

Its hinges were well-oiled, and it moved smoothly, despite its weight.

As it opened, a soldier appeared at the end of the corridor behind him.

"Halt," he cried and fired two shots.

Lance fired back, and the man fell to the ground.

More men were coming, and Lance went through the door and swung it shut behind him, just as the soldiers appeared at the corner and opened fire. Their bullets struck the steel door and bounced off it, and Lance spun the locking mechanism from the inside until he heard the loud clank of the lock creating its airtight seal.

Through a small window, filled with twenty-inch thick, bullet-proof perspex, Lance could see dozens of soldiers appearing in the corridor outside the door.

There was an emergency deadbolt system that was only operable from Lance's side of the door, and he locked it, then jammed the barrel of the Glock into the mechanism that controlled it, making it impossible for it to be opened from the other side.

Lance could see the soldiers outside the door, and they could see him, but there was nothing they could do now to stop him. The only way through that steel door was with explosives, which they were already gathering, but by the time they were ready to blast the door, it would be too late.

Lance looked around. He was in a small service room, deep underground, and it didn't look like the layout had been altered at all during the eight decades since the blueprints had been captured.

There was a light switch next to the door, and he turned

it on. A single, incandescent bulb lit the room from its wire cage on the ceiling. The room was about fifteen by fifteen feet, a solid, concrete box, and the walls were wet to the touch.

In front of him, in the center of the room, was the municipal-grade natural gas intake. Behind it were valves for controlling the flow and shutting it off, and from the top was a series of smaller-gauge pipes leading to the various boilers and furnaces scattered throughout the building.

In the ground was a small metal grate for drainage, and from the grate, Lance could hear the distinctive sound of squeaking rats.

Outside the door, a loud clanging noise began. The soldiers were trying to break their way in. Lance knew how long it would take for them to get explosives brought down from the armory, and he got to work.

He went to the gas intake, found the pressure release valve located next to the mainline, and placed both hands on the valve handles.

He knew it was going to be difficult. Decades of rust and neglect had sealed every bolt and screw, but he heaved against the handles and began trying to open the valve with all his might.

He couldn't get it to budge.

He removed the jacket of his uniform and tied it around two opposing handles to provide himself with some leverage, then heaved again.

He pulled, harder and harder, until he thought he was going to dislocate his shoulders, and eventually, just as he was growing faint from the effort and was afraid he'd pass out, the valve, ever so slightly, began to budge.

At first, he could barely hear the sound of it, but as he continued to open the valve, the slight hiss gave way to a deafening gush as hundreds of pounds of gas filled the small room at high pressure.

It took about ten seconds for the room to be turned from an empty cube into an enormous bomb.

Lance knew he had about ninety seconds before he ran out of air.

That was all the time he needed.

He set up the EPX-1 explosive next to the valve, attaching it to the body of the intake, then fitted a detonator to the explosive.

The detonators had the ability to be activated remotely. There was a radio transmitter, a small, black plastic device that looked like the remote control for an old television set, but Lance had nowhere to go.

There was no way out of the room.

He set the timer on the detonator to three-hundred seconds, the time it was pre-programmed for, and then slumped to the ground. As more and more gas entered the room, he found it difficult to keep his balance and his vision blurred.

He wasn't worried about anything the soldiers could do. Even if they came back with their explosives now, anything they did would ignite the gas and set off the explosion.

There was nothing they could do to stop him.

He lay down on the ground and squinted up at the light bulb. He could see a green halo around it.

This was it, he thought.

The end of the road.

He'd always known it would come down to something like this. Trapped in an underground bunker.

About to be vaporized by an enormous explosion.

It wasn't such a bad ending.

He was a soldier, and he'd seen a lot of better men than him come to worse endings.

This was no better and no worse than he deserved.

The end was coming for him quickly, and he welcomed it.

He couldn't breathe, and the gas had grown so thick that even the rats in the grate by his feet had stopped screaming.

There was silence.

93

R oth, the president, and the other cabinet members watched in awe as an enormous explosion lit up their screen. The explosion was so large and so powerful, it actually caused the satellite feed to flicker for a moment.

It began beneath the triumphal arch, right where the two wings of the building met, and was followed rapidly by a series of follow-up explosions as a chain reaction was set off, and the furnaces distributed around the building were ignited by the fuel in the gas lines.

"No one's walking out of that," the president said, his eyes fixed on the screen as fires engulfed the entirety of the enormous building.

"If that doesn't stop them," Schlesinger said, "I don't know what will."

Roth nodded.

The entire command of Russia's Western Military District had just gone up in smoke. This action, combined with the airstrikes already being launched, would make it impossible for the Russians to continue with the invasion.

"Well done, Levi," the president said. "I think your man made the right call."

Roth nodded.

Lance had calibrated this attack so as to be devastating enough to stop the Russian invasion but not so great that it would trigger a general war.

"I think you're right, sir."

"I hope so, Levi."

Roth hoped so too.

Because if a general war did break out between Russia and the United States, the consequences were unthinkable.

It could be game over for everyone on the planet.

The outbreak of World War Three.

"I think the Russians will stand down now, sir," Roth said. "The Russians didn't want a general war. Everything they did suggested they wanted a quick, limited engagement."

Roth didn't say what everyone in the room was thinking.

That the Russians had been testing the president for weeks, testing his resolve, measuring his responses as they gradually ratcheted up the stakes.

They'd also laid the groundwork for their false flag operation so carefully, ensuring that all communications in Latvia were down, and even taking out US satellite surveillance, so that they'd have a pretext for the invasion.

They'd wanted to hide their intentions.

They'd wanted the world to believe they had a legitimate reason to be in Latvia.

And only after they'd given themselves that intricately planned pretext did they dare cross the border into Latvian territory.

The Russians didn't want all-out war.

Why would they?

They couldn't possibly win.

They'd bet that the United States, and the rest of NATO, wouldn't be willing to go to war over a country as small as Latvia.

And maybe they'd been correct in that bet.

Because Roth still wasn't sure that President Montgomery, not to mention his counterparts across western Europe, would have been ready to engage in all-out war for Latvia's sake.

Latvia was, after all, a country of just two million people that could fit handily inside the shores of Lake Superior.

Luckily, thanks to what Lance had managed to do, the president didn't have to make that decision.

The Russian command had been wiped out.

The US airstrikes were a proportional response to the missile attacks Russia had already made against targets inside Latvia.

War was averted.

Roth was confident of that.

What scared him was how narrow the victory had been.

How close the Russian president had come to calling NATO's bluff.

On the screen, the entire General Staff Building was engulfed in flames. No one would ever be able to prove for certain who'd been behind the attack. Lance would have been vaporized the instant the gas ignited.

This crisis was over.

And so, it appeared, was Lance Spector.

Roth smiled thinly.

This was a victory of sorts, but it didn't feel like one. For one thing, the man responsible for it was being burnt to a crust on the screen in front of them.

Roth watched the screen. He saw clearly as the roof of

the building collapsed in on the top floor, raising a cloud of dust and ash as the flames continued to spread around Palace Square and along the stores and shops of the Bol'shaya Plaza.

"All right, gentlemen," the president said, "We're not out of the woods yet. No one is to leave this building. I want reports every fifteen minutes on the progress of our airstrikes, and if there's any sign whatsoever that the Russians are not backing down, I want to know."

As the president and cabinet members filed out of the room, Roth slumped back into his seat at the table.

He waited until everyone was gone, then reached for the controller of the satellite and zoomed in on the burning building. He knew it was futile.

In the first minutes after the explosion, people had staggered out of the building, into the Palace Square at the front, or the Bol'shaya Plaza at the rear, where ambulances and paramedics were waiting for them.

But Lance wasn't going to come out.

There would be no such miracle.

He was in the basement, in a sealed concrete box, and the only one way in and out would have been blocked by soldiers.

He was at ground zero of the explosion, at the very source of a fireball as hot as the surface of the sun when it first ignited.

Survival was impossible.

There was a rap on the door, and Roth looked up to see the president.

"I thought you might still be here," he said.

"I was just making sure," Roth said.

"I know, Levi. And I'm sorry. I really am."

"No one could have survived that blast," Roth said to himself.

The president nodded. "But your man, you were right about him all along. All the shit I gave you. All the push-back. You always stood by him. You never once threw him to the wolves. And your instincts were right, Roth. This situation was resolved because of that man, what he was capable of, and there isn't a man alive who could have done for us what Lance Spector did today."

Roth nodded sadly.

"You were right when you selected him, Roth. You were right when you trained him. And you were right when you stood by him."

"Thank you, sir."

"Now come on," the president said, hitting him on the arm. "There'll be other assets. There'll be other fights. War was averted today, but the fight will never be over. It goes on and on. It takes new forms. It puts on new masks. But it continues down through the decades, and nothing any of us does will ever truly change that."

Roth let out a long sigh. He was getting old, and suddenly, more than ever before, he felt it.

94

Tatyana and Laurel were at the diplomatic terminal of Riga international airport, waiting for the jet that would take them back to DC.

Tatyana looked out the window at the plane as it refueled. A few others from the embassy were waiting for the same plane. The events of the past few days had led to dozens of recalls, and the president had named a new ambassador and an entirely new diplomatic team in Riga.

He was also beefing up the CIA's presence in the region and had announced that the US would be maintaining a significantly larger military presence in the Baltic zone to deter further Russian aggression.

Regarding the massacre, the Council of the European Union had announced the establishment of a multilateral inquest into the events that had taken place in the village of Ziguri. Its mission was to find out what had truly happened there, and it was to be named the Agata Zarina Inquiry in honor of the Latvian policewoman who first raised the alarm.

The Russians opposed the inquiry and protested vehemently that the victims had been ethnically Russian. It was becoming increasingly clear however, that they were the ones responsible, and Tatyana thought that the sooner they shut up about the victims being Russian, the better it would be for them.

There was a television in the departure lounge, and Tatyana looked up at it. The news networks were streaming live footage of the NATO airstrikes. The rockets flew out like a hail storm, like a Katyusha barrage, over and over. Fighter jets took off from aircraft carriers in an impressive display of prowess.

Laurel was over at the kiosk, getting them coffee, and Tatyana turned back to the window. She looked out at the drizzly expanse of concrete, the planes taxiing and fueling, and felt a shudder. All of this, an entire country, had almost been swallowed up in a matter of hours by the Russian army.

How could anyone, anywhere feel safe if that had been allowed to happen?

Tatyana wondered what would have happened if Lance hadn't taken out the Russian command. Would the mobilized Russian units have fought back? Would the tanks have rolled on into Riga?

And in the face of resistance, would the US president have backed down rather than get drawn into an all-out war?

Tatyana suspected he would have.

Ingram Montgomery was a good man, but he was no match for the world Vladimir Molotov inhabited.

Molotov wasn't encumbered by the moral and humanitarian considerations that the US president prioritized.

And when it came to a fight, he wouldn't care about the

costs, about the sacrifice in blood and tears, that would be required from his own people.

How could the Americans stand up to that?

How did you fight someone who had a death wish?

"What are you thinking?" Laurel said, handing her a cup of coffee.

Tatyana shook the thoughts from her head. "That was a close call," she said.

Laurel nodded. "Things could have gone south fast."

Tatyana ran her hands over the thin fabric of her skirt. They'd been provided with fresh clothing at the embassy, but it was a far cry from what she usually wore.

She looked at Laurel and smiled.

They trusted each other now.

Looked out for each other.

They liked the same things, expensive clothes, fine restaurants, fancy hotel rooms.

But they weren't the same.

Laurel had signed up for the military as a way to get back at the men who'd killed her father.

She believed in what she was fighting for.

She believed in the world that would emerge from it.

For Tatyana, the reason was simpler. Less inspiring.

Money.

She couldn't bear the thought of being reliant on a man for her security, so she joined the GRU.

For Tatyana, the expensive clothes, the jewelry and perfume, it wasn't for fun that she bought those things. They were necessities, as urgent as oxygen, symbols of her security, an armor with which she protected herself.

She'd grown up in communism. She knew what it was to be hungry. She knew what it was to fear for her survival, for her sustenance. She knew what it meant to struggle in a world that didn't care whether she lived or died.

She'd watched her mother die when she was four years old. She'd spent six days locked in the apartment with her corpse.

She knew that the American view of the world, that happy, orderly place portrayed in television shows and Hollywood movies and on the covers of glossy magazines, wasn't the only world that could exist.

There was a meaner world.

A world in which unspeakable things happened.

And she wasn't sure that Laurel knew just how dark that world could get.

And how could she?

She was an American, a US citizen, born and brought up in a nation that was successful, and optimistic, and materially secure. She knew hardship, that was true. Her mother died during childbirth, and her father was killed in Afghanistan when she was fourteen.

Tatyana knew she'd refused to attend his funeral.

She knew there was a wound there, somewhere beneath the surface, that festered.

They'd both been hurt by the world. They both knew what it meant to want to get even.

But for a girl who grew up pledging allegiance to the flag of the United States, who grew up under the security and prosperity of a democratic government, who loved her country, Tatyana didn't think she'd be able to understand the rules of the game played by the Kremlin.

Even the American president didn't understand those rules. When Tatyana saw how he faltered in the face of Vladimir Molotov's challenges, the way he hoped that things would be better than they were, she was shocked.

President Montgomery's optimism was a problem.

A problem that was only going to get worse.

Because between Washington and the Kremlin, there was an unbridgeable gulf in which lurked dangers the US leadership had never fathomed.

Where Washington still believed in hope, and optimism, and a world that was secure and peaceful, the Kremlin was determined to see that such a world never came to pass.

And the things they were willing to do to achieve that, things Tatyana had seen with her own eyes, would have made President Montgomery's hair stand on end.

Tatyana knew Laurel was going to need her help.

And she'd already decided she was going to give her that help. She would stand by her side. She would help carry the burden.

Because Lance was dead, and the world Laurel was walking into was darker and meaner than she could ever imagine.

"Are you all right?" she said to Laurel.

Laurel wasn't all right. She'd been crying earlier, in the cab on the way to the airport, and she was crying again now. Her eyes were red, and no matter what she did with her mascara, it kept getting ruined.

"I'm fine," she said. "It's just...".

"I know," Tatyana said.

"I'm heartbroken," Laurel continued.

"Of course you are," Tatyana said again.

Tatyana didn't like this sort of conversation. Displays of emotion made her uncomfortable. They were as foreign to her as so many other things Laurel took for granted.

Tatyana took a sip of the coffee. It was good. Strong.

"I think..." Laurel said, then broke down into a fit of weeping.

That was something Tatyana hadn't seen before.

"You were in love with him, weren't you?" Tatyana said.

Laurel looked up at her, and in the midst of all that grief, Tatyana saw a flash of something else. It was a look of gratitude. Gratitude for letting her say out loud, something she'd been keeping locked inside for so long.

"Yes," she said before bursting into more tears.

Tatyana nodded. She reached out and put her hand on Laurel's shoulder.

Laurel leaned into her and then clung to her in a tight hug, burying her face in Tatyana's neck.

Tatyana held her, looking out the window as if suddenly very interested in the planes on the tarmac.

"You were in love with him too, weren't you?" Laurel said into Tatyana's ear.

Tatyana took a step back. She should have expected the question, but the words still came as a shock.

"Women like me," she said, "we're not really capable of love."

"What is that supposed to mean?" Laurel said.

"I fucked for money," Tatyana said.

"You did what you did for your country."

Tatyana let out a quiet laugh. "I did it for the money, Laurel. You know that."

Laurel said nothing. She was looking into Tatyana's eyes, searching, probing in a way that made Tatyana feel like she had nowhere to hide.

"Excuse me," she said.

She walked, almost ran, across the lounge to the women's washroom, went into the first stall, and locked the door.

Then she put her fist into her mouth and silently, without emitting the slightest sound, wept bitterly.

95

R oth stood by the side of the grave and listened to the chaplain drone on. Across the grave, Laurel and Tatyana stood in black dresses, under black umbrellas.

Laurel wept openly.

Tatyana was as still and lifeless as a statue made of granite.

But Roth knew that, however they showed it, both their hearts were broken.

The funeral was small. Just the three of them, and the servicemen and chaplain stationed at Arlington. Everyone knew the coffin, draped in a flag, was empty, but that did nothing to lessen the pain or sense of loss.

When the chaplain finished his sermon, the bugler played the wailing triplet of notes that had been used to honor dead soldiers since the days of the Civil War. Then, the officer-in-charge issued his order, and three soldiers fired three volleys into the air.

The sound of the guns brought tears even to Tatyana's eyes.

The casket team stepped forward to lower the coffin into the ground.

"Before you fold up the flag," Roth said, "I want to say something."

The men stood back respectfully, and Roth cleared his throat. He looked up at the chaplain, then across the grave at Laurel and Tatyana.

"The world will never know the man we're burying here today," Roth said. "They will never know who the star on the Memorial Wall at Langley commemorates. The Distinguished Intelligence Cross, and the Intelligence Star, which were both awarded this morning by the president himself, will never bear his name."

Laurel and Tatyana's weeping grew louder with every word.

"But we know," Roth said, looking directly at Laurel and Tatyana. "The three of us know. And we won't forget the sacrifice he made for this country and for the world. He died as so many soldiers before him. He died alone, uncelebrated, doing his duty, holding back the horde that threatened our very existence. He stood and faced the monster, so the rest of us would never have to know what it looked like."

Roth reached into his pocket and took out the two medals that had been awarded by the president, anonymously and posthumously. They were in ceremonial boxes, and he opened each of them, looked at the medals, then stepped forward and slipped them inside the coffin.

"All right," he said, and turned and walked down the slope to his car, which was waiting on the gravel drive, engine running, wipers running.

96

Alex Sherbakov knew he'd fucked up.

He knew he was in trouble.

He hadn't meant to kill that girl. He was only supposed to scare her.

But in the heat of the moment, something came over him.

A feeling of power.

He could remember so clearly, so viscerally, the look in the girl's eyes when she realized what he was going to do to her.

He was a man who knew all too well what it was like to be powerless. He knew what it was to be an insect, insignificant, under the thumb of others.

When that girl realized he had the power to kill her, when she realized that it was real, she'd looked at him in a way no other woman ever had before.

It wasn't love, but it was just as intoxicating.

It was a drug.

And once he'd tasted it, he was hooked.

He'd done things to that girl, to the body, disgraceful things, things he hadn't even known he wanted to do.

But power was a potent mistress, and now that he'd tasted it, he wanted more. Like a dog that's tasted blood, there was no going back.

He could feel it, crawling inside him like an itch that needed to be scratched.

He'd hurt that girl, and he wanted to do it again.

When he got back to New York, he never called Kirov like he was supposed to. He never went back to his apartment.

He knew Kirov would send men looking for him.

And Kirov had.

For a time.

But that had stopped.

Sherbakov had been watching. Three weeks passed, and no one had been to his apartment.

It was then that he found out that Jacob Kirov was dead, and he dared to wonder if, maybe, he'd get away with what he'd done.

Sherbakov had grown in confidence. He carried a gun, and more importantly, he knew he could use it.

He'd been visiting nightclubs, strip clubs on Cypress Avenue, watching the women with a new interest.

A new hunger.

He knew the girls thought of him as an easy target. They saw him as a city worker with a suit and an office and more money than dick.

An easy lay.

An easy paycheck.

He didn't imagine that any of them would ever talk about him, but if they did, he knew what they'd say.

They'd call him pathetic.

Flaccid.

Impotent.

Now, all he thought about was making them pay.

A month had passed since he'd killed the girl in Montana, and he was ready to do it again.

He was going to take out years of frustration and humiliation on one lucky girl. He could already picture it.

Just the anticipation was making him hard.

He'd gone over every detail of what had happened in Montana a million times. He'd luxuriated over every excruciating detail. He knew exactly how he would do it next time, what he would change and what he wouldn't.

He wouldn't rush so much.

He would savor it.

He wanted it to last longer.

He wanted to drag it out.

He wanted her to know the full limits of his control over her.

He got out of the cab and walked into the bar. It was still early in the evening, about six, and the place had yet to pick up.

There was a girl leaning on the pole, half-heartedly swaying to some eighties rock. A fat bartender with gray stubble stared at her with his mouth slightly open.

Sherbakov sat at a table in front of the stage, and the girl came closer. She got down on her hands and knees and gave him a closer look at what she was selling.

There were plenty of strip clubs in New York that obeyed the laws around prostitution, human trafficking, and drug use, but this was not one of them.

Sherbakov watched her dance and imagined sliding a knife deep into her stomach. He imagined reaching inside her until he felt her organs.

The bartender came over, and Sherbakov ordered a beer.

He drank the beer fast and ordered another.

He wasn't going to do it tonight. He would have to prepare. He would need plastic to line the floor. He would need a plan to dispose of the body.

And he would need to go back to his apartment. He needed a place to commit this crime, and his apartment at the Oceanic was perfect.

He would have to be careful. Kirov may be dead, but some henchman might still be cleaning up old jobs.

Sherbakov didn't think so, but he would take precautions all the same.

He had the cab drop him off at the Oceanic and looked around the lobby for a long time before going to the elevator.

He took the elevator up to his floor and looked out at the corridor. It was empty.

He waited a few minutes before approaching his door. He listened before unlocking it, and he pushed it open without stepping inside.

The place was silent.

There was a light switch in the hallway, and he slid his hand along the wall, searching for it.

He found it and flicked it on.

The light didn't come on.

He wondered for a moment what was wrong, maybe a bulb had blown, or a breaker had tripped in his absence.

Then he heard the click of a gun being cocked.

Inside the apartment, sitting on a sofa in the dark, sipping Sherbakov's scotch, was Lance Spector.

"Come in, Sherbakov," he said, pointing a gun at the man. "Don't be shy."

There was a lamp next to Lance, and he switched it on.

"Come on, Alex," he said.

Reluctantly, Sherbakov entered the hallway.

"Shut the door," Lance said.

"Who the fuck are you?" Sherbakov said.

Lance smiled. His journey to that sofa had not been an easy one. He'd almost died in that hundred-and-eighty-foot-long tunnel, filled with rats and sludge and more than a century of shit. He'd opened the iron grate in the floor of the concrete room in time to escape a fireball as hot as a blast furnace.

He'd followed the rats and found a pipe full of sewage where he submerged himself entirely for four minutes before daring come up for air. At that point, he didn't know what would be waiting for him above the surface, but he had no choice.

He had to breathe.

And in any case, the heat from the explosion was raising the temperature of the sewage so quickly that if he didn't move, it threatened to boil him alive.

Surviving the burns, choking in the smoke, swimming in the shit had not been easy.

Getting out of those sewers, and then getting out of Saint Petersburg, had not been easy.

Getting back into the United States without the government or the CIA tracking him had not been easy.

But those were the things Lance had done.

And he'd done one other thing too.

Before coming to New York and tracking down the apartment in the Oceanic Building in Little Odessa that belonged to one Alex Sherbakov, before picking the lock and seating his ass on Alex Sherbakov's custom-made, Italian leather, art nouveau sofa, he'd gone to Montana.

Not for long. Just a few days.

He'd gone to the cemetery in Beulah, Montana, and he'd found Sam's grave. Everything had been taken care of. A nice headstone. Flowers. A stately slab of marble bearing the image of a dagger on top of a spearhead.

On the headstone was Sam's name and the years of her life, and beneath that, where a prayer might be found, or the words of a psalm, was an inscription.

It read simply, "De Oppresso Liber."

It translated from Latin as '*To Liberate the Oppressed*' and was the motto of the First Special Forces Operation Detachment, Delta Force, the unit her father had served in, and died in, saving Lance's life.

Lance had sworn an oath that day. He'd sworn to protect Sam.

And now, there he was, standing at her grave, alone, in a

gray mist that came down off the mountains like a time-lapse sequence of cloud movements.

"Alex Sherbakov," Lance said. "I've been waiting for you."

He knew from the look on Sherbakov's face that he didn't need to explain who he was.

Or why he was there.

"How did you?" Sherbakov stammered.

"How did I what? Find you?"

"I thought...".

"You thought what?" Lance said, motioning with the gun for Sherbakov to come further into the room.

Sherbakov entered the living room and stood there, staring at Lance like a cow looking over a fence.

His gaze was vacant, but Lance knew there was more to this man than the docile idiot before him now. This man had done some terrible things to a woman.

And he hadn't been ordered to do those things.

Lance knew enough about human nature to know that if he did them once, he would do them again.

It took a very sick mind to do the things Alex Sherbakov had done to Sam, and there was only one way to handle it.

"As it is with dogs, so it is with men," Lance said.

"What does that mean?"

"You know what it means."

Sherbakov shook his head.

"Sit down," Lance said.

Sherbakov sat on the sofa across from him, and Lance leaned back and crossed his legs. He knew Sherbakov was armed, but there was no way he'd be able to draw fast enough. Lance already had his gun trained on him and, by rights, should have killed him already.

It was pain that caused him to stall.

The pain of losing Sam. The pain of knowing he'd failed in the one thing he'd sworn to do.

"You don't look like an assassin," Lance said.

Sherbakov shook his head.

"You're American?"

"My parents were Russian," Sherbakov said. "I've never been there."

"But you did this."

Sherbakov said nothing.

"You did sick things, Sherbakov. Real sick things."

Sherbakov said, "What did you mean when you said, as it is with dogs, so it is with men?"

"I meant that if a dog did what you did, it would be put down."

"And that's why you're here now?"

"That's why I'm here now, Alex Sherbakov. You're going to meet your Maker this night."

Sherbakov nodded at that, like he'd already known it was coming, like it was normal to him to hear those words.

It was nothing more than a bill that had to be paid.

A debt that had to be reckoned.

Lance drained his glass and raised his gun.

"Any last words?"

Sherbakov tried to reach into his pocket, and Lance held up the gun. "Whoa there."

"No," Sherbakov said. "I'm not going for the gun."

He reached very slowly and pulled out a necklace. It was the necklace that had belonged to Sam's father. The one Lance had given to her before he left.

Lance shook his head. He'd never felt so utterly hopeless. So forlorn.

What was it all for?

He stood up and took the necklace, then pointed his gun

at Sherbakov's forehead.

He didn't ask why he'd mutilated the body.

He knew there was no reason, other than some sickness in the core of his body that Sherbakov understood no better than anyone else.

Lance was about to pull the trigger when Sherbakov spoke again.

"Wait," he said.

Lance clenched his jaw. He was in no mood for groveling. He seemed to know he needed to die as well as Lance did.

"You asked if I had any last words."

"All right," Lance said.

"There was a woman."

"What are you talking about?"

"There was someone in my life once."

Lance said nothing.

"She loved me. At least, she pretended to."

"Good for you," Lance said, raising the gun and pressing it against Sherbakov's forehead.

"Her name is Tatyana."

"I see," Lance said, then pulled the trigger and Sherbakov's head jerked backward over the back of the sofa.

Lance looked down at him. Then he looked at the necklace in his hand. A gold crucifix on a chain.

He knew then that if he'd never gone back for Sam, if he'd simply left her where she was, that none of this would have happened.

She would still be alive.

She was dead because of him.

Because of his vanity.

Because of the belief, or hope, that he, of all people, could do something good in the world.

AUTHOR'S NOTE

First off, I want to thank you for reading my book. As a reader, you might not realize how important a person like you is to a person like me.

I've been a writer for fifty years, and despite the upheavals my industry has faced, the ups and downs, the highs and lows, one thing remains constant.

You.

The reader.

And at the end of each book, I like to take a moment to acknowledge that fact.

To thank you.

Not just on my own behalf, but on behalf of all fiction writers.

Because without you, these books simply would not exist.

You're the reason they're written. Your support is what makes them possible. And your reviews and recommendations are what spreads the word.

So, thanks for that. I really do mean it.

While I have your attention, I'd like to give you a little bit of background into my opinion on the events portrayed in this book.

Writing about politics is not easy, and I hope none of my personal thoughts and opinions managed to find their way into this story. I never intend to raise political points in my writing, and I never intend to take a stand. I'm one of those guys who stays out of politics as much as possible, and I would hate to think that any political ideas raised in my book hampered your ability to enjoy the story or relate to the characters.

Because really, this is your story.

These characters are your characters.

When you read the book, no one knows what the characters look like, what they sound like, or what they truly think and feel, but you. It's your story, written for you, and the experience of it is created by you when you read the words and flip the pages.

I write about people who work for the federal government. The nature of their work brings them up against issues of national security and politics, but apart from that, I truly do try to keep any views I might have to myself. So please, don't let any of my words offend you, and if you spot anything in my writing that you feel is unfair, or biased, or off-color in any way, feel free to let me know.

My email address is below, and if you send a message, while I might not get back to you immediately, I will receive it, and I will read it.

saulherzog@authorcontact.com

Likewise, if you spot simpler errors, like typos and misspellings, let me know about those too. We writers have a saying:

To err is human. To edit, divine.

And we live by it.

I'm going to talk a little about some of the true facts that this book is based on, but before I do, I'd like to ask for a favor.

I know you're a busy person, I know you just finished this book and you're eager to get on to whatever is in store next, but if you could find it in your heart to leave me a review, I'd be truly humbled.

I'm not a rich man. I'm not a powerful man. There's really nothing I can offer you in return for the kindness.

But what I will say is that it is a kindness.

If you leave me a review, it will help my career. It will help my series to flourish and find new readers. It will make a difference to one guy, one stranger you've never met and likely will never meet, and I'll appreciate that fact.

Now that those formalities are out of the way, let's talk about some of the events in this book.

One thing that might have stuck out to you is the reference to *Germania*, Hitler's planned new capital for Germany. This was a real project pursued by the Third Reich, and Hitler's 'First Architect,' Albert Speer, made enormous, detailed models of the new city for Hitler's review.

Between 1938 and 1943, construction on the project began, with large areas of the city being demolished to make way for enormous new streets and government buildings. Thousands of Berliners were forced from their homes as the government bought up properties and began clearing them. Stone was brought in from quarries at the Gross-Rosen, Buchenwald and Mauthausen concentration camps to make use of slave labor. In Berlin itself, 130,000 prisoners of war were used as forced labor. It is estimated that tens of thousands of workers died on the project, and labor was in such demand that beginning in June 1938, the Berlin police force was ordered to round up all male beggars, tramps, Gypsies, and homosexuals to work on the various projects.

The plans included a grand new four-mile-long north-south avenue for victory parades. At each end of the avenue would be a new railway station, and along it would be some of the largest buildings ever constructed. The Great Hall, which was to be based on the Pantheon, was going to have a dome sixteen times higher than that of St Peter's in Rome, and would have been the largest covered space in the world. It was planned to host crowds of over 180,000 people.

There was also to be a gargantuan Triumphal Arch, three times the size of Paris's Arc de Triomphe.

The buildings would have been in the Nazi Intimidation Style of architecture, as seen in the Ministry of Aviation building which appears in the book, and beneath which Prochnow keeps Laurel and Tatyana captive. The city would have demonstrated the power of the Nazi state, while presenting a nightmarish and hostile environment for its inhabitants.

In present-day Berlin, parts of Speer's plan can be seen from the layout of the grand Straße des 17 Juni and the positioning of the Berlin Victory Column.

Another real event mentioned in the book is Hitler's attempt to erase the city of Warsaw from the face of the earth. According to the *Neue Deutsche Stadt Warschau* plan, also known as the Pabst Plan after its architect, Friedrich Pabst, detailed plans were drawn up for the complete destruction of Warsaw. The plan envisioned replacing the city of one-and-a-half-million with a new provincial German town of 130,000 inhabitants. The new city, centered on a People's Party Hall, built on the ruins of the Royal Castle in Warsaw, would be the new home of Poland's ruling elite. It was envisioned that all traces of Warsaw's cultural patrimony would be completely erased.

These plans were put into full motion following the Warsaw Uprising in 1944, which enraged the Nazis. Following the uprising, Heinrich Himmler ordered a sixty-three-day artillery and air attack that destroyed most of the city.

Following the bombardment, a large camp was constructed at the Pruszków Train Repair station, and 650,000 people, the bulk of the city's remaining population, were sent to it. There they were segregated and deported, with thousands being sent to Auschwitz and other concentration camps.

By October 1944, the city was a ghost town, and it was at this point that the Germans created special engineering groups, known as *Sprenkommando*, or demolition units, to sift through the ruins and demolish any remaining buildings. These were followed by *Verbrennungskommandos*, or burning detachments, whose job was to burn any combustible material.

By Christmas, ninety percent of all structures had been razed, with careful attention being paid to the destruction of museums, libraries, schools, statues, government buildings, and buildings of cultural or historical significance. All books, documents and government records had been burned.

Another part of the book that is based on real history is the massacre scene, which in the book takes place in the village of Ziguri, which is located less than ten miles from Latvia's border with Russia.

However, the massacre is based on records of events that took place at the Rumbula forest close to Riga, between November 30 and December 8, 1941. During those days, twenty-four-thousand Latvian Jews from the Riga Ghetto were marched out of the city and shot in the manner described in the book. The killing was carried out by the Nazi Einsatzgruppe A, with the help of local collaborators. A man named Friedrich Jeckeln had experience with such killing, having carried out similar massacres in the Ukraine, including that at Babi Yar. Rudolf Lange, who later played a role at the Wannsee Conference, where the implementation of the Final Solution was decided by Nazi leadership, was present at the massacre.

Many other incidents in the book are based on historical fact. For example, the character of Alex Sherbakov is based on the Russian Illegals Program, which placed ten deep-cover sleeper agents in the United States without official cover. In June 2010, the FBI made ten arrests, with all agents being Russian nationals planted in the United States by the Russian Foreign Intelligence Service, or SVR. The arrests led to a prisoner exchange in July 2010, and formed the inspiration for the television show, *The Americans.*

These events are brought up in the book to highlight one of its themes, which is that, "Those who cannot remember the past are condemned to repeat it." Those words, attributed to George Santayana, are written in Polish on a plaque at Auschwitz. I believe them to be one of the reasons why fiction of this kind can be useful, and to anyone who says the events depicted in the book are far-fetched, the sad reality is that they are not. Such things, and things much worse, happened before.

And as is said many times in the book, anything that happened once, can happen again.

Finally, I'd be remiss if I didn't tell you that Book Four in the Lance Spector series, *The Sleeper,* is now available for pre-order.

So grab your copy now. I promise, if you enjoyed the first three, you're only going to be drawn into these characters more deeply!

God bless and happy reading,

Saul Herzog

Made in the USA
Las Vegas, NV
10 January 2023

65386323R00353